An eerie feeling wafted through Cate, as if this wasn't real.

As if she was looking into the mirror and seeing into the past.

Joan cleared her throat, her nervousness growing. "Can I help you?"

Cate kept looking at the woman in the bed, searching for some foolproof sign. All the while knowing that there wouldn't be one. "That all depends."

"On what?" Joan whispered the words, now clearly fatigued.

Cate took a step toward her then stopped. She was afraid that the woman would pass out if she came any closer. Did she know? On some instinctive level?

Cate put her thoughts into words. "On whether you're willing to admit that you're my mother."

Dear Reader,

The editors at Harlequin and Silhouette are thrilled to be able to bring you a brand-new featured author program for 2005! Signature Select aims to single out outstanding stories, contemporary themes and oft-requested classics by some of your favorite series authors and present them to you in a variety of formats bound by truly striking covers.

We want to provide several different types of reading experiences in the new Signature Select program. The Spotlight books offer a single "big read" by a talented series author, the Collections present three novellas on a selected theme in one volume, the Sagas contain sprawling, sometimes multi-generational family tales (often related to a favorite family first introduced in series) and the Miniseries feature requested previously published books, with two or, occasionally, three complete stories in one volume. The Signature Select program offers one book in each of these categories per month, and fans of limited continuity series will also find these continuing stories under the Signature Select umbrella.

In addition, these volumes bring you bonus features...different in every single book! You may learn more about the author in an extended interview, more about the setting or inspiration for the book, more about subjects related to the theme and, often, a bonus short read will be included. Authors and editors have been outdoing themselves in originating creative material for our bonus features— we're sure you'll be surprised and pleased with the results!

The Signature Select program strives to bring you a variety of reading experiences by authors you've come to love, as well as by rising stars you'll be glad you've discovered. Watch for new stories from Janelle Denison, Donna Kauffman, Leslie Kelly, Marie Ferrarella, Suzanne Forster, Stephanie Bond, Christine Rimmer and scores more of the brightest talents in romance fiction!

The excitement continues!

Warm wishes for happy reading,

Marsha Zinberg

Marsha Zinberg
Executive Editor
The Signature Select Program

SAGA

Searching
for Cate

MARIE
FERRARELLA

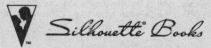

Published by Silhouette Books
America's Publisher of Contemporary Romance

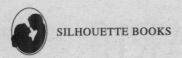 **SILHOUETTE BOOKS**

ISBN 0-373-28525-6

SEARCHING FOR CATE

Copyright © 2005 by Marie Rydzynski-Ferrarella

Dear Reader

What if, one day, you wake up to discover that everything you believed to be true, wasn't? That the parents you'd always loved really weren't your parents? How would you feel? These are the emotions that FBI Special Agent Cate Kowalski finds herself facing. She'd gone into law enforcement to honor and emulate the father she'd always adored, the father who was killed in the line of duty while she was still in her teens. Now, she finds the very reason for who and what she is has been based on a lie. This is the premise behind *Searching For Cate*. It is Cate who is searching for herself, the way that, in part, we all search for ourselves, except that in her case she has to begin from scratch. The search for her birth parents brings her to Southern California and eventually, into the life of Dr. Christian Graywolf, a selfless physician who is also one of the walking wounded. Together, slowly, they each heal the gaping hole in the other's soul.

I hope you enjoy reading this as much as I enjoyed writing it. And, as always, I wish you love.

Marie Ferrarella

To Marsha Zinberg, who asked,
and Patience Smith, who said yes.
Thank you.

Chapter 1

"What do you mean it's not compatible?"

Special Agent Catherine Kowalski stared at the short, husky lab technician before her. A basket filled with vials, syringes and other blood-letting paraphernalia was looped over his arm and he looked at her as if she were a deranged troll who had wandered out of a fairy tale.

The drone of voices in the hospital corridor outside her mother's single-care unit faded into the background as she tried to make some kind of sense of what the man had just told her.

It's a mistake, a voice whispered in her head. But still, there was this terrible tightening in the pit of her stomach, as if she was about to hear something she didn't want to hear.

This was absurd, she thought. Just a small foul-up, nothing more.

"She's my mother. How could my blood type be in-compatible with hers? There has to be some mistake," Cate insisted.

There was no sympathy on the technician's rounded, pockmarked face, just a weariness that came from doing the same laboratory procedures day after endless day. There was more than just a touch of indignation in his eyes at being questioned.

His voice was flat, nasal. "No mistake. I tested it twice."

Her stomach twisted a little harder. Somewhere in the distance, an alarm went off, followed by the sound of running feet. She blocked it out, her mind focused on what this new information ultimately meant.

No more surprises, I can't handle any more surprises. Cate had graduated near the top of her class at Quantico. In the field, there were few better. But on the personal front, she felt as if her life had been falling apart for the past few years.

And this might be the final tumble.

Cate's eyes narrowed. Her voice was low, steely. "Test it again."

Submitting to the blood-typing test had been nothing more than an annoying formality in Cate's eyes. She'd thought it a waste of time even as she agreed.

Time had always been very precious to her.

Ever since she could remember, for reasons she could never pin down, she'd always wanted to cram as much as she could into a day, into an hour. It was as if soon, very soon, her time would run out. Over the years, every so often, she'd tried to talk herself out of the feeling.

Instead, she'd been proven to be right. Because there hadn't been enough time, not with the father whom she adored. Officer Thaddeus Kowalski, Big Ted to his friends, had died in the line of duty, protecting one of his fellow officers during the foiling of an unsuccessful liquor store robbery. She was fifteen at the time. It seemed like the entire San Francisco police force turned out for his funeral. She would have willingly done without the tribute, if it meant having her father back, even for a few hours.

When she was a little girl, they used to watch all the old classic westerns together, and her father always told her that he wanted to die with his boots on. She'd cling to him and tell him that he could never die. He'd laughed and told her not to worry. That he wasn't prepared to go for a very long time.

He'd lied to her and died much too soon.

As had Gabe Summer.

Special Agent Gabriel Summer, the only man she had ever allowed herself to open her heart to. Gabe, who had stubbornly assaulted the walls she'd put up around herself until they'd finally cracked and then come down. Gabe, who somehow managed to keep an upbeat attitude about everything in general and humanity in particular.

Gabe, of whom nothing more than his arm had been found in the rubble that represented a nation's final departure from innocence on that horrific September 11 morning in 2001.

Like her father, Gabe had left her much, much too soon. They never had the chance to get married the way they'd planned, or have the children he wanted so much to have with her. The lifetime she'd hoped for, allowed herself to plan for, hadn't happened. Because there wasn't enough time.

And now, with her mother diagnosed with leukemia and her bone marrow discovered not to be a match, Cate had thought at the very least she could donate blood to be stored for her mother so that when a match would be found—as she knew in her heart just *had* to be found—at least the blood supply would be ample.

But now here was this stoop-shouldered man myopically blinking at her behind rimless eyeglasses, telling her something that just couldn't be true.

"I can't test it again," he informed her flatly. "I've got work to do."

Lowering his head, he gave the impression that he was prepared to ram his way past her if she didn't let him by.

Cate planted herself in front of him. At five foot four, she wasn't exactly a raging bull. To the undiscerning eye, she might have even looked fragile. But every ounce she possessed was toned and trained. She was far stronger than she appeared and knew how to use an opponent's weight against him.

She temporarily halted the technician's departure with a warning glare.

"Look, a lot goes on in the lab. You people are overworked and underpaid and mistakes *are* made. I need you to test my blood again. And then, if you get the same results, test hers. Just don't come back and tell me they're incompatible, because they're not. They can't be."

The small man stepped back, his eyes never leav-

ing her face. "Lady, you're AB positive. Your mother's
O. I don't care how many tests you want me to run,
that's not going to change. You give her your blood, she
dies, end of story." He drew himself up to the five foot
three inches he came to in his elevator shoes. The vials
in the basket clinked against one another. Annoyance
creased his wide brow, traveling up to his receding
hairline. "Now, I've got other patients to see to."

"Problem?"

Cate recognized the raspy voice behind her immediately, even before she turned around. It belonged to Dr.
Edgar Moore.

Doc Ed.

Tall, with a full head of thick silver hair that added
to the impression of a lion patrolling his terrain, Doc
Ed had been her family's primary physician long before the term had taken on its present meaning. It was
Doc Ed who had held her and comforted her when
she'd found out about her father's death. And it was Doc
Ed who had called her at the field office to tell her to
come home, that her mother needed her even if Julia
Kowalski was too stubborn to get on the phone and
place the call herself.

Cate had gotten herself reassigned to the San Francisco field office, where she'd initially started her career. That allowed her to see to her mother's care. It
didn't help. Her mother's condition was worsening by
the week. By the day. Time was slipping away from her
and there wasn't anything she could do about it.

On the verge of feeling overwhelmed, Cate sighed
with relief. Reinforcements had arrived. Doc Ed would
put this irritating person in his place.

She refrained from hugging the doctor, even though she felt the urge. Instead, fighting for control over her frayed emotions, banking down the scared feeling growing like an overwatered weed, Cate brushed aside a strand of straight blond hair that had fallen into her face.

"Doc Ed, could you please tell this man that his infallible lab *has* made a mistake."

The doctor's warm gray eyes looked from the annoyed technician to the young woman he'd known since her first bout of colic. "How's that?"

Cate took a breath and collected herself. She hadn't realized that her temper was so close to snapping. The restraint she'd always valued so highly was in short supply.

She gestured toward the technician and stopped to read his name tag. "Bob here is telling me that I can't donate blood to my mother. That our blood types are incompatible." The laugh that punctuated her statement was short and mirthless. And nervous. "We both know that can't be true."

The moment the words were out of her mouth, they tasted bitter. Like bile. Instincts honed on the job pushed their way into her private life. Once again whispering that something was wrong. Very, very wrong. That the twisting feeling in her gut was there for a reason. There were no planes flying into buildings, no bullets firing, no cells mutating and turning cancerous, but something was still wrong. She could feel it vibrating throughout her whole body.

Because Doc Ed's affable face had taken on a look of concern.

Cate suddenly felt like throwing up. Like running down the hall with her hands over her ears so she couldn't hear anything, anything that would further shake up her already shaken world.

She did neither. But it was all she could do to hang on. She'd spent a good part of her life trying to be tough, trying to live up to Big Ted's reputation. He'd had no sons and she felt she owed it to him, because in her eyes, he'd been the greatest father to ever walk the earth.

But she wasn't sure just how much more of life's sucker punches she could take and still remain standing, remain functioning.

"Can't be true, right?" Cate heard herself asking quietly. Holding her breath.

Doc Ed sighed. "Cate, maybe it's time that you and your mother talked."

Every bone in her body stiffened, braced for an assault. She could feel the hairs on the back of her neck standing up.

"We talk all the time, Doc." Her voice was hollow to her ear.

Behind her, Bob, the lab technician, took his opportunity to hurry away. She heard the rattle of the vials as he escaped down the hall. But her mind wasn't on the other man. It was centered on the expression on Doc Ed's face, which did nothing to give her hope.

She wasn't going to like whatever it was that she was going to hear. She was willing to bet a year's salary on it, and she had never been a betting person.

"At least," she added, "I thought we talked. But I guess I thought wrong."

Doc Ed made no answer. Instead, he lightly cupped her elbow and guided her back into the room she'd vacated several minutes ago when she'd seen the technician making his rounds. Her mother had been dozing off.

Cate had waylaid the lab tech in the hallway, once again stating her impatience. She wanted to begin donating blood, the first of what she intended to be several pints. Frustration had assaulted her even before he'd opened his mouth to tell her the bad news.

Ever since she'd learned that her mother had leukemia, Cate had felt completely frustrated. There was nothing she could do to change the course of events. When her bone marrow turned out not to be a match, it had just fed her impatience, making her that much more determined to be able to help somehow. She'd immediately taken it upon herself to spearhead a search amid the San Francisco bureau personnel and their families for a donor. So far, there had been none who matched.

More frustration.

And now, this, whatever "this" was.

"Julia." Doc Ed's gravelly voice was as soft as Cate had ever heard it as he addressed her mother.

The pale woman in the bed stirred and then turned her head in their direction. The look on Julia Kowalski's face told Cate that her mother was braced for more bad news. Resigned to it.

Don't be resigned, Mama. Fight it. Fight it!

Cate found herself blinking back tears as she approached her mother's bed and took the small, weak hand into hers.

She could almost *feel* time slipping through her fingers. Her soul ached.

Julia tried to force her lips into a smile as she looked at her daughter. "Yes?" The single word came out in a whisper.

"Cate just found out that her blood doesn't match yours." Moving over to the bed, Doc Ed took his patient's other hand and held it for a long moment. "Julia, it's time."

"Time?" Cate echoed. A shaft of panic descended, spearing her. She fought to push it away without success. Her heart hammering, she looked at the man who, over the years, she'd regarded as her surrogate grandfather. "Time for what?"

"Something that you should have been told a long time ago." His words were addressed to her, but Doc Ed was looking at the woman in the bed as he said them. "I'll leave the two of you alone now." Releasing Julia's hand and placing it gently on top of the blanket, Doc Ed made his way to the door. Pausing to look at them for a moment longer, he added, "I'll be by later to look in on you, Julia. And Dr. Conner will be by shortly."

Cate was vaguely aware of the reference to her mother's oncologist as she watched the door close behind him.

Sealing her in with her mother and whatever secret the woman had kept from her all this time.

Chapter 2

Juanita Graywolf was nursing a cup of the black tar she liked to call coffee when her son, Dr. Christian Graywolf, entered the small house in Arizona where he'd grown up. Hearing the soft creak of the front door, Juanita Graywolf barely stirred in her seat. Instead, she looked at the reflection in the kitchen window directly opposite her. The window faced the garden, and west. Dawn was still making up its mind as to just how large an entrance it was going to make this morning. Darkness remained with its face pressed against the pane, helping to define her son's image in the glass.

He was such a handsome boy, she thought. He looked like his father. Tom Graywolf had turned out rotten to the core, but he had been a handsome devil, there was no denying that. Christian was twenty-nine years old now, but he was still her boy. And once, he had been her golden child.

Until *she* had stolen his smile from him. His smile and his soul.

Her face gave away none of her thoughts as she took another sip of coffee. Juanita smiled at the reflection instead of at her second born. "You're up early this morning, Christian."

It was Monday morning and she'd risen early to have a little time with him before he returned to Bedford, California, which he and his brother now called home. But Christian's bed was empty when she'd knocked and looked into the room. And she'd known where he had gone.

"So are you," Christian Graywolf pointed out.

She sat up straight, like a young girl, he thought. People seeing them together mistook them for siblings, not mother and son. He was proud of her for taking care of herself. Proud of her for never giving up the way so many here did. She had always been the source of strength to him. She and Uncle Henry.

"I have a flight to catch," he reminded her.

The flight had nothing to do with where she knew her son had been. For a moment longer, Juanita held her peace, even as her mother's heart ached.

"And I have a schoolhouse full of students to prepare for," she said. Turning around now to face him, she nodded toward the old-fashioned stove. It was the same one that had occupied that space when she was growing up in this same house. "Coffee's hot."

"And hard as usual," he joked. Taking a cup, he filled it only halfway.

At the other end of the small house, they heard Henry stirring, mumbling to himself as he obviously ran into something in the dark. The words were all in Navajo and hard for Christian to catch. He saw his mother smiling to herself as she listened.

Henry Spotted Owl, his mother's older brother, had come to live with them years ago, to take the place of the father he hardly remembered. And to help straighten out Lukas before his older brother was forever lost to them. Henry, an ex-boxer among other things, had done such a good job with Lukas, he'd decided to stay on and offer his own brand of rough-handed counseling to some of the other troubled teenagers on the reservation. He built a gym and gave them a way to work off their anger productively. In his late sixties and fifteen years' his mother's senior, the man gave no sign of letting up despite the emergency bypass surgery he'd received from Lukas some years back.

Grit and determination against all odds ran in the family. Henry had pulled himself out of a self-destructive lifestyle that would have killed him before he reached forty. Lukas had become the first of their family not just to graduate high school and college, but to become a doctor. And Christian was the second.

Christian's mouth curved slightly. He and Lukas both owed a great deal to their mother, who had refused to follow a path of self-indulgence and self-pity, the way so many other of her contemporaries had. Just to put her sons through school, she'd worked two jobs without a word of complaint, behaving as if it was the norm.

At fifty-three, Juanita Graywolf looked younger now than he remembered her looking while he was growing up. Back then, he thought of her as just his mother, who was also a schoolteacher. Now she was principal of the school where she'd once sat in the back row as a student. It was the reservation's only school, taking children from kindergarten to twelfth grade. His mother had almost single-handedly brought up the standard of teaching there, so that now the school was held up as an example to other reservations.

She was a remarkable woman, and he had grown up thinking that all women were that strong, that determined not to allow life to best them.

His late Alma had shown him how wrong he was.

Juanita suppressed a chuckle. "It sounds like your ride is grumbling," she said as she nodded toward the rear of the small house.

There had been just three rooms when Henry had come to live with them, a combination living room and kitchen and two small bedrooms. The first thing Henry had done was add on his own room. After that, he'd built on another room and expanded the living room, then added a porch. Henry liked to say that he left his mark wherever he went. Truer words were never spoken.

Christian finished the remainder of the black pitch in his coffee cup and set it on the table. "Uncle Henry wouldn't be Uncle Henry if he didn't grumble."

Juanita looked at her son, her mother's heart tugging hard. He looked so sad, so different from the boy he'd once been. Her brain told her to avoid the subject, to let it slide, because to raise it would serve no purpose, heal no wounds. The fact that Christian had gone there told her that the wound he bore was far from healed.

Seasons had gone by. And it was time he let go of the past.

Long past time.

Juanita almost wished that Christian wouldn't come home as frequently as he did. She dearly loved seeing him, loved seeing both her sons when they came to work at the clinic to tend to the sick and the forgotten. But whenever Christian came, he was also returning to the scene of his greatest heartache.

She would rather never see him again than have him relive his pain, time and again.

He needed to put it all behind him. And she couldn't hold her tongue any longer. It wasn't in her. She set down her cup again and looked into his eyes. "You went there, didn't you?"

"Why shouldn't I?" He met her gaze unwaveringly. Of her two sons, Christian was the more sensitive one. The one more like her.

"Why should you?" Juanita challenged. She spoke quickly, before he could answer. Before he could defend actions that to her were undefendable. "Christian, every time you go, you come back with this look on your face, as if your heart has been torn out of your chest all over again. As if," she emphasized, "what happened that day was your fault."

He looked at her sharply with blue eyes that proved their lineage had allowed an interloper. "It *was* my fault. I was her husband, Mother. I should have seen it coming. I should have known."

The words might be different, but the conversation

was not new. They'd had it before. Many times in the past three years. It never got any better.

"The blood of the shamans runs through my veins," Juanita reminded him. "And *I* did not know, did not see." She leaned forward at the table, a new urgency in her voice as she pleaded with him. "Alma was an unhappy girl all of her life, Christian. We all saw that. We all knew that. How could we—how could you—have known that she would do such an awful thing?" she demanded.

Awful thing.

Words that could have been used to describe so many events. Somehow, they didn't seem nearly adequate enough to apply to what had happened. Because what had happened that morning was beyond awful. Beyond anything he could have ever imagined.

Afterward, every night for a full year he'd wake up in a pool of sweat, shaking, visualizing what he hadn't been there to see. Alma, their six-month baby girl in her arms, walking out onto the train tracks, the very same tracks that had run by the reservation ever since he could remember.

The same tracks where they'd foolishly played as children.

Except that morning she hadn't been playing.

They were staying with his mother and Uncle Henry for a few days. He'd brought Alma and the baby with him on a working holiday, brought them so that his mother could visit with the baby. Alma had bid him goodbye as he'd gone to the clinic to work with Lukas. Both he and his brother returned as often as they could manage, to give back to the community where so many of their friends had remained.

That last trip, Alma had asked to come with him. He'd thought nothing of the request, except that perhaps she was finally finding a place for herself in the life they were carving out together. He was hopeful that she finally had put the baggage from her past into a closet and permanently closed the door on it. Because he loved her so much and tried every day to make up for the childhood she'd endured. The shame she had suffered at her father's hands.

Alma had seemed happy enough to accompany them. Happy enough when he'd left that morning. He'd turned one last time to wave at her before climbing into the car. She was holding the baby in her arms. Picking up one of Dana's tiny hands, she'd waved back.

There'd been no hint of what was to come in her manner.

Alma had waited until everyone was gone, his mother to the school, Uncle Henry to the gym he still ran, and then she'd taken their daughter and walked onto the train tracks. To wait for the nine-thirty train. Not to leave the reservation, but to leave life.

A life she could no longer tolerate, according to the note she'd left in her wake. She hadn't wanted her daughter to grow up without a mother, the way she had, so she had taken the baby with her.

Lukas was the one who had broken the news to him. He remembered screaming, cursing and not much else. Except that there had been a burning sensation where his heart had been. For days afterward, he'd thought about following Alma, about making the same journey she had. Lukas kept him sedated and Lydia, his brother's wife, kept vigil over him, making sure to keep him safe when the others weren't around.

His whole family loved him and rallied around him. Eventually, he saw the reason for continuing to live. His tribe needed him. His patients needed him and his family loved him. So he continued. That was all the life he'd once relished with such gusto had become to him, a continuance.

He set up his practice and was affiliated with the same hospital that Lukas was. Blair Memorial in Bedford. He banked close to every cent he made, bringing it back with him whenever he came to the reservation. With the money, he purchased much needed equipment for the clinic that retained only nurses now that Doc Brown had died. He, his brother and the handful of doctors they'd gotten to volunteer their time came whenever they could.

The clinic needed so much, even now. The closest hospital to the Arizona reservation was more than fifty miles away. That barely amounted to a trip for most people, but in an emergency, it was a considerable distance, especially since most of the vehicles on the reservation were old and unreliable.

His dream was to someday have a hospital on the reservation. But until that time, he did what he could. And worked until he dropped so that he didn't have to think, or remember.

Except that some days, it couldn't be helped.

Moving her cup and saucer aside, Juanita reached across the table, her hand covering her son's.

"Christian, beating yourself up isn't going to change anything. Isn't going to bring her or Dana back. And it's wrong. It's as futile as Alma constantly reliving everything that happened to her. She couldn't let go of the past and it killed her. Don't let what happened kill you," she pleaded softly. "Learn from it, my son. Learn from it and grow."

He knew his mother wasn't giving the advice lightly. She'd been through a great deal herself. Married at seventeen to a man who betrayed her on a regular basis, she found herself suddenly widowed at thirty-two when Tom Graywolf had been killed in a barroom brawl. From somewhere, Juanita Graywolf had summoned an inner strength and made a life for herself and her two sons. Christian was well aware that he wouldn't be where he was if it hadn't been for her.

But right now, he didn't want advice, didn't want to be told what he should or shouldn't do. The pain was there whether he stood over Alma's grave, attended one of Blair Memorial's surgical salons, performed an operation. It was always there to press against his chest when he least expected it and steal away the very air he breathed.

He'd married Alma, promising her that he would always be there for her, to protect her from everything. And he had failed. Failed to protect her from the inner demons that haunted her. And that failure was something he was going to have to carry around within him for the rest of his life.

He offered his mother what passed for a smile. "I'll do what I can, Mother."

Out of the corner of his eye, Christian saw his uncle entering the room. Short, squat and built like a bull even at his age, Henry had a vivid three-inch scar across his right cheek that he liked to refer to as his badge of courage. He'd gotten it as a young man, and in all these years, it hadn't faded. And neither had Henry.

He helped himself to some of Juanita's coffee, draining the cup in one long swig as if its bitterness was nothing. "You about ready, boy?" He put the cup down on the counter. "I've got miles to cover today, miles to cover."

"I'm all set, just let me get my bag."

Juanita rose from her chair, embracing Christian before he could leave the room. "Try to be happy, Christian," she whispered.

For her sake, he smiled and nodded, even though he knew that wasn't possible. "I'll try, Mother," he repeated. There was no feeling behind the words.

Chapter 3

For a moment, Cate remained where she was, near the door. Looking at her mother.

Ever since she could remember, she'd always believed in challenging herself, in seeing just how brave she could be. Her father had been her very first hero and she'd wanted to be just like him, an officer of the law who put herself out there, protecting people. Keeping them safe the way he made her feel safe.

Being brave, testing that bravery, was the first step to getting there. It wasn't something she even thought about in the beginning. She just did her job. Even now, she would draw a line in the sand and dare herself to cross it. When one of the other field agents had recently referred to her as being fearless, she'd taken it as the highest compliment.

It was only privately that fear had gotten such a

huge toehold in her life. Until the day he died, she had always thought of her father as being ten feet tall and bulletproof. Nothing could happen to him. Ever. When her mother would worry on those evenings that he was late coming home, she'd comfort her, saying it was just some loose end on the job that was keeping her father, nothing more. She never once thought that her father's life might be in danger, that something could happen to him to permanently keep him from coming home.

When it did, the very foundations of her world cracked. They became so badly damaged that they were never quite the same again.

And neither was she.

Like the snake that had entered paradise and ultimately brought about the loss of innocence for Adam and Eve, fear entered her life the day her father was killed, forever robbing her of her innocence.

Losing Gabe had brought about another upheaval, another magnitude-nine earthquake that destroyed the foundations she'd so painstakingly repaired. Older, wiser, she was still that fifteen-year-old girl who had sobbed her heart out the July night her father was shot.

She hadn't bothered to attempt to repair her foundations a second time. She just patched the gaping cracks as best she could and went through the motions of living her life.

Eventually, because she knew how badly her state affected her mother, she tried harder. Her enforced routine took, and while she didn't exactly enjoy life, Cate found she could once again draw breath without pain.

She rallied for her mother once again. Because the woman needed her.

Receiving news that her mother had leukemia threatened to throw her down into the bowels of hell again. Secretly, Cate clung fiercely to the threadbare hope that her mother would survive, that this was some kind of trial she had to endure, but that she would ultimately emerge on the other end of this long, dark tunnel victorious. Cate refused to entertain the thought that her mother might not make it. That Julia Kowalski's light would be extinguished and that the sweet-tempered woman would no longer be a presence in her life. She'd lost her father and her lover. The thought of possibly losing her mother as well was too heinous to contemplate, even for a second.

And now, something besides death hovered between them. Something that threatened to destroy her world for a third time.

Or maybe it was death—not of a person, but of a belief. A belief upon which her very world had originally been founded. Each time she'd rebuilt, it was on that belief, that truth. That she was Catherine Kowalski, Big Ted and Julia's daughter.

Was that going to be taken away from her, too?

Cate curled her fingers into her hands, as if to clutch what little power she had left. Silence blanketed the room. The only break was the sound of her mother's labored breathing.

Say it isn't so, Mama. Tell me I'm your little girl, your own flesh and blood. Yours and Daddy's.

Cate remained by the door for a moment longer, trying to absorb everything she could about the woman.

Holding off that first bite from the apple a moment longer.

She was acutely aware, not for the first time, that her mother and she didn't look at all alike. Julia Kowalski was a short woman with dark brown hair and lively hazel eyes. Until this illness had begun to eat away at her, her mother had been pleasantly plump and large boned, like her husband.

Cate had always been thin, delicate, even as a little girl, despite all her attempts to bulk up and be just like her father. She was small boned and deeply frustrated by it when she was younger. To comfort her, her father told her she took after his only sister, who had died before she reached her twentieth birthday.

"Josephine was a real beauty, just like you," he'd tell her time and again.

And she'd been content that she looked like his sister, Josephine. Even when he could produce no photographs to back up his claim, it never occurred to her to doubt him.

Cate doubted him now. Doubted everything they had ever told her, and yet she still desperately hoped that she was just being paranoid. That her imagination was running away with her.

Years on the job did that to you, Cate thought. It heightened your senses and made you ready to take on anything. It also made you see things that weren't really there. Full-blown figures where in reality only shadows existed.

Please let there be only shadows.

Cate took a deep breath and braced herself. It was time to test her bravery again. Time to cross another line in the sand. God knew she didn't want to. But she had to.

"Mom, what was Doc Ed talking about just now?" To her own ear, her voice trembled slightly. She fisted her hands harder, dug her nails into her palms more deeply. "Why is our blood type incompatible?"

The smile on Julia's lips was thin, weary, and yet somehow still just as warm now as it had been when Cate had been a little girl of eight. Back then, thunderstorms would frighten her, causing her to crawl into the shelter of her mother's arms, begging to hear stories that would distract her. Her mother always obliged.

She wasn't eight anymore, Cate thought sadly.

"You're a smart girl, Catie." Julia's voice was thin, reedy. "You know why."

Yes, Cate thought, she knew in her soul. But until she heard the actual words, she would remain in denial. She needed that kick in the butt to make her stop playing games with herself.

Cate pressed her lips together, hating this. "Tell me."

Julia sighed. Passing a hand over her eyes, she willed her tears back. A couple seeped out, anyway. Because she was tethered to an IV, her movement was restricted. With another bracing sigh, Julia dropped her hand to the bed. It fell as if it was too heavy to hold up.

God, how she wished Teddy had listened to her. She'd told him that it was wrong to keep this from Catie. But he'd begged. It was one of the very few times he'd asked anything of her and she couldn't deny him, even though she knew it was wrong. Teddy had been and always would remain her childhood sweetheart, the man with the key to her heart.

With effort, Julia forced words past her lips, trying not to let the very act exhaust her. "Your father and I loved you from the moment we saw you."

"Tell me, Mama."

And so Julia said the words she'd promised her husband never to say. But he wasn't here now, and if Teddy was looking down, she told herself he'd understand. "You were adopted, Catie." She channeled every last bit of strength into her voice, determined to make Cate understand. And forgive. "You came into our lives when you were just a week old, but you were always part of us."

In her heart, she begged Cate not to be angry at the grave omission that had been made. Julia fisted one frail hand and placed it against her breast.

"I didn't get to carry you beneath my heart, the way your birth mother did. But I held you there when you cried because the other kids made fun of you, or when that boy you liked so much asked another girl out. I held you to my heart when your father died—and he *was* your father. Just as you are my daughter, Catie. In love, in spirit and in fact. In every way but the mechanics of birth." Pushing a button on the hospital bed, Julia drew herself up as best she could, a pale shadow of the vivacious woman she'd once been. "No one could have loved you more than your father and I did. *No one,*" she underscored as fiercely as she could.

"It's okay, Mama, it's okay."

On legs that were less than solid, Cate crossed to the lone bed in the room and took her mother's hand. She didn't want her to become agitated and waste what precious little strength she still had left.

Even as Cate held her mother's hand, she could feel everything around her cracking, breaking. Shattering and raining down around her like tiny shards of glass. Cate struggled to understand why her parents would keep this from her. Were they ashamed of her, of how she had come into their lives?

Julia wrapped her fingers tightly around Cate's, afraid to let go. Afraid that the young woman she'd loved for the past twenty-seven years would walk out the door and never come back.

But that isn't my Catie. Catie would never leave.

"But why didn't you ever tell me?" Cate asked.

A ragged sigh escaped Julia's lips. "That was your father's decision. He was afraid to let you know. When I tried to argue him out of it, he made me promise that I would never tell you." Julia tried to read her daughter's expression, but Cate had on what she'd once teased was her special agent face, the one that gave nothing away. Julia proceeded cautiously, as if every step on the tightrope might be her last. "Your father loved you so much, he said it would kill him if someday you wanted to go away to find your real parents."

Digging her elbows into the mattress, Julia struggled to sit up. Shifting pillows, Cate propped her up. Julia offered her a weary smile of thanks. "*We* were your real parents, your father and I."

"I know." Cate said the words because her mother expected them. Because up until a few minutes ago, they had been true. But they weren't now. There was a hollowness opening up inside of her, a hollowness that threatened to swallow her whole. It took everything she had not to let it register on her face.

Doggedly, Cate pressed as much as she dared. "But after Daddy died...?" She paused, searching for words. Trying desperately to absolve the woman she'd thought of as her mother. "Why didn't you tell me then?"

A helpless look entered the hazel eyes. "You were fifteen and I didn't know how to tell you. I did try, though, several times. But every time an occasion opened up, I realized that, like your father, I was afraid, too. You have to understand, after he died, you were all I had. I didn't want to lose you."

After her father died, she and her mother had grown closer. So close that when it came time for her to go away to college, she opted to go to the University of San Francisco instead of a school back east the way she'd originally planned. She didn't want to be far from her mother in case she was needed.

They'd taught her that family was everything.

How could they have said that to her, knowing what they'd known?

Cate battled back the bitter anger as she lightly squeezed her mother's hand. Trying to remember only the good times. "You wouldn't have lost me, Mama."

The look in Julia's eyes said she knew better. "I've lost you now."

She couldn't allow her to think like that. If Julia was going to get well, she needed only positive energy in her life. Cate was determined to provide it. She knew she owed it to the other woman.

"Shh, don't talk nonsense. I'm here and I'm always going to be here." Cate took the once robust woman into her arms. Julia felt as if she weighed next to nothing and it broke her heart. "You just make sure that you do the same, understand?"

"I'm trying, Catie," Julia whispered hoarsely. "I'm trying."

"Yes, Mama, I know you are."

The problem was, Cate thought, she was afraid that it just wasn't enough. A cold fear gripped her heart once again.

Chapter 4

When her mother fell asleep, Cate slipped out into the parking lot and drove the five miles over to Doc Ed's office.

Rhonda, the nurse who had been with him for the past ten years, looked somewhat surprised to see her and even more surprised when she asked to speak with the doctor. The nurse obligingly sandwiched her in between patients.

Cate ignored the exasperated look the woman in the waiting room gave her as she walked by and went into the inner office.

The doctor's terrain was as familiar as the back of her own hand. Three exam rooms huddled together, with Doc Ed's personal office at the end of the tiny hall. All three charts were in the slots that hung on the outside of the doors. It reminded her of Goldilocks and the

Three Bears, except that she was in search of something far more important than porridge and comfortable sleeping accommodations.

She knocked once on Doc Ed's door and let herself in before he gave his permission. If he was surprised to see her, he hid it well.

Cate struggled to hold in her hurt and anger. "You knew, didn't you?"

Doc Ed put down the file he was reviewing and indicated that she should take the chair that was before his scarred desk. Old-fashioned in his methods, he put the patient before the fee and there was no computer on his desk, challenging his mind and his time. He liked only what he could put his hands on, like the files that littered every flat surface within his office.

"Yes," he told her, scrutinizing her reaction, "I knew."

Somehow, that seemed like the ultimate betrayal to her. Had no one in her life been honest with her? "For how long?"

"From the beginning. I was the one who put them in touch with the private agency."

Cate reminded herself that she was first and foremost a special agent with the FBI. That meant she had to conduct herself professionally. She was supposed to be able to gather information under the worst situations, and heaven knew, this one qualified. "What was the name of it?"

Doc Ed shook his head. "Angels From Heaven," he told her. "But it's long gone." He saw the protest rise to her lips, as if she thought he was lying. "From what I'd heard, the lawyer handling all the private adoptions was killed in a freak accident. Stepped off a curb and right in front of a bus. Died instantly."

That sounded like the punchline of a bad joke. "When?"

Doc Ed thought for a moment, trying to pin down a year. He remembered reading the story in the paper and wondering what was going to happen to all the files of the babies who had changed hands. He'd even gone so far as to try to find out. But the address on the card the lawyer had given him turned out to belong to a dry cleaner's now. All trace of the dead man's small office was gone.

"Twelve, fifteen years ago. Without him, there was no agency."

She watched the doctor's eyes for signs of nervousness. Seeing none still didn't convince her. He could just be a convincing liar. After all, he'd allowed her to believe a lie all these years. "You're sure?"

Doc Ed spread his hands wide. "I have no reason to lie to you, Catherine."

"You had no reason to keep my adoption from me, either," she pointed out.

"Not my call, Catherine." He leaned back in his chair, an old leather chair that had long since assumed his shape. It creaked slightly as he studied her. She was a strong-willed girl, she always had been. She would get through this, but not easily. "For what it's worth, I thought your father was wrong, keeping this from you." He laughed softly to himself. "Big Ted was absolutely fearless, but you were his Achilles heel."

Her eyebrows drew together. That didn't make any

sense to her. Achilles heels signified a weakness. She'd never held Big Ted back. "I don't understand."

"If you had wanted to call someone else 'Dad,' it would have killed Big Ted. You were the sun and the moon and stars to him."

How could her father have even thought that she'd turn her back on him and all their time together? Turn her back on the man who'd taught her how to ride a dirt bike, how to play baseball, how to fish. She'd been the best boy she could be for her father, and all the while the relationship she'd believed in didn't even exist.

"But he didn't trust me."

The accusation surprised Doc Ed. "What?"

"He didn't trust me," she repeated. "My father didn't trust me not to leave him, not to think of him differently once I knew that I didn't have his genes in my body." She leaned forward, trying to make Doc Ed understand what she was still trying to grapple with herself. "Don't you see, if my father had told me I was adopted, it would have been no big deal. I knew a couple of kids in school who were adopted and they were okay.

"But he didn't tell me. Neither of them did, and *that* made it a big deal. That they couldn't tell me the truth. And the truth I knew was a lie." Restless, she ran her hand through her hair. "Now I'm not really sure about anything anymore, least of all who I am."

Doc Ed reached for her hand and forced her to look at him. "You're still Catherine Kowalski," he told her firmly. "You can call yourself Watermelon, it makes no difference. You're still Cate."

Despite herself, her mouth quirked in a half smile. "Watermelon, huh?"

"Watermelon," he repeated.

Her smile faded and she shook her head. "It's not the name that matters, Doc. It's the truth that makes a difference. And the truth is that someone else gave birth to me, that there are genes inside of me that didn't come from the people who, until a couple of hours ago, I'd thought of as Mom and Dad. The truth is, I thought there was no secret in my family and there is. And it's a whopper."

Doc Ed folded his hands on the desk and looked at her over his glasses. "So what are you going to do? All the records that might have given you a clue are long gone."

Maybe not, she thought. Maybe someone had claimed them, stored them. Something. But she wasn't going to deal with that now.

"For the time being, I'm going to stay where I'll do the most good, right here with my mother." She noted how he smiled when she still referred to Julia as her mother. "I'm putting in for a leave of absence so I can be with her for as long as I can. After she gets well, we'll see."

Unlike his colleagues, he believed in dispensing hope if there was even so much as a shred to be had. But even he couldn't find it within his heart to allow her to deceive herself like this. "Cate, you know that she might not get well."

Cate squared her shoulders, the look in her eyes forbidding him to say anything more. "Please," she whispered the word quietly, "I'm dealing with one truth at a time."

* * *

Two and a half weeks later, Cate found herself standing at her mother's gravesite. It was raining, which seemed somehow fitting. She'd been angry at the sun for daring to shine the day of her father's funeral so many years ago.

She was only vaguely aware that her partner, James Wong, was holding an umbrella over her head, keeping her dry. Vaguely aware of the world in general. She felt as if she was walking along on the outside of a huge circle, looking in.

She'd refused the Valium Doc Ed had offered her just before the ceremony. She didn't want to be any more numb than she already was. Numb from the loss of a woman she'd loved with all her heart and had thought of as her mother to the very end, despite everything.

Numb from the realization that she'd been lied to for the past twenty-seven years of her life.

Numb because there were no foundations beneath her feet, no walls around her to protect her. She was bare and exposed. Completely and utterly adrift in dark waters. And for the first time in her life, she had no sense of identity. She had no idea who she was, or who she might have been meant to be.

She wouldn't know anything until she found the answers to the questions that had been battering her brain for the past two and a half weeks.

Ever since that day in her mother's hospital room.

Just before the end, her mother had begged her to forgive her and of course she had. She bore no malice toward the people who had done everything in their power to make her feel loved and secure. But it didn't negate her desire to discover her birth parents and, with them, her roots.

Cate realized that the priest had stopped talking. The ceremony was almost over. Someone handed her a white rose. She went through the motions, kissing a petal and then throwing the flower onto the deep-mahogany casket that lay nestled in the freshly dug grave.

As she looked down, she felt her heart tightening within her chest.

Julia Kowalski had died three days ago. And now she and Big Ted were together again.

And she was alone. Completely alone. With no family to fall back on.

Neither one of her parents had had any siblings. Cate had always thought of herself as the only child of only children. Now she no longer knew what to think, what to feel.

Except for alone.

Everyone gathered at her parents' house after the funeral. Betsy Keller, her mother's best and oldest friend, had taken over and handled all the arrangements. Had insisted on it.

"You have enough to deal with, poor thing," she'd clucked sympathetically several times during the past three days.

The mother of six and grandmother of nine, Betsy took to traffic control easily. Rather than call in a caterer, she'd summoned the collective resources of all of Julia's friends. The women had brought over casseroles, pies, cakes and enough food to feed two armies.

"You've got to eat something," Betsy insisted. She paused to deliver the same entreaty every time their paths crossed within the crammed house filled with people who had loved Julia and Ted.

And each time, Cate would respond the same way. "Maybe later."

Betsy would peer at her through her red-rimmed glasses. "All right, but I'll be watching you."

Cate forced a smile to her lips. She tried to cheer herself up with the fact that her mother had been well loved by a great many people. Both her parents had been. And she was going to miss them terribly, but it was going to take her some time to get over the fact that they had deceived her. That they hadn't had enough faith in her to know that she wasn't about to pick up and go searching for her birth parents the moment she knew of their existence.

She wouldn't have then. But, she had to now. Now that she had no roots. No family to call her own. Maybe it was a failing, she thought, but she needed to feel part of something. Something other than the bureau.

She made eye contact with James, who was there with his wife and oldest son. Her partner started to come over, but she shook her head and James faded back, giving her space.

As she stood, looking at people exchanging pleasantries, catching up on one another's lives, she became aware that someone had come up to join her. She began to move away but felt something being slipped into her hand.

"What's this?" Cate looked down at the brown manila envelope Doc Ed had just given her.

"Everything that I know about your adoption. It's not much, but it might give you a start." Slipping his arm around her slim shoulders, he said, "I know you people at the bureau have ways of finding things out as long as you have some kind of starting point."

The envelope was light. It couldn't contain much. "We don't use government resources for personal ends."

His gray eyes twinkled for the first time in three days. He gave her a fatherly squeeze. "Yeah, and I'm sure there are ways around that, too, Catherine. Now, eat something before I have you strapped down to a gurney and fed intravenously."

She looked down at the manila envelope again. The smile that rose to her lips was only slightly forced, far less than what she'd been displaying all day as well-wishers pumped her hand, gave their condolences and told her stories about her parents.

"Yes, sir."

He took hold of her arm and steered her toward one of the two tables laden down with food. "If you think I'm going to be taken in by that, then you don't really know me, either."

She appreciated the irony he'd tossed her way.

Chapter 5

Dr. Lukas Graywolf quietly tiptoed up behind his wife in the Wedgwood-blue tiled bathroom of their modest Southern California home. He slipped his arm around her waist and buried his face in the nape of her neck. Taking a deep breath, he inhaled the fragrance that still clung to her skin from her morning shower, an event he sorely regretted missing.

"So how's the bureau's sexiest extra-special agent this morning?"

He'd startled her. Lost in thought and rushing, Lydia Wakefield Graywolf hadn't realized that her husband was behind her until she'd seen his reflection in the slightly fogged mirror a second before he'd wrapped his arm around her waist.

Lucky for him that she had, otherwise he might have found himself sprawled out on the floor, flat on his back. She wasn't trained for pleasant surprises, only the other variety.

Lydia had had every intention of going in to the office early today. Certain new things had come to light regarding the case she was working on and she wanted to go over the details. And they were getting in someone new today, a Catherine Kowalski from up north. The assistant director wanted her to take the woman under her wing as if she was some kind of mother hen instead of one of their top operatives.

She didn't have time to babysit anyone.

She didn't have time for this, either, Lydia thought, but she allowed herself to linger for a moment in the embrace of the man she loved more than life itself.

His bare chest pressed against her back and heat penetrated the bath towel she'd wrapped around herself. She could feel the heat stirring her. Tiny tongues of desire began to burn away at logic and resolve. Her mascara wand slipped from her fingers.

Lydia smiled at his reflection, their eyes meeting as she covered his arm with her hand. "The bypass surgery went well, I take it?"

He hadn't mentioned the operation to her yesterday at breakfast. Their schedules were so busy lately, especially hers, that they barely had time to see each other. He didn't want to waste what time they had together with shop talk. Neither did she.

He wished they could both take some time off and just spend it with each other, going away to some reclusive beach where the next warm body was miles away.

She'd probably go stir crazy within two days, he thought with a silent laugh. Lydia always had to be doing something. Most of the time that involved making the country safe for tomorrow.

Pressing a kiss to the side of her neck, Lukas thought for the umpteenth time how lucky he was to have found Lydia. Everything had changed since she'd come into his life, including him. He never knew he could feel like this, that love could be so uplifting, so empowering.

He felt her sigh as it rippled through her. "You add clairvoyance to your job description, Special Agent Graywolf?"

With a small laugh, Lydia turned around to face him, her body brushing against his as she did so. Her heart quickened a little, the way it always did when they were so close together.

Her husband had the vaguest hint of stubble on his rugged, handsome face, and there was still a trace of sleep in his vivid blue eyes. Right now, he looked more like a boy than the skilled surgeon that he was. She didn't know who she loved more, the boy or the man.

Because her towel felt as if it was slipping, she tugged it back into place, then threaded her arms around his neck. "Not that I couldn't use that kind of an added boost, especially with this case, but clairvoyance has nothing to do with it. You always act like this whenever a bypass goes well."

He didn't mind being predictable, but she'd aroused his curiosity. "Like what?"

She cocked her head. Her smile bathed over him. "As if you just won the brass ring and all's well with the world."

"All *is* well with the world and the brass ring I won

doesn't have anything to do with Mr. Sellers, the man whose life yours truly saved yesterday." His sentence was punctuated with two light, almost chaste kisses, delivered to first one cheek, then the other.

A sound akin to a purr escaped her lips. Lydia moved her hips against his, her body silently teasing him, drawing him out.

"Oh?" There was nothing short of mischief in her eyes. "Then what?"

He'd started this, but now he was the one who was hopelessly trapped. Trapped by the look in her eyes, by the smile on her face. By the feelings that were always there, just a hairbreadth beneath the surface, waiting to be summoned and pressed into service.

"You know damn well, what." Lukas pressed a kiss to her temple. "It has to do with a certain sexier-than-hell FBI operative."

Gazing up at him, struggling not to melt right there in his arms, Lydia batted her lashes at Blair Memorial's leading cardiac surgeon like an old-fashioned femme fatale. "Anyone I know?"

"Maybe." Ever so lightly, he brushed her lips with his own and ignited a fire in his veins. "Someone I definitely know better than you do."

Because she was so well trained, Lydia didn't stiffen, didn't react. Lukas had said that before. That he knew her better than she knew herself. Until recently, she wouldn't have taken exception to the point.

Until recently, she would have been the first to say that Lukas could see into her very soul, a soul that had been driven and troubled until she'd allowed him into her life.

But now, well, now he didn't know her as well as he thought he did. Didn't know that she was keeping something from him and would continue to do so for at least a while longer, even though it killed her to do it. But there were reasons for what she was doing, reasons she knew that her husband wouldn't understand.

"Speaking of which," Lukas murmured, his words heating the hollow of her throat just before he kissed it, "something bothering you?"

It was a struggle to keep her eyes from fluttering shut. She really did need to get down to the Santa Ana field office and Lukas was making it very, very difficult for her to keep her mind on her goal. She'd been rigorously trained to withstand anything the enemy might have to throw at her. But this was torture of an entirely different variety. Lukas was her weakness as well as the source of her strength.

"Other than the chaos of the world as we know it?" Lydia could feel her very core tightening. Yearning. Her husband had one hell of a bedside manner.

She heard him laugh softly as he took another pass at her throat. "Other than that."

His hand cupped her breast, pressing lightly. Her mind began scrambling. "No, why?"

"You were talking in your sleep last night. I couldn't make out the words." He raised his head to look at her, a faint line of concern between his eyes. "And you were tossing and turning like a top. That's something new."

Anyone else would have used a far more modern comparison, she thought. But Lukas had spent his childhood living on a Navajo reservation in Arizona.

It was a life that had deprived him of so many things that children even in his generation had taken for granted. For lack of other toys, he had probably played with a top as a boy. It might have been something that had been handed down from generation to generation, because on the reservation there was nothing else to give a child beyond love, which she knew her mother-in-law did with abundance.

Without realizing it, Lydia caught her bottom lip between her teeth. The answer to her husband's question was very simple. But she couldn't give it to him. God, but she hated keeping anything from Lukas. Still, there might not even *be* something to tell him. She wasn't certain. But there was no way she could share her thoughts with Lukas. She knew him. The second he found out, he'd want her to restrict her duties. As would the department. And she couldn't, not yet. Not until this case was over.

She was personally invested in the case, had been right from the start. If she was taken off the case or relegated to some desk, it would probably kill her. Or come very close.

Lydia gave him a half truth. "Just the case," she answered vaguely, then before Lukas could comment, she added, "and frustration."

His eyes narrowed as he looked up at her, momentarily abandoning the slow-moving siege he was laying to her body. "What do you mean?"

Her mouth curved wickedly. "Well, there I was, lying alone in that big, empty bed. My husband was gone, working late—"

He'd had plans of being home by six. Instead, he'd

gotten home after eleven. There'd been complications. When he'd walked into the bedroom, Lydia had already gone to bed and was asleep.

"The operation ran over. Way over."

Lydia nodded. They'd made a promise when they were first married that neither would upbraid the other because of the demands of their careers. Each felt that what they did was of paramount importance.

She smiled seductively now, not wanting him to think she was complaining in the true sense of the word. An intentionally dramatic sigh escaped her lips before she said, "Maybe if I'd had someone there with me last night, I wouldn't have been so tense or tossed around 'like a top.'"

When she looked at him like that, there was very little he could do to resist her. And there was no desire to. He could feel his body hardening in response to the look in her eyes.

He'd been exhausted when he'd walked in last night. Exhausted, but exhilarated. There was nothing he'd wanted more than to make love with her then. Disappointment had nibbled away at him when he'd found Lydia asleep. But it never occurred to him to wake her to satisfy his own needs.

Right now, he pretended to lament the lost opportunity. "If I'd known that, I would have woken you up."

Lydia sniffed. "Yeah, yeah, big words after the fact." She placed her hands on his biceps, loving the way the muscles felt under her palms. "I guess I'll just have to take a rain check." Lukas dropped his hands from her waist and lightly tugged on the towel she had wrapped around her. She raised her eyes to his face, barely keeping hers straight. "What are you doing?"

"Unless I miss my guess," he said, giving the towel a final tug, "preparing for rain."

Lydia laughed as her damp towel hit the floor, pooling around her feet. Along with her resistance. Still, she was honorbound to make an attempt at a protest. "Luke, I have to get to the office."

He filled his hands with her hair, bringing her mouth to his. She felt his breath on her lips as he promised, "You will."

Everything inside of her was turning to the consistency of oatmeal. "I mean, like soon."

Amusement etched itself into his features. "I'll be quick, I promise."

Any kind of resolve she might have been able to muster on short notice evaporated like icicles in the hot August sun. She had never been able to resist Lukas, not even from the very first. And then she'd been armed with determination, resolved not to allow herself to fall for the tall, dark, handsome surgeon. As if she had any say in the matter, even then.

They'd met under the most dire of circumstances. She'd burst into the hospital E.R., accompanying a man she'd shot not fifteen minutes earlier. He'd been the grief-stricken parent of a young girl who had overdosed on drugs she'd gotten from someone dealing at the mall. Extremists had tapped into his grief, making use of his knowledge of demolitions. Only timing and a huge amount of luck had allowed her and her former partner to partially foil his plot to blow up the mall.

She'd arrived at the hospital determined to bring her

wounded "suspect" to justice. Lukas was only concerned with saving his life.

All in all, it hadn't been the best setting for love to take root, but it had. Strongly. But then, she hadn't counted on the determination of a man like Lukas. Despite their years of marriage, she could feel her head beginning to spin, her pulse beginning to race as his lips roamed over her shoulders. God, she hoped that would never change.

"Just not too quick," she cautioned.

Stripping off the pajama bottoms that had just barely been clinging to his hips, Lukas caught her up in his arms.

"Your wish is my command," he told her just before he brought his mouth down on hers.

And made the world disappear.

Chapter 6

The moment she got behind the wheel of her vehicle, Lydia transformed. She was no longer Lydia Graywolf, the proud, contented and very much in love wife of a prominent cardiac surgeon. She was Special Agent Lydia Wakefield Graywolf, a dedicated operative who had given her all to the bureau.

At times, she found the system restrictive, the regulations frustratingly binding. But when she came right down to it, no better system existed within the country, certainly not outside it. And until a better one did, she was determined to remain working for the bureau in one capacity or another. That meant being a field operative, and she wanted nothing to change that. Not yet.

Again, a pang of guilt slipped through her. She banked it down.

Not now, she told herself sternly. There was time

enough for that later, when she was a hundred percent certain.

Lydia glanced at her watch. Silver-banded, blue-faced, it had been a gift from Lukas on their first wedding anniversary. The irony of it was, without knowing his choice, she'd bought a similar one for him.

Just showed that they thought alike, she mused. Kindred spirits that had found each other.

She wasn't late—yet—but she certainly wasn't going to be early the way she wanted to be, either.

Pressing down on the accelerator, Lydia gunned her engine. She made her way from Bedford to Santa Ana taking surface streets. The Santa Ana Freeway was a bear at this hour of the morning. Traffic was known to come to a dead stop with a fair amount of regularity. She didn't have the patience for that this morning.

Lately, there was very little patience to draw on.

Periodically, Lydia glanced up in the rearview mirror, keeping an eye out for any policeman who might have a quota to fill. Luck was with her. She managed to fly through a number of amber traffic lights before they turned red and kept her from getting to the office on time. Any hope of getting there early died the second Lukas had kissed her that morning.

No, she amended, they'd died the moment he'd come up behind her.

She didn't exactly hold it against him. Lydia knew she was one of the lucky ones. Like her mother had been before her.

Love was a funny thing. The right kind of love lit things up, made even the worst that life threw at you bearable. Made life exciting. She didn't take it, or Lukas, for granted for one moment.

She realized that she'd had love all her life. First from her parents, from her mother who'd doted and from her father, whom she'd emulated by entering the world of law enforcement. And then from Lukas. She didn't know if she would have turned out to be the same person had she grown up the hard way. Without love.

Main Street, which went from Bedford straight through to Santa Ana, lost a lane, when she entered the latter city. While every bit of Bedford was modern, Santa Ana was comprised of both the old and the recently renovated.

Traffic moved slowly on the older streets, and there was no use fighting it.

Her mind turned to the case, where some young girls' lives were over before they had even begun. Their hope, their very souls, were stolen from them, leaving behind empty shells. Girls barely into puberty who did what they could to survive in a world they hated.

The task force she headed was trying to break up a teenage prostitute ring that had far-reaching tentacles. In some cases, the girls weren't even teens yet. Just yesterday, it had come to light that kiddie porn was involved. Videos depicting awful, awful things that little girls shouldn't even know about, much less take part in.

She knew most of the girls had either run away from intolerable conditions at home, or been sold into the life by a family member. Somebody needed crack but had no money, so he passed around a daughter, a younger sister, any means to an end. It happened more often than she wanted to acknowledge and made her sick to her stomach.

And if it was the last thing she did, she was going to break up the ring and send whoever was responsible to prison. But first, she wanted to hang them upside down by their genitals. And leave them there for a week. Maybe longer.

She owed it to her cousin Susan.

Traffic cleared up a block away from the civic plaza. The difference between the blocks that housed the federal buildings and their surrounding area was astounding, like going from one world to another. Every so often, like today, it hit her anew.

After making a left, Lydia drove into the structure, not even bothering to look for a place in the open lot. You had to arrive at six to get a spot there. She parked her car, made her way back into the daylight and hurried across the grounds to the second federal building. She took the stone steps leading to the glass doors two at a time. The doors parted automatically, and she sailed right through. It was a quarter to nine and already busy.

The second she got off the elevator on the seventh floor, she walked into Mike Santiago, narrowly avoiding his jelly doughnut. Considering that Mike's reach cleared him to over seven feet, there was little danger of jelly smearing across the navy blazer she had on today.

Once he lowered his prize, he took a bite, then nodded his head toward the rear of the room where the A.D. had his office. "New girl's here. She's in with Sullivan."

Lydia made her way to her desk. They were all out in the open here, unrestricted by cubicle walls. That was both good and bad, depending on which side of a private conversation you were on.

"We're not girls, Santiago," she told him mechanically, knowing he expected it, "we're women."

Married, with two kids and one on the way, Santiago was as faithful as they came. But he liked perpetuating the image of a Romeo. "You can say that again. This one makes me glad God made me a man."

Lydia deposited her purse into the bottom drawer of her desk, then shut it with her foot. Looking at the tall, slightly rumpled agent, she shook her head. "God's not finished yet."

Mike did his best to imitate a leer as he spread his hands before him. "Any time you want to sample the goods, Graywolf…"

They'd known each other ever since she'd joined the field office some six years ago. And had been friends for almost as long.

"Death would be preferable." Taking off her jacket, she draped it over the back of her chair. Her blond hair was caught back in a clip and worn up, her style of choice while on the job. "Besides, I have something really special at home."

"Brag, brag, brag." Tommy Hawkins came up behind her, munching on another doughnut, a plain glaze. Tiny bits of sugar broke off, marking his path from the common room. In his late fifties, widowed with one estranged son who lived on the opposite coast, Tommy seemed to be counting the days to retirement. And dreading it. "Morning, Beautiful."

She gave him her best deadpan expression. "That's sexist, Tommy."

"That's observant," he corrected, then winked broadly at her. "I won't tell if you won't."

A smile curved her mouth. "You win again." She indicated the doughnuts both men were consuming. "What's the occasion?"

"I didn't ask," Tommy said. "That way, nobody can tell me they're not meant for everyone."

Mike wiped his lips and tossed the napkin into the basket by Lydia's desk. "New girl—excuse me, woman, brought them."

"She trying to bribe us?" Tommy asked.

"Works for me," Mike responded. "Wouldn't mind having another." He glanced toward the common room. From here, he could just barely see into it. The large box of doughnuts was on a table near the rear of the room.

Lydia looked in the opposite direction, toward Assistant Director Aaron Sullivan's office. She could see a poised, young blonde in a teal-blue suit sitting in the chair beside Sullivan's desk. The new special agent. *Her* new special agent if she were to believe Sullivan. The A.D. had said the young woman would be working with them. And specifically, she would be taking Patterson's place. Her partner had put in for a leave of absence shortly after he'd been wounded. It was his second time and he thought that perhaps it was an omen that he should reevaluate his career choice. Over the years, they had come to work like a well-oiled machine. She'd known him longer than she'd known Lukas. Although the time interval since he'd left had been short, she already missed him like crazy.

Welcoming his substitute, even his temporary substitute, was not going to be easy.

Lydia looked back at the men she worked with. "Anyone know anything about her?"

Tommy shrugged, finishing his doughnut. "Just that she's a transfer from San Francisco."

Lydia sighed. "Which means she's probably a hot-shot, or thinks she is."

Santiago laughed. "And we all know that you're the only hotshot around."

Playing along, Lydia patted Mike's face. "And don't you forget it."

All three saw Sullivan rising from his chair. He'd be summoning them soon. Tommy straightened his jacket, but it still looked wrinkled. "Time to make nice, Lydia."

Plucking her own jacket from the back of her chair, she slipped it on again. "Yeah."

Instinct had Cate glancing over her shoulder a second before the three people entered the assistant director's inner office.

These would be some of her new co-workers.

They looked friendly enough, she decided. The woman seemed to be sizing her up. Undoubtedly wondering if she was going to be competition. Well, she'd put the special agent's mind at rest soon enough. She had no desire to compete on any level, except possibly against herself. All she wanted to do was her job.

That and find her birth mother.

The day after the funeral, she'd gotten down to work, though still on leave. She utilized everything

she had at her disposal, determined to track down any
shred of information regarding her birth parents and her
subsequent adoption. What Doc Ed had said to her was
true enough, she would still be Cate Kowalski at the
end of the journey. But depending on what she found
out and the effect it had on her, she very well might be
a different version of herself.

And if for some reason that didn't happen and she
remained just as she'd always been, that was all well
and good. But the bottom line was that she needed to
know why she'd been given up. And most of all, she
needed to know the identity of her biological parents.

Doc Ed had given her her start, handing her names.
Thanks to Jeremy Kovel, a computer wizard she'd
briefly dated, and his almost uncanny ability to pluck
things out of cyberspace, she'd managed to find Ava
Gerber. Ava was the secretary who had handled all the
details for Larry Lieberman, the lawyer who had arranged for her adoption.

Retired and desperate for company, Ava needed no
prodding to get her to talk about her days with Lieberman. The woman turned out to be one of those
secretaries who ran the entire office and was up on
everything that had ever crossed not just her desk, but
her boss's as well. Thanks to Ava and her incredible
memory, made more accessible over wine and dinner
at the finest restaurant in San Francisco, Cate wound
up getting the names of not just her birth mother, but
her birth father as well.

"I got the feeling that he didn't know anything about
it," Ava confided over her third glass, her head nodding
dangerously. "But she put his name on the baby's birth

certificate." She'd grinned broadly at her. "That would be you, I guess."

Her last name, it turned out, was Blue. Bonnie Blue. Like the old sea chantey about the ocean. In any event, the name didn't really fit, and there was a reason for that. As it turned out, the name wasn't really her birth father's, either. He'd been a would-be musician who'd billed himself as Blue in his short-lived career of going from one half-baked band to another. His real name was Jim Rollins, and his so-called career had lasted long enough to attract the attention of one Joan Haywood.

Instead of becoming a successful musician, Rollins had wound up going into life insurance and was a salesman for Gotham Life when he'd died in a three-car pileup on I-15 on his way to Las Vegas for a three-day weekend. Twice divorced, he had no children, no family that she could unearth.

Cate turned from that dead end to searching for her birth mother, Joan Haywood. The trail had brought her to Bedford, California.

Since the bureau had field offices in Santa Ana and Los Angeles, she'd decided to put in for a transfer. She'd needed a change of scenery, anyway. The Santa Ana office was closer to Bedford and to her birth mother's last-known address, so she'd chosen the one city over the other.

Cate realized that she was gripping the arms of the chair she was sitting in when the trio walked into the office. She dropped her hands into her lap. She was going to have to work at learning to relax. Otherwise, by the time she did find her birth mother, who had moved several times in the past twenty-six years, gotten married and was now Joan Cunningham, she was going to be far too stressed out to have something good come out of the meeting.

Chapter 7

After a very poor night's sleep during which she had woken up every hour on the hour, Cate finally gave up and stumbled into the living room of her garden apartment. She narrowly avoided tripping over a small box she'd opened some time earlier. It took her a minute to remember where the light switch was. Boxes impeded her progress to the opposite wall.

There were boxes everywhere within the two-bedroom ground-floor apartment. She'd been here almost a week now and it still looked as if she'd just arrived from San Francisco.

Cate tried to remember if she'd unpacked any paper yet besides the sheets that were with her printer. Frustrated, she went into the second, smaller bedroom, which would eventually become her office, and took a sheet right off the top.

It had taken her two trips to get everything together in one place. She'd brought her car down first, then flew back to rent the U-Haul. Whatever she couldn't cram into it, she'd left behind. She wasn't much on possessions, anyway. Her mother used to tell her that if you owned too much, it wound up owning you.

Fiercely independent, Cate liked being in control of everything, had been that way since her father, since Big Ted—she amended with an ironic smile—had died. She'd controlled the timing of her move down here, the method used to do everything.

Control, however, didn't extend to unpacking within a given amount of time. That she did on a need-to-have basis. So far, beyond her computer and printer, she'd unearthed a week's worth of clothing and her coffeemaker. Everything else she'd brought with her, besides the small amount of furniture that was now disbursed within the rooms, was still sealed away within the boxes.

Her furniture might have still been on the truck if it hadn't been for Lydia. To her surprise, when she'd mentioned in passing that she planned to spend the weekend unloading her U-Haul, Lydia had volunteered to come over with her husband and help. She'd also volunteered Santiago and Hawkins, much to the agents' surprise.

Cate had tried to turn down the offer, saying that it wasn't necessary, but Lydia wouldn't take no for an answer. From anyone.

Sometimes pushy had its place, Cate thought with a smile. She had no idea how long it would have taken her to unload the U-Haul by herself.

Making her way to the kitchen, paper still in hand, she went to the refrigerator to take out the can of coffee she kept there. If she wasn't going back to bed, she needed a cup of coffee. Maybe several cups.

She got along well with her new partner, which was a nice bonus. And the woman's husband was a sweetheart. The two looked perfect together, like the figures on top of a wedding cake, except far more lively and animated. Anyone looking at them knew they were in love.

She envied Lydia, envied her because she would never know what that was like, being married to someone she adored who adored her back. Her one chance had come and gone with Gabe.

"So you're the new special agent. Read your file." There'd been no expression on Lydia's face when the woman had initially greeted her.

Lydia seemed to have materialized out of nowhere and looked her carefully up and down. Cate knew she was being sized up. But she didn't have long to wait to discover what the verdict was. A smile entered Lydia's eyes at the same time it curved her mouth.

"Pretty impressive" had been her verdict about what she'd read. "Reminds me of me." One of the other agents in the room had punctuated her statement with "Ha!" and she'd nodded behind her. "That would be the bull pen. Don't mind them. All thumbs and male testosterone." She winked and her smile widened. "Nice to have another female on the team. They can get pretty rowdy sometimes."

She wasn't sure if Lydia was serious or joking, but she liked the woman's friendly manner. Liked her almost instantly because Lydia didn't seem worried about guarding her territory, she'd made it instantly clear the job was about teamwork. Lots of it.

"This thing gets uglier by the day," Lydia had warned her, dropping off a thick-looking file on her desk. She discovered that all the notes taken on the case that hadn't made it onto the computer were stuffed in there. "It's about all the awful things in society the rest of the world doesn't want to hear about. Kidnapping, child prostitution. The worst of it is, we still don't have much, despite all the hours we've all put in." Lydia placed her hand on the file before Cate had been able to open it and asked, "Are you up to it? Because if you're not, I can recommend having you transferred to something that isn't quite as gut-wrenching to deal with."

It was a first. No one had ever given her a choice, considered her reaction before. It made her feel instantly accepted. She'd looked at Lydia and said, "I'm up to it."

Lydia had nodded and smiled. "Good." She removed her hand from the file.

In a way, Cate thought now, Lydia reminded her of a slightly older version of herself. Very together, very efficient, and driven. All qualities she could relate to. Except perhaps the "together" part, she mused. She still tried to project that image, but inside she felt like a little girl lost, waiting for someone to find her.

Knowing that no one would.

It was up to her to find *them.* Or in this case, her birth mother. Until that was resolved, she felt as if she was just hovering around, unable to find a place to really settle.

Which, she supposed, was one of the reasons most of the boxes still remained packed. It wasn't that she intended to pick up and go somewhere at a moment's notice, but she couldn't quite get herself to unpack and make herself at home here, because she wasn't certain that "here" would be home.

Besides, she was far too busy to unpack more than a few things at a time. Whatever time she had away from the job and the man-hours it demanded, she spent on the computer, trying to track down the whereabouts of one Joan Haywood, now Cunningham.

It was far from easy. She was good, but she wasn't in Jeremy's league. From what she had managed to piece together, both while in San Francisco and now here, her birth mother had gone on to have a regular life after she'd given away her firstborn. Joan Haywood had attended a local four-year college, gotten married in her senior year and then moved down to Southern California.

Her husband, Ron, a former air force pilot, now aerospace engineer, had gone where the jobs were. There'd been five addresses in the past twenty years. And a sixth she couldn't find. The last known address had been in Bedford, even though he was working for an aerospace company in El Segundo. Having gotten familiar with the area, she could appreciate that it was quite a drive. One he didn't have to make for long. Raytheon had laid him off. And then he and Joan, along with their children, had disappeared, going down somewhere beneath the radar. They'd moved, leaving no forwarding address.

Facing a dead end, she'd turned to Jeremy, her computer fairy godfather. In part, he was responsible for her broken night's sleep. Jeremy had called yesterday, saying that he'd managed to hack into records that were far off the beaten path. The records testified that a Ronald Cunningham had undergone a top-secret clearance check a little more than two years ago. The check had been requested by one of the leading companies in defense. When Jeremy had mentioned the name, she'd recognized it instantly. A major branch of the company was domiciled in Orange County, just north of Bedford.

It took Jeremy a little while to ascertain that the social security number for Ron Cunningham and Ronald Cunningham were one and the same. To elude detection, his "break-ins" could last only ninety seconds. Gleaning information had been slow-going. He'd waited until he had more before calling Cate.

When he did, it was well past midnight. Closer to two in the morning. "Got an address for you, Cate. You ready to take it down?"

She'd been in a deep sleep when the phone rang. It had taken her a couple of breaths to get her mind reasonably in gear. It took a little longer to find a writing utensil and paper.

"Don't you ever sleep?" she asked.

Jeremy was a self-described insomniac who prowled chat rooms in the dead of night when nothing else presented itself as a diversion. This was a diversion.

"Not when something's on my mind. I've been looking for this woman for you since you left our field office. By the way, how is it down there?"

Her first response would have been "chaotic," but

that would have been describing her life, not conditions. She gave the standard reply. "Weather's perfect."

Jeremy made a little disparaging noise with his teeth and lips. "Huh. It has no character."

She thought of the cold, clammy winters, the sticky, humid summers she'd left behind. Watching leaves turn color did not balance out the minuses. "That's okay. I've got character enough to spare."

There was no paper to be had, but the local newspaper caught her attention. Scooting off the bed, Cate bent down to capture a corner of the paper and pull it back to her.

In a pinch...

She spread the paper on her lap, her pen poised over one of the margins. "Okay, shoot."

Jeremy recited the address and phone number he'd found in the top-secret files. He turned down her offer to pay him for the information. This was what he did, he told her, he challenged himself. Not for any personal or monetary gain, but just to see if he could do it.

Grateful for his help, Cate jotted the address and phone number down along the margins of the newspaper. She did her best to print carefully. Someone once told her that her handwriting looked as if a spider had been dipped in ink and then allowed to run pell-mell over a page. Cate fervently hoped she'd be able to make it out in the morning.

"That's it for now," Jeremy had concluded.

She put the pen back down on the nightstand. "Thanks, Jeremy. I owe you one."

She heard him laugh shortly. "After all the work I've put in, you don't owe me just one. You owe me your firstborn."

There was a slight pang in her stomach. She tried not to think of Gabe. "Since there's little chance of there ever being a firstborn, let me take you out to lunch the next time I'm up there."

"You're coming back?"

He sounded eager, which she thought was sweet. She'd always liked Jeremy, thinking of him as a slightly unkempt younger brother, even though in reality he was a couple of months older than she was.

As to what she'd just said to him, she'd meant coming back to Frisco for a visit. His question made her stop to consider. And realize again that from where she was standing, her future was undecided and murky.

"I don't know. Maybe. We'll see." She knew nothing was going to be decided until after she'd met with her birth mother and eradicated the hollow feeling she'd been carrying around inside of her for the past three weeks. "First I need to take care of these loose ends."

Everyone who knew Cate knew she was like a bulldog with a bone. Once she clamped down on something, she wouldn't let go until it was resolved to her satisfaction.

"Just don't let them strangle you. Pleasant dreams, Cate."

"Yeah, you, too."

But even as she hung up the receiver and stifled another huge yawn, Cate knew she wasn't going to get any sleep, not tonight. If she forced herself to remain in bed, all she was going to wind up doing was counting the minutes as they trickled their way into dawn. And then count more minutes as she waited for a decent time to arrive before she showed up on her birth mother's doorstep.

Glancing at the address and phone number she'd written in the newspaper margins, she decided that she needed to transcribe both while they still looked reasonably readable.

After that, she promised herself, she'd see about maybe unpacking a few more things.

Cate's hand felt damp on the receiver as she gripped it, her fingers tightly holding the mouthpiece. Her hand was so sweaty, she was surprised that the receiver didn't just slip out of it.

The line on the other end was ringing. She silently counted the number of rings.

She'd waited until eight o'clock, forcing herself to shower and get dressed before she made the call. To hear the voice of the woman who had rejected her. Granted, she'd wound up in a home most kids only dreamed about, rich in love if not possessions, but it could have easily gone another way. She could have landed in an abusive home.

Or worse.

Her birth mother had no way of knowing what her fate was to have been when she gave her away. Right now, it was very hard not to be resentful, if not downright angry with the woman.

"Hello?"

The high-pitched female voice that answered the telephone on the fourth ring sounded way too young to be the woman she was seeking. Joan had been seventeen when she was born. That would make her forty-four or forty-five now. The person on the other end of the line was definitely *not* forty-five.

Her mouth felt like cotton. Cate forced herself to speak. "Hello, this is Catherine Kowalski. Is this Joan Cunningham?"

There was a short, breathless, nervous laugh. It was as if the girl was unaccustomed to speaking to people. "No, this is Rebecca."

That would be Joan's daughter, Cate thought. There was a pause, after which Cate pressed on. "Then may I speak to Joan, please?"

"Sorry, she's not here."

Damn it, she'd waited too long. Joan had left the house for the day. According to what she'd found, her birth mother worked as an interior designer in one of those small, trendy stores along the Pacific Coast Highway. *Athena and Daughter.*

With effort, she managed to rein in her impatience. "What time will she be back?" Cate asked politely.

"I'm not really sure," the girl responded. "My mom's in the hospital."

Chapter 8

Christian flipped the chart closed and frowned. This was the downside of his job and he hated it.

He never minded being roused out of bed at some ungodly hour of the night or predawn to help bring a new life into the world. Even in his worst moments, when the futility of life got to be too much for him, there was something indescribably exhilarating about holding a brand-new human being in his hands. About seeing eyes open for the very first time. About seeing a tiny chest rise and fall as a baby took its first breath. All of it humbled him.

And made him feel hope.

Hope was what he tried to dispense now to Joan Cunningham, the woman in room 527. Hope that the life she cherished so much was not going to be cruelly yanked away from her now, in the prime of her life.

He knew she was frightened. Who wouldn't be in her place? She'd come to his office two days ago with huge eyes and a tremor in her voice. Even as she spoke, there was a silent plea in her eyes, a plea for him to tell her that her fears were unfounded.

He wished he could. But the test results indicated otherwise.

Walking into her hospital room, he tried hard to appear upbeat. It wasn't easy for him. The moment she saw him enter, the woman stiffened as if she were anticipating a physical blow.

He spoke quietly, softly, hoping to soothe her. "Joan, I'm afraid there's no way to say this except to say it, so we're going to get the bad part over with first." Christian realized that he was bracing himself as much as his patient was. "The tumor appears to be malignant."

Joan's long, delicate hands flew up to her mouth as she tried to keep the sob back. She paled, growing whiter than her sheet. He knew one could be braced for the worst, but never fully be prepared for it. Losing Alma had proven that to him.

"Oh God," Joan cried. "Oh God, oh God."

"But," he continued gently, taking her hand and holding it tightly, as if to anchor her to the world, "there is every indication that once we remove it, everything'll be fine."

"It?" Her voice was hollow, numb, as she repeated the single word. Her hand went to her right breast, covering it protectively. Joan was terrified. "You mean my breast?"

He empathized even if he could not relate. "No, just the tumor."

It would have been prudent to add "For now" and cover his bases, but Christian refused to do that to the woman. Refused to hedge at her expense. They'd cross each bridge when they came to it. And they might not have to make that final journey. For now, that was all he was going to focus on.

"It's very, very tiny," he assured her. "I've already spoken to the surgeon. You can be scheduled for surgery as early as this afternoon." He saw fear rise in her eyes. She had to be feeling that things were careering beyond her control. In her place, he knew he would. Christian did what he could to make her feel that it wasn't all out of her reach. "The final decision, of course, is yours."

Joan nervously passed her tongue over her lips as she raised her eyes to his. "What's your opinion?"

He gave her the benefit of his experience—and all the extensive reading he'd done on the subject. Christian didn't believe in entering into a situation unprepared. "I think an aggressive course of action is the most effective way to go. Have the operation and recover. Your life'll be on track again soon."

Joan swallowed hard. The lump in her throat was almost choking her. That's all she needed, another lump, she thought cynically. Her fingers dug into his hand as her eyes searched his face. "Do you promise?"

His profession had long since gotten away from making promises. The day of the promise had gone the way of exchanging medical services for a chicken and three potatoes. These days, people were far too eager to sue over the smallest of things, and this was by no means a small thing. But he couldn't divorce himself from his patients, couldn't think of them as merely names on a file, statistics in a computer, the way so many of his colleagues did.

That wasn't his way. His way was to care. Usually too much.

Christian closed his hand around hers and looked into her eyes. "I promise."

Joan let out a shaky breath. Nervously, she ran her hand through her pale reddish hair and wondered if she was going to lose it in the treatment. She'd always been so proud of her hair. So vain. "I should discuss this with my husband."

He moved over to the telephone on the nightstand beside her bed, picked up the receiver and handed it to her.

"Call him." And then he nodded toward the door. "I'll be back in a little while. I have a few other patients to see to."

Joan nodded mechanically. She looked like a woman whose whole world had been turned upside down, and who could blame her? he thought. It had. And he of all people could identify with the helpless feeling that had to be coursing through her veins.

With any luck, though, all this would be temporary and they *would* have her back on her feet soon. In his case, the helpless feeling was permanent. Nothing was ever going to change that.

He heard Joan begin to press the numbers that would connect her to her husband's telephone at work. He moved out of the room to give her privacy.

Preoccupied, Christian walked right into a woman standing directly outside Joan's door. The impact was sudden and startling.

He had close to a foot on her and nearly knocked her to the floor. Instinct had Christian's hand shooting out to grabbed her and keep the woman from falling. Pulling too hard, he wound up pulling her into him. He was vaguely aware of soft breasts brushing against him a second before he stepped back.

He was also mildly aware of the buzz of electricity just before contact was broken.

"Sorry."

The woman, blond, twenty-ish and dressed for business, shrugged and forced a smile to her lips. "My fault."

He could feel her eyes sweeping over him, as if she was trying to place him. Did he know her? No, he was fairly confident he would have remembered a woman who looked like her.

Christian sank his hands deep into the pockets of his lab coat. The almost pleasant hum throughout his body had yet to cease, even though he willed it to. "Are you looking for someone?"

Still staring at him, she appeared to hesitate before finally answering. "An outpatient here."

Only two of the patients on the floor were his. The others were in the maternity ward two floors up. The woman with the soft smile would do best to ask for her friend's room number where the names were listed.

"The nurses' station is right over there." He pointed it out to her.

Cate had already been there. It was her first stop off the elevator, despite the fact that she had asked for Joan Cunningham's room number at the information desk on the ground floor. "I know. They sent me here."

He had a full schedule even without assisting at Joan's lumpectomy this afternoon. But he noticed that the young woman was looking at the door behind him as if that was her intended goal. The small bit of curiosity he still retained got the better of him. "Who is it you're looking for?"

"Joan," she told him. "Cunningham," the woman added after a moment, as if the surname was difficult for her to work her tongue around.

Moving slightly for a better light, he looked at her more closely. And realized that, despite the different hair color, there was a resemblance between the two women, especially around the mouth and eyes. Younger, fixed up, Joan Cunningham must have been a very pretty woman.

This woman, however, was beautiful. Even in the muted lavender suit, with her silver-blond hair pulled back and away from her face, she was more than just striking. With very little effort, she could have been— what was it that his brother John called it?—drop-dead gorgeous.

He'd never met any of Joan's relatives. Was this her daughter? A younger sister? They seemed to be too far apart for the latter, too close for the former. But then, anything was possible these days.

"Are you related to Joan?"

As he watched, the woman straightened her shoulders, pulling them back as if she was bracing herself for something.

"Yes."

At least, that was what she thought, Cate added silently. If the woman in the room behind this door turned out to really be the Joan Cunningham, nee Haywood, that she was looking for.

Nerves danced through her. Taunting her. She hadn't felt this unsettled even on her very first day out of Quantico, facing her first real boss. But she'd had confidence in herself then.

This was different.

The more he looked at the woman, the more he was certain that she *was* related to Joan. And if she was a relative, she couldn't have timed her appearance better. Joan looked ready to fold when he'd talked to her. There was no doubt in his mind that she was going to need all the support she could get. Even with all the positive feedback he'd given her before she'd gone in for her test, and despite the fact that the numbers were increasing every day regarding survival rate, this news had to be devastating for Joan.

"She's on the phone right now," he told the woman. "Trying to reach her husband with the news. But any encouragement you can give her will be very good."

"Encouragement?" Cate didn't like the sound of that. "What's wrong with her?"

Telling her wasn't his call. His role here was limited, which at times frustrated him. "You'll have to ask her."

Cate nodded, really expecting nothing less by way of an answer. Joan's daughter hadn't been very informative, either, when she'd spoken to her on the phone earlier. But that was probably because she really didn't know what was going on. The girl was eighteen, too young to be burdened with anything that might be happening behind hospital walls. Her mother was undoubtedly keeping this from her. Whatever "this" was.

"I will," she told him. Moving around him, Cate rapped once on the door, then opened it. She assumed that the dark-haired doctor with the electric-blue eyes had gone on his way.

The moment she slipped into the room and closed the door behind her, Cate forgot all about the physician she'd encountered. Forgot about everything except for the woman she saw sitting up in the hospital bed.

The irony of the situation was not lost on her.

A little more than four weeks ago, she was entering another hospital room more than four hundred miles to the north. Entering it to say goodbye to her mother, although she didn't realize it at the time. Her mother slipped into a coma that evening and died twelve days later.

And now here she was, walking into another hospital room, attending possibly another sickbed; this time, though, it was to say hello to her mother. Another mother.

A host of emotions charged through Cate, riding horses with jagged hooves. There was anger, sorrow, joy and so much more. Too much to sort through and catalog. She felt as if she had no room in which to think.

The woman in the bed—was that really her birth mother?—was talking on the phone just as the doctor had told her. Unable to help herself, Cate listened. The redhead's voice was shaky. As shaky as the hands that were desperately clutching the receiver.

"I'm going through with it," she said to the person on the other end of the line. "I just wanted you to know. Dr. Graywolf said it was important to do it as quickly as possible."

The familiar name had her snapping to attention. Dr. Graywolf? Was her partner's husband this woman's doctor? Just how small was the world? Cate wondered.

The fact that there was someone in the room, silently watching her, slowly penetrated the wall of fear around Joan. She murmured "I love you" to her husband and then hung up the phone, her eyes now on the young woman in her room. An eerie feeling wafted through her, as if this wasn't real. As if none of this ever since she'd first detected the thickness on her right breast was real.

As if she was looking into the mirror and seeing into the past.

Joan cleared her throat, her nervousness growing. "Can I help you?"

Cate kept looking at the woman in the bed, searching for some foolproof sign. All the while knowing that there wouldn't be one. "That all depends."

"On what?" Joan whispered the words, now clearly frightened.

Cate took a single step toward her, then stopped. She was afraid that the woman would pass out if she came any closer. Did she know? On some instinctive level, did Joan sense that she was her mother?

Cate put her thoughts into words. "On whether you're willing to admit that you're my mother."

Chapter 9

The woman in the bed drew in a sharp breath. "Excuse me?"

Cate's heart was in her throat as she confronted a piece of her life. The very air felt still, despite the soft *whoosh* made by the air-conditioning system.

Was this woman lying in a hospital bed, looking small, frightened and disoriented, really her biological mother, or had Jeremy's information led them in the wrong direction?

She searched for signs of resemblance and thought she saw a few, but her desire to belong could have colored her perception. Maybe she looked like her father. So far, the only picture she'd managed to find of Jimmy Rollins was his last DMV photo. In true DMV fashion, the photograph was terrible.

"My mother," Cate repeated. The word tasted chalky

on her tongue. Part of her felt disloyal to Julia for even addressing someone else by that name, but part of her felt this need to connect, to still be someone's daughter. The confidence with which she'd helmed her life was nowhere in sight.

Joan pressed the button on the side railing, moving the bed into more of an upright position. She struggled to get hold of herself.

This can't be happening, it wasn't real.

She was still reeling from what Dr. Graywolf had just told her, she couldn't handle this on top of that.

Despite the reading about breast cancer that she'd done, despite having talked to several women at her club who had lived through the horror that she now faced, she'd discovered in the last five minutes that she wasn't prepared at all. Not emotionally. Not for this horrible gut-twisting feeling that threatened to cut off her very air. She felt trapped, unable to know which way to run or where.

And Ron, well, Ron didn't know how to deal with anything that couldn't be solved with some kind of an elaborate mathematical equation. Her husband of the last twenty-two years had all his emotions stored somewhere in a bank vault and she had no idea what the combination to it was.

Her nerves frayed, her future uncertain, Joan was in no condition to field this latest shock.

Avoiding the young woman's eyes, Joan grasped at a lie. "I'm afraid that you must have me confused with someone else."

Then why won't you look at me? Cate silently demanded. People lied to her all the time, attempting to avoid the consequences of their actions. Part of her job was to see through the lies and get down to the truth.

She saw through Joan's.

Cate moved closer to the bed. "Are you Joan Cunningham?"

The woman's breathing became more audible. Like a cornered animal, Cate thought.

"Yes, but—"

Holding up her hand, Cate didn't let her finish. "And are you formerly Joan Haywood?"

The look of panic in the woman's eyes increased. "Yes, but—"

Cate pushed on, refusing to allow the woman a chance to regroup. "And did you live in the San Francisco area twenty-eight years ago? Did you know someone named 'Blue?'"

Joan dug her fingers so deeply into the bedclothes that she was pulling loose not only the white blanket, but the sheets beneath it. Panicked, unable to cope, she cried, "Get out."

Cate remained where she was. Rather than triumph, she felt anger welling up inside of her. This was the woman who'd given her away. People gave away things they didn't want, not children.

Her voice was deadly calm, even though her insides were in turmoil. "Well, did you?"

"I said get out!"

The order came out in almost a high-pitched scream. Frantically, Joan searched for the buzzer to summon a nurse, an orderly, someone, anyone, to come and help her. To come and save her.

This couldn't be happening. This wasn't real. She

was back in her own bed in her own bedroom and this was some nightmare she was having. If she could only scream, Ron would shake her awake and tell her that this was just one of those awful dreams she sometimes had. Dreams of small girls with huge green eyes looking up at her.

It had been a mistake ever to hold that baby, to even look at it. If she hadn't, she would have been able to sweep this out of her life forever, like the nightmare it was.

But she *had* held her little girl. Against her mother's wishes, she had held her baby. Held Bonnie Blue to her breast. And left a piece of her heart wrapped up in those small, curled fingers when the nurse came to take her away.

The woman looking at her had green eyes. Accusing green eyes. Joan shrank back in her bed, still frantically trying to locate the call buzzer that had somehow gotten loose.

"I just need to know that I'm right," Cate said, struggling to remain calm. To keep from crying because the hurt went down deep, scraping against the bone.

Shaking now, Joan felt as if she was falling completely apart. "I don't know what you're talking about. I'm too upset to deal with this—"

"I'd like an answer, please." It was hard keeping the emotion that choked her out of her voice.

"Get out!" Joan screamed again. Finally finding the buzzer, she clutched it in both hands as she pressed the button frantically. Her entire body was trembling. Any moment, she thought she was going to begin convulsing.

The door flew open.

"What's going on here?" Christian demanded as he

strode into the room. He looked accusingly at the young woman by his patient's bedside. He'd been right outside, about to go in when he'd heard Joan's raised voice. Coming in, he recognized the other woman as the one he'd bumped into earlier.

Just who the hell was she and why was she agitating his patient?

Joan looked ready to collapse. "Oh, God, Doctor, please get her out of here," she sobbed, covering her face with her hands. "I can't deal with this right now, I just can't."

Christian had no idea what was going on, only that his patient was on the verge of hysteria, which didn't do her present condition any good.

He turned his attention to the blonde. "I'm afraid I'm going to have to ask you to leave. Mrs. Cunningham obviously doesn't want you here."

Cate continued looking at the woman fate and genetics had made her mother. Despite the frustration she felt at the moment, she was still determined to find out all she could about Joan. "I'm sure she'd rather I wasn't anywhere. She should have thought of that twenty-seven years ago."

Christian had no idea what was going on, only that he needed to have the blonde leave before Joan became even more agitated. "Don't make me call Security."

Cate suppressed a sigh. She didn't want to create any trouble. And getting tossed out on her ear wasn't going to get her what she wanted. At this point, she wasn't completely clear what it was that she *did* want, other than recognition.

Acceptance, she supposed. Something to make this

awful restless feeling in the pit of her stomach go away, to help dam up this gnawing, gaping hole in the center of her being. She didn't expect to have the space filled, but at least the rent could be repaired before she began hemorrhaging.

Angry, frustrated, Cate turned on her heel, away from Joan and under her doctor's watchful eye.

It was hard not to succumb to the dark mood that was vying for possession of her. It wasn't supposed to go this way. She wasn't supposed to have lost her temper like this.

But then, she supposed her nerves had been on edge ever since she'd discovered that she had been adopted. And now it was as if she was waiting for something else to happen, something to further tear down the foundations of her world.

What foundations? she mocked herself. What was left? Between Gabe's death and her mother's deathbed confession, there *were* no foundations. Only empty air under her feet. And, unlike the cartoon characters who could walk on air until they realized what they were doing, she couldn't. She was plunging down swiftly. Toward what, she didn't know.

Maybe the chasm was bottomless.

No, damn it, it wasn't. She was going to stop feeling sorry for herself and rally. Because Joan Cunningham was going to give her some answers.

Reaching the door, Cate looked back over her shoulder toward the woman who refused to admit to being her mother. "This isn't over yet," she warned, then left the room.

"Yes, it is," Joan insisted. Her voice broke as she attempted to raise it. A sob followed and then she began to cry.

"Calm down, Joan," Christian instructed, his voice low, soothing.

The tears continued to come. Joan looked from the door toward her doctor, her eyes pleading with him again. "She's not coming back. She can't come back."

Who was this woman to her? The question echoed in his head. He knew his asking would only contribute to Joan's agitation. He wanted her calm.

Reaching over to the nightstand, Christian picked up the small box of tissues tucked behind the telephone. He held it out to her.

Instead of taking one tissue, Joan took the whole box and held it against her chest, as if having it there somehow comforted her. She looked up at him, the same silent plea in her eyes.

"No, she's not coming back," he told her. Christian crossed to the door. "I'll send in a nurse in a couple of minutes with a tranquilizer for you. You need to calm down."

He saw gratitude enter her face as she silently nodded her thanks.

Once outside the room, Christian looked up and down the hall. The blonde was just disappearing around the corner. Hurrying to catch up to the source of his patient's agitation, he passed Joan's nurse and gave her his instructions on the fly.

"Hold on a minute," he called after the blonde.

Cate didn't hear him. Or if his voice registered at all in the recesses of her mind, she didn't realize that he was talking to her.

That certainly went well, she upbraided herself. If she'd interviewed suspects the way she had her birth mother, the bureau would have had her mowing lawns instead of where she was.

She did her best to calm down. Part of that entailed focusing on a plan. Now that she had located her birth mother, she was going to have to try talking to her again. Later, after both she and Joan had an opportunity to collect themselves.

As she approached the elevators it occurred to Cate that she still didn't know what the woman was doing in the hospital. She needed to get a look at Joan's medical records.

Christian lengthened his stride. He had considerable more leg than the woman did, but she moved quickly. He managed to finally catch up to her just as she pressed for the elevator. Rather than call out to her again, he simply got in front of her. She looked surprised, and almost as agitated as his patient.

"Excuse me."

She could feel herself growing defensive. Was he about to lecture her on behalf of his patient? Right now, she was in no mood to have to listen. If he wasn't careful, this good-looking doctor was going to find he had bitten off more than he had bargained for. "Yes?"

There were a great many diplomatic ways to begin. Since Alma's death, he'd lost the ability to be diplomatic and patient. Christian went straight to the heart. "Who are you?"

Blunt. She admired blunt. Sometimes.

"Ah, the million-dollar question," the woman he'd just chased down said sarcastically. Christian saw the same tears he'd just witnessed in Joan Cunningham's eyes now making an appearance in the blonde's. It struck him that they had the same light green color. "I wish to God I knew," she whispered. It sounded as if she'd said the words more to herself than to him.

Chapter 10

Because it seemed as if tears were about to spill out of her eyes, Christian took out his handkerchief and held it out to her.

"Is that some philosophical statement," he asked, commenting on her statement, "or do you have amnesia? Don't worry—" he nodded toward his handkerchief which she still hadn't taken "—it's clean."

Instead of accepting it, she passed an index finger under each eye, wiping away the excess moisture that had managed to leak out despite her best efforts to will her tears back.

Cate had never liked crying in front of people, certainly not in front of strangers. She liked losing control over herself even less. And she had done both just now, one the result of the other.

She sniffed, then blew out a breath, collecting herself.

God, but she wished she was ten again. Ten years old and sitting in the family room, watching reruns of some old western series her father had discovered on one of the cable channels. She remembered fondly that her dad always gave a running commentary on what was going on in case she didn't understand. She'd understood far more than he thought, but she loved listening to the sound of his voice. It made her feel so protected, so safe from everything.

And now she wasn't safe from anything.

"Neither." The retort to his question sounded a little sharp to her ear. She dug deeper for control.

He wondered if perhaps he should have summoned Security. The woman wasn't making any sense. "Then what…?"

The elevator car arrived, and Cate ignored it. "Joan Cunningham is my birth mother."

The moment she told him, she upbraided herself. She had no idea why she'd just shared that. No one else down here knew the mission she'd set out on. She hadn't even mentioned it to her partner. Her acquaintances would think she'd simply just wanted a change of venue after her mother died. It went against her natural grain to share anything but the most trivial of information. Even Jeremy had had to prod her repeatedly before she had told him what she was really looking for.

Christian looked at her very skeptically. Granted, Joan Cunningham hadn't been his patient long, just for the past two years, but she seemed like a fairly open woman. By her second visit, he knew the names of her three children. The Christmas card he'd received from her last December had carried their likenesses. None of them had been this woman. Joan had never mentioned having a fourth child.

"Are you sure?"

Damn it, she was going to cry again. What was the matter with her? She'd thought that she'd used up the last of her tears at her mother's funeral. There shouldn't have been any moisture left inside her, not after all the tears she'd shed over her mother and over Gabe. Where was all this water coming from?

Cate sighed, jabbing her index finger at the elevator keypad again. "Right now, I'm not even sure if the sky is blue."

The woman before him looked pale and shaken. His main concern in Joan's room had been getting her away from his patient. Now that he had, he should just let her go on her way. But there was something about the look on her face, especially in her eyes, that kept him from murmuring some trivial phrase and walking away. He saw pain there. It held him fast.

Christian glanced at his watch. He had a little time before his first patient was due. With his office located on the hospital premises, he didn't have far to go. He made up his mind.

"Why don't you come this way with me?" Without waiting for her to answer, he took hold of her arm, about to lead her over to the nurses' lounge.

Cate interpreted his actions in her own way. "Don't worry, I'm not about to cause any trouble." Moving her arm out of his hold, she began to dig through her purse. A minute later, she produced her wallet and opened it to her ID. She held it out to him. "I'm a special agent with the FBI."

Just like Lydia, he thought, although he refrained from saying so. *Small world.* "Then this was bureau business?"

"No, it's private, like I said." She looked down at his hand. He'd taken hold of her again. Was he afraid she was going to go running off to Joan's room? "You're holding my arm again, Doctor. I told you, I'm not about to cause any trouble."

His expression didn't change. She didn't like the fact that she couldn't read it. "Then you'll come this way." He began walking.

There were a hundred different ways to separate herself from him. For the moment, she employed none of them. Curiosity had gotten the better of her. "Which will lead me where?"

He brought her to a door and indicated the sign. "To the nurses' lounge."

As far as she knew, only nurses were allowed in the nurses' lounge. She'd had a friend at one of the local hospitals in San Francisco who'd been very territorial about the small room that bore a similar sign.

"I'm not about to change professions," she quipped.

The half smile that came to his lips intrigued her. She wondered what he looked like when he actually allowed his mouth to curve. Some people had smiles that were better left unused, others had the kind that lit up a room. She had a hunch that he leaned toward the latter.

"They have coffee there," he told her as he pushed open the door.

"And you're prescribing a cup?"

"That—" he continued to hold the door for her, waiting "—and maybe a slight change of attitude."

She looked at him sharply as they crossed the threshold into the lounge. The room was small, no bigger than nine by twelve, and for the moment, empty. A few chairs were scattered around with no apparent pattern in mind.

The doctor walked over to the small table where a pot of coffee sat on a burner. The pot was half full.

And she felt half cocked. Where did he get off, judging her?

"What would you know about my attitude?" she asked. It took effort to keep her anger under wraps.

After pouring the coffee, Christian turned around to face her. "Not a thing," he admitted, his expression still giving nothing away. "How do you take it? The coffee," he prompted when she made no answer.

Cate pursed her lips. She supposed she had nothing to lose by accepting the cup of coffee. She hadn't eaten since this morning and that had only been a piece of toast. "Black."

Nodding, he handed her the cup. He took coffee the same way, the way he took life. Unadorned. "Anything else I can get you?"

Taking the cup from him, a slight smile curved her lips. "The truth would be nice."

He took half a cup of coffee for himself, then placed a dollar into the empty coffee can beside the pot. "Truth is all relative."

Cate rolled her eyes. Philosophy, that was all she needed. "Oh, please. What is that, Zen?"

His shrug was careless. He lifted the cup to his lips and drank before answering. "Navajo."

Cate looked at him sharply. A Native American. Like Lydia's husband. There was a resemblance, she realized. The same rugged planes and angles making up the face, the same high cheekbones and straight, almost blue-black hair, worn a little long, no doubt in tribute to their heritage. The only thing that threw her was that she would have expected his eyes to be brown or almost black. They weren't.

"You have blue eyes."

Christian shrugged casually. "Yes, I do." His mother's father had been only half Navajo. The other half had been an Italian woman who hailed from the northern region, where Italians were fair-skinned, fair-haired and blue-eyed, unlike their Sicilian brethren to the south.

The doctor looked comfortable in his own skin, she decided. And why shouldn't he? Life probably held no surprises for him, threw him no curves out of nowhere. "I take it you know your family history?"

Christian thought it was rather a personal question, but given the situation, he allowed for it. When they were both younger, his brother had had no use for stories of the Dine, which was the name the Navajo gave themselves. At the time, heritage hadn't meant anything to him. In one of the few times that he could remember, their mother had grown stern and laid down the law to him. He was to learn and be proud of who and what he was. The lessons had stuck.

He nodded. "Yes, I do."

She laughed softly. He heard no humor in the sound.

"That makes you one up on me. I thought I knew mine—until a month ago."

As she spoke, he studied her. He had the impression that she ordinarily kept rigid control over her reactions. When people like that finally let go, it was a fearsome thing to witness. He wondered if she had some sort of a release valve.

"What happened a month ago?" he asked.

She pulled her shoulders back, as if bracing for a blow. "I tried to donate blood for my mother and the lab technician told me that mine wasn't compatible with hers."

Since he was a doctor, he honed in on the part of her statement that was most relevant to him. "What was wrong with your mother?"

"Leukemia." The momentary hesitation and the slight press of her lips together was his only hint at the extent of her inner turmoil. The woman took a breath before she continued. "She died a little more than a week after that."

"I'm sorry." The words were not said automatically. Christian meant them genuinely. He had never learned how to separate himself from the sting of death, and though it made things difficult for him, he hoped he never could. If he were anesthetized to loss, it would rob him of his compassion.

Cate tried to shrug nonchalantly and couldn't quite pull it off. The wound her mother's death had caused was still too new, too raw. Even when she was angry with Julia Kowalski for the secret she had kept too long, there was still this huge hurt in her heart that her mother, the woman she'd loved and cherished, fought with and learned from for twenty-seven years, was gone. The thought, too, that she was no longer anyone's child, but an adult in every sense of the word, was still new, still unwelcome.

"Yes," she said quietly, "me, too."

"Did your mother make a deathbed confession before she died?"

The irony of that still got to her. "She wouldn't have even made that if it hadn't been for the blood incompatibility."

Not for the first time, she thought about how Julia Kowalski might have gone to her grave with the secret and she would have never known the truth. And subsequently she would have been at peace instead of feeling betrayed.

Maybe the truth was highly overrated. But now that she'd begun this, she couldn't back away. She always needed to know. Everything. That had always been both her failing and her strength, the need to know, to fit in every piece of the puzzle.

Cate looked at him, her eyes capturing his. "How would you have liked to wake up one day to discover that your whole life was a lie? That you weren't who you thought you were? That your parents weren't your parents, that you weren't a hundred percent Polish with just a hint of French, but God only knew what?"

Her eyes were stinging again. When was she going to get over this? she demanded silently. When was her anger going to burn away the tears?

"Do you have any idea how many stupid Polish jokes I had to endure while I was growing up? And I did it all for no reason. I'm not Polish. There was no great-great-grandmother who was an impoverished French countess. There's nothing but this huge question mark," she added.

She had an energy about her when she became animated. He found it difficult to look away. "So you've set out to erase that. The question mark in your life. What makes you think Joan's your mother? Did your adoptive mother tell you?"

"No." Cate's mouth curved ever so slightly in a self-deprecating smile that did not reach her sad eyes. "I tracked her down. It's what I do."

And at least that much she was sure of. She was sure of her abilities. Everything else was up for grabs.

"Then you are sure."

The deep baritone voice echoed in the room. Cate set down the coffee cup. There was a restlessness stirring within her. Cate attributed it to her less-than-successful encounter with her birth mother and was annoyed with herself. She usually had better control over herself than that.

She was also vaguely aware that the stirrings became more pronounced when Joan's doctor was looking at her. It had been a long time since she'd even noticed a good-looking man.

Cate shifted in her seat. It did no good. She felt as uncomfortable in her own skin now as she did a moment ago. "I'd need a DNA test to be positive, I suppose. But Mrs. Cunningham didn't exactly look inclined to submit to one of those."

He could only imagine how having one bombshell after another dropped so quickly must have affected Joan. "This isn't a good time for her."

She looked at the doctor for a long moment. He hadn't told her before when she'd asked, but the boundaries had changed. She tried again. "Why is she here?"

He was surprised that he was actually tempted to tell her. Christian attributed the momentary lapse to the sad look in the young woman's eyes. A look he doubted if she even knew she possessed. A look he was particularly vulnerable to. But vulnerable or not, there were ethics to adhere to. "I'm afraid I can't tell you that."

Cate blew out a breath, banking down frustration. "Doctor-patient privilege, yes, I know all about that stumbling block." *If at first...* She tried another approach. "What kind of a doctor are you?"

"A good one, I'd like to think."

The hint of amusement in his eyes got to her for a second. It was almost as if there'd been a tiny tidal wave in the middle of her stomach. The meeting with her birth mother had *really* shaken her up more than she was willing to admit. She focused on fact finding, something she usually did well.

"From the sound of it, at least a slippery one. Normally I'd attribute that kind of an answer to a shrink, but psychiatrists generally don't walk around with stethoscopes slung around their necks—unless they're into shock therapy," she added dryly.

The seconds ticked away and he had to be getting down to his office, but something about her made him linger just a few minutes longer. He saw no harm in telling her his discipline.

"I'm a gynecologist."

Her mind quickly flipped through the conditions attached to his specialty. "Only two things would have a woman as upset as Mrs. Cunningham looked even before I told her who I was. A change-of-life baby…" Her voice trailed off as something far worse occurred to her. "Oh, God, it's cancer, isn't it?"

He saw distress before she could mask it. He thought of what had to be going through her head. To find her birth mother, only to think she was losing her again. It made him want to tell her that things were being handled. But to say that, he would have had to admit that there was something wrong. And his allegiance was to his patient, not the blonde sitting beside him.

Christian shook his head. "I can't tell you."

She hated not knowing, hated being shut out. Frustration had her fisting her hands in her lap. "What *can* you tell me?"

"That if this is on the level and for some inner peace you need to have Joan accept you as her daughter, that you take this slowly. Let her get used to the idea," he advised.

That would be his approach, it always had been. Slow and steady. Only once in his life had he jumped in with both feet, and that was to threaten Alma's father to keep away from her.

"If Joan is your mother the way you say," he added as he saw the protest rise to her lips, "she probably thought she'd never see you again. She certainly didn't expect you to pop up on what she undoubtedly feels is one of the darkest days of her life."

Was he doing that on purpose, teasing her with information he wouldn't give her? No, she doubted that. Gut instincts told her that this was a man who didn't tease. *Too bad.* The thought came from nowhere and she had no idea why it materialized in her brain. She began to entertain the thought that, just possibly, she was going a little crazy. Who could blame her?

Cate sighed, regarding him a moment in silence. Wondering what made him tick. Wondering what she could use to her advantage. He seemed nice enough, or else why would he be here, talking to her now? But his allegiance was clearly to his patient. "You won't tell me if I guess right, will you?"

"I took an oath."

"To what, torture the bastard daughters of your patients?" This time, Cate was certain she saw a hint of a smile quirk his lips.

"No, to keep my patients' confidences just between us." Christian debated for a moment, then decided to tell her the little that he could. "I will tell you this, though. Joan never mentioned having another daughter besides Rebecca."

The laugh that left her lips was completely without humor. Her eyes challenged his. They were flashing with barely suppressed anger. He had to admit, the sight was compelling.

"And you would tell me if she'd filled out on her patient history form: 'Gave away one daughter because I wasn't ready to be a mother yet.'"

In her position, he was pretty sure he would have felt the same. But he wasn't in her position. And his position was to guard Joan's privacy. "If she had, I wouldn't say anything. But since she hadn't, I can tell you. I can also tell you that maybe you should think about signing up for an anger-management class."

And who the hell was he to tell her what to do? She could feel her temper rising dangerously close to the surface. Cate squared her shoulders. "I can manage my anger just fine, thanks."

Instead of getting up and walking out the way she'd expected him to, her mother's doctor took her wrist and placed his fingers against her pulse. Her anger square-danced with a strange surge of warmth that washed over her.

"That's not what your pulse is saying." His eyes held hers. "It's accelerated."

Cate yanked away her wrist. The warm feeling stayed, but it was being smothered by a wave of anger fueled by indignation. "Maybe that's because a good-looking man is holding it."

Christian took it as a sarcastic remark. If there was the tiniest part of him that reacted, he attributed it to a trying morning, nothing more. He'd hoped that Joan's tests would have returned negative from the lab.

"You have better control over yourself than that" was all he said. He took his cup, rinsed it out and placed it on the counter again. "I've got to go to my of-fice." After drying his hands, he put back the towel and saw that she was staring at him. "What?"

His comment about her having better control over herself than that left her momentarily speechless. Rallying, she searched for something plausible to say. Cate glanced at the mug draining on the counter. "I never saw a man rinse out his own cup before, that's all."

He had a feeling she was lying, but he went along with it. "Part of being allowed to use the nurses' lounge. I remove all traces of having been here."

"Except for the money you leave in the can." She nodded toward it.

"Except for that." It occurred to him that maybe the woman needed more time to pull herself together, although she didn't look it. But he was the first to know that the exterior didn't always give away what was happening beneath. People thought of him as stoic and he was anything but. It was only a role he took on. "You can stay here as long as you like," he said as he began to open the door.

But Cate was already on her feet. She quickly rinsed out the cup he'd given her and was beside him in less time than he would have thought possible.

"I just took a few hours of personal time to try to resolve this." The expression on her face was contrite. She realized that something this huge required more than "a few hours of personal time." "I need to be getting back, too."

Christian held the door open for her.

"Thanks," she murmured. "For the coffee and the talk."

"Even if it wasn't fruitful?"

"Everyone's got their own interpretation of 'fruitful,'" she replied.

He couldn't quite read the smile on her face. He supposed that was why the word *enigmatic* was created.

They parted in the hallway. He had a feeling deep in his gut that this wasn't going to be the last time he saw her. The FBI special agent didn't strike him as the kind of woman who gave up easily. She reminded him a great deal of his sister-in-law.

Christian hadn't lied about needing to get to his office. He had patients scheduled all morning. But the first up was an annual exam with Sally Jacobs, who'd had no particular complaints when she'd made the appointment with his nurse. Christian decided that the annual exam could wait a few minutes.

Instead, he went back to Joan's room to check on her. He wanted to see if the sedative had taken hold yet and if she was doing better than when he had left her.

Knocking once, he opened the door when he heard the muffled, "Come in."

Joan was sitting up in bed, shredding a tissue into a hundred tiny pieces. Out of habit, Christian picked up the chart hanging off the edge of her bed to see if the right dosage had been given. There had never been any mistakes of major consequence at Blair Memorial, just a few minor inconveniences. Delays in lab results, a food menu lost, things of that nature. Nothing to warrant any anxiety. Checking the chart was a pretext.

His real concern was Joan.

After a beat, Christian set the chart back where it belonged and approached her. "Is the sedative helping any, Joan?"

For a moment, she didn't appear to hear him. Joan seemed lost in thought, lost in her own world. A world that, if he read the signs on her face correctly, caused her a great deal of anxiety.

And then, just as he was going to ask her something, she suddenly said, "I got pregnant at seventeen." There were tears in her eyes when she glanced up at him. "I'd only done it that one time."

"Once is all it takes."

She laughed sadly as she began to shred another tissue.

"I found that out fast enough. I was so scared." When she turned her eyes on him again, he saw the frightened girl she'd once been. "One minute you've got the whole world up before you, the next, there are all these responsibilities. A baby." She shook her head in wonder, remembering. "I was only a baby myself."

Her breathing grew shaky as she relived that time again. "I had to tell my mother. Had to watch the disappointment on her face. And my father…" Her voice drifted off. There were things she was just unable to put into words, even after all this time. "They didn't want me to have an abortion, so I went through it. The whole nine months." She closed her eyes for a moment. A tear seeped through. "The checkups, the first kick, everything. Everyone said the labor would be hard, but it wasn't."

Joan opened her eyes again, looking at him. Silently asking him to understand, to forgive the sin that seeing her daughter again reminded her she was carrying. The years had made her forget.

"Giving her away was hard. Hardest thing I ever did. But there wasn't anything I could give her. If I kept her, both our lives would have been over. I did the right thing," she insisted.

"No one's judging you, Joan," he said kindly. "You did what you felt was right. But why don't you admit to her that you're her mother and finally put her mind at ease? You might put your own at ease, too."

He wasn't prepared for the fear he saw wash over her face. She shook her head from side to side. "I can't, oh, I can't."

Was she afraid that her daughter would ultimately reject her because she'd been given away at birth? He doubted that Cate would have gone to all this trouble for that. He could be wrong, but he didn't get the feeling that the special agent was a vengeful person. "She'd forgive you in time, Joan."

Joan looked at him in confusion, and then she realized what he was saying. "But my husband's family wouldn't." She began to explain quickly. "It's taken me all these years to have them accept me. They never thought I was good enough for Ron, that he was marrying beneath him. If they found out that I'd had a baby before I met Ron—"

"People don't stone women for having babies out of wedlock in this country, Joan."

She laughed shortly. "You don't know my in-laws. They make the townspeople in *The Scarlet Letter* look like the Muppets. If my husband found out—" She thought of Ron's face and how it would look. His disappointment would be too much for her to bear. "No, they can't find out. Nobody can." She grabbed the doctor's hand, clutching it as she implored, "Promise me you won't tell them."

Christian did what he could to set her mind at ease. "Joan, I'm your doctor. In this case, it's kind of like being your priest, listening to your confession. I'm not about to tell anyone anything. That's up to you. Although I think you'd feel a lot better if you did."

There was no way she would feel better. She was too old to start over. "I never felt good poor, Doctor. I've been poor. Rich is much better."

Money was one thing, but it was far from the answer

to everything. Joan Cunningham was a good woman. Would her conscience let her have any peace, now that her daughter had made a reappearance in her life?

"Right now, I want you to put everything out of your mind," Christian instructed her. "I need you upbeat for the surgery."

She'd forgotten about that for a minute. The specter of the surgery moved forward, casting its shadow over her. A firm believer in yoga, Joan closed her eyes, trying to picture herself walking along a long, winding beach. Searching for peace. Holding desperation at bay.

"I'll do my best," she whispered.

Chapter 11

The surgery went well.

Christian had lined up the best surgeon for Joan and assisted during the procedure. Sample tissues were rushed to the pathology lab while Joan was still under the anesthetic. The results were what they expected and they went ahead with the procedure that had been decided on.

Although the tumor turned out to be cancerous, it seemed to have been caught in time. Before it could begin spreading its poison. To be on the safe side, lymph nodes surrounding the area were removed. The prognosis was positive.

When he told Joan that she was going to be all right, she'd cried tears of joy. Of relief.

Her husband was in the room with her. The tall, gray-haired man had stood over her when the news was delivered and had stoically squeezed her hand. Christian remembered thinking that there seemed to be a great deal of bottled-up emotion within the man.

Not unlike himself, he thought as he left the room.

Taking the elevator, he went down to the first floor and out to the parking lot. It was still chilly, but the rain that had been promised had slipped away. This was their rainy season and it had only done so a handful of times. Looked like another dry year, he mused.

Christian got in behind the wheel of his car. He still drove the same car he'd had in medical school, the one he'd almost single-handedly resurrected at Henry's behest. He could afford a better one now, but the car still ran and it suited his purpose of getting from here to there. Wealth and its trappings had never meant anything to him, the way they did to Joan.

Because it was Friday and he found himself needing to touch base, he drove to the private airfield instead of his small apartment.

He was going home. His real home. Where he had grown up. Where they still needed him.

As he drove, he wondered if Joan's husband would react the way she thought he would if he found out her secret. The man in the hospital room had looked relieved, even though he'd actually said nothing. Ron Cunningham had struck him as someone who cared deeply but couldn't bring himself to say it. Had probably been raised that way, to keep things bottled up. It was obvious that Joan would benefit from having some of those feelings released.

Every woman needed to hear words of endearment, words of comfort. Had he said them enough to Alma?

Had he told her he loved her enough? Had he done everything he could have to get through to her?

Would she still have killed herself if he'd talked to her more, said those words more often? He pondered this as he sat back on the commuter plane that was taking him to Mesa Roja, the closest town he could reach before the reservation. He and Lukas had a standing arrangement with Jake Anderson, the man who ran the used-car dealership in Mesa Roja. They'd rent a vehicle for the duration of their stay at the reservation. The man did it as a gesture of good will—and because he knew that neither one of the Drs. Graywolf would do anything to cause damage to his precious property.

A slight tremor went through the plane as turbulence challenged the pilot's skill. The first time it had happened, Christian remembered getting violently ill. Not so much from the swaying as from the thought of crashing. But withstanding turbulence had become so commonplace for him, Christian hardly noticed it now.

His thoughts were elsewhere.

With a girl who'd had a heart-shaped face and the saddest dark eyes he'd ever seen. Her eyes were so dark, they looked almost as black as her long, shining black hair.

He couldn't remember a time when he hadn't loved Alma. Most likely, it was love at first sight. They'd grown up together on the reservation. He with his partial family, she with hers. He used to joke that between them, they had a complete unit. Because in Alma's case, it was her mother who was no longer there. Death hadn't claimed her the way it had his father, she'd walked out.

And left her daughter with her husband. The man, he later learned, quickly turned to his daughter for comfort. From the time she was seven years old she'd been used by Alan Three Feathers as his surrogate wife. Scarring her forever.

When she had finally confided in him what her father was doing, Christian had been filled with such rage, he could barely see. Going to him, he'd threatened to kill the man if he ever laid so much as a finger on her again. As it happened, Uncle Henry had overheard the exchange and had his own talk with the man. Shortly thereafter, a very bruised-and-battered Alan Three Feathers disappeared off the reservation. Permanently.

Because he'd begged her, his mother took Alma in. He'd hoped that with a loving home around her, Alma would bury the past and the damage it had done. She'd fooled them all into believing she was getting better. Only sometimes, when the two of them were alone and talking, he'd see that look in her eyes. That look that belonged to a whipped dog who had no hope, no inner resources to draw on. It made him feel powerless. He tried harder to make it all up to her, to love her with every fiber of his being.

He went to college close by, but medical school was another story. He had to go where he was accepted. He remembered how terrified Alma had been when she found out he would be going away. She'd begged him to take her with him. To get her away from the reservation because she was afraid that someday, her father would come back for her.

Christian could never say no to her. They lived together in a little one-room flat close to the campus.

For a time, she worked as a waitress in the same restaurant where he tended bar nights and he thought they were happy. He knew he was happy, despite all the hard work and the long hours. But long hours at night by herself made Alma sink further into the abyss she'd created. Further into the bottle she chose for comfort.

He'd married her his last year in medical school, praying that the official piece of paper would make a difference to her, would somehow pick up her self-esteem. He tried every way he could to show her what she meant to him. Again, things were good for a time. But then she began slipping back.

And then she became pregnant. The day she told him the news, she swore that she would be the world's best mother. That things would be different from now on. He believed her because he wanted to. He felt his life was perfect. The girl he'd loved since childhood was bearing his child. All was right in the world.

His world, not hers.

As a doctor, he should have realized that. As a man, he hadn't. And because he hadn't, because he hadn't insisted that she get counseling, hadn't found a way to reach in and slay the demons Alma was always wrestling, the demons killed her.

And she killed their baby.

How could he have been so blind?

A hand was on his shoulder, shaking him. Bringing him back to the inside of the small passenger plane and the present. Bill Preston, the pilot who ferried his brother and him back and forth from Bedford to Mesa Roja, was standing over him, looking befuddled.

"Hey, Doc, you thinking of taking the trip back?"

Christian shook himself free of the memories that were dragging him down. "What?"

Bill pointed out the window beside him. "We've landed. You're usually the first one off the plane. Something wrong?"

After unbuckling, he quickly rose to his feet. Bill stepped back to get out of his way. The other passengers had already disembarked. He hadn't even heard them. Christian picked up his luggage. "No, just lost in thought."

"Oh." Bill followed him down the narrow path to the door. "Happens to me sometimes. When I got a thought to get lost in," the man chuckled, pushing his hat back on his head. "Sunday night or Monday morning?" he asked.

Christian got off the plane. "Make it Sunday night."

"Right. Sunday," the pilot called after him.

Turning back around, he left the field and walked to Anderson's A-1 Cars. He'd called the used-car dealer from the plane to tell him he was coming. A car was waiting for him in front of the lot. Like clockwork. The key was in the left rear wheel well. Christian unlocked the driver's door, threw in the small suitcase he'd brought with him and got into the vehicle. As he turned on the ignition, he blew out a long, cleansing breath. He had to stop doing this to himself. Had to stop reliving everything. There was no sense to it, no changing anything no matter how many times he did it. It had been three years since Alma had died. Three years. He needed to move on.

Easier said than done.

* * *

It always seemed that whenever he, his brother or one of their physician friends from Blair came to the clinic, the amount of patients doubled or tripled the second word was out. It got so bad that at times patients literally poured out the front door and down the path.

He'd gone to the clinic at seven, and patients were already waiting for him. The first in line said he'd seen a "strange car parked in front of Juanita's house," so he knew one of her doctor sons was here. Christian took it as a compliment and ushered the man in.

Other patients quickly followed. The clinic's one retired nurse and midwife, the only other staff, showed up at nine.

He put in far longer hours here than he did at the hospital, starting early, staying late, pausing only to grab a bite to eat when he remembered. His only compensation was a strong handshake and a show of gratitude. It was more than enough. Enough to know he was doing some good.

Although, there were times he wondered if he was really getting through to some of the patients.

He put down the new file he was reviewing, the one that had been filled out by his new patient, Lily Windwalker. His mother had sent the girl to him, insisting that she come.

Lily had sauntered into the tiny office, a palpitating cross between sullen and seductive. She was all of fifteen going on trouble. His mother had been blunt with him, saying that she was afraid Lily might have contracted something. It was no secret that girl had been sexually active for a while now.

He ran a preliminary test and conducted an exam, then gave Lily the results after she'd gotten dressed.

"You're lucky, you know."

"You want to get lucky, Doc?" Lily moved forward on her chair, her skirt barely covered the legs that were parted invitingly.

Trouble, he thought, any way you spelled it. Before he'd had her disrobe for the exam, Christian had made sure that not only the nurse who ordinarily assisted him with these exams was present but the midwife as well. He could see that Lily was unpredictable and he wasn't about to take any chances.

"I meant that you haven't contracted any sexually transmitted diseases so far. But you keep this up the way you are and you're just playing a game of Russian roulette." He could see he wasn't getting through to her. "You know what Russian roulette is?"

"Couldn't care less," Lily informed him. And then her smile grew wicked. "I bet I wouldn't 'contract' anything from you, Doctor. You're squeaky clean."

He wondered how many men and boys had fallen victim to that smile. There was no denying that Lily was beautiful, with the body of a woman ten years older. Another ten years like this, and she'd look like a burnt-out shell. He'd seen it before.

"Don't do that, Lily," he told her angrily. "You're worth more than that."

"How would you know what I'm worth?" she smiled wickedly. "Oh, I forgot. You saw me naked. Whet your appetite, Doctor? Did you like what you saw?"

She reached out to touch him, but he stopped her

with a look. Lily slid back in her chair. "Stop it, Lily, I'm your doctor."

"You're also a man." She tossed her head, sending her hair over her shoulder. He wondered how long she'd practiced that in the mirror. "You can't separate the two."

"You can if you take an oath and believe in it."

He rose from his desk and walked over to the cabinet he and the others always kept locked, except when they were in the office. Reaching in, he took out a handful of samples that had been donated to the clinic. That had been Alix DuCane's work. The pediatrician knew which drug companies to approach and she approached them tirelessly. The result was a good size supply of almost every medication needed to treat patients at the clinic.

"If you're going to continue what you're doing, I want you to at least exercise some common sense." He placed several small boxes in front of her. It was a three-month supply.

She looked at the boxes, making no effort to take one. "What's that?"

"Birth control pills."

She snorted, waving a hand at the boxes. "I'm not going to have a baby."

"Not if you use these, you're not."

Lily stuck out her lower lip. "Why would you care if I do or not? My mother doesn't."

His mother had filled him in about that, too. Lily's mother worked two jobs, trying to provide for herself and her daughter. Any free time she had was spent in the company of prospective husbands. She was rarely home. "Is your mother even aware of what you're doing?"

There was contempt on Lily's face.

"Not since the day I was born. Look, Doc, I'm only here because your mom said she wouldn't let me come back to class until you gave me a note. She's pretty hard-assed, if you ask me."

He might have entertained similar thoughts in his time, although not quite in those terms. There was no denying that in her career, Juanita had set more than just his brother straight. "She knows her way around kids."

Lily waved away the words. "Yeah well, am I getting my note?"

He'd already written it out. He held it now, just out of her reach. "Will you take the pills?"

Opening her purse, she leaned forward and with one sweep of her arm, brushed the stack off his desk and into the black bag. "Consider them taken."

He let her have the note. "You might try abstaining, too."

She grabbed it from his hand before he changed his mind. The look in her eyes was enticing. "And you might try not."

The next minute, she was gone.

Chapter 12

"You know, we have a saying—physician, heal thyself."

Christian looked up from his plate and smiled at his mother. She had purposely delayed dinner until he walked through the door. Uncle Henry and John fairly pounced on their meals the second he did.

As for him, he had to concentrate to work up even a ghost of an appetite. Food didn't interest him, even the traditional meals that his mother made, not for more than three years now.

A faint smile touched his lips. "I don't think that's a Navajo saying, Mom."

Juanita looked unfazed by her son's correction. "It could be. It's wise enough for one." She eased an ear of corn onto his plate. There was hardly anything on it besides that. "Now, the question is, my fine young son, are you wise?"

He was wise enough to see through one of his mother's webs. But because he loved her, he tolerated her burrowing into his life. "What are you driving at, Mother?"

She spooned out a serving of grilled chicken tenders onto his plate, then passed the bowl to her uncle. "Well, a wise man—like my grandfather was—knows that each man has something to add to the sum total of the community. You, like your brother, are a wonderful doctor. The people are grateful for you, for your frequent trips back to the reservation to care for them when you could just as easily turn your back on life here."

She was setting up for her argument. It was like watching a craftswoman. He knew from experience that it could take a while and today his patience wasn't the best. "The point, Mother, where's the point?"

"At the top of your head, it would seem." She nodded at his plate. He was pushing food around with his fork, wearing out the beans in their circular travel. "You don't eat enough to keep a bird healthy."

She'd slipped up, Christian thought. "You're the one who knows that birds eat twice their weight in food. If I did that—"

The sound of muffled laughter had Juanita looking sharply to her left. Toward John, the boy she had taken into her home when his parents were killed in a car accident. To show his gratitude, when he wasn't going to school, John helped Uncle Henry at the gym.

Right now, the seventeen-year-old was working

hard trying to hide the laughter that had bubbled up. Despite his efforts, a small noise had managed to eke through. His eyes on his plate, John pretended to be involved with his meal.

"All right," Juanita conceded. "Then eat like a human being." She waved a disparaging hand at his plate. "A healthy human being. Or you are going to become ill," she warned with the voice she used whenever she made one of her "vision" prophesies. "And then who will treat these people?"

Normally, he'd let it pass. But tonight, he had an answer ready for her. A certain perverseness, utterly foreign to him, urged it out. "Lukas and the other doctors who donate their time—"

Juanita was quick to cut him off. "Lukas has a wife, a practice and a life. We can't expect him to sacrifice himself and do without any sleep at all. The others are in the same position. They're married, they come when they can…"

A blind person could see where this was going. Food had only been her starting point. They were going to the field where they always went. To duel without weapons, armed only with love.

"But I have no wife or life, so I'm here more often," Christian concluded.

She looked at him for a long moment. He couldn't tell if she was annoyed because he had seen through her, or because he'd interrupted her.

"That really wasn't where I wanted the conversation to go," Juanita informed him quietly. She looked accusingly at her older brother and John. "You two, don't just sit there like grazing cattle, help me."

Henry raised his eyes to his nephew. "Eat something," he said, then focused back on his meal.

A hint of exasperation echoed in Juanita's voice as she watched him incredulously. "That's it?"

Henry raised his eyes again, this time to look at the woman he referred to as his baby sister, but only in private. The stoic expression on his face never changed. "That's what you want him to do, isn't it?"

Juanita sighed and shook her head. One look at John told her that he wasn't even about to try. She knew the boy idolized Christian. Left without soldiers, Juanita attempted to use diversion, hoping that Christian might wind up eating without realizing it. She really did worry about him. "How did it go with that girl I sent you? Lily?"

Christian noticed that at the mention of the girl's name, John seemed to snap to attention despite the fact that he continued staring at his plate.

"I can see where you'd have your hands filled with that one," Christian commented.

"Did you talk to her?" Juanita pressed.

Christian broke a bit of bread and dipped it into bowl of hot sauce his mother had prepared. "I talk to all my patients."

Juanita snorted, although she was pleased to see him eating something without prompting. She felt a small surge of victory. Christian had a weakness for her bread and the hot sauce she liked to make.

"If I had wanted you to be a lawyer, Christian, I would have sent you to law school." Her eyes narrowed. "Stop sounding like one."

He wiped his fingers on the napkin beside his plate.

"Mother, you know I can't talk about my patients." He saw impatience crease her unlined brow. He told her as much as he could. "But I gave her all the information someone in her position needs."

"Her position?" The question came from John. Three sets of eyes turned his way. Even Henry's deeply hooded eyes took on a smattering of interest. "I know her," John explained evasively. "I was just curious what you meant, that's all."

Christian hadn't thought about that. About the fact that John might have interacted with Lily. He was too busy thinking of him as the younger brother he'd never had. Of course, it stood to reason that Lily would invite his advances. John was extremely good-looking. Tall, slender, with sensitive eyes.

It stunned him as he recalled that those very words had once been applied to him. By Alma.

He watched the young man pointedly. "If you know her, you undoubtedly know that she gets around." He saw John's jaw harden. The boy was getting defensive. On Lily's behalf? Or his own? "This day and age you can't be too careful." Christian paused, letting the words sink in. Knowing that John didn't want him to get into any kind of detailed explanation. "That goes for guys, too."

"The good thing about our skin color," Henry commented, talking to the string beans on his plate, "is that you can't tell when one of us is blushing."

It was getting too uncomfortable for her men. Juanita decided that it was a good time to change the subject. "Will you be staying the whole weekend?" she asked her son lightly.

Christian nodded. "Same as usual. Except that I'll be going home Sunday night instead of Monday morning."

Never a greedy woman, Juanita took what she could get.

"What's bothering you, Christian?"

The question came out of the blue, as Juanita and her younger son stood in the kitchen, doing the dishes later that evening. She'd let the dishes slide for a while, preferring to partake of the company of her men. But then she'd slipped away after John had gone to bed and Henry had dozed off in front of the television set. Christian followed her into the next room, silently taking up his post at her side the way he'd done so many times while growing up.

He knew better than to look into his mother's eyes. He glanced at the rack instead as he took out another dish to dry. "What makes you think there's something bothering me?"

She smiled in triumph. "You didn't deny it, for one," she pointed out. "And, I'm your mother. Some mothers, the ones who have a connection to their children, can tell these kinds of things." She paused for a moment—for effect he was certain—before adding, "Besides, I had a dream…."

And how many times had he heard that before? He couldn't begin to count. Every time his mother had wanted to make a point, she'd claimed she'd had a dream, underscoring what she was about to say.

"You had a dream."

She knew he meant no disrespect, but still, she was

required to reprimand him. "Don't humor me, Christian. I come from a long line of shamans and seekers, you know that. Sometimes spirits whisper in our ear when we are asleep."

He teased her, but he knew that there were people like his mother among his kind. And they were revered. He didn't doubt that his mother was a seer. He just doubted that she "saw" as often as she said she did. At least, he doubted the dreams she claimed to have had about him. "And what was this dream of yours?"

Facing him, Juanita grew very grave. "That someone would come into your life. That no matter how much you resist, she would make you happy again."

He humored her for a minute. "And why would I resist being made happy?"

Juanita was deadly serious when she answered him. "Because you don't think you deserve it. But you do, you know. No one I know deserves it more." She paused, drying her hands for a moment to cup his cheek. "You were always my happy one. I always used to think if only Lukas was like you..." Her voice trailed off, almost wistful for the old days.

He knew what it was that she wasn't saying. He'd been her son far too long not to. "And now you think, 'If only Christian was like Lukas.'"

Juanita pressed her lips together, wishing she could do something to change things around. She hadn't fabricated the dream. She'd had it. But even in her sleep, she'd felt Christian's resistance. He truly didn't believe he deserved another chance at life and what it had to offer.

"I want you to be happy, Christian."

"I am, Mother." He'd found a peace of sorts, a purpose. He no longer thought about oblivion and joining his wife and child. Too many people needed him here. "As much as I can be."

"It's been three years, Christian. Time to let go of the past and move on." Juanita sighed, folding the dish towel. "I seem to be saying that a lot to you. But I have hope that if I say these words in just the right way, you'll listen." A fond smile enhanced her features, making her look young again. "You always used to listen to me when you were a boy."

When he was that boy she was talking about, he'd thought his mother the wisest woman in the world. He still deferred to her, but he knew that she was human and, as such, fallible. Especially in her beliefs that he would someday find someone. How could you find someone if you weren't looking for them?

"Things are more complicated now."

"No, we are still the same people inside, here," she said, tapping his chest. "The young boy who found that he could love everyone and everything is still there. Just let him out."

But to let that boy out meant to subject himself to pain. Because love ended in pain. Only his brother seemed to have escaped that fate. His mother hadn't; from the little he knew, Uncle Henry hadn't. And heaven only knew, he hadn't.

But for his mother's sake, he smiled. "Well, if your dream is right, someone will be along to do that." Draping the dish towel he'd used on the side of the sink, he headed for the front door.

Juanita made no move to follow, but her voice called him back. "Where are you going?"

At the front door, Christian paused to look at his mother over his shoulder. He didn't answer. He didn't have to. The look in his eyes told her that she already knew where he was going.

She could only nod. A mother couldn't live her children's lives for them or take on their pain no matter how much she wanted to.

"Be careful where you walk," she cautioned, "we've been having trouble with coyotes lately. Sabrina Cool Water lost her little dog the other week."

He imagined that some of the neighbors probably saw that as a blessing. Sabrina's pet had been a yappy little mongrel, barking from sunup to way past sundown. Still, he didn't like thinking that it had made a meal for some coyote, no matter how hungry the animal had been.

"I'll be careful, Mom," he promised, shutting the door behind him.

Maybe that was just the problem, Juanita thought, walking to her own small bedroom. Christian was being too careful. Afraid to live life again, afraid of being hurt. She hoped that the woman she had seen in her vision would come soon.

Even if she wasn't one of the People.

Chapter 13

Days went by.

Cate felt as if she were on the brink, waiting for something to happen, to break wide open.

She also felt as if she was being eaten up alive by frustration.

She refused to believe that was the end of it. That she had managed to successfully track down Joan Haywood from her early home in San Francisco through several residences across the state down to her present home in Bedford, and that after one brief, unsatisfactory meeting, that was that.

There was going to be more. There *had* to be more.

Just not immediately, no matter how impatient she felt. Cate grudgingly acknowledged that perhaps both she and the woman who had turned out to be her mother needed a breather. That Joan Cunningham needed time to come to grips with the fact that her past had suddenly, without warning, come up to invade her present, just as her doctor had suggested.

And Joan also needed time to deal with her diagnosis. Through careful maneuvering, Cate had found her way into her birth mother's medical records and followed what was happening, knowing things as soon as Joan did. Maybe sooner.

And on the small chance that her mother's doctor had been right in his suggestion that perhaps she'd made a mistake in thinking that Joan was her mother, Cate had checked her facts over again.

There was no mistake. Joan Cunningham née Haywood *was* her mother. She just needed to find a way for the woman to accept that and acknowledge her. What would happen after that, she didn't know. Maybe she could move on. She'd know once the time came.

Right now, she had a case to concentrate on. The task force she'd been assigned to had been in existence for more than six months, but things were beginning to finally move and fall into place. On her first day, she'd familiarized herself with as much of the background as time permitted.

The child-prostitution/white-slavery ring had come to light like so many other cases, by accident. A routine complaint about too much noise called in by neighbors in the area led police to an apartment that was supposed to be empty. Two underage girls were found chained to beds in the trashed quarters. The people who had been their captors had just managed to flee the premises a few minutes before the police arrived.

The girls, frightened, bruised and abused, were almost incoherent. Neither could give an adequate description of their jailers even after they had sufficiently calmed down. Both girls had claimed to have been kidnapped, although one had turned out to be a runaway. The runaway had told them that she'd been taken to a place with more girls like her. Many of the girls didn't speak English and their native tongue didn't sound as if it was Spanish. More than that, the girl couldn't tell them, except that every so often—she had no way of knowing if it was days or weeks—they were transported in a truck to another location.

That was when the FBI had been called in and the task force set up. Thanks to another tip, they managed to conduct another raid a couple of months later. But the information had come too late and no one was found. The only thing that had been discovered was a video accidentally left behind. It seemed to have been dubbed from a master tape, undoubtedly for sales. The operation was expanding.

It was obvious that Lydia Graywolf was living and breathing the case, dedicated to bringing down the people behind this ring. Cate discovered she got along well with the woman. They had a great deal in common, including the fact that they both had fathers in law enforcement who had been brought down in the line of duty. It was because of her father that Lydia had become a special agent. When Cate told her that she had felt the same way, a silent bond was formed between them.

Traffic was heavier than usual this morning. An overturned big rig had reduced the flow of vehicles down to a trickle and had turned a fifteen-minute drive into an hour-and-a-half ordeal. She called into the office twice, once to say she was going to be late, once to follow up, saying she was still trying to get to the office. Side streets had become unbearable as well.

Not in the cheeriest of moods when she finally walked into the room, Cate tried to head straight for the coffee in the common room. She'd only made it halfway across the floor when Lydia popped to her feet, hanging up the phone she'd just been on.

The look on Lydia's face was positively vibrant as she made eye contact with her. "Okay, people, let's look alive. We've got ourselves another hot tip."

"That mean we're going to the track?" Santiago pretended to guess even as he donned his jacket. "Because I could sure use a little money."

"Then here's your chance to earn it," Lydia cracked. She looked at the others who'd gathered around her desk. "Just got a call from an officer responding to a domestic dispute. Wife went crazy when her husband came home after being out all night, partying. The story she beat out of her husband—"

"Hell hath no fury like a woman scorned." Hawkins muttered under his breath as he jammed his arms through the sleeves of his jacket.

Lydia ignored him. "—was that he and his buddy went to an old office-supplies warehouse and got more than just a box of pencils."

"Paper cuts in unmentionable places?" Santiago hazarded a guess.

"Little women," Lydia replied grimly. It was the term she used to refer to the underage pawns within the floating prostitution ring. She nodded at Cate, indicating the door as she began to hurry out. "Let's hope they haven't pulled up stakes yet."

"Here."

Cate looked down and realized that Santiago was pushing a lidded, foam cup into her hand. Despite the foam, the contents felt hot.

She raised a quizzical brow as she looked at him. "What's this?"

He grinned broadly at her, never missing a step. "Coffee."

Cate smiled to herself. Funny how people here had picked up on her habits so quickly. It was almost like having a surrogate family. She wasn't worth a damn without a heavy dose of caffeine to kick-start her morning. Because her own coffee-making skills lacked a little something, she usually got her first real cup first thing in the office.

Returning his grin, she gave Santiago a little salute. Though she wanted that first long sip badly, she knew better than to attempt it on the run. And to stop moving long enough to take a drink would be tantamount to asking to get run over.

Coffee was going to have to wait until she was in the car. Every second that went by might be *the* second they needed to make the bust.

Lengthening her stride, Cate fell into place behind Lydia as they all hurried to get out of the building and to the warehouse in time.

The smell of rain was once more in the air. The atmosphere was pregnant with promise. Taking a full breath was a challenge as they hurried into cars and vans. A haze accompanied them all the way there, making it a thoroughly unpleasant morning.

They got there in record time.

As they approached the edge of the warehouse, a bead of perspiration trickled down Cate's back. She was uncomfortably aware of the vest she was wearing beneath her lightweight jacket. The latter proclaimed her to be a member of the FBI, white letters on a deep navy-blue fabric. The former was there so that she could remain a member. A standard-issue bulletproof vest—a heavy and constant reminder that her career of choice was dangerous and often came down to a situation where it was "them" against "her."

Not to mention the fact that there were enough crazies out there willing to take her down just for the sport of it.

Cate looked around the perimeter of the warehouse. It was surrounded by more than a dozen members of the SWAT team. There was a lot of manpower here.

Her weapon already drawn, she held it up as she leaned her head toward Lydia. "You sure about this?"

Lydia nodded. "The officer calling it in said the wife was very adamant, very specific and sick to her stomach that she'd been married to a guy like this without a clue."

"And she beat it out of him?" Cate asked incredulously. Most men wouldn't have admitted to that, no matter how badly things went against them. And she also couldn't see any man volunteering the kind of information this woman's husband had, especially since the way the ring operated was in strict secrecy.

Lydia released the safety on her weapon, then held

it aloft—ready and poised. They inched forward until they were next to the warehouse's front entrance. "The officer said it had something to do with the sharp end of a boning knife."

"Oh." That would explain it, Cate thought. A knife could be a great equalizer, just like a gun.

They stepped to the side, allowing the SWAT team to position themselves ahead of them. One of the men held a battering ram, ready to swing into action at the first sign from Lydia.

The battering ram turned out to be unnecessary. An old-fashioned padlock hung on the outside of the door.

"Talk about cheap," Lydia muttered. She beckoned forward another one of the team. The officer held bull cutters. One quick movement of the wrists and the lock fell to the ground.

Cate held her breath as she entered the warehouse. The doors were wide enough for more than two of them to enter at a time. They still went in single file, just in case.

Her senses were on heightened alert. Adrenaline coursed double-time through her veins as her eyes swept over everything, trying to take it all in at once. The darkness and the light intermingled, making the officers indistinguishable from one another. Turning everything into a murky brown.

The warehouse looked empty.

Cate felt an acute sense of disappointment warring with the energy throbbing through her body. They fanned out, checking every corner, every abandoned aisle.

And then Santiago called out, "Lydia, back here!"

The others moved quickly, converging at the back of the warehouse. There were several tiny, makeshift rooms lining the rear wall, separated by planks of wood meant to act as partitions. Each makeshift room had a door. At first glance they looked like storage rooms within a storage facility.

Except that these storage rooms were outfitted with beds.

Cate and the others opened door after door, all with the same results. There was no one there. The only indication that there ever had been someone there were the chains found in a couple of the rooms. Chains that were undoubtedly used to hold the young girls captive.

Lydia swallowed a curse as she holstered her weapon. "We're too late, damn it. Someone tipped them off again." They had been playing musical residences now for the last month and she had yet to get ahead of the game.

There was one more slim door located off to the side. Too small to be a room, it might have been a bathroom of sorts. Finding it, Cate tried to open the door. It was stuck. She tried the doorknob again, but it wouldn't budge. Was it locked? Why?

The logical answer was that someone had to be in there.

"I need a shoulder here," she called out.

Santiago came up behind her and moved her aside. "If I dislocate this, you're picking up the excess medical tab," he warned.

Bracing himself, the heavyset man applied his full weight against the door. It gave easily, the rusted hinges separating from the wall on the other end like so much cardboard. They opened the door on the side of the defunct hinges. Santiago moved it out of the way just as Lydia came up behind Cate.

Inside the bathroom, chained to the pipes and slumped on the floor, was a crumpled figure. A girl. There was a pool of blood all around her. She was no more than fourteen, if that much.

"Son of a bitch, they killed her," Lydia cried.

Cate was on her knees beside the body, her fingers pressed against the girl's neck. The girl's blood began to soak into her skirt.

"I got a pulse!" she cried. "It's faint, but there's a definite beat."

Lydia was already on her cell phone, calling for an ambulance. "I need a wagon here, now! We've got a live one, but just barely." She rattled off the location and then snapped the phone shut.

For just a second, the girl's eyes fluttered open. Terror came into them less than a second later. She looked as if she was trying to shrink into herself, whimpering. Cate heard Santiago curse behind her.

"Hang on, honey, we're the good guys," Cate told the girl.

The girl's head jerked in her direction. The next moment, the girl had slipped out of consciousness again.

Chapter 14

Once a week, Christian put in a four-hour stint in the E.R.—from 7:00 a.m. until eleven. He felt it kept him on his toes as far as emergency medicine was concerned, something that proved very handy while working at the clinic on the reservation.

He usually pulled duty on Wednesday mornings. Wednesday was his short day, barring an unexpected delivery. He only had afternoon hours, going into his office after one.

E.R. duty varied. Some days, he couldn't draw two breaths in succession, other days went so slowly they felt like a week. This morning had been in the latter category. Other than a down-on-his-luck house painter who came in with a bad case of the shingles and one small boy who had tried to break some kind of record for the amount of berries he'd pushed up his nose, the E.R. had seen no activity.

Christian had treated the painter, then given him the name of one of his friends who was looking to paint the outside of his house. The painter had been extraordinarily grateful as he left. As to his other patient, Christian spent more time calming down the little boy's mother than he did separating the boy from the berries.

Given a choice as to the type of day he would have picked, Christian preferred working under the gun to marking time. After the minutes moved by like molasses in an ice cube tray, his shift was finally over.

"You've got empty beds, Jerry," he told the physician who came on to take his place. "If it was any slower, we'd have to be giving patients back."

The moment he uttered the words, the rear electronic doors leading into the E.R. burst open.

"Looks like things are about to change," the other physician commented.

Christian raised his hands, as if to ward off any involvement. "All yours. I have a date with a ham-and-cheese sandwich in the cafeteria."

He had every intention of keeping that date as he turned toward the side exit. The back elevators were just around the corner. There was nothing unusual about paramedics bringing in patients. It happened all the time. Paramedics routinely brought in emergency cases if they occurred within the fifteen-mile radius of Blair Memorial's jurisdiction.

Reflecting on it later, he couldn't have said if it was instinct, curiosity or something else that made him look over his shoulder toward the parking lot. His mother would have said it was fate, but he didn't subscribe to all of his mother's beliefs.

Whatever caused it, he looked. And found himself surprised by what he saw.

Doubly so.

His sister-in-law Lydia was rushing alongside the gurney that the two paramedics were guiding in through the doors. He remembered Lukas telling him that the first time he'd met her, Lydia had just burst into the E.R. and was running alongside a gurney. Back then, it had been a suspected terrorist strapped to the moving bed. This time, a battered young woman whose dark brown hair looked to be matted with blood lay on the gurney.

That caught his attention.

What really nailed him, however, was that on the other side of the gurney, moving right beside the shorter of the two paramedics, was the woman he'd met in Joan Cunningham's room last week.

Cate something, he recalled. At the time, he'd wanted to ask her if she knew Lydia but had discarded the impulse the moment it came to him. Just because they were both special agents for the bureau didn't mean they knew each other. It was like having someone from the East Coast assume that since he came from Southern California, he knew Tom Cruise.

And yet, Cate obviously did know Lydia.

And they both looked agitated.

"I've got this one, Jerry," he announced, waving the young physician back.

"But you're not on duty anymore, remember?" Jerry protested, although not too vehemently.

"Clock me back in," Christian instructed the nurse behind the central desk.

By then, the gurney was almost on top of him. He quickly nodded at Lydia, then at Cate, but his main attention was on the unconscious young girl he now saw was little more than a child.

"What have you got?" he asked.

The paramedic in charge quickly rattled off the girl's condition when he'd come on the scene, then added her vital signs. They hardly met the criteria for sustaining life.

Lydia didn't seem surprised to see him there. More like relieved. "Christian, you've got to keep this kid alive," she cried.

"That's the name of the game." He'd never seen his sister-in-law in action before and wondered if she was so personally involved in all her cases, or if the girl's age was responsible for the extreme agitation he saw on her face. "Put her in that room," he ordered the paramedics, pointing to the first empty room rather than just a vacant bed used to treat the more common complaints.

"She stopped breathing!" Cate cried.

Instantly, nurses seemed to swarm in on either side of the gurney as Christian began applying CPR. A young Hispanic nurse hurried in with the crash cart. Seconds ticked by as paddles were charged and then quickly applied.

It took two efforts, with the jules being raised to six hundred before the girl's heart finally responded and began beating again.

To Cate, it seemed the level of activity never decreased. The moment the crash cart was moved aside, a caravan of machines were brought into the room. Each direction she turned, she found herself getting in the way. Machines were hooked up to monitor the girl's blood pressure and newly revived heart as well as to keep track of a host of other body rhythms.

Though she wanted to remain in the thick of it, watching, absorbing everything that was going on, Cate found herself forced to step back or be the unintended target of swiftly ebbing and flowing hospital personnel. She joined Lydia, who watched her brother-in-law's every move with rapt attention.

Cate couldn't shake the impression that Lydia was willing the girl to hang on.

A noise had Christian glancing up, his eyes meeting Lydia's. The orderly had almost crashed into his sister-in-law.

"Lydia, you're going to have to move out of the way," Christian instructed, then glanced toward Cate. "You, too."

Cate began to step back, but Lydia remained where she was, unwilling to leave the tight circle around the gurney. "Will she be all right?" Lydia's concern was audible.

You would have thought that Lydia was the girl's mother instead of the special agent who had brought her in, Cate thought. Was there some kind of special connection between her partner and the girl? Or was it just the sight in general of young flesh being peddled that got to Lydia? Cate made a mental note to ask the first opportune moment that presented itself.

Christian made no answer at first. He concentrated

on getting a tube down the girl's throat, intubating her until she could breathe better on her own. It was only when he was finished that he looked up again. His answer was honest. Lydia wasn't the girl's relative, so there was no need to phrase things in order to soften the blow.

"I don't know yet."

Cate stared at the end of the lengthy tube that had gone down the girl's throat. If she woke up and had something to tell them, there was no way she was going to be able to.

"How long does that thing have to stay in?" Cate asked.

Christian turned and looked at her a moment longer than he should have. Every second still counted. The next beat, he was back fighting to stabilize the girl's vitals. Her pulse jumped all around and he was afraid that she might start having seizures.

But the tube did the trick. The regular flow of air allowed her breathing to become steady.

One problem down, a myriad to go, he thought. The girl would have to go to X-ray as soon as possible. It wasn't a stretch to assume that there was internal damage. The real question was, how much and where was it? There was no way for him to know without films.

"Until she's breathing better," he finally answered Cate.

"We've got to question her as soon as possible," Lydia told him. "There could be a lot of other lives at stake."

That had to be her bureau voice, he thought. He'd never heard her this serious, this official before. "She has to be conscious for you to question her," he pointed out. And then he nodded over toward Cate. "Best thing you can do for her right now is to get back there with your friend."

Lydia opened her mouth to protest, both the order and Christian's assumption. But then she realized that in the short time she and the other woman had been working together, she'd found herself getting close to Cate. She supposed that qualified the latter for the term "friend." In any event, female friendship didn't happen to her very often. For the most part, because of her relationship with her father and the career she'd chosen, Lydia had always had an easier time getting closer to men than to women. Cate Kowalski was proving to be the exception.

As for his instruction, she knew Christian was right. She was just in the way here and had to step back to let the others do their jobs. She couldn't always control every situation. Lydia blew out a breath, and did what she was told.

A tense smile quirked her lips as she glanced at Cate. "He likes to give orders, like his brother."

Not a hundred percent sure she followed her, Cate looked at Lydia, confusion creasing her brow. "Who's his brother?"

"My husband, Lukas." She nodded toward the center of the activity. "That's his brother, Christian." *Please, Christian, don't lose her.* Her eyes never left her brother-in-law's hands. "The baby of the family, if you don't count John."

Knowing that they both needed to keep their minds occupied for the moment, Cate played along. "Who's John and why shouldn't he be counted?"

"Because he's not strictly a blood relative. John's an orphan Juanita took in. Juanita's their mother." This time her smile was genuine, if distracted. "One hell of a woman, let me tell you. First woman who had me shaking in my shoes."

Lydia didn't realize that her remark had carried over the din. Christian never looked up, but nonetheless he had heard her.

"She'll be happy to hear that," he called out. "She always thinks of herself as a pushover," he added.

There was no way Lydia was about to believe that. The woman could probably instill fear in a mountain lion with just one look. "Yeah, right. She's the original matriarch."

Cate would have been tempted to picture the typical "mother-in-law from hell" except that there was a note of fondness in Lydia's voice as she spoke about the other woman.

Because it was noisy and she had no desire to shout, Cate lowered her head, bringing her lips next to Lydia's ear. "I take it you two get along."

"Yes. Now." Lydia lowered her own voice because this part she definitely didn't want Christian to overhear. She needn't have worried. The noise volume began to increase as more monitors were brought in. "Once she realized that I loved Lukas and wasn't there just to amuse myself with a Native American lover."

She paused for a moment as she studied Cate. She knew the other woman's mother had died recently, which put her at emotional loose ends. She knew how she'd felt when her father had been killed. It wasn't so much a matter of substitution as in finding a way to help fill a void, even temporarily.

"I'd like you to meet her sometime. She's the school principal on the reservation. Got a heart as big as all outdoors. She took in John when his parents were killed in a car accident. His parents were friends of hers. She's that kind of woman," Lydia added with a pride that could only come from feeling as if she was a member of the family. Cate envied her, missing that feeling. Missed feeling as if she was part of something instead of just being adrift, part of nothing. Barred from everything. "She raised two terrific sons," Lydia concluded, still watching Christian's every move intently.

Christian stripped off his gloves and stepped back. For the moment, according to the monitors, the girl was stable enough to be taken to the X-ray department. He looked at the tall orderly who had brought in the last monitor.

"Take her up to X-ray. Tell them I said she gets first priority. I want chest, pelvis, spleen—the works. She looks like she attended one hell of a party. Tell them to put a rush on it and get the films back to me as soon as possible."

The orderly nodded, kicking back the brakes from the gurney's back wheels. A nurse fell into place, doing the same to the wheels in the front of the gurney. A minute later, the gurney was being guided out the door again.

Lydia stepped back as the gurney passed. "You're staying?" she asked Christian.

He had some time before his first patient. And if the

X-ray results took longer, he'd make adjustments. Lydia seemed invested in this girl's survival. The least he could do was his part.

"Until I know what's up, yes. My patients are used to having my schedule reshuffled." He thought of all the women who had gone into labor during his office hours. "Babies don't punch clocks, either."

Babies. Lydia suppressed a sigh, but it escaped, anyway. She'd been meaning to call her brother-in-law this past week, but she hadn't gotten around to it. There was something she needed to ask.

She realized that Christian was looking at Cate. Was that interest or just curiosity? "Sorry, Christian, this is my new partner, Special Agent Cate Kowalski. Cate, this is my brother-in-law, Dr. Christian Graywolf."

Both Cate and Christian said "We've already met" at the same time.

So it wasn't curiosity she'd seen on Christian's face, Lydia thought. That meant it was interest. Despite what was weighing heavily on her mind, the thought intrigued her.

Chapter 15

Any other time, Lydia would have attempted to explore the possibilities that might be present. She dearly loved her brother-in-law and knew all about the tragedy he'd endured. It had happened just after she and Lukas had gotten married. But right now, she had other things on her mind.

She looked down the hallway as the gurney disappeared around the corner. "How long before the films come back?" she asked.

"They haven't even gotten her into X-ray yet," he said. "Half hour, maybe more." Was it his imagination, or was Lydia distracted? He couldn't shake the feeling that she just didn't seem to be herself. "Why?"

She moved a little closer to him, cutting out Cate. "Can I see you, Christian? Privately?" she added. "In your office."

Now he knew something was up, and she sounded unsure of herself. This definitely wasn't the Lydia he knew. Ordinarily his sister-in-law came on like gangbusters and he'd often thought, wistfully, that his brother had more than met his match in the vibrant woman.

Christian nodded. "Sure, let's go."

Lydia looked back at her partner, suddenly remembering she was there. "Cate, can you wait here for me?"

Cate had already gotten the message that whatever Lydia wanted to talk to her brother-in-law about, it wasn't for general knowledge. There was a chair in the hallway and Cate suddenly realized that she felt wired and drained at the same time. It wouldn't hurt to sit down for a little while.

"Sure, I'm not going anywhere."

Lydia flashed a smile of gratitude at her partner. "This won't take long," she promised.

"What won't take long?" Christian asked when they were safely inside the elevator car.

Lydia let out a nervous breath. "Why don't we wait until we get into your office?"

A small shrug of his shoulder told her that was fine with him. And then he looked at her.

"You're being awfully mysterious about this, Lydia." A smile softened his features. "I thought *we* were supposed to be the ones who had a lock on that."

For the first time since this morning, Lydia relaxed a little. "Maybe being married to 'one of you' has rubbed off," she teased.

Something was definitely wrong, Christian thought.

She just wasn't herself. Even her smile looked tight. He tried to distract her. "So, how long have you had this new partner?"

"Three weeks." She decided to lay a little ground-work to get her mind off her dilemma. "I didn't think I'd like working with a woman," she admitted, "but Cate's different."

He'd been the quiet one in the family, developing just as keen an eye in his way as his mother had. "You mean she reminds you of you."

Lydia began to protest, then rethought Christian's words. He was probably right. They did have a lot of things in common and seemed to think the same way on a lot of subjects. "Something like that, I guess." She paused for a second as the floors blinked by. "Where do you know her from?"

Christian slanted a look in her direction. "Who says I know her?"

"Give me a little credit, Christian. I notice things for a living."

The similarity in their phrasing struck him. "Funny, she said she tracks down things for a living."

Good, he admitted meeting Cate. Next question. "When did she say that?"

He couldn't help wondering why Lydia seemed so interested. Was there something about Cate he should know? He remembered that when his brother had met Lydia, she was assigned to a terrorist task force. After they'd gotten married, her concession to him was switching departments. Lydia's mother told Lukas that he had immediately earned her undying gratitude.

"She was here the other week, visiting one of my patients."

The elevator doors opened and he placed his hand to the small of her back, ushering her out.

"That's odd. I wasn't aware she knew anyone here. She just transferred in from San Francisco." Because she thought it might make Cate a little more accessible to Christian, a little more human, she added a more personal note. "Her mother died recently and she thought she needed a change."

"Her mother?" he echoed. For a moment, he'd forgotten, but then recalled that Cate had told him that herself the one time they'd talked.

"Yes, you know, like what Juanita is to you."

Turning a corner, they approached his office. He noticed that Lydia was looking up and down the hallway, as if she was afraid of running into someone.

Lukas?

It didn't seem plausible, yet he couldn't shake the feeling that she was being incredibly secretive and that it had something to do with his brother.

Rather than take the first door that led to his office, he used the second one, the one that admitted him in the back. He saw his nurse, Lisa, looking his way, to see what was going on.

Christian nodded at her and put his finger to his lips. "I'm not here," he whispered, then explained, "I'm still on call at the E.R."

"Someone go into labor?" Lisa guessed.

Rather than get into the circumstances right now, Christian felt it was easier just to nod and agree. He'd fill his nurse in on the details later.

"Tell my patients if they want to reschedule, they're welcome to do that. Right now, I'm not sure how long I'll be."

Already opening the scheduling book, Lisa nodded. She glanced once last time toward the rear of the office. "Nice to see you again, Mrs. Graywolf," she mouthed.

Lydia forced a smile to her lips. "Same here."

She only wished it was under better circumstances, Lydia thought as she followed Christian into the last examination room.

Christian closed the door behind her. "That didn't look very genuine."

Suddenly very nervous, she fingered the paper sheet covering the examination table. This was it. She was going to get her answer. "What didn't?"

"Your smile." And her voice had a slight tremor in it, now that he noticed. Christian crossed his arms before him. "Okay, what's up?"

She didn't blurt it out, although it was hot on her tongue. Instead, her FBI training kicking in, she gave him a little background information first. "My doctor recently retired. Dr. Alicia Price," she added.

"I know. The hospital was sorry to lose her."

Lydia ran her hands along her arms. The room temperature was low, but definitely not chilly enough to warrant her actions, Christian observed.

She moved around the room, a hummingbird trying to find a place to perch if not land. "I'm not too comfortable with who she recommended take her place."

"Okay." He waited, watching her struggle, the silence stretching out until he finally broke it. "Lydia, is something wrong?"

Yes, something's wrong. I'm supposed to be happy, but I can't be. Not yet.

Lydia searched for inner strength. Turning to face him again, she said, "I think I'm pregnant."

Abandoning his role as doctor, Christian threw his arms around his sister-in-law and hugged her. "Lydia, that's wonderful." He thought he felt a little resistance on her part, as if she just couldn't relax. Stepping back, he studied her face.

Lydia didn't look the way he thought she would under the circumstances. He'd always thought that she wanted children. He knew his brother did. "It is wonderful, isn't it?"

Lydia dragged her hand through her hair. It fell about her face, straight and long. "Yes, and no."

He leaned against the examination table. "Tell me about the no part," he said gently.

He's probably going to think I'm horrible, Lydia thought. "If I'm pregnant, they're going to put me behind a desk."

"As they should." And then a light began to dawn on him. Lydia had never been the type to sit back and let others do the work. She was a hands-on type of person.

"Yes." Under normal circumstances, she thought, although it would make her antsy. But these weren't normal circumstances. Not to her. "But I'm right in the middle of this case."

He was trying to put the pieces together. "The case have anything to do with the girl in X-ray?"

Lydia nodded. "It has everything to do with the girl in X-ray."

She didn't ordinarily talk about cases. You never knew who was listening. But it was only Christian in the room. She trusted him. That was why she'd come to him in the first place. And she needed him on her side.

"We found her unconscious and chained to a toilet, for God's sake. We think she's part of a juvenile-prostitution ring. We're working on something big, Christian, I can feel it. And I have to be out there, at least until we find out who's pulling the strings. This isn't just an isolated incident. Sitting this one out, working behind a desk, doesn't do it for me."

He could sympathize with her, but as a doctor and as her brother-in-law, his concerns took him elsewhere. "You have to think of the baby."

Restless, she prowled around the small space, forming semicircles around the examination table. "I know, I know, and I am, but I'm also thinking of Susan."

"Susan?" The name was unfamiliar to him. One of her friends?

"My cousin." Funny, bright, beautiful Susan had been born late to her parents. A generation and a half separated them. "She would have been thirty this year." After all this time, she could still feel a tightening in her throat when she talked about her cousin and what had happened to her. "It's the usual story. Susan got to a certain age and suddenly she and her mother didn't get along. She got fed up and ran away one summer when she was about that girl's age. Her parents were frantic. They put up flyers, offered money, hired a private detective. Nothing."

She sighed, looking beyond Christian. Into the past.

"I saw her about three years later. I wasn't even sure it was her at first, she looked so different. So old and worn out. She'd gotten mixed up in prostitution and took drugs so she could tolerate living inside her own skin. I gave her money and helped her escape—yes," she said when she saw the look on Christian's face, "escape. The guy pimping her would have killed her rather than let her go. When she finally could talk about it, she told me that she'd been kidnapped, made a virtual prisoner forced to do things for this guy who 'kept' her. God, the horror in her eyes when she talked—" Lydia felt tears forming and blinked them back. "Susan finally killed herself because she couldn't live with what she'd done, what she'd gone through. Someone took advantage of her, of her teenage rebellion. And someone's taking advantage of these girls. I've got to stop him."

He understood how she felt, but Lydia was talking as if she was the only one who felt this way. "You're not alone in this."

Lydia pressed her lips together. He was making sense. But she was talking from her heart, not her intellect. "I know, I know, there are lots of people to take my place. I'm sure that Cate's more than good for it. But don't you see, this is something I have to do, something I feel that I owe Susan?"

Christian got to the heart of the matter. "Does Lukas know? About the baby?"

"No." She took a breath, fortifying herself. She knew she was asking a great deal of Christian. "And you can't tell him." She fell back on a technicality. "You're my doctor."

But Christian shook his head. "Lydia, I don't think I should be the one to examine you. I don't think either one of us would be comfortable with that."

"But you can give me a test."

He looked at her incredulously. "You haven't taken any?" He would have thought that would be the first thing she would have done.

Lydia held up her hand, fingers spread. "Five," she told him. "But I've never trusted anything that comes out of a box."

He saw through her. "You're hoping the test I do will tell you otherwise."

"That's the hope."

He sighed, taking a plastic cup from the rack and handing it to her. "Bathroom's that way. You know the drill."

She nodded, leaving the room.

Ten minutes felt like forever.

"Well?" She fairly pounced on Christian when he walked back into the room.

He gave her the answer with mixed feelings. Ordinarily, he would have been delighted to say this to her. "You're pregnant, Lydia. As for a doctor, Dr. Sheila Pollack is excellent." The woman was head of the obstetrics department and was well known for her skill and her bedside manner. "I suggest you see her as soon as possible. I also suggest you tell my brother as soon as possible."

Lydia nodded, but first she needed to buy herself some time. With any luck, she could push the investigation into high gear. There had to be someone who knew something but wasn't saying. More cages had to be rattled. More informants had to be questioned. Sullivan was letting her handle this on her own. She *had* to get results.

"I promise, Christian, and this is a good thing, it really is. I want to have lots of babies."

"Just at a more convenient time," he said, filling in the unspoken part.

She smiled at her brother-in-law, grateful he understood. "Something like that. You won't tell Lukas?"

He sighed. "It's against my better judgment, but it's your call. I won't break your confidence even if I'm not comfortable with this."

She kissed his cheek, relieved that she'd made the right call. "You're the best."

"Be that as it may, just make sure you tell him as soon as possible."

"I will," she promised.

He wanted to believe her.

Chapter 16

"Any word yet?" Lydia called out to Cate as she and Christian approached.

Cate stopped in midpace and shook her head in response. Rather than a few minutes, Lydia had been gone for almost half an hour. She couldn't help wondering what was going on. Lydia looked a little more somber than when she'd left. As for the good-looking doctor, he was a shade away from scowling. Was something going on between them?

It didn't seem possible. When Lydia and Lukas had been over to help her move in, they'd seemed as if they were still very much in love. They'd hit that enviable rhythm that sometimes occurs between a husband and wife—the lucky ones. Lydia didn't seem to be the type to jeopardize that for a little extramarital thrill.

And though she knew nothing about him, she didn't

get those vibes from Christian Graywolf, either. There was just something so upstanding about him. He was the kind of man to make flags stand up and salute as he walked by.

None of her business, Cate told herself.

The doctor stood behind her partner, giving no indication that he was taking his leave. Was he going to stick around until the girl they had found was brought back?

She was surprised to realize that she wanted him to stay. The next minute, she was shrugging the thought away. If she wanted him to remain, it wasn't because of any physical reaction to him, but because Christian Graywolf was the only doctor she knew in the area and it always helped to have an in. Besides, since he was Lydia's brother-in-law, that made the whole thing more personal and easier for all of them. Graywolf was their way of being able to find out what was going on without having to bring in a doctor from the bureau.

Generally speaking, except for Doc Ed, doctors were far too closemouthed for her liking.

Doctors weren't the only ones, she thought. These days everyone had some kind of little clique, a small group they owed allegiance to. Doctors, FBI agents, everyone thought their territory was primary.

And what of her? Cate silently asked. What kind of a group did she ultimately belong to? None that she could think of.

Granted, she was a special agent, but this was a new team she was on, and although Lydia and the others had done what they could to make her feel welcome, the others had history together.

She had… What?

No history with anyone anymore, Cate realized. Again she felt that she needed roots. Someplace to have sprung up from, a point of origin. And again, she thought of Joan Cunningham. Thoughts of Joan brought her back full circle to Christian Graywolf.

She raised her eyes to his, more than vaguely aware of the fact that with his chiseled features and his dark, dark hair, the man was too damn attractive for his own good.

And maybe yours? a small voice inside her head whispered.

She blocked the voice out. Yes, he was handsome, but he was also Lydia's brother-in-law, which somehow also put him off limits. His life had to be full of women. Women were known to develop crushes on their doctors. There was no doubt in her mind that Christian Graywolf probably had three times his share. Maybe four.

Cate forced herself to focus. Lydia had asked her a question when she'd approached. Something about the girl. And then it came back to her.

"They haven't come back from the X-ray facility," she told her partner. "I sent McClure up there with them, just in case someone was watching the warehouse and realized their mistake."

It had been totally her call. The other agent had been about to go back to the field office when she'd asked him to play bodyguard. He didn't look as if he liked taking orders from the task force newbie, but all things taken into account, she had more time on her sheet than he had on his. And she was also speaking for Lydia in the woman's absence.

Cate caught herself watching in silent fascination as two perfect, midnight black brows drew together over the bridge of his nose.

"Mistake?" Christian asked.

She was going to have to learn to eat on a regular basis. Her blood sugar had to be much too low, she upbraided herself. Her head spun just enough to make her feel unstable.

"That they left her alive instead of dead." Had they not arrived when they did, Cate was sure that the girl would have died.

Christian paused, scrutinizing his sister-in-law's partner. The two were obviously cut from the same cloth, even the same bolt, he thought. They even talked alike. Had he not been looking at her when she spoke, he would have been hard-pressed to say which one of them had just answered him.

A memory came to him out of nowhere, burrowing in. When Lukas had first brought Lydia around, he'd had what he later recognized to be a minor crush on her. Not that he would have ever done anything about it despite the very difficult patch that he and Alma were going through at the time. Lukas was his older brother and loyalty meant more to him than anything.

But he could still envy Lukas because Lydia was everything any man would have ever wanted in a woman. Not only did she have intelligence, wit and a charm about her, but she was damn beautiful to boot.

And Lydia's new partner reminded him a great deal of her.

They were both blond, both intelligent, independent and self-assured. And both were apparently very dedicated to their work.

Not only that, but Cate was just as beautiful as Lydia was. He blinked. It had been a long time since anyone's physical appearance had even registered with him. He supposed, if his life had been different, if there had been no wife to rip out his heart, he might have been somewhat interested in this woman. Maybe even more than just somewhat, he amended silently.

But there had been a wife. And Alma had left a permanent mark on him. He'd read once that you never got over a loved one's suicide, never really made peace with it. The best you could hope for was a co-existence that wasn't too markedly painful.

Alma's suicide would dictate his behavior for the rest of his life.

Otherwise...

He shook himself free of a sweet fragrance that somehow seemed to separate itself from the clean, antiseptic scent of the hospital. The scent whispered softly through him like a long-forgotten melody.

Perfume? Shampoo? Soap? It didn't belong to Lydia because he'd only just now become aware of it.

Cate?

"I'll go check on her for you," Christian abruptly told Lydia.

As he started to go toward the service elevators that were used to take inpatients to the various labs and X-ray facilities, he realized that her perfume followed him.

Cate had fallen into step beside him.

"Mind if I tag along?" Cate glanced over her shoulder and called "I'll be right back" to Lydia.

Christian looked quizzically over the woman's head toward Lydia for an explanation. But his sister-in-law merely spread her hands, indicating that she had no more of a clue than he did why her partner was asking to accompany him.

"They won't tell you anything," he informed her shortly.

"I know that. That's what I have you for." She smiled broadly at him and he caught himself thinking that his sister-in-law's partner had one of those unexpected smiles that seemed to light up the entire area. In a single moment it transformed her face from serious to charming, bordering on ethereal.

Not to mention damn sexy.

If she wanted to come, he had no reason to refuse her. So he shrugged and resumed walking toward the elevators. "Suit yourself."

"I usually do." Before he could change his mind, Cate quickly slipped through the swinging door he held for her.

His laugh was short, leaving his features completely unchanged. She caught a cynical note in his voice.

"Somehow," he said, "that doesn't surprise me."

She wondered what else he thought of her and why that should matter. But it did, and that bothered her.

The elevator car that arrived a couple of moments later was empty, save for the padded drop cloths hanging on all three of the walls. It made her think of a padded cell.

"Looks like someone's moving," Cate commented.

"They're bringing new equipment into the sixth-floor research lab."

Reaching over her, Christian pressed for the third floor. Cate stepped back to get out of his way and somehow managed to do the opposite because he moved as well. She found herself with her back up against his chest, his right arm forming a semicircle around her as he reached for the keypad.

Something fluttered through her, unsettling her. Making her feel flustered for no apparent reason.

She couldn't remember when she'd felt that way last. High school? *Flustered* wasn't a word that an FBI special agent enjoyed entertaining anywhere except maybe on a Scrabble board.

Cate cleared her throat, more out of nerves than any real need. "Sorry," she murmured.

"My fault."

God, they sounded like characters trapped in a play about awkwardness. It wasn't a feeling he welcomed or was all that familiar with. Maybe his hours were finally getting to him. His mother's words, "physician, heal thyself," mysteriously materialized in his head.

He went on the defensive. Against everything. "What are you doing here?" he asked her suddenly.

Humor had always been her way out. "Define *here.*" Cate turned to look at him and decided that the padded walls made the elevator car feel very small and oddly intimate. She didn't need that right now. "*Here* as in the elevator, *here* as in the hospital, or *here* as in Southern California—"

He held his hand up, stopping her. He had a feeling she could go on indefinitely. And then he surprised them both by laughing. She stared at him quizzically. Or maybe she thought he was crazy. Maybe he was. A little. Not that anyone could blame him with the schedule he kept.

"My mother recently accused me of talking like a lawyer. She should have been here for your response, then she'd realize what legalese *really* sounds like." He looked down at her. A strange urge wafted through him that he refused to recognize as anything but the result of lack of sleep on his part. "Okay, to be very specific, what are you doing in this elevator in this hospital, riding up to the X-ray lab with me?"

Unable to resist, Cate deadpanned, "And by that you mean—" The incredulous look on his face made her laugh and give up the ruse. "Sorry, couldn't help myself." Her smile broadened, filtering into her eyes. And into him. "And thank you."

His mind was wandering again. Her smile seemed to do that to him. He struggled to pull his focus back on the subject and away from her. "For what?"

"I don't think I've laughed for weeks now." Longer than that, she thought. Maybe not even since Gabe died.

"You should," he told her quietly. "It's a nice sound."

A pleased feeling sprouted from nowhere. She didn't usually take compliments to heart. Maybe she was just needy right now, she reasoned. And maybe the good doctor wasn't as anal as she'd originally thought. After all, Lydia seemed to like him and she had already learned that her new partner didn't suffer fools or humorless people.

"Thank you. I guess I just actually wanted to corner you and ask how Joan was doing." She saw the guarded look that came into his eyes. "I am allowed to do that, right? Ask how she's doing?"

"Without my getting specific?"

"Be as vague as you like." But she wouldn't have been Cate if she hadn't added, "But feel free to be specific if you have a heart."

"I have a heart, agent—" He stopped abruptly. "What is your last name, anyway?"

"That's my whole problem," she reminded him. "My quest, if you will," she added. "I'm trying to find out my last name. My *real* last name."

Chapter 17

Christian knew all about quests. Because he was a Native American, a Navajo, the word had special meaning for him. A great many of his people, not to mention the members of other tribes, went on personal quests. On private journeys where no one else could follow them. To find themselves. To seek guidance and answers.

In a way, he supposed that he was still on a quest of his own. He needed to find a true purpose to his existence. The death of his wife and daughter had shattered his firm grasp on life. He knew he was a healer, had wanted to be one all his life. When Lukas preceded him into the field of medicine, it had just intensified his drive to become a doctor, even though the odds were against him and money was scarce.

But as to who and what Christian Graywolf the man

was, that had somehow evolved into a mystery for him. He used to know, or at least thought he knew. But Alma and their baby's deaths had changed all that, had him questioning everything he used to take for granted. Since he hadn't followed them into the Great Beyond the way he'd initially wanted, there had to be a reason why he was still here.

He needed to ascertain that reason and make his peace with it.

Looking at Cate tempted him to tell her more than he should. More than he could. There was some kind of connection working between them, some kind of current traveling on a level he didn't want to acknowledge. And yet, he could feel it, feel a pull toward this woman that seemed to transcend his will and logic.

But his training managed to overpower his inclination and the coaxing look in her eyes. For now. "Joan's doing well."

As well as could be expected under the circumstances, or really well? Had the woman been given a clean bill of health? Cate wondered. She hadn't been able to get her hands on positive documentation yet.

"Despite the cancer." she said.

It was a leading statement and he was never one to be led. "I never said—"

"No, you didn't." He hadn't even hinted that Joan had cancer. She wondered how the man would have stood up in a witness stand, being grilled by a thousand-dollar-an-hour lawyer. Probably well. His honor wouldn't have let him do anything else. She had no idea why she found that sexy, but she did. "But government work has its perks."

He looked at her for a long moment, trying not to get lost in her eyes. Was she telling him she'd hacked into the hospital's records? He doubted she'd go that far, but the truth was, he didn't really know what this woman was capable of. On the other hand, she could just be fishing.

"Not legally," he said.

He couldn't read her expression. The desire to run the back of his hand along her cheek came out of nowhere. He banked it down.

"Sometimes there's a fine line between legal and moral," she countered.

The elevator had finally made its slow way up to the third floor. The doors seemed to open arthritically. Christian waited for her to get off first. The moment he stepped out of the car, the doors suddenly closed with unexpected verve. Startled, he took another step, bumping against her. A current zigzagged through him. Through her as well, he thought, because for just a moment, a stunned look flashed across her face.

He forced himself to focus on what they were discussing and not the sensations, so long dormant, that were attempting to chew their way out of a steel-caged prison. "Not according to the law," he reminded her.

Cate made no comment as to her feelings about legality. Having him bump against her had her dealing with a warmth that had sprung out of the shadows. It worried her. She moved the conversation to a lighter venue. "Your mother was right, Dr. Graywolf, you should have been a lawyer."

"No, what my mother said was that if she'd wanted me to be a lawyer, she would have sent me to law school."

They turned down a long corridor. Arrows of vary-
ing colors pointed to different departments. She felt as
if she was dealing with those same arrows inside of her,
pointing off in different directions. And right in the
middle was this physical reaction to the man walking
next to her. She had to get a grip. "Lydia tells me that
your mother's an amazing woman."

He was proud of his mother, extremely proud, but
not blind to her faults. "That's one word for her."

"I'll bite, what's another?"

Christian smiled, and Cate felt something in her
stomach tighten. "In Lydia's case, she would have
probably used the word *formidable*."

Cate could easily envision that. A clash between
two strong-willed women who loved the same person.
Especially if they came from different cultures. "I take
it your mother didn't like the fact that her new daughter-in-law wasn't one of the Dine."

He looked at her, impressed. Most people that he
knew weren't familiar with the name that his tribe applied to itself. "Been doing homework?"

"I just like knowing."

He waited for more, but it didn't come. He turned
down a second corridor, then made another right.
"Knowing what?"

"Just knowing," she replied innocently. "As much as
I can about everything I can."

Most people only took in as much as they had to,
no more. That made her a very unusual person. But
then, he'd already sensed that. On all levels. "Knowledge is power?" he guessed.

Only if you could hold it over someone's head, she

thought, shaking her own. "I don't care about power, I care about knowledge for its own sake."

It was a specialized world they lived in, with only enough time to focus on very specific things. No one had a chance to even approach being a Renaissance person anymore. There was just too much to know, to learn. But he had to admit that trying was admirable. "I thought they stopped making people like you in the Middle Ages."

She grinned. She would have never survived that era. Except for a few isolated souls, women were regarded as utterly inferior. If she'd lived back then, she would have had to have been a man. "A few of us managed to survive."

"Good to know."

She could tell he meant what he said. Cate had no idea how but there was something in his eyes—and he did have beautiful eyes. Almost as if a bit of the morning sky had fallen and managed to somehow channel through him.

Cate suddenly pulled herself together. What was going on here? Fantasizing about a man's eyes was *not* what she was being paid for.

Christian paused in the hallway for a moment, standing before the X-ray facility where he'd sent his patient. Inside him, ethics and morality warred with each other. He bent the former to allow a little leeway to the latter.

He lowered his voice. "Look, Joan isn't as strong as you are."

"You think I'm strong?" Cate pressed her lips together. The man probably thought she was fishing for a compliment. She wasn't, but he'd surprised her. The confident, strong woman she'd once been had been steadily crumbling for the last few years now. All that was left was a facade and a charade.

He smiled at her even as he attempted to distance himself from this woman who seemed to be getting to him far too quickly and on levels he wanted to keep sealed off. "Let's say you remind me of Lydia."

She took it on approval and it warmed her. "Nice company to be in."

"The best." He thought back to the beginning of this part of the conversation. They'd only been together for a few minutes and it seemed as if there were several fragments he had to pull together. "And by the way, my mother loves Lydia. Initially she was just worried that maybe Lydia was slumming."

She couldn't come up with a proper meaning to the word in this context. "Slumming?"

"There are women who are drawn to men they feel are socially inferior but can still serve as trophies. A theme and variation of the rich girl and the bad boy," he elaborated. "Native American men fit under that category."

She didn't think of him in terms of a category. She did think of him as a threat, though. He was making her mind wander far too much. She took a deep breath, as if that would reinforce her professionalism. "You need a better crowd to hang around with."

Christian shook his head. "You wouldn't understand."

"Until I walk a mile in your shoes?" she guessed flippantly. She'd do him one better. "At least you know what shoes are yours. I don't. Technically," she added when he looked at her, confused. "Not until I hear Joan Cunningham admit that she's my mother."

Hers was just a matter of switching heritage. Ancestors didn't mean all that much in the Caucasian world, not the way they did in his. Didn't she understand that? "And will your whole way of thinking suddenly change if you find out you're Irish instead of Polish with a drop of French blood?"

He remembered, which surprised her. The exchange between them about the people she'd thought were her family had occurred days ago, and from all appearances, the man had an extremely busy life. Yet he'd remembered that she'd thought she had a great-grandmother who'd been an impoverished French countess. Something inside of her felt pleased, although she couldn't have explained why. Or maybe she could, and just didn't want to.

"No, but it might open up things for me, make sense about things I've felt. I can't explain it unless you're standing in *my* shoes," she told him. "And it's Norwegian, not Irish."

"What is?"

"Joan's heritage." She'd yet to piece together her father's background. There'd been several surname changes and she was still tracing those back. "Both her parents came from Norway. First generation."

"So you already know."

"Like I said, 'technically.'"

She moved out of the way as a woman and her son walked up to the door. The woman was carrying several pages in her hand and looked nervous. The little boy was whining about wanting to play. Envy shimmered through her. The boy had no idea how lucky he was.

Graywolf really wasn't interested, Cate decided, glancing toward him. But she'd started this, so she put it as succinctly as possible for him. "It was a blood test that blew my world apart, made everything I knew about myself turn out to be a lie. It's going to take another blood test to start putting things back together for me."

"You said you had documents you've obviously tracked down."

"Yes?"

"Aren't they enough for you?"

How could paper take the place of flesh and blood? She didn't want answers so much as she wanted acceptance. She wanted a family, a feeling of belonging somewhere instead of this awful rootless feeling that kept cropping up over and over again. She wasn't meant to be a loner, and yet that was what she was right now. And she hated it.

"It's paper," she said simply. "There could always have been a mistake made."

He supposed, in her place, he might have felt the same way. Angry at having been rejected, needing to hear that he was accepted. But he wasn't in her shoes, he reminded himself. He was in his own shoes. The shoes of a doctor. Specifically Joan Cunningham's doctor.

"I think you should let this go."

"Could you?" she asked. "Honestly?"

She had him there.

Christian opened the outer door and walked in. The receptionist behind the counter looked up, saw his lab coat and stethoscope and nodded a greeting.

"Does Lydia know her new partner is pigheaded?" Christian asked.

"We haven't butted heads yet, so I doubt if she suspects." She wasn't about to allow herself to get sidetracked. "You didn't answer my question, Doctor. If you were me, this close to finding out, could you back away?"

"I'm not you."

"But if you were?" she pressed.

Christian took a breath, knowing he could either take the easy way out and lie, or answer the question and leave his patient and this woman open to further complications and interactions.

But before he could answer, the inner door to the X-ray area burst open and he heard a nurse cry out, "She's having a seizure."

Gut instinct told him the nurse was talking about the patient he'd sent up.

Chapter 18

Christian hurried through the doors that took him into the rear of the X-ray facility. Deceptively small-looking from the front, the interior of the department was catacombed with rooms where technicians performed various tests with a variety of imaging machines.

"Where is she?" he demanded of the nurse who'd called for help.

Seeming relieved that a doctor was there to take over, the young woman quickly turned on her heel, beckoning for him to follow. "This way."

As he hurried behind the nurse, he realized that Cate was still right behind him.

"Stay outside." He shot the order over his shoulder and stepped up his pace. The nurse was almost running.

Cate lengthened her stride to keep up. "The hell I

will," she retorted. "This might be the only time I get to talk to her."

She was *exactly* like Lydia, Christian thought. Under different circumstances, he might have admired Cate's grit. Right now it just annoyed him. But he had no time to waste arguing with her. He needed to get to his patient. The rooms were purposely constructed small and tight for maximum efficiency. Usually there was just enough space for the technician, a table and whatever scanning apparatus was being used on the patient. Cate was going to have to stay out by default.

"In here." The nurse pointed to a room, stopping short of one of the doorways.

Cate peered inside and caught her breath. Two male technicians were attempting to hold down the girl she'd found in the warehouse and having a tough time of it. The girl was arching and bucking, her entire body convulsing with uncontrollable spasms.

Christian never hesitated. He called for a medication that, when injected into the girl's arm, instantly made the spasms cease. As Cate watched, the girl fell back against the table, unconscious and limp. For a second, the very air around her seemed to freeze.

Almost afraid to say anything, Cate raised her eyes to Christian. "Is she—?"

"Dead? No."

Whipping his stethoscope from the back of his neck and inserting the earpieces, he listened to her heartbeat. It was settling down. He needed to stabilize her if he was going to operate, and there was no doubt in his mind that she needed surgery. He returned the stethoscope to its original position and stepped back.

Into Cate.

An annoyed sigh hissed through his teeth. "Why are you still here?"

Cate took a single step back and no more. There was no way he was going to get her to leave. "Because I have a job to do."

Christian glared at her. "Since when is getting in the way a job?"

She thought his ancestors must have been formidable opponents if they could cast thunderbolts from their eyes the way he did. "You only tripped over me once," she pointed out.

Placing his fingers on the girl's wrist again, he resumed monitoring her pulse. It was getting stronger. Good.

Christian slanted a glance at his sister-in-law's annoying partner. "Did you expect her suddenly to sit up and tell you everything you wanted to know?"

"I don't know what to expect, that's why I'm here," she retorted. "Sometimes people experience a moment of lucidity just before the end."

That was for movies and books. Reality didn't arrange itself nearly as neatly. "And most of the time, they don't."

"But it's not a sure thing," she countered stubbornly.

The woman just didn't give up. Christian got the distinct impression that, given half a chance, she would probably try to argue God out of Armageddon.

The situation temporarily calm, Christian stepped back from the table. Glancing toward Cate, he studied her for a moment, trying to delve into her thoughts. He got nowhere. "My sister-in-law seems to be wound up around this case, too. Is it personal for you, as well?"

A glimmer of a smile took over her lips as she reflected. All of her work had always been very personal to her. She'd had to work on that. She'd come very close to burning out the first year in the field. It had taken her time to learn how to appear to keep things under wraps. There had been nights, especially in the early days, when she'd come home from work and just cried. Until Gabe had come into her life and let the sunshine in. He had a way of looking at things that didn't just put them in their proper perspective, but somehow managed to keep them light.

She missed Gabe in so many ways.

"If you let something get to you, you're not going to be any good to the bureau, not accomplish any good for the people you're trying to protect and help. The picture's bigger than just a close-up." Gabe had been right, of course, and she'd tried to remember that. But at times, it just wasn't easy.

"Anything done to a child is personal to me," she told Christian stiffly. She didn't like being questioned. It made her feel as if she was on the defensive. "And under that misapplied makeup—" she waved at the still, small form on the table "—is a child. A child who never got the chance to be one."

Christian read between the lines. "So you're a crusader."

"I'm anything I have to be to bring the bad guys in." Realizing that her answer sounded rather flippant, she watched to see if he took offense.

One of the X-ray technicians approached him. "Doctor, we managed to get a few films done before she began having seizures. They've just finished developing them." He nodded toward the door on his right. "If you want to see those…"

"Absolutely." Christian walked into the next room where the X-ray films could be viewed more easily. Behind him he heard Cate following, matching him step for step. This had to stop.

Christian halted abruptly. Unable to stop in time, Cate walked straight into him. "Are you planning on following me into the men's room, too?"

"Only if that's where you're reading the X-rays," she deadpanned. She could see the humor fell on deaf ears. It was obvious that the man's patience was wearing thin. "Look, I need to see those X-rays."

"Why?" he demanded. "Are you going to try to assist in the surgery?"

"No, that's your department."

"Thanks at least for admitting that."

She could have gotten frostbite from the sarcasm. "Look, I need to find certain things out."

"What possible difference could it make to you what's on those X-rays?" he asked.

She went toe to toe with him. "You want to know, all right, I'll tell you. And it's not a pretty picture I'm painting. Maybe whoever kidnapped her or bought her from her parents for the price of several ounces of drugs didn't just use her as a prostitute. They could also be using her as a mule." She saw that the term momentarily threw him. "Mules are made to bring cocaine into the country by either swallowing small balloons filled with the drug, or having them inserted in various body cavities." Even after all this time, the thought of that made her stomach turn. "One balloon leaking—"

Christian cut her short. "I know all about what happens, Special Agent. I watch the Discovery Channel, too."

"Yes, but I live it."

She said it as if she was ready to defend truth and justice, challenging the dregs of society. With little imagination, he could almost envision a cape flapping behind her in the wind.

Christian knew that if he called for Security, they would remove Cate quickly enough, but it didn't seem worth the effort just to win. Growing up Navajo had taught him not to compete, that trying to best his fellow person wasn't polite. It was only when he'd become Americanized that winning had taken on some kind of meaning.

So he'd focused on winning victories against diseases and injuries instead. And right now, he had to prepare for another battle. There was no time to waste arguing with a woman with a rosebud mouth and flashing green eyes.

Without another word, he went through the door the technician held open for him.

Cate followed, feeling a little triumphant. She'd won a battle. The house was on his side, not hers, and she'd still won a concession. It reminded her how much she'd liked beating the odds.

The technician had all the X-rays that had been developed mounted against the screens. Backlighting illuminated them. The problem was easy enough for even a layman to spot. The girl had three cracked ribs. In addition to that, her spleen had been damaged and her kidneys were bruised.

"That's not right, is it?" Cate asked, pointing to the cracked ribs.

"No," he said quietly, "that's not right. A girl her age should be daydreaming about her first boyfriend, not being manhandled by some scum with the price of a good time in his wallet." The girl was small boned with dark hair. She made him think of Alma at that age. It was becoming personal for him, too, and he struggled to resist the feeling. "If we don't tape her ribs, one of them might just pierce her lung." He blew out a breath, looking at the radiologist who had come into the room. "It's a wonder that it didn't happen while she was having her seizure episode."

"We got lucky," Cate said softly.

He supposed that was one way of seeing it, although how the word *luck* could be applied to this girl was nothing short of a mystery to him.

Christian surveyed the X-rays one last time. "I need her in surgery right away," he told the radiologist.

The latter nodded and began gathering together the X-rays as he shut off the backlight.

Christian searched for the nurse who had initially brought him back here. She was nowhere in sight. With an impatient shrug, he crossed to the wall phone himself. After yanking up the receiver, he pressed the three numbers that connected him to the scheduling desk.

"This is Dr. Graywolf. No, the other one," he corrected. He noticed that Cate was trying to suppress the smile that rose to her lips. Somehow, the sight of it seemed to counterbalance the drama of the situation. He forced himself to look away. "I need an operating room. ASAP. No, not good enough. I mean *now*. A girl's life might be hanging in the balance." There was a pause as he listened to the woman on the other end. "I need an internal surgeon," he told her, cutting in. "Is Dr. Bendenetti on call? He is, good, get him. Tell him it's an emergency. Yes, I'll assist. Operating room 3? Right."

Cate watched him drop the receiver into the cradle. He seemed satisfied with the answers he'd gotten. "I thought you were a gynecologist."

"I am. But I'm cleared to assist." He paused, glancing at her. "Anything else you'd like to question?"

"What are her chances?"

"Slim. We'll know more when we open her up. Go back and tell my sister-in-law that there's nothing she can do right now, short of lighting a candle."

His comment surprised her. "You believe in prayer?" He didn't seem like the type.

"Lydia does. As far as I'm concerned, whatever sees you through the night is okay."

She couldn't have really said, in the midst of all this, why it seemed important to her to get a handle on him. But it was. "So you don't believe in prayer."

He looked at her for a moment that seemed to stretch out indefinitely. So much so that she decided he wasn't going to answer her, other than to make her feel that it was none of her business.

And then she heard him say, "No."

He didn't believe in prayer. Because prayer had failed him. Over and over again. He'd lost track of the times he'd prayed, prayed that Alma would get over her demons, prayed that they could have a normal life together.

And he'd prayed for the life of his little girl as she waged a infinitesimally short war against death that awful day. His beautiful daughter hadn't died with her mother on the tracks. Somehow, she'd managed to survive long enough to be taken to the hospital, and he'd hoped, prayed...

But ultimately, she'd died at the hospital before a single doctor could come to attend her. If there was a God up there, His answer had been no and he didn't want to carry on communications with someone who didn't want to take his calls.

But he kept that all to himself, because to breathe a word of it was far too personal, far too hurtful.

Cate nodded her head. She thought of how hard she'd prayed the morning of September 11. Prayed that Gabe would survive the awful catastrophe. After all, some people had come out of the buildings alive, why not him?

But he hadn't.

God had not taken her call.

"Me, neither."

Christian paused for a moment.

He was tempted to ask her why she didn't believe that praying did any good. He didn't usually experience curiosity, not about strangers. And asking her something so personal would only pave the way for more personal information to be rendered. Something he neither wanted nor welcomed from people who were not his patients. Because that meant getting involved, and the only thing he wanted to be involved with was the vocation he'd taken an oath to uphold. That and his family.

Maybe that was why his curiosity had been aroused. Because Cate reminded him of Lydia and he cared about his sister-in-law. About what she felt and what she thought. She made a dynamic impact on the lives of everyone she came in contact with.

He wondered if Cate did. This woman seemed somehow darker than Lydia had been. Was it just because she was plagued with doubts that had to do with her parentage? Or was there something else, something more?

And why the hell should any of that matter to him? More than likely, he'd never see her again after today.

Even as he thought it, something inside of him whispered that it wasn't true. That there would be more.

Christian shut the thought out. He had no time for this. There was a life to save and that was far more important than satisfying a smattering of idle curiosity, which was all it was. If he was reacting to her on any other level, wanting to touch her and see how soft her skin was, it was just because he was tired, nothing more.

"Tell Lydia I'll call right after the surgery's over and give her an update."

She looked at him for a long moment. There'd been something in his eyes just then, something that had nothing to do with hospitals, or the case. Something that spoke to the very heart of her. Cate shut away the wave of warmth that passed over her body. She was imagining things. Imagining his look, imagining her response. She refused to give either any credence. She was all about the case, nothing else. Nothing more.

More. The word hovered in her brain. She forced herself to focus on what he'd just said.

Cate nodded. "Okay, but Lydia'll probably call you first."

He laughed shortly, shaking his head. "You're probably right." As she began to leave, he called after her, "Know how to get back?"

It seemed to her an unusually thoughtful question, especially given the circumstances. In her experience, the stereotype was true. Most men didn't think about directions.

"I've got a natural sense of direction," she assured him.

Christian nodded in response. He found himself watching her leave longer than he should have, the sway of her hips drawing him in.

The next moment, he was issuing orders to get the girl in the next room ready for surgery.

Cate felt Christian's eyes on her as she left. Knowing when she was being watched had developed into almost a sixth sense for her. She felt her mouth curving as she retraced her steps to the service elevators. Maybe it wasn't all just her imagination.

A movement out of the corner of her eye caught her attention and she glanced over to her left just before turning a corner.

Cate stopped dead.

Joan Cunningham was no more than twenty feet away.

Chapter 19

Her biological mother was so close and about to enter one of the rooms on the opposite side. A tall, young man was with her. Rangy, with reddish hair that seemed to echo Joan's own darker red, the young man was dressed too casually to be a hospital employee.

Joan's son?

Cate's pulse quickened. Was that her half brother? The thought throbbed in her brain as she changed her direction and quickly stepped up her pace.

"Joan?" she called out. When there was no reaction, she raised her voice and called again. "Joan?"

This time, they heard her. The woman's son stopped first. Joan appeared almost reluctant to acknowledge that someone was calling to her. When Joan looked over in her direction, her complexion, still pale from her ordeal, faded to the color of newly fallen snow.

The man beside Joan appeared to be mildly curious as he looked at her. He had an easy smile, Cate noted. Like her.

"Friend of yours, Mom?" Cate heard him ask.

She was right. He was Joan's son. She had a half brother. She had a family. She'd been aware of that already, but only on paper. It was different, seeing the evidence in the flesh.

Would he reject her, too, once he knew?

"How are you feeling?" Cate called out before she even reached the stricken-looking woman.

The woman looked like a deer caught in the headlights of an approaching car. She wanted to run, but she couldn't. Cate had never seen that look outside of a fugitive's eyes. Until now.

Joan's sharp intake of breath told her she was right. Caught, Joan undoubtedly knew she couldn't urge her son to rush away without causing a scene, without raising questions in his mind.

"How are you feeling?" Cate repeated as she joined the duo. It took everything she had not to fire more questions at Joan. Not to ask why she refused to admit she was her mother.

I'm giving you another chance. Don't keep rejecting me.

But there was no mistaking the distress in Joan's eyes, the silent pleading. So the questions she had, about all the minor details she hungered to find out about this woman, especially about how she'd felt about the man who'd been her father, had to be put on hold. Cate hoped not indefinitely.

They burned on her tongue.

But working for the bureau had taught her restraint.
She dug deep into her reserve and forced a smile to her
lips as she looked at the young man standing beside her
birth mother.

*Hi, I'm your half sister, Cate. Didn't know I existed,
did you?*

She put her hand out, her smile warm, all the while
scrutinizing his face, searching for similarities between
this handsome young man and herself. "Hi, I'm Cate
Kowalski."

Joan's son leaned over and took her hand. His fingers dwarfed hers as they wrapped around them.

My brother has a firm grip.

"I'm Alex. Where do you know my mother from?"
It was a question to which he supplied his own tenta-
tive answer. "The cancer support group?"

"No." She saw fear rise in Joan's eyes.

I'm your dirty little secret, aren't I, Joan? The
thought stung. *I didn't come all this way, looking for
you to cause trouble. All I want is to know who I really
am. And maybe get a family in the bargain.*

She hated feeling this alone, this adrift.

But there would be no answers if she wound up
completely alienating this frightened-looking woman
standing before her.

Cate thought of Christian and had her excuse. "We
both have the same doctor. Dr. Graywolf," she told
Alex. "We met in his waiting room one late afternoon
and just got to talking. I didn't expect to run into her
today." At least that much was true, Cate thought.

The look in Joan's eyes was one of guarded relief,
as if she still couldn't relax. As if she still expected her

to suddenly say something that would bring her house of cards tumbling down.

Smiling had never felt quite as painful before, Cate thought as she looked at Joan again. "So, you still haven't told me. *Are* you feeling better?"

"Not when she has the chemo," Alex volunteered when his mother said nothing, "but the doctor says everything's going to be great. It looks as if they got everything when they went in." A puzzled expression creased his otherwise smooth brow as he looked down at Joan. It was obvious that he didn't understand why she wasn't saying anything to her friend. "Mom's one of the lucky ones, aren't you, Mom?" Draping one arm around her shoulders, he gave the woman a half hug.

"I'd certainly say she was." Her eyes met Joan's. Joan lowered hers.

Look at me, damn it. I'm not some leper, I'm your daughter. I've got your eyes.

It was difficult maintaining this degree of cheerfulness. "Well, I won't keep you. It was nice seeing you again, Joan. Maybe we can get together sometime and actually get a chance to talk a little." Cate began to turn away.

Joan licked her lips, as if they felt too dry to form any words properly. "Maybe." Cate froze, afraid she'd imagined the woman's response. She looked at her, waiting for a sign that she wasn't hearing things. "When I'm feeling better."

"The treatments take a lot out of her," Alex confided to her. There was a degree of protectiveness in his voice. "That's why I took the day off, to bring her here and take her home."

"Where's your dad?" *What kind of a man did you wind up marrying, Joan? Why isn't he here for you?*

Alex raised a broad shoulder, shrugging off her question. "Dad has a hard time dealing with this kind of thing. He likes to think we're all perfect." Affection shone in his eyes as he looked down at his mother. "I keep telling Mom he's just afraid of losing her and doesn't know how to show it." A rueful smile played on his lips as he looked back at Cate, as if he were sharing a piece of information they were both aware of. "That generation of men is still stuck in the Dark Ages."

"Lucky for Joan that you're not," Cate told him.

Alex grinned at the compliment. She liked his smile. It was quick, guileless.

"Well, I'll be seeing you." On impulse, she took out her card and pressed it into Joan's palm. "Call me sometime." It was half a command, half a plea. "When you feel like talking."

Looking over his mother's shoulder, Alex glanced down at the business card. Surprise lifted his brow. "You're an FBI agent?"

"Special agent," she corrected with a smile. "They like to call us that. That's supposed to make up for all the heat we're sometimes required to take." She looked at Alex for a moment longer, trying not to seem as if she was studying him. Doing just that. He had his mother's hair, but most of his features had to be his father's. Like her. "Again, nice meeting you."

She meant that from the bottom of her heart. Wondering if she would ever get the chance to meet her other half siblings.

Taking a breath, Cate turned on her heel, picking up her pace as she made her way toward the back elevators.

Before she was tempted to remain. And tell Alex everything.

"Did she die?"

Those were the first words out of Lydia's mouth when she finally got back. A moment before her partner had looked up to see her approaching, she'd been glancing at her watch. Probably wondering what the hell had happened to her, Cate surmised.

Reaching Lydia, her mind on her unexpected meeting with Joan, Cate realized that the "her" Lydia was referring to was the young girl they had brought in.

Cate shook her head. "No, why?"

"Well, for one thing, you took a long time getting back." Lydia looked down the hall, but there was no sight of Christian. "What happened to Christian?"

"I left him upstairs. Our 'witness' is going in for emergency surgery. Your brother-in-law's assisting. Someone named Bendenetti's operating."

Lydia nodded, looking relieved. "Reese." The surgeon and his wife had been to their home a number of times, and vice versa. She got along well with both of them. "He's a good man."

"Your brother-in-law said not to wait. That he'd call us, you," she corrected, "when the surgery's over."

Lydia sighed, nodding. "I suppose he's right. We can leave one of the men here, just to be sure nobody shows up to finish what they started." She stopped talking. "Is anything wrong, Cate?"

"No, why?"

"Because you look like you've seen a ghost."

She shook her had. "Just ran into someone from my past."

Lydia looked surprised. "I didn't think you lived here before."

"I didn't. This was someone who moved down here from San Francisco. Like I did."

She didn't want to talk about it, didn't even want to think about it just yet. Not until she was alone and had a chance to sort this all out for herself.

Christian knew all about it, of course, but she doubted he would say anything to Lydia. He didn't strike her as the type to find her secret quest worthy of repetition.

She'd tell Lydia about it in her own good time. Once she got Joan to openly recognize her.

Chapter 20

Lydia and Cate rode back to the field office together, accompanied occasionally by intermittent static coming from the dispatch radio. Each was lost in her own thoughts, only vaguely aware that the other was not talking.

Lydia was busy trying to assuage her conscience. She'd already made a silent vow to herself that if the case wasn't wrapped up in a month's time, or at least very close to it, she would tell first Lukas, then Assistant Director Sullivan, that she was pregnant. She'd act as if this was all news to her as well. Neither man needed to know that she would have known of her pregnancy for a while. That she'd suspected the fact almost from the first moment because her body felt slightly out of sync.

The state of her emotions had been her first clue.

They had been all over the map right from the start. She was usually focused, not feeling as if she were spinning out of control. At first, she'd gone into a state of denial, blaming it on stress, on anything except what she knew in her heart was the reason. Birth control had obviously failed her.

Sitting in the passenger seat, Cate took the lack of dialogue as a blessing. Not that she found talking to Lydia taxing in any way, but right now she was desperately trying to get her head together. She'd reacted to that doctor today, to Lydia's brother-in-law. It wasn't her imagination. In the elevator, when she'd backed up into him, something had gone on between them. Something she couldn't put her finger on.

All she knew was that it made her feel uneasy and she couldn't say why.

She'd been pushing herself too hard, Cate decided. That was why she was feeling things. She was just stressed out and at the end of her rope. Ever since Gabe had been killed, she'd worked almost nonstop, only taking time off to be with her mother when Julia had become ill. It wasn't exactly the kind of lifestyle a doctor would heartily recommend for her nerves, she thought.

When they were less than three blocks away from the bureau, Lydia glanced away from the road and at her partner.

"So what did you think of my brother-in-law?" she asked.

The question caught Cate off guard. Why would Lydia ask her that? Was there something in her face that told her partner something—whatever that "something" might be—was up?

Cate tried to buy herself some time as her mind scrambled about, searching for a plausible response. "Excuse me?"

Lydia's mouth curved. She recognized a stalling tactic when she heard one and it pleased her. If Cate was stalling, that meant she was searching for the right thing to say. Which either meant that she was trying to be polite, or trying not to say anything that might give away the fact that Christian had left a more-than-favorable impression on her.

Lydia put her hopes on the latter. It was about time Christian started seeing someone other than his patients. And as for Cate, there were still gaps that the younger woman hadn't filled in, but she had a feeling a relationship had gone sour in Cate's past. She never talked about anyone special. Someone as attractive as Cate had to have had someone in her life at some point. The fact that she didn't mention anything just convinced Lydia that her partner needed to have someone in her life.

Why not Christian? That would solve both their problems. At least for a little while.

"Christian," Lydia prompted. "What did you think of him?"

That he has the most unsettling blue eyes I've ever seen. They seem to look right through you. That he's the first man I've noticed since Gabe died. That he's sexier than hell and probably has a ton of women hanging all over his stethoscope.

Cate shrugged carelessly, as if she hadn't given the man a thought. "He seems very capable."

Dead giveaway, Lydia thought smugly.

Cate was very descriptive with her words. Her response was entirely too vague to be in keeping with what Lydia knew of her partner's character.

Stopping at what she could only assume was a red light, her vision blocked by the huge supermarket delivery truck in front of her, Lydia decided to build her brother-in-law up a little.

"He's more than that," she said with pride. "He's the best. Christian could probably write his own ticket anywhere he goes."

Doctors like that usually went where the money was, Cate thought. "So why does he stay at Blair Memorial?"

"Because Lukas is here."

That had been Christian's main priority when he first began medical school. He'd wanted to practice where his older brother was. After Alma killed herself, Lukas had insisted on it because he'd wanted to keep an eye on him, afraid of what Christian might do if he were alone in another city.

"And don't get me wrong," she said quickly. "Blair Memorial is a fantastic hospital. It's ranked as one of the best in the country. I just meant that somewhere else, they might have already made him head of the Obstetrics Department despite his age. Sheila Pollack is young," she went on, referring to the present department head. "Unless something happens and she moves, she's going to be head of the department for a good many years."

Cate listened, thinking that after all those years of sacrificing to become a doctor, the name of the game would be getting ahead. "So why doesn't Christian go somewhere else?"

A fond look entered Lydia's eyes. "He's not ambitious. Not in that way, anyway. Neither of them are. He and Lukas just want to be the best at what they do. The money, the prestige, none of that means a thing to either one of them."

During tiny pockets of time, Cate felt as if the world was made up of people so busy pursuing goals that they didn't have time to enjoy what they'd gained so far. She supposed that she was just as guilty as the rest when it came to that. To know that some people approached life differently was comforting.

"That's kind of refreshing," she said to Lydia.

Lydia readily agreed. Life with Lukas had taught her how to go through life at speeds less than ninety miles an hour. At least part of the time. "Yes, I guess it is. It's part of their heritage."

Finally, the truck ahead of them began to move. Lydia took her foot off the brake and only let it hover over the accelerator. They were going no faster than ten miles an hour on the narrow, one-way streets that eventually led to her destination.

She glanced toward Cate and saw that the other woman looked puzzled. "You know how in some cultures, you're encouraged to compete against everyone else? In the Navajo culture, that's considered impolite."

It was a wonder they had ever survived, Cate thought. And then she thought about what she'd witnessed so far. Christian seemed completely dedicated to his work, to his patients, both established and new.

"But it's okay to compete against yourself?" It wasn't a question on Cate's part so much as an assumption based on his behavior.

Lydia nodded. She saw an opening in the lane beside her and quickly eased the nose of their vehicle into it. Anything to get away from the truck. "Yes. Which is what makes them so good—if not rich. Christian spends a lot of time going back to the reservation where he and Lukas grew up."

Going back to his roots, Cate thought. She made the only connection she could. "Searching for himself?"

"Giving of himself," Lydia corrected. Cate raised an eyebrow in a silent query. "They have a clinic on the reservation. It was hardly more than just four walls and a blood pressure cuff until Lukas organized a drive at Blair to get some of the doctors to donate their time. A lot of his friends fly to the reservation a couple of times a year or more to work there for free. Christian goes there probably two, three weekends a month."

"Doesn't his wife protest? Or does she live on the reservation?" Her curiosity had gotten the better of her, but she couldn't help it. If she'd come right out and asked if he was attached, Lydia would misunderstand why she was asking.

So why *are* you asking? a small voice whispered inside her head. She had no good answer. Because she didn't know.

"There is no wife," Lydia told her. She bit back a curse of frustration as she reached the next light only to have it turn red. "Not anymore."

"Divorced?" Lydia guessed.

"She…died." It was on the tip of her tongue to tell Cate the whole story, as she knew it, but then she decided it really wasn't her story to tell. It was Christian's.

"Oh." Death was something, despite the nature of

her work, despite what had happened to Gabe, that she didn't ordinarily associate with people her own age. She felt Lydia looking at her and explained, "He doesn't look old enough to be a widower."

Christian definitely wasn't old enough to be as haunted as he was, Lydia thought. "Yeah, well, unfortunately, it happens." She pulled up in the spot that was designated for her vehicle. "I guess we'd better get to work." After getting out, she closed her door, then activated the security lock. "You're sure he said he'd call about the girl?"

Cate nodded. "The second she was out of surgery."

"Well, that's good enough for me." They began to circumvent the lot to get to the front of the building. Wheels were turning in Lydia's head and she welcomed the momentary diversion. "Say, what are you doing this Friday night?"

Cate didn't really have to think. Evenings found her in her apartment, the computer and television both on for company. "Nothing I can think of."

"Good, you can have dinner with Lukas and me." It was an impulsive decision, but Lydia knew Lukas wouldn't mind. He'd told her that he liked her new partner. The tricky part would be to get Christian to come. "Eight sound good to you?"

Cate usually ate the moment she walked in through the door. Meals consisted of anything that happened to be in her refrigerator or pantry, or on rare occasions, what she bought on her way home. Eight was a little late for her taste. But she did like Lydia and she welcomed the opportunity to get to know her off the job.

So she smiled and nodded. "Eight sounds fine."

"Good. I've got this new recipe I've been wanting to try." She laughed. "Lukas will be pleased that he won't be the only guinea pig at the table."

Cate pretended to slant her an uneasy look. "I think I suddenly remembered a previous appointment."

"Too late. Your word is your bond, Kowalski. Can't back out once you give it."

She had no intention of backing out. She'd left a great many friends in San Francisco and she wasn't accustomed to spending her nights alone. It was time she began laying the foundation of her life here if she was going to remain for any length of time. "I'll remember that the next time you ask me anything."

That evening, after she left the field office, instead of going home, Cate drove back to Blair Memorial. True to his word, Christian had called Lydia earlier to say that the surgery had gone well, but that the girl still hadn't regained consciousness. When Lydia pressed him, he told her that there was no way to predict anything about her present condition, other than that internally, she was on the road to recovery.

Christian had promised to keep both of them posted before he hung up.

Cate certainly didn't doubt him. She just felt sorry for the girl who was lying in that bed. After parking in the visitors' north parking lot, she rushed into the hospital.

Several minutes later, as she looked down at the unconscious teenager, Cate imagined there was a mother and father who had spent God knows how much time anxiously waiting for a phone call, worried sick about their daughter.

"Or are you a runaway?" she asked the still, pale face.

Outside the room, as a safeguard, one of the rookie agents—the not-so-special-special agents as they used to refer to them in her old office—was posted just in case one of the people involved in the underage prostitution ring somehow found out that she was still alive and wanted to make the girl's comatose state a permanent one.

Cleaned up, their silent witness looked more like a child than ever. A nurse had taken the time to comb and pull back her jet-black hair, securing it with a dark blue ribbon. The girl's lips still had the soft dew of pink that faded after years of lipstick were applied to them. Her eyes were closed, and long black lashes rested against her pale skin like two soft, dark crescents.

Looking at her made Cate think of a description of Snow White she'd once read.

"Did anyone ever read Snow White to you?" she asked in a soft whisper. "Or was your life so awful, so unbearable, that you couldn't wait to get away? Couldn't wait to start living it on your own instead of under someone's thumb?"

Unable to help herself, Cate feathered her fingertips through the girl's bangs, brushing them back the way her mother always did with her.

Her adopted mother, she reminded herself.

A pang of guilt shot through Cate. What was she doing here, trying to get her birth mother to own up to her? It was Julia Kowalski who'd been with her through the crucial years. Julia whom she still loved. Julia whom she missed more than she could stand.

With a start, Cate realized that her anger over the sin of omission that had been committed against her was beginning to abate in the face of all the happy times she'd spent, believing herself to be Cate Kowalski.

What was in a name, anyway?

The name on the chart by the girl's bed had dubbed her "Jane Doe."

"Not a very original name," Cate said softly to the unconscious girl. "You don't look like a Jane." Her features looked too exotic for such a mundane name. "Why don't you wake up, honey, and tell me who you are?" Cate coaxed.

Chapter 21

"On another quest?"

Cate swung around, her hand instantly going to the hilt of the gun holstered inside her jacket.

Blowing out a breath, she silently upbraided herself for letting her guard down as she made eye contact with Christian. She hadn't even heard him open the door or come up behind her. If he'd been someone who meant the girl harm, he could have gotten the drop on her. What was the matter with her? She was getting sloppy and there was no excuse for it.

Withdrawing her hand from inside her jacket, Cate looked at him grudgingly. "That's a good way to get yourself shot."

"Making my rounds?" he deadpanned. Taking the girl's limp wrist in his hand, he glanced at his watch and took her pulse. "Haven't you heard? Bedford is supposed to be one of the safest cities in the country."

Yes, she'd heard that. She also knew that this girl had been found in a Bedford warehouse. "There are always exceptions to everything and nothing ever stays constant."

"I know."

Was that sadness she heard in his voice? Cate told herself she was imagining things.

She stepped to the side as Christian slipped in to take her place beside the girl's bed. After taking his stethoscope from around his neck, he began to listen to his patient's heart. His methods struck Cate as almost old-fashioned in the face of all the state-of-the-art monitors jammed into the small intensive care unit.

"Don't trust the monitors?" she asked, nodding at the gaggle of technological marvels.

The smile that crossed his lips was fleeting, but she found it potent nonetheless.

"I'm hands-on," he explained.

She couldn't have said why the term made her think of those same hands on her, other than it had been a long time since she'd been with a man. A long time since she'd wanted to be with a man.

She didn't want to now, she insisted silently.

"I like checking things out for myself," he added, taking up Jane Doe's chart.

Looking at the entries on the bottom of the second page, he nodded to himself. Everything was going along the normal postsurgical path. Except that the girl still hadn't woken up, not even once. At least, not during any of the nurses' interactions with her. She'd remained unresponsive even after prodding. That bothered him.

Christian returned the chart to the foot of her bed and sighed. And then he looked at the woman standing here. "It's late. What are you doing here?"

A little on the defensive, she lobbed the question back at him. "I could ask you the same thing. I have it on the best authority that doctors do go home."

There was nothing at home for him except time to think. Sometimes he spent nights right here in the hospital, stretched out on the sofa in his office, because he didn't want to be alone with his thoughts. "I don't keep banker's hours."

"Neither do I."

He laughed shortly. "I guess that gives us something in common."

"That," she conceded, "and knowing Lydia."

Cate tried not to stare at him.

What's your story, Doctor? What is it about you that keeps getting to me? Was something inside of me ready to crack and you were just there at the right time?

God, she felt as if she was losing her mind.

He didn't notice the change in her expression. His attention had been drawn back to his patient. By rights, the girl belonged to Reese now. Bendenetti had performed the surgery and was best suited to care for his patient from here on in. But there'd been something about the child-woman that reminded him of Alma. And made him want to save her.

As if that could somehow atone for his having failed to save Alma. And Dana.

He realized that Lydia's partner was looking at him and that he'd lapsed into silence. "Speaking of Lydia, I'm surprised she's not here instead of you."

"I headed her off." It was his turn to look puzzled. "She seemed really wiped out," Cate told him, "so I told her I'd look in on Jane here."

Wiped out. Yeah, he just bet she was. One of the classic signs of pregnancy. God, he hoped that she'd come to her senses soon and tell Lukas that she was pregnant. Lukas worshipped the ground his wife walked on, but he wouldn't let her be foolish. He'd make her take a desk job.

Christian realized he'd lapsed into silence again and that Cate was regarding him curiously. He grasped at the last thing she'd said. "Jane?"

"Jane Doe," she explained. "At least according to her chart." She frowned, shaking her head. "The name seems so cold, so impersonal."

There was a solution to that. "If it bothers you, why don't *you* give her a name?" he suggested mildly. "Although you know what Shakespeare said."

She told herself that she'd made a mistake in coming back tonight. She told herself that she should be leaving. She told herself a lot of things she didn't seem to be paying attention to because she was still here, sharing the small space with a collection of machines, an unconscious girl and a man who, just by breathing, made her come alive again, inch by unfreezing inch.

And that, she knew, could be dangerous.

"No, I'll bite," she said gamely. "What did Shakespeare say?"

"A rose by any other name—"

From somewhere amid all the trivia she'd collected in her lifetime, the line came back to her. "Would smell as sweet." *Romeo and Juliet.* It figured. "A doctor who quotes Shakespeare?"

He could recite entire passages, and had. To Alma. On long, hot, still nights that stretched out into oblivion. She'd liked listening to the sound of the words she didn't quite grasp. He'd loved seeing the wonder in her eyes when she looked at him.

Christian shrugged evasively, not knowing if she was amused or amazed or how he should respond to either set of circumstances.

"We all have our guilty pleasures. When I was a kid, I'd read anything I could get my hands on. We didn't have much of a library on the reservation, so I'd wind up rereading a lot of what was there." He watched her face for her reaction, but the mention of where he'd lived out his childhood had garnered no particular response from her. No covert disdain the way he'd seen mark so many other faces. "Care to hear Marc Antony's speech from *Julius Caesar?*"

The suggestion made her laugh and for that she was grateful. A little of the tension she'd felt building up since he'd walked into the room drained away. "Maybe some other time."

His grin was fast, guileless and lethal. "Don't know what you're missing."

The words felt as if they were dancing along her skin long after they faded from the air.

He was standing too close, she thought.

Or maybe just close enough.

Close enough for her to feel something humming

between them. Something she hadn't really felt for a very long time. Chemistry? Electricity?

A physical craving?

She wasn't really sure what to call it, only that she'd missed feeling it. And that it frightened her at the same time that it enticed her.

Her smile faded just a little, growing serious. "No," she agreed quietly. "I guess I don't."

He was unprepared for the jolt he felt, looking into her eyes. Unprepared for the sudden longing that came out of the recesses of his being where it had dwelled, unattended, far too long.

For one insane moment, he felt like…

Christian shook himself free, clinging to the one word that had burst upon his brain with clarity.

Insane.

It was utterly insane to feel this pull, this need that was even now gnawing away at his gut. Desire, with its accompanying passions, had left him the day Alma had died. As if all those feelings had been surgically excised out of him. At the very least, all the nerve endings connecting him to that part of his being had been ruthlessly severed.

Nerves that were cut never regained their feeling. He believed this to be true until a moment ago.

She needed to leave, Cate thought urgently. She needed to get some air to clear her head of all the strange thoughts that were crashing into one another.

Cate took a step toward the door. "I'd better be going. I just stopped by here because…because she has no one." Why did she feel she had to continue to justify her actions to him? She'd already said she was here instead of Lydia. That should have been enough. "At least, no one we can contact. And I didn't want her to be alone." Cate willed her mouth to stop moving, but for some reason, she kept on talking. "Stupid, isn't it? I mean, she doesn't know I'm here. She probably wouldn't even recognize me if she did open her eyes."

Cate's last words caught his attention. "Should she recognize you?"

Who knows if she'd even been processing any information that one split second back in the warehouse? Cate shrugged. "I was the last person she saw before she blacked out. She clutched my hand and cried. I couldn't make out any of the words, they were badly garbled, but the meaning was crystal clear. She was terrified and she wanted to be saved."

His eyes met hers and she felt another tidal wave coming on, navel level. "Well, you saved her."

"Maybe." She was the one who'd found the girl. That wasn't quite the same thing. "No, I didn't," Cate amended abruptly. "You did. You and that surgeon you called in."

"Reese Bendenetti," he told her. "But I wasn't talking about that. There's saving the body and then there's saving the soul." That much he had picked up from his mother and the old ways. "She probably saw something in your eyes that helped her hang on."

That was almost spiritual. Cate stared at him. Graywolf was definitely a hard person to pigeonhole. She supposed that wasn't such a bad thing. In her line of work, she had a tendency to want to file everything and everyone neatly under a heading. Some people, the interesting ones, defied that.

"I thought you said that you didn't believe in prayer."

"Not prayer, but something. Sheer force of will." Christian shrugged. Some things just defied being labeled. "Something," he repeated, leaving it at that.

She studied him in silence for a moment. "You're a very complex man, Doctor." *And I'm letting myself get sidetracked much too much.* With renewed energy she headed toward the door. "Well, good night."

Cate had every intention of leaving the hospital. But as she placed her hand on the doorknob, she found herself pausing. Wrestling. Finally, she looked at him over her shoulder. "Would you like to go somewhere for a cup of coffee or something?"

His first impulse was to say no. He'd turned down a great many invitations from women in the past three years. In that time, he'd grown almost reclusive except for his frequent trips to the reservation. But now, for reasons he could not fathom, a tiny slit of light had opened up inside of him. Warmed him. He didn't want it to close just yet.

"That depends."

Her eyes met his. The soft hum of the machines faded into oblivion. "On what?"

She saw his mouth curve. Felt her pulse rise in direct proportion. "On whether or not you're going to pump me for information."

Cate shook her head. "No pumping. Not tonight. Just coffee."

He'd had next to nothing to eat since breakfast. Lunch had been nonexistent and dinner had been a sandwich of some kind of mystery meat from the cafeteria. He'd forced half down before giving the rest of it away to some birds outside the cafeteria. The birds had enjoyed the sandwich far more than he had.

Coffee sounded pretty good right about now. Something to fill the gnawing emptiness in his belly. "All right. There's a coffee shop down the block. I think it's still open if you want to give it a try."

She didn't want him thinking this was any big deal. Part of her was already regretting having asked. *Because it might lead somewhere?* She didn't even try to answer that. "The cafeteria'll do. I'm easy."

He glanced at his watch. "The cafeteria's closed at this hour."

"There's always a vending machine." She vaguely remembered passing one that touted coffee, hot chocolate and chicken soup.

He'd never met anyone who would have opted for vending-machine fare over something from a coffee shop, especially since the former usually tasted like lukewarm, murky-colored water.

"You really are easy, aren't you?" he asked.

The response was on her lips automatically. "I'm a cop's daughter. My father taught me to roll with the punches." Abruptly, her expression changed. "I mean, I thought I was a cop's daughter—"

He could see in her eyes that she'd made no peace with this yet. "Biology doesn't make a person a parent. Being there for the scraped knees, the heartaches and the small joys, that's what makes a parent."

"Yeah, well I'm still having a little trouble sorting all that out." She eyed him. It had been a mistake to act on impulse. She needed to back off. "Maybe we'd better take a rain check on that coffee."

He paused for a long moment. She had no idea if she'd just insulted him, or taken him off the hook.

"Maybe," he finally said.

Cate left the room before she changed her mind again and ruined her retreat. As she hurried out of the building and to her car, a wave of disappointment assaulted her, mixing with the cooling night air.

Chapter 22

Lukas walked into the kitchen and came up behind his wife as she stood at the stove. He could see she was frowning as she stirred a large pot of her version of marinara sauce. He wrapped his arms about her waist, pulling her against him.

Pressing a kiss to her neck, he inhaled the light fragrance he always associated with her. A feeling of contentment wafted through him and he nuzzled her, thinking how perfect his life had become these past few years.

The only thing that would make it even more so was if they had a child. They'd talked about having children, several times in the last few months, and Lydia was open to the idea.

She'd said, "Soon."

The thought about making babies was on his mind

a great deal lately. He wanted to be young enough to enjoy them, to run with them and be their companion in every sense of the word.

"You know," he proposed, his voice low and husky, "we still have time for a quickie."

He was outlining the shell of her ear with his tongue and Lydia found it really hard not to melt against him. He had this drugging, hypnotic effect about him that always got to her.

"A very quick quickie," she pointed out, struggling to keep stirring. Their guests were due soon.

Raising her hair, Lukas brushed his lips against the other side of her neck. "I do some of my best work under pressure."

Any second now, her eyes were going to drift shut and she was going to be a goner. Lydia gripped the stirring spoon harder. "Luke, what if one of them comes early?"

"Then they'll just have to entertain themselves for a while by ringing the doorbell." He turned her around so that she faced him, his arms still resting around her waist. Something was wrong, he'd sensed it for a while now, but he just couldn't put his finger on it. "I thought a little lovemaking might help relieve your tension."

It took everything for her not to stiffen and give credence to his words. Instead, she just laughed lightly. "What tension?"

"The tension that brings out the faint little line between your eyes." To illustrate, he traced the line with his fingertip.

Lydia curtailed her impulse to pull her head away. She didn't want him delving too hard. Their marriage wasn't about lies and she didn't want to begin now. Besides, she always felt that he could see right through her. With a mighty effort, she rallied, gave him a quick kiss on the mouth, wiggled free of her confinement and went back to stirring the temperamental sauce.

"The tension's not going to go away until I close up this case." That much was true, she consoled her conscience.

"And if you don't close it?"

He saw her shoulders stiffen with determination. "I *will*," she insisted.

"Never let it be said that you lack confidence."

Lukas stepped back from her and leaned his hip against the sink. His eyes on her profile, he studied her in that quiet way of his that always got under the layers of her skin and saw straight into her heart. Every time.

Except that this time, she made very sure she kept the barriers up.

"Lyd, is that all that's bothering you?"

She'd known this was coming. With all her heart, she hoped she sounded convincing.

A little more time, I just need a little more time. She flashed a quick smile at him. "Sure, what else could there be?"

He spread his hands wide, frustrated. "I don't know, that's why I'm asking. It's just that lately, you've seemed preoccupied, as if there was something else on your mind."

"I have a lot of things on my mind." She reached for the container of Parmesan cheese and shook out some more to thicken the sauce. She had the heat on low, but even so, tiny bubbles burst along the surface of the sauce like miniature erupting volcanoes. Lydia turned the heat down another notch to avoid having tiny streams of sauce shoot out like lava. "Carrying off this dinner without a hitch, for one." She slanted him a look. Diversion had always been her best asset. "Wondering if some hussy is after my husband, for another." That had hit the mark. There was a look of surprise on his face. "Lots of women fall in love with their doctors."

Lukas laughed incredulously, shaking his head. Even if he was given to roving, which he never had been, she had absolutely nothing to worry about in that department.

"Most of my patients are over sixty," he pointed out.

She leveled a warning look at him. "Never underestimate a sexy grandma." When he laughed, she took umbrage, suddenly realizing that her insecurity did actually reside in the recesses of her brain, thanks to the emotional roller coaster she'd found herself on these last four weeks. "Hey, I'm serious."

"No, you're not," he scoffed, refusing to believe that she could possibly entertain such an absurd idea. "Because you know damn well that you've got my heart wrapped up around your little finger." His eyes held hers for a moment, communicating things that couldn't be put into words, at least not when they had guests arriving in minutes. "You have since the day I met you."

She knew she should be convinced, but something kept her from shutting the door on the thought. She was turning into her own worst enemy. This was supposed to be a diversion, not an inquisition based on real insecurities. She had to get hold of herself before she allowed this to get out of hand.

Lydia tried to keep her voice playful, even if the question was not. "You never had any desire to see if the grass is greener on the other side?"

"In my experience," he told her, "if it's greener, it means it's just crabgrass, or weed grass."

She pretended to look at him over the top of an imaginary pair of glasses. "And by experience, you would mean…?"

"I read a lot." Okay, enough was enough. There was something else going on here. He knew her. This whole act was camouflage. "Lydia, really, what's wrong?"

Covering the large pot, she turned off the burner and let the sauce stand there, absorbing the residual heat. "I already told you—"

"You're actually worried about me having an affair with a patient?" he asked, not believing it for a minute. Lydia wasn't one of those insecure, jealous women.

She retreated to a more plausible. immediate explanation, hoping Lukas would back off for now. Until she could tell him the truth. "No. I know I can trust you. I meant about this little dinner party."

For the time being, even though it seemed out of character for her, he decided that maybe this really was what was preying on Lydia's mind, at least for the past couple of days. Ever since she'd had him invite Christian and said that she was asking Cate to come over as well. His own reaction to it had been lukewarm at best, but he'd always been the type to let fate take over. After all, fate had brought her into his life, hadn't it?

"Four people is not exactly a party, but I can see your point." He picked up one of the canapés she'd made and pulled away before she could hit his hand to make him drop it. "I didn't know you had this match-making bug in you. Is this something all women are born with and it just comes out later in some than in others?" He popped the canapé into his mouth. "Mmm, good."

She leveled a gaze at him. "Thanks, and define 'later.'"

As a male, he knew he was perilously close to having stepped in it. "Not twenty-one."

"Good answer." She nodded her approval. "Nice recovery."

"I thought so." He debated having another canapé, but Lydia was armed with another large spoon. He wouldn't put it past her to use it, so he saved his appetite. "Seriously, Lydia, I'm not sure how Christian is going to react to being set up with Cate."

"It's not a setup," she protested a bit too heatedly, "it's food. Away from the hospital and the field office," she added, then shrugged. "I thought they looked good together."

The old line about the best-laid plans of mice and men drifted through his brain. "On paper, so do salt-water fish and freshwater fish, but I wouldn't go putting them in the same tank together. One of them is bound not to make it."

After putting on an oven mitt, Lydia opened the oven door. A curtain of steam escaped, then cleared away so that she could check on the veal chops she'd stuffed and breaded earlier. They were turning the right color, thank God. Golden brown instead of charred black like the last ones she'd attempted.

"Is that your sneaky way of saying that you'd rather be fishing than here?"

He laughed. "I'd rather be anywhere you are, but since you mentioned it, Dr. Amos has invited us to go deep-sea fishing next weekend. I've got someone covering my rotation. Are you up for it?"

Ordinarily, she would have said yes without hesitation. She loved going out on the water with him. But the thought of being out on a rocking boat at sea, no matter how large it was, almost made her stomach rise up in her throat. She took off the oven mitt and tossed it on the counter. "I'll get back to you on that. Our witness might regain consciousness before then," she added for good measure, in case he asked why she was stalling.

Lukas sighed. Maybe this case *was* the only thing on her mind. And if it was, he was afraid that she was letting it become an obsession. "I know how important this case is to you. How important they all are to you, but you're letting it consume you—"

The sound of chimes interrupted anything else he might have said.

"Doorbell," Lydia declared cheerfully, finally understanding the full import of the phrase, "Saved by the bell."

Lukas tabled what he had to say. For now. He passed her and crossed to the kitchen's threshold. "Yes, I can still distinguish sounds, Lydia. I haven't gotten that old yet."

"No," she agreed, a wicked look coming into her eyes. "I'd say you've still got a few miles left in you." Lydia punctuated her statement with a sexy wink.

He stopped where he was. If he lived to be a hundred, he was never going to fully understand women. He'd never seen Lydia so mercurial before.

"I can still put the chain on the door—" Lukas offered, comically raising and lowering his dark eyebrows like a silent film would-be Romeo.

"Go." She shooed him off with her free hand. "Make yourself useful."

He gave her one last glance over his shoulder. "I thought that's what I was offering to do. My husbandly duty." His voice floated back to her as he made his way to the front door.

Lydia laughed as she took the sauce off the burner and then began ladling out some of it into a serving dish. God, but she loved that man. And she absolutely hated keeping this pregnancy from him. All right, so it wasn't an outright lie, it was just omission, she told herself. But she knew he'd see it as a lie if he ever found out that she knew she was pregnant and hadn't told him.

Just a little longer, I promise, she swore to him.

All the leads they'd had regarding the case had suddenly dried up. The game of musical residences had temporarily halted, or at least they'd ceased to leave an identifiable trail. It was as if the girls and the people responsible for pimping them out had fallen off the face of the earth.

She knew that was impossible. Scum had to be cleansed before you could get rid of it. Like mildew, it would return again and again unless you eradicated it once and for all.

Sullivan had called in a few favors and pressed more people into undercover work. They in turn put out feelers, pretending to be eager johns looking for "tender, young flesh." The very idea turned her stomach, but if you wanted to catch the bad guys, she told herself philosophically, that's what it took. You had to cover yourself with filth to avoid detection.

More than anything in this world, she desperately wanted to catch the bad guys.

Hoping for some good news, she'd called the hospital just before she'd begun cooking dinner. But the guard they had posted outside the ICU room said that there'd been no change in "Jane's" status. The young teenager was still clinging to life, still unconscious.

Every cage the department had rattled so far had come up empty.

The frustration was driving her crazy. Not to mention that she didn't know how much longer she could hold out against Lukas and her own conscience.

"Smells good, whatever it is," Christian said, walking into the two-story house with its recessed windows, stucco exterior and vaulted, beamed ceilings. He'd told Lukas the house reminded him of some of the haciendas he'd seen in Arizona. And the interior always made him feel as if he'd stepped onto a western movie set.

Lucky for Luke that Lydia had the same taste as he did, Christian thought.

He handed his brother the bottle he'd brought with

him. Lukas looked at it, then at Christian, raising an eyebrow. "Sparkling cider?"

He knew what Lukas was thinking. He usually brought Wild Turkey. But this wasn't a time for hard liquor. He shrugged casually. "Alcohol-free. I thought we'd try something new."

When he'd gotten the invitation, he'd hoped that Lydia had changed her mind and was going to make an announcement about the baby at dinner. But one look at Lukas's face told him that if she was making any announcements, she'd kept her secret from her husband.

"I'm game for anything," Lukas said, leading the way into the living room.

From there, Christian could see into the dining room. The table was set for four instead of three. "Someone else coming to dinner?"

Before Lukas could answer, they heard a car pulling up in the driveway.

Chapter 23

In the past few hours, Cate had come close to picking up the phone, calling Lydia and begging off. Each time, she'd stopped herself, recognizing that scrambling feeling inside of her for what it actually was.

Fear.

She was afraid to get close. To anyone. Even Lydia. Looking back, it felt as if everyone she had ever built a bond with had abandoned her. Not of their own free will, but the end result was the same. She was alone. Gabe had been taken from her. Her father had died, her mother had died. Even her identity had died.

It was hard putting herself out there again. Hard to risk incurring that devastating feeling that cut you off at your knees and sucked out all your air again. But she had to admit, she really did like Lydia, and the one time she'd met Lukas, she thought he was exceptionally nice. And perfect for Lydia. They had the kind of marriage that she'd once thought she'd have, if Gabe had lived.

The bottom line was, it was too late to put on the safety features. She already felt close to Lydia. She might as well enjoy some of the perks.

The moment she'd given herself the freedom to do that, the knot in her stomach loosened and she found herself actually looking forward to getting together with Lydia and Lukas for dinner.

She supposed that in a sense Lydia and Lukas were becoming more her family than the one she'd been trying to get close to. Cate's mouth curved. Just went to show, life never neatly laid itself out the way one hoped it would.

After glancing at the map she had opened on the seat next to her, Cate made a left turn at the next corner. Lydia's address was written on a piece of paper she'd placed on her dashboard. She'd committed it to memory, but it made her feel better to have it handy. Just in case.

As an only child, she'd often fantasized about having siblings, especially a sister. And now, in actuality, she had one. Rebecca. A sister she couldn't seek out or speak to without causing problems. She wondered if she ever could speak to the girl.

Well, until then, she had Lydia. And, to be honest, so far they seemed to be getting along far better than most sisters did. It had taken her less than a day to feel comfortable around Lydia, to feel a rapport setting in. The kind of thing that sometimes took years to develop, if ever, had happened in almost a matter of hours.

YOUR PARTICIPATION IS REQUESTED!

Dear Reader,

Since you are a lover of fiction – we would like to get to know you!

Inside you will find a short Reader's Survey. Sharing your answers with us will help our editorial staff understand who you are and what activities you enjoy.

To thank you for your participation, we would like to send you 2 books and a gift – **ABSOLUTELY FREE!**

Enjoy your gifts with our appreciation,

Pam Powers

SEE INSIDE FOR READER'S SURVEY

HOW TO VALIDATE YOUR

EDITOR'S FREE THANK YOU GIFTS!

1. Complete the survey on the right.

2. Send back the completed card and you'll get 2 brand-new Romance novels and a gift. These books have a combined cover price of $11.98 or more in the U.S. and $13.98 or more in Canada, but they are yours to keep absolutely FREE!

3. There's no catch. You're under no obligation to buy anything. We charge nothing—ZERO—for your first shipment. And you don't have to make any minimum number of purchases—not even one!

4. The fact is, thousands of readers enjoy receiving their books by mail from The Reader Service. They enjoy the convenience of home delivery…they like getting the best new novels at discount prices BEFORE they're available in stores…and they love their *Heart to Heart* subscriber newsletter featuring author news, special book offers, book reviews and much more!

5. We hope that after receiving your free books you'll want to remain a subscriber. But the choice is yours—to continue or cancel, anytime at all! So why not take us up on our invitation, with no risk of any kind. You'll be glad you did!

YOURS FREE!

We'll send you a fabulous surprise gift absolutely FREE, simply for accepting our no-risk offer!

YOUR READER'S SURVEY
"THANK YOU" FREE GIFTS INCLUDE:

▶ Two BRAND-NEW Romance Novels
▶ A lovely surprise gift

PLEASE FILL IN THE CIRCLES COMPLETELY TO RESPOND

1) What type of fiction books do you enjoy reading? (Check all that apply)
   ○ Suspense/Thrillers ○ Action/Adventure ○ Modern-day Romances
   ○ Historical Romance ○ Humour ○ Science fiction

2) What attracted you most to the last fiction book you purchased on impulse?
   ○ The Title ○ The Cover ○ The Author ○ The Story

3) What is usually the greatest influencer when you <u>plan</u> to buy a book?
   ○ Advertising ○ Referral from a friend
   ○ Book Review ○ Like the author

4) Approximately how many fiction books do you read in a year?
   ○ 1 to 6 ○ 7 to 19 ○ 20 or more

5) How often do you access the internet?
   ○ Daily ○ Weekly ○ Monthly ○ Rarely or never

6) To which of the following age groups do you belong?
   ○ Under 18 ○ 18 to 34 ○ 35 to 64 ○ over 65

YES! I have completed the Reader's Survey. Please send me the 2 FREE books and gift for which I qualify. I understand that I am under no obligation to purchase any books, as explained on the back and on the opposite page.

193 MDL D37G   393 MDL D37H

FIRST NAME	LAST NAME

ADDRESS

APT.#	CITY

STATE/PROV.	ZIP/POSTAL CODE

◀ DETACH AND MAIL CARD TODAY! ▶

(SUR-SS-05) © 1998 MIRA BOOKS

The Reader Service — Here's How It Works:

Accepting your 2 free books and gift places you under no obligation to buy anything. You may keep the books and gift and return the shipping statement marked "cancel." If you do not cancel, about a month later we'll send you 3 additional books and bill you just $4.99 each in the U.S., or $5.49 each in Canada, plus 25¢ shipping & handling per book and applicable taxes if any.* That's the complete price and — compared to cover prices starting from $5.99 each in the U.S. and $6.99 each in Canada — it's quite a bargain! You may cancel at any time, but if you choose to continue, every month we'll send you 3 more books, which you may either purchase at the discount price or return to us and cancel your subscription.

*Terms and prices subject to change without notice. Sales tax applicable in N.Y. Canadian residents will be charged applicable provincial taxes and GST.

She'd always been lucky when it came to partners—after her first one, of course. She and Joe Wong, her second partner, had gotten to a point where they could finish each other's sentences. He'd told her that the bureau wouldn't be the same without her when she left. She missed him a great deal.

Once she transferred down here, she was certain that she'd never be able to get that close to another partner again. She'd held her breath, anticipating another Jack Powell. Jack had been her first partner and highly resentful of having to team up with a woman, one who was thirty years his junior to boot. After nine months of picking away at everything she did, he'd retired, to her everlasting relief. She wasn't sure how much longer she could have held on.

It was only human nature to expect a repetition of the bad rather than the good when she transferred to the Santa Ana field office.

Cate laughed softly to herself. The interior of the car echoed with the sound. It was nice to be wrong and still have things turn out so right.

Evening had long since crept in and swallowed up the landscape, leaving it in darkness as Cate pulled up in the driveway. She parked beside a car she didn't recognize.

Lydia drove the Crown Victoria they used during the day. When she and her husband had come over that first weekend to help her move in, Lukas had been driving an old Mustang he'd lovingly restored. The car to her right was a two-seater.

Getting out, she gave the small vehicle the once-over. It was an original, she decided, a car created out of the odds and ends of other vehicles. Lukas was handier than she thought. Low to the ground and not very comfortable-looking, the sporty-looking car was probably built for speed. She wondered if he raced it.

Cate reached inside her car and got her purse, then, closing her door, she aimed her remote key chain at it. The car gave a little squawk, telling her it was secured.

She'd stopped by the hospital on her way over here in the hopes that she'd have something positive to tell Lydia about their witness. She knew she could have called instead, but there'd been that secret hope that if she showed up in person, something good might happen.

The power of Me.

She smiled to herself. It was something Big Ted had taught her. The secret of getting ahead. Positive thinking. Firmly believing that you made a difference, that given enough effort, you could do anything you wanted to. In essence, that things happened just because you willed them to.

When she'd looked up at the big man, wide-eyed, completely enthralled at the ripe old age of five, and said, "Me?" he'd laughed and told her that was a good name for it. From that day forward, he referred to his theory as "The power of Me."

In a way, Cate supposed that she still subscribed to the philosophy. If she didn't, she wouldn't be butting her head so hard against the wall with Joan.

No, I'm not going to think about that tonight. No negative thoughts. I'm just here to have fun with two very nice people I really like.

Cate rang the doorbell. The door opened before the

chimes had a chance to complete their melody. She dropped her hand to her side as she grinned at Lukas. He was wearing jeans and a pullover, and she was grateful she hadn't decided to put on anything remotely formal. Casual made her comfortable.

Walking in, she handed him the pink box embossed with the logo of one of the pricier bakeries in the area. Things moved inside the box as he took it from her.

"I couldn't decide what to get, so I got a little of everything," she explained. "Sorry I'm late."

Habit had him looking at the clock over the mantel. "Not late, right on time. Here, let me take your coat and purse."

Once she shrugged out of her coat, she surrendered both to him. "I didn't realize that among all your other accomplishments, you're a juggler, too."

He looked at her, puzzled. "What other accomplishments?"

"Building cars." She followed him into the living room. "That's a real beauty you have out in the driveway. What kind is it?"

"That's not mine." Lukas hung her coat and purse inside the hall closet and closed the door.

"Then whose—?"

"It's mine. I built it out of whatever I could find in the junkyard while I was going to medical school. It took almost a year."

She turned toward the source of the voice, although she didn't have to. The moment she'd heard the first word, she recognized it.

Lukas continued holding on to the box she'd brought, studying the two that Lydia seemed so sure were meant for each other. Had to be a female thing, he decided. They didn't particularly look like a matched set to him. Or happy to see each other, for that matter.

"You know my brother, Christian?"

"Yes, I do." The words stuck like cotton in her mouth.

From the look on his face, she could see that Lukas's brother was just as surprised to see her here as she was to see him.

Christian nodded, his eyes on her. Giving nothing away. "We've met."

Okay, this might get sticky. "Lydia," Lukas called over his shoulder, "I think it's time to stop babying the sauce and come out here."

"I'm not babying the sauce," Lydia informed him as she walked in from the kitchen. "It's ready. And so is everything else."

As if the statement needed a little fanfare, she pulled off the apron that still hung loosely to her waist, thanks to Lukas's toying with the strings.

"Hi, you made it." The comment was addressed to both of them. Her voice was warm and cheerful and Cate thought it sounded just a tad hopeful. Why?

"Cate brought dessert," Lukas told her, indicating the box.

"Something decadent, I hope," Lydia heard herself saying. Where the hell had that come from? She didn't even care for dessert. Was she nervous? But why? This was just Cate and her brother-in-law, no reason to have this strange unease vibrating through her. Where had all this uncertainty come from suddenly?

Another new sensation she was completely unfamiliar with and didn't remotely welcome. She knew it was all due to her condition, which in a way was a relief because prior to confirming her pregnancy, she'd begun to think she was losing her mind.

She wasn't all that happy about things as they stood, though. Whoever had drawn up the original blueprint for pregnant women had done a poor job of it. From one minute to the next, she never knew what to expect from herself. It felt as if all her emotions had gone completely haywire inside of her, threatening to short circuit.

Like now.

She dug deep for the old Lydia, the one who could plow through anything and still remain unruffled. It was getting harder and harder to drag her to the surface at times like this.

Lydia took the box from her husband and brought it to the kitchen. She put it in the refrigerator after moving a few things around to accommodate it. That done, she turned to the next order of business.

"So, what would everyone like to drink?" she asked cheerfully when she reentered the living room.

"Christian brought sparkling cider," Lukas told her, producing the bottle. He shook his head incredulously as he regarded the offering.

It was obviously not something Christian usually brought, Cate thought. She caught the sharp look that went between Lydia and Christian. On his way into the kitchen for glasses, Lukas missed it.

Again Cate wondered if there was something going on between the two that she was missing.

"This thing need a corkscrew?" Lukas called back to Christian. They could hear him opening a drawer and rifling through it.

"I don't know," Christian answered.

He was staring at her, she realized. What was going through his head? Did he resent being set up this way? Did she? She would have thought her immediate response would have been yes, but she honestly didn't know. Evening was the wrong time for her to think about this. The night made her feel far too vulnerable.

"I never bought a bottle of that before," Christian added.

"What made you buy it now?" Lukas asked.

"Impulse," his brother answered as he walked into the kitchen to join him.

Lukas turned from the counter, an exaggerated expression on his face. "You? Impulse? That'll be the day." He looked beyond his brother at Cate, who still remained in the living room, the last holdout. "Christian maps out everything."

Unfazed, Christian seemed to take the observation in stride.

"It's good to have a game plan." He glanced at Cate as he said it. "That way, there are no surprises."

Her father used to tease her that they should have named her Mary, as in the nursery rhyme once said to be secretly about Mary, Queen of Scots and that began "Mary, Mary, quite contrary." Cate always seemed to relish taking on an opposing point, just for argument's sake, even if she didn't believe in it.

She did it now. "Don't you like surprises?" she asked.

In his experience, the only surprises he'd had tended to knock the air right out of him. "Some are better than others, I guess. But in general, no, I don't like surprises. I don't like not being prepared."

The optimist that still existed in her liked to believe that surprises were usually positive occurrences. "Sometimes spontaneity is a good thing."

"I'm sure my wife thinks so," Lukas interrupted, thinking how quickly Lydia had thrown this evening together. Although he loved his brother, after the week he'd put in he would have been happier wearing his oldest clothes, stretched out in front of the TV, one arm around Lydia, one hand within easy reach of a bowl of chips.

Unwrapping the gold foil, he found that there was no unadorned cork underneath, only a plastic top with a cork attached. He removed it easily enough, no struggling or deletable words necessary. Lukas poured a little of the bubbling liquid into each of the four glasses.

After setting the bottle on the table, he handed out the glasses, then took his own. He looked from one face to another. Was it just him, or did everyone around him seem tense?

He could understand why Cate and his brother were tense. Any way you sugarcoated it, they were in the middle of a not-so-blind blind date. But as for the orchestrator of this possible disaster-in-the-making, he simply wasn't buying Lydia's earlier answer to him. At least not completely.

Although he firmly believed that everyone needed their space, he intended to find out just what it was that had his wife behaving so strangely. Maybe it was just the stress of the job getting to her. If that was the case, he had just the medicine to prescribe. A nice long cruise, with him in attendance. That would melt the tension right out of her. Unless the ship's name was the *Titanic*.

His fingers curved around the fluted glass. "All right, what do we drink to?" He paused, waiting, looking from one face to another.

"New life?" Lukas suggested tentatively.

Cate was positive she saw Lydia turn a shade paler. What the *hell* was going on?

"You mean new friends, don't you?" Lydia corrected lightly. As Cate watched, color returned to Lydia's face. *The power of Me,* she couldn't help thinking. To Cate's surprise, Lydia turned her face and her glass toward her, then raised the latter.

"To my new partner and what looks to be the beginning of a beautiful friendship."

Nice recovery, Cate thought, silently congratulating Lydia.

The admiration didn't stop her from continuing to wonder what, if anything, was going on between Christian and Lydia. Whatever it was, Lukas was oblivious.

The husband's always the last to know. Unless, of course, it's a trusting daughter.

Chapter 24

Lydia turned away from the front door after having locking it behind her departing guests.

It was a little after ten. Both Cate and Christian had left somewhat sooner than she'd expected, less than an hour after dinner was over. Neither one had seemed overly comfortable this evening. But comfortable or not, she couldn't shake the feeling that there was chemistry between the two of them just waiting to explode. She mentally crossed her fingers that she'd pushed something a little further along.

Leaning against the door, she smiled hopefully at her husband.

"Well, that went well."

Lukas gave her a look that all but said, "And what planet are you living on?"

Moving away from the door, Lydia lifted one shoulder in a hapless half shrug. "Okay, maybe not exactly well. But it wasn't awful. And I just know there's something going on between them. I can feel it."

Lukas merely shook his head, a fond, indulgent expression on his face.

"Just promise me you won't quit your day job anytime soon." When she frowned, he laughed. He took her hand and laced his fingers through hers. He led her into the living room. "You do a hell of a lot of things well, Lydia. Matchmaker just doesn't happen to be one of them." He motioned her toward the stairs, pressing a kiss to her temple before whispering into her ear. "Now, what do you say we go up to bed and you can do one of those multitude of things that you *do* do well?"

Lydia gave him a skeptical look. "I thought you have to get up early tomorrow."

"I do." Despite the fact that it was a Saturday, he had surgery scheduled at seven-thirty tomorrow morning. Which meant he wanted to be at the hospital no later than six-thirty. But thanks to the dinner party breaking up earlier than anticipated, that gave him a little leeway. "We're wasting time."

Lydia looked toward the kitchen. She hated facing cleanup first thing in the morning. "But the dishes—"

Lukas continued ushering her off in the opposite direction. "Will still be in the dishwasher tomorrow morning, unless we're blessed with elves, or druids, or some kindly spirits from my ancestors decide to stop by." Her protest grew halfhearted, especially when that intimate smile of his curved his mouth, the one that was only meant for her. "News flash, I didn't marry you for your housekeeping skills or your culinary skills, which, by the way, have improved vastly." He liked nothing better than flattering her. "Dinner was excellent."

"Thank you."

He'd already said that to her, as had Cate and Christian, so at least the meal itself had been a success. It was nice to know that something had gone right. The rest, apparently, was going to take a little more time.

Lydia realized that Lukas hadn't finished his train of thought. She looked up at him innocently. "What did you marry me for?"

Very slowly, Lukas applied his thumb to the side of the first button on her blouse and coaxed it out of its hole, then went on to the next. His eyes remained on hers. "Guess."

Lydia was tired, wired and worried—definitely not in a state primed for lovemaking. Yet when Lukas was close to her like this, when the scent of his skin filled her head, the casual touch of his hand heated her body, all she could think of was making love with him. When they made love together, nothing else mattered. The rest of the world, its chaos, its problems, all disappeared. Everything disappeared.

Except for him and her.

It was her precious corner of the world. *Their* precious corner of the world, she thought, her heart quickening. Warmth filled her. "How many chances do I get?"

He was on her last button. Her blouse parted, giving him a glimpse of the light blue lacy bra she wore underneath. It was one of his favorites. "If you don't get it right on the first try, I'm going to have to show you."

She widened her eyes, doing an imitation of a vapid woman without a thought to call her own. "Um, is it my smile?"

"Close, but no cigar." The next moment, filling his arms with her, he lifted her up.

With a whoop of delighted laughter, Lydia laced her arms around his neck. Her head was spinning as if she'd imbibed something a lot more potent than sparkling cider with dinner.

She began to nibble on his neck as he approached the stairs, then drew her head back for a moment.

"You really don't think they hit it off?"

Her eyes searched his face, hoping for a positive response. Her own thoughts kept fluctuating and it wasn't entirely because of the two people involved. Damn, she couldn't wait until this part of the pregnancy was in the past. She hated this vacillating feeling. It just wasn't like her. She was accustomed to making gut calls about almost everything.

"Not like we're going to," he promised. And then he sighed. "I guess there's only one way to shut you up tonight."

His smile was enticingly wicked a second before he captured her mouth with his.

Lydia surrendered herself to the moment. And to the thrill.

Her key in her hand, Cate stood beside her car in the driveway where she'd parked it. The evening had ended a bit abruptly with both of them practically vying for the honor of being the first out the door.

She supposed it really hadn't been that awful. She

just balked at having things arranged for her without her knowledge or consent. That *really* took control away from her, and right now, it was all about regaining control of her life.

Cate looked at Christian over the roof of her car.

He pulled his door open. As if sensing that she was watching him, he glanced in her direction.

"I guess that was kind of awkward," she murmured.

Her smile was almost shy. Had she been embarrassed? He hadn't thought of that. He'd been too busy dealing with his own reaction to think of hers.

"I've been in more comfortable situations," Christian admitted. If she had been embarrassed, she was certainly being a good sport about it, he thought. Christian paused, debating his next move as he fingered his car's ignition key. He supposed that Cate was just as much a victim of Lydia's unexpected foray into matchmaking as he had been. That gave them something in common. "Want to get that cup of coffee we never wound up going out for the other evening?"

Cate had one foot inside the car and nearly stumbled. His question, coming out of the blue, caught her completely by surprise. As did the little shaft of pleasure she felt swirling through her, leaving a tiny pinhole in its wake. A little ray of light began to push its way through.

Getting out of the car again, she stared at him. His question replayed itself in her head. This was without orchestration, entirely spur-of-the-moment.

Impulse.

Somehow, the very fact that it was impulsive sanctioned her reaction. Cate inclined her head, allowing a faint smile to surface. "All right."

"Or would you prefer getting a nightcap instead?" He'd deliberately passed on the wine that Lukas had offered him at dinner, wanting to make it easier for Lydia to abstain without drawing attention to herself. "I know this small restaurant not too far from my place…" Looking at her, Christian let his voice trail off.

His place.

Was he asking her something? Suggesting something? That maybe she…

She was reading too much into it, Cate told herself. One of the drawbacks to being an FBI agent. Nothing ever seemed simple anymore.

And sometimes, every once in a while, some things were. Like maybe now.

She widened her smile and nodded. "Sure. That sounds good. Why don't you lead the way? I'll follow you in my car."

He tried not to think about where this might go and what he might have started. For now, it was just one foot in front of the other.

Gingerly, Christian folded his six-foot-two frame into the small interior of the car that had been as much therapy for him as a project. He'd begun work on it two months after Alma had killed herself. Not because he'd wanted to, but because Uncle Henry had presented it to him as a challenge.

"You need to do something with your hands, boy," his uncle had said. He'd half expected a pair of boxing gloves to be dropped in his lap. Lukas had taken it up at Uncle Henry's behest all those years ago and it had turned him around.

But instead of gloves, Uncle Henry had given him a book on building his own car. At first he'd resisted, but Uncle Henry kept prodding and pushing. He'd begun working on what ultimately turned out to be his car in self-defense, never thinking it would amount to anything.

But bit by bit, the vehicle began to take form. Eventually, he looked forward to working on it, to scouring junkyards, searching for the right parts. It took time, especially with his workload. He made time. Silently, he dubbed the car Phoenix because it had emerged out of hundreds of discarded, broken parts.

Just the way he finally did, rising out of the ashes of what had been.

After a time, the car was finished. He was not. He doubted if he ever would be completely whole again. He knew it was something that his mother prayed for, but the world, his world, was sorely short on miracles.

For now, he congratulated himself each evening for making it to the end of another day. He doubted if he could ever expect more than that. To expect was to be disappointed and he had more than his share of that.

Christian adjusted his rearview mirror, making sure to keep the woman driving behind him in his sights. He drove slower than usual. If a light began to turn yellow as he approached it, he'd ease up even more, coming to a stop rather than taking a chance on crossing the intersection and leaving Cate behind at a red light.

Twenty minutes later, he was pulling up his sports car into the Red Balloon's parking lot. It was already three-quarters full, but there were a few empty spaces away from the front. Cate was right behind him. And then right next to him as she stopped her vehicle in the spot beside his.

"Do you always drive that slowly?" she asked him as she shut the door behind her.

He had to admit that the slower speed had been an effort for him. "I didn't want to lose you." Securing his own door, Christian led the way to the Red Balloon's entrance. "Why?" He held the door open for her. "Too slow?"

A wall of warmth greeted her the moment she stepped inside the restaurant. Music pulsed from the interior, just loud enough to enjoy, not loud enough to destroy conversations. The lighting was dimmed to a soft, intimate glow.

She liked the place instantly.

Christian held up two fingers as they approached the hostess. The woman led them to the rear of the dining area.

"I think I coasted half the way here," Cate told him, following the hostess. She glanced over her shoulder to look at Christian. "It took everything I had to keep from running up your tailpipe."

The hostess took them to a booth that was tucked away on one side, away from foot traffic.

Christian moved up behind Cate. "You're one of those drivers that speeds, I take it?"

The hostess placed a menu at each place setting and discreetly withdrew.

"I've always had a tendency to do everything fast," Cate confided. It tied in with her need to know things as soon as they occurred. She always read the end of a mystery before buying the book so that she could spend her time appreciating the technique being employed rather than trying to figure out who had "done the crime." "I hate wasting time."

He laughed as he took his seat. "The CSI people must drive you crazy."

Cate slid in from the opposite side and found herself beside him. There wasn't enough booth and too much of him. She slid back a little.

"Yes, as a matter of fact, they do. How did you know?"

"Lydia complains about the same thing, although she's slowed down a little since she married Lukas." He thought of life on the reservation. Of time that seemed to stand still for weeks on end. "Where I come from, time seems endless. Minutes are to be enjoyed as they stretch out into the day."

A bright, bubbly waitress came up to the table. Before she could say a word, Christian handed her his menu and Cate's. "Just drinks for now," he told her, then looked at Cate for her order.

She wanted something smooth to cut the edge off what she was feeling. "I'll have a white Russian."

"Make mine a black one."

The young woman nodded, making a notation in what appeared to be a Palm Pilot. "One white Russian, one black Russian. Appetizers?" Her bright eyes danced from Cate to Christian and then back again.

He raised a brow in Cate's direction, but she waved away the suggestion.

"If I have anything else to eat tonight, I'll explode." With a nod of her head, the hostess withdrew. Cate picked up the conversation. "What you said before sounds good in theory, but I don't think I could put it into practice."

"You mean about enjoying the minutes?"

She nodded. "I'm too goal oriented."

"And your goal now?"

"Is to close the case I'm working on."

He looked at her for a long moment. She felt as if he was actually seeing *through* her, into her thoughts. Into her soul.

"And nothing else?" he asked.

She could almost feel his eyes touching her. Could feel the air all but wrapping itself around her, sealing her in. With him.

The booth was much too intimate, Cate realized. Maybe this was a bad idea.

Maybe it wasn't.

She cleared her throat, as if that would somehow also drown out the small, annoying voice in her head that so often played devil's advocate with her.

"You know my other goal," she told him as she wrapped the fingers of both hands around the tall glass of water before her. "Getting Joan Cunningham to admit that she's my mother."

He studied her face, trying to imagine himself in her place. Wondering what he would feel, if he'd suddenly found out that he had another set of parents some-where. Parents who, for whatever reason, had given him away. He wasn't convinced that he would *want* to find them. "Isn't it enough that you believe she is?"

"No." Cate let go of the glass and looked up at him. Was it her imagination or were his eyes suddenly sym-pathetic? Probably had to do with the soft lighting.

Everything looked better in soft lighting. "I can't really explain it, but—no, it isn't."

And she was going to push this to its conclusion, he thought. His loyalty to his patient had him siding with Joan. His sympathies, however, were leaning toward the woman beside him. A woman who very well might be setting herself up for a lot of grief and heartache.

"Did you ever stop to consider that openly recognizing you might cause problems in Joan's life?"

Cate pulled her shoulders back. "I don't want her to take out a full-page ad on the front page of the *L.A. Times* proclaiming the fact. I don't need her to tell her husband or her children about me, although I have to admit I really would like to get to meet them, maybe even have a chance to get to know them.

"But that would be just icing on the cake. I grew up as an only child. For almost half of that time, I was fatherless. I'm used to a small family. I just want her to admit it to me. To look at me and say, 'Yes, I'm your mother.'"

"And that would be enough for you? Just her saying that?" he asked.

The waitress returned with their drinks. Christian nodded at the effervescent young woman. He took out the appropriate amount of money from his wallet, added a healthy tip to it, and then handed the money to her. When she saw the size of the tip, the waitress's eyes fairly glowed.

Cate waited until the waitress retreated, her feet hardly touching the floor. And then she said, "I think it would be enough. Yes."

He wasn't as convinced as she was. Maybe because

he'd had a chance to see the less-than-noble side of man. He didn't lump Cate in with some of the lower life forms he'd known, but human nature was human nature. "Ever hear the one about the fisherman's wife?"

Her brows drew together for a second as she thought. He could see her as a student, pondering a question, surrounded by half a dozen open textbooks. He'd always had a healthy respect for intelligence.

He had no idea why the image aroused him.

"Is this a limerick," she asked, "or are you talking about the fairy tale?"

"Fairy tale," he answered. "I'm afraid I don't know any limericks."

Neither did she, except for the classic one dealing with Nantucket which she wasn't about to repeat. But his reference to the fairy tale left her just as much in the dark as the other would have.

"That's the one where a fisherman catches a magic fish that promises to grant him wishes if the fisherman just puts him back. Not wanting a reward, the fisherman asked for something simple, a good meal. The woman told him he was a fool to wish for something as ordinary as that. She kept making wishes and every time they were granted, she wanted something more. Is that the one?"

He nodded. "That's the one. And that's the word. More."

She toyed with her drink, trying not to take offense at what he was implying. After all, he really didn't know her. "I can't honestly say that I wouldn't want more, but I at least want that."

He'd expected her to refute him, to drown him in a

sea of excuses and rhetoric. He liked her honesty. Christian folded his hands in front of him as he regarded her. "I think that's what Joan might be afraid of. That if she admitted to you that she was your mother, you'd want more. You'd want her to introduce you to her family. And she's not prepared for the sacrifice that might cost her."

All of this was focused on Joan, on his patient. But there were two of them involved in this. Or maybe he'd forgotten that little fact. "What about what it's cost me so far?"

The light at their table caressed her skin, darkening her hair until it almost looked strawberry instead of golden. He had to admit he was having trouble keeping his mind on the conversation.

"Tell me about the people who adopted you."

She thought of Big Ted and Julia and her heart immediately ached. God, but she missed them. "They were terrific people—and I know what you're doing."

Christian snapped his fingers. "Damn, and here I thought I was being subtle and mysterious." And then he smiled at her.

He had perfect teeth, she thought. To go along with his perfect chiseled looks. Although she tried to block it, she wasn't fast enough. A longing stirred inside of her, reminding her how happy she'd been once. And how lonely she felt these days when she let her guard down even for a moment.

Cate struggled to reinforce the barriers she kept up around herself. They wobbled dangerously. She played along with what he'd just said.

"Sorry, but I'm afraid you failed miserably." To un-

derscore it, to show him that she was perfectly fine with
how things were going and that she wasn't about to
back away, Cate forced a smile to her lips.

It immediately went straight to his gut, delivering if
not a mortal blow, one that sent him momentarily reeling. For a second, he even lost his ability to think
straight.

"Would you like to dance?" he asked.

She realized that while they'd sat here, nursing
drinks and skirmishing, the fast music she'd heard
when they'd entered the restaurant had given way to a
soft melody she didn't recognize. Recognition wasn't
necessary. What was important here was that it seemed
to permeate every single corner of the dining area.

And her.

Cate looked around and saw that there was a small
dance floor just past the bar. Only one couple was
dancing. They looked to be well into their seventies.
Childhood sweethearts celebrating their golden anniversary? Or a newly matched couple rejoicing that
they'd found each other after all this time?

Where were all these romantic thoughts coming
from and why wouldn't they leave her alone?

Instead of answering his question, she countered
with one of her own. "You dance?"

"Navajos have been known to dance with partners
on occasion."

Cate stared at him, confused. Why the hell would
he say that? Did he think she was prejudiced? Someone incapable of seeing things in living color, but rather
fell back on two-dimensional stereotypes? She didn't
know whether to laugh or be insulted.

"I wasn't thinking about your heritage, Dr. Graywolf," she informed him. "I just didn't think you were the type to dance."

"Why?"

"You look too serious." And dancing was something that freed the spirit, that fed the soul. And that let you relax. None of which she associated with him.

"I take dancing very seriously."

She could see a smile creep onto his face. Maybe he was more laid-back than she gave him credit for.

Cate rose to her feet, her eyes on his. "I guess I'll have to see that for myself."

"Guess so." Taking her hand, he led her to the dance floor.

The soft, bluesy song gave birth to another one, its tempo just as dreamy, just as slow. He curled his fingers around her hand, resting it against his shoulder as he slipped the other hand around her waist and drew her closer. His hips fit against hers as they swayed in time to the rhythm.

Another mistake, her inner voice whispered.

A mistake because it felt so good to be held by a man. If she closed her eyes, she could almost pretend that her life had been untouched by tragedy. That this was Gabe and everything was all right.

The bad thing about pretending was that eventually, she had to stop.

But not just yet, that same voice inside her head begged.

So she shut her eyes, rested her cheek against his chest. And pretended all was right with her world as the music and the evening took her away.

Chapter 25

Christian closed the door to his apartment slowly. After a beat, he flipped the lock into place.

The sound reverberated in her head and she turned immediately, her eyes as wide as sunflowers when they searched for the sun.

"It flips the other way to open," he told her quietly. "Whenever you want."

She felt silly for panicking. Sillier because she knew it showed.

Cate pressed her lips together, nodding in response. What was she doing here? Why wasn't she in her car, heading for home? Why was she here instead, heading for disaster?

Because it didn't feel like disaster. It felt exhilarating.

Fear and excitement undulated through her, its

rhythms mixing, creating something all its own. She realized that she felt this way whenever she was on the verge of charging onto a scene to make a bust, to take down a felon.

Adrenaline raced through her.

Building.

She tried to level it off. To find something to ground her. She forced herself to look around the apartment. The kitchen was small. Nothing was out of place. The same went for the living room.

"You're a lot neater than I am," she told him, aware of every word crawling up her throat, out of her mouth. "Of course, you seem to have a lot less."

"I'm not home enough to get attached to anything."

"Lydia told me about the hours you keep." She turned around to face him. "Between the clinic on the reservation and your patients here, it's a wonder you're not worn out."

Funny she should choose those words to use. That was what he'd tried to accomplish at one point. To wear himself out until there wasn't anything left. But somehow, he still managed to exist. So he put one foot in front of another, riding each day into the next and the next. Making a difference, he hoped, as he struggled to keep the emptiness inside of him from consuming him, body and soul.

That was what had prompted him to invite her to his apartment tonight after the waitress had cleared away their glasses. Because, for whatever reason, being with Cate had made him forget the emptiness for the first time in three years.

"But then," she added, transfixed by the strange

look that had come into his eyes, "people are usually a lot stronger than they give themselves credit for."

He didn't want to talk anymore. Didn't want to think. It always hurt to think. Christian brushed back her hair from her face. "I've heard the rumor."

Her heart had stopped. Totally and completely. She had no idea why she wasn't passing out. How she could continue standing here, looking up into his hypnotic eyes instead of crumbling to the floor. Wasn't that what you were supposed to do when your heart stopped? Crumble? Die?

He moved his head and she knew he was going to kiss her. Panic spiked up, ten feet tall.

Just before his lips touched hers, she abruptly began talking. "Look, I'm not about to get close to anyone. Every time I have, I get the rug pulled out from under me." She pressed her lips together. "I just wanted you to know that."

"Well, that's a first." He smiled, shaking his head. "I never had anyone issue a disclaimer before I kissed her. Don't worry." He framed her face with his hands. "I'm not looking for forever."

Her heart started up suddenly, beating wildly. "Good, because neither am I."

Liar.

The single word echoed in both their heads as they began their race toward oblivion.

If asked, Christian would have said that he would never feel this way again. That he would never have that fire in his belly, that urgent pull racing through his body as desire built on desire, seeking an outlet. Yet here it was, capturing every part of him.

When Alma died, when the full impact of what she had done, ending not just her life and their daughter's but tearing apart his, had really hit him, everything within him had shut down. In the early stages, he couldn't even summon any feelings surrounding his core family. His capacity to love, to empathize, to hope, had all been burned away, leaving nothing but ashes in its wake.

He had nothing to draw on, nothing to cling to as one day swam into the next.

Slowly, from deep within, and with his family's love and support, he'd managed to find the will to live, to continue in a world that had been so cruel to him as to build him up only to tear him down. And eventually, some measure of feeling did return, at least for the people who had stood by him through all this. He loved his mother, his uncle, his brother and the woman Lukas had taken as his wife, Lydia. And he loved his work, because it allowed him to help, to make a difference. It was what he cleaved to in the worst moments.

The first time that he'd held a newborn in his hands after Alma's death, tears had rushed to his eyes. Cleansing tears that had allowed him to cautiously take his real first steps back among the living. The journey was grueling, but he made it.

And so it was tonight.

As the passion rose within him, Christian could feel his soul defrosting by infinitesimal increments. It left him in bewildered awe at the process, because he'd firmly believed that it would never be this way for him again. That he was too numb to ever physically want a woman, too numb to ever want to become lost within her essence.

He'd been wrong.

Without fully realizing how it happened, only that he'd experienced a heated explosion that seized him within its grip, he found himself urgently pinning Cate against the wall. His mouth slanted against hers over and over again as he felt every movement of her body against his. Could feel the full imprint of it on his own torso and limbs.

The flames licked higher, the urgency grew, reminding him just how long it had been since he'd taken the shackles off, since he'd made love with a woman. Those were the key words. Not had sex, but made love. Because he had never been one to merely go through the motions of anything—except perhaps for breathing those first few days—but now the motions were going through him. Urging him awake, suddenly taking by storm what they hadn't been able to remotely even coax out up to this point.

He wanted her.

The thought throbbed through his head as he examined it from all sides. Examined it in wonder, with relief—and with no small amount of fear. He told himself that his reaction was due to a natural physical occurrence after enduring self-imposed celibacy for so long. Tried to convince himself that feelings, true feelings, deep feelings, were things that took years to develop.

He'd only known Cate for what amounted to a blink of an eye.

No, it was just her body that captivated him, that pulled him out of the deep freeze where he'd been living his life, nothing more. Because physically, she was magnificent, her body wondrously firm, gloriously supple. What man wouldn't have wanted to sleep with her if he could get the chance?

And tonight, there'd been this look in her eyes....

As he ran his hands over her, desire took on form and rhythm. Tilting her head back with his hand beneath her chin, he pressed his mouth over hers again, unable to get enough. Trying desperately to become sated. Cate tasted of something sweet, something seductive, and it made his head spin even as it fed the needs within him.

Cate dug her fingertips into his shoulders, trying desperately to anchor herself. To keep from getting swept out to sea.

Everything was being sucked out of her.

She was having trouble drawing in enough air to sustain her. Her lungs felt depleted, almost to the point that she could swear she could feel them collapsing. She would have collapsed if she wasn't holding on to him. Her knees weren't working right.

She wasn't working right.

It was almost as if, traveling in a tiny boat made of paper, she'd come to the edge of the world. Any second now, she was going to fall off.

And fall into him.

Into this man who had made her open up everything she'd kept so safely locked away in storage. She'd kept all her feelings there, along with a secret hope buried deep in her heart that perhaps someday, someday the dead would rise and she would be able to feel again. To love again.

Raised as an optimist, Cate had still taken longer

than most to trust anyone with her heart. It was very precious to her and she didn't surrender it lightly. She'd given her father her heart and he had died, breaking it. Gabe had always teased her that he'd wage a long, hard campaign to get her to agree to marry him. He was right. But that was because, after her father's death, an inherent fear of being left behind had always kept her from agreeing to make that final transition, that final leap that would take her from lover to wife.

It wasn't that she was afraid of commitment, she was afraid of having that commitment broken.

And now, no matter what she'd told herself, how safe she wanted to remain, she couldn't go on hiding any longer. The walls she'd hidden behind were crumbling. She'd always thought she'd had that much control over herself, that nothing could ever happen without her mentally giving her permission. She'd been secure in her belief that if she didn't allow her feelings to rise up, they wouldn't.

But sometimes, it wasn't a matter of allowing things to happen. Sometimes, they just did.

Such as now.

Desire raced through her body like a raging forest fire. Everywhere that desire touched ignited her. Just the way his hands were setting fire to her as they brushed over her. As they found their way to her breasts, her hips, her flesh.

Cate moaned, wanting more.

This was too much to hold out against. For at least one moment, she wanted desperately to feel whole again. To feel that final intense burst within her body, bathing her in euphoria.

She couldn't, wouldn't think beyond that. Beyond the fact that this was, after all, a single moment in time. She didn't want to think about consequences. She wanted to think about him, about Dr. Christian Graywolf. She twisted against him as he kissed her, sinking deeper and deeper into the hallowed ground he'd created for her.

For them.

Desire so consumed her that she was only vaguely aware of stripping his shirt from him, or that she was running her fingers along his smooth, hard chest, feeling the taut biceps, the muscles that were as hard as rocks. And she was only vaguely aware that he had pulled her sweater up over her head and thrown it to the side. She had no memory at all of helping him. Of lifting her arms up over her head so that he could yank the sweater away.

And she was only marginally aware that she'd held her breath as he undid the hook at her back, allowing the soft fabric to sigh away from her breasts and fall to the floor. She was focused only on the feeling that he was bringing out of her, only on the light that burned brighter and brighter within her.

The fire grew.

Clothing flew right and left, his, hers, a strip-poker exhibition caught up in a fast-forward mode until there was nothing between them except for the people they had been before this moment had overtaken them.

Lost in his embrace, feeding on the incredible surges that vibrated through her, Cate blocked out everything—the newly born insecurities that plagued her, the past that had once seemed so good before it was destroyed—everything but the feelings running through her.

Everything but the man who had brought them all unexpectedly to fruition. And even as she wanted to race to the climax, to feel that wondrous explosion within her, she dearly wanted to prolong the journey that would take her there.

With sweeping fingers she explored his body, employing the tenacity of an investigator who knew that rewards lay at the end of a job well done. And when he matched her, stroke for stroke, or outdistanced her, bringing her to the brink of the precipice, pleasure screamed through her body, begging for release.

Begging for more.

To her everlasting surprise, he turned her body into an instrument, playing songs upon it she'd never heard before, never been aware of before. As they echoed through her, Cate realized that the corners of her eyes had become moist.

Damn, she couldn't cry at a time like this. Crying made one more vulnerable and she was already far more vulnerable, far beyond any line in the sand she'd ever drawn for herself.

A ray of determination suddenly flashed within her.

She couldn't just take without giving. Couldn't be at his mercy without bringing him to hers.

Breathing heavily, trying to focus her eyes on his face, Cate wrapped her fingers around his thickened shaft, striking a rhythm of her own.

Surprise imprinted itself on his features. A sense of triumph marched through her. The next moment, his hand was closing over hers. But instead of urging her to continue, Christian was drawing her fingers away.

She didn't understand. Was she doing it wrong? But before she could protest or question, he'd parted her legs with his own. The next moment, he drove himself into her. Her breath caught in her throat, standing still.

The rhythm never began slowly. It was frantic right from the start and she rushed to embrace it with determination and joy. At one point, her hips were moving so quickly, so urgently, she managed to push them both up off the ground.

She thought she felt his smile against her mouth, but she wasn't sure.

And then there was no space for thought, no space for anything but this huge bonfire raging within her.

The earth and sky disappeared. The room faded. Everything vanished except for the tiny sphere within which they were captured.

And when the final climax came, stars rained all around her, bathing her in the most wonderful sensation of euphoria, of hope, she'd ever experienced.

She held on to him as tightly as she could, afraid of falling back to earth alone.

Chapter 26

Slowly, like someone coming out of a half dream, Cate became conscious of her surroundings. Of the rug beneath her back. Of the slight press of weight hovering just above her body.

She realized that Christian was balancing himself on his elbows, mindful of her even at the most intimate, most crucial of moments. And then he shifted. He lay beside her, their union dissolved.

The earth and sky came rushing back to her much too quickly.

Oh, God, what had just happened here? What had she done? Pinpricks of panic jabbed her skin like icicles in a macabre dance. She felt naked, exposed.

He felt her stiffen beside him. Could almost feel the warmth draining away from her. Was regret burrowing in, creating a space between them so quickly? And was that his regret or hers?

Part of him wished that she would leave. Just disappear. Taking all traces of what just happened with her. But that wasn't possible. And even if it were, he wasn't completely convinced that he truly *did* want that. Because just for a moment back there, he'd felt alive again. More alive than he had in a long time.

Christian had to admit, being alive was far better than the alternative. The feeling was also seductive.

Cate moved. He could swear that she was trying to withdraw into herself.

"Cold?" he asked.

He glanced at the blanket draped over the back of his sofa and contemplated getting it for her. The brightly woven fabric depicted a history of the Navajo people. His mother had made the blanket for him when he came out here to live, so that he would never forget where he came from. As if that was ever possible.

Cate pressed her lips together. No, she wasn't cold. If anything, the opposite was true. Heat emanated from her every pore. He'd brought her body temperature up so high, she could probably warm a small Third World village for a year.

"Not cold. Bewildered," she finally said.

He looked at her thoughtfully. "I don't know if I have a blanket for that."

Her mouth twitched as a hint of a smile surfaced, then faded.

Lying flat, Cate stared at the ceiling, her mind going at the speed of light. She tried to harness her thoughts. She admitted she'd wanted this to happen. Wanted to stop feeling this paralysis, this overwhelming malaise when it came to her personal life.

Wanted to feel alive.

But right now, she felt guilt and fear. Guilt because she'd betrayed Gabe's memory. And fear was taking on a life of its own within her. She never, ever wanted to feel so bereaved as she had that September morning.

There was no danger of that, she reminded herself. Christian had indicated that he didn't want anything to come of this. And in a strange way, that was comforting to her. Because it meant no risks were involved. She had all the benefits of a campfire without needing to know how to tend it. Without the fear of accidentally burning the campgrounds down.

But she still had to deal with the impression she had probably made. This might have been a one-time thing, but she worked with his sister-in-law. Because of that, they were bound to run into each other again. She didn't want him getting the wrong idea.

Clearing her throat, Cate turned her head, forcing herself to look at him. He was too close. Her thoughts scrambled a little. So much for remaining cool under fire. "I just want you to know that despite modern mores, I, um, don't do this kind of thing."

Humor shone in his eyes as he regarded her. He went from solemn to incredibly appealing. She could feel her pulse accelerating. Cate pinned the blame to the lack of proper attire.

"For a novice—" his eyes were skimming over her "—you have a hell of a natural talent."

She found it difficult not to respond to Christian, to keep her body from flowing into his again. She did her best. "No," she tried again, "I mean that I don't sleep around."

His smile deepened. He had been struggling with his own conscience, but Cate's apparent dilemma had pushed that into the background. "We weren't sleeping."

Was it her imagination or were his eyes teasing her?

She took a deep breath and became alarmed as her breasts brushed against his arm. "I don't make love with someone I don't know, either," she replied tersely.

He appeared to take in what she was saying, but at the last moment, his serious demeanor failed him. "If that's the case, then whatever they slipped me in that restaurant, I am definitely going back for seconds."

For a moment, she said nothing. The quiet stretched between them, allowing small sounds to make their way in. The ticking of his wristwatch close to her head. The sound of his breathing.

Finally, drawing in a deep breath, she tried to explain. "I had a fiancé."

"Had?"

Cate pressed her lips together, afraid that a sob might betray her. But when she spoke, her voice was incredibly calm given the turmoil she felt inside. "He died in Tower Number Two."

No more of an explanation than that was needed. The tragedy had captured an entire nation, holding them transfixed before their television sets for hours, for days. Trembling in anger and disbelief that this had happened to them.

"I'm sorry."

She nodded, accepting the words that had echoed

within her own soul so often since that day. Summoning her courage, she turned her face toward Christian again. Something quickened inside of her as it reached out to him.

"And I haven't been with anyone since." She wasn't even sure why she was telling him this and what, if anything, it actually meant. To him. To her. She couldn't sort it out now. Her mouth was dry. "I just wanted you to know," she repeated.

This was where he told her about Alma, Christian thought. It was the perfect opening. He either told her about his wife's suicide, or he said something flippant and distanced himself.

Bonded or retreated.

He did neither.

Instead, he chose a third path. Sympathy. He slipped his arm around her and drew her closer to him. Not to make love with her, but to hold her. And to offer her whatever mute comfort he could.

She dealt very well, very efficiently with anger, both her own and what was aimed at her. Kindness was another matter. Kindness undid her. Cate could feel tears forming again. She blinked hard, trying to push them back, to erase them. This wasn't fair. She'd expected him to say some trivial thing, or even suggest that perhaps she'd want to leave. All the ingredients for an awkward moment were there, to intensify her regret over what she'd done with him.

That he just held her, that he gave her mute solace in memory of her grief, was almost too much for her to bear. She wanted to pull away from him.

Instead, this pulled her to him.

Cupping his cheek, Cate kissed him. In gratitude and in need.

The single kiss built, until it flowered into another. And another. Growing until the passion that they both had thought had been quenched suddenly rose up again, full-bodied and demanding. They had no choice but to give in to it and each other. And found themselves being swept out further into the night.

Dawn dragged itself in at six-fifteen. Rays of light probed the corners of his bedroom. They had ended up here last night, after making love one more time in the living room. He'd sensed she'd wanted to leave, but he hadn't wanted her to go. It took almost nothing on his part to get her to change her mind.

As he watched her fall asleep against him, he remembered thinking that some of the jagged edges had come off the pieces of his life. He'd fallen asleep with his arm around her. His arm was empty now as he pulled consciousness tightly to him.

She was gone.

Lying flat on his back, Christian dragged his hands over his face, as if wiping away the last traces of sleep. He strained to hear a sound, something to indicate that she was still here, roaming through another room in the apartment.

There was nothing. He was alone.

In a way, he was relieved. If she was gone, he could simply blot out last night as if it had never happened. But it had. In truth, he wasn't sure exactly what it was that he *had* experienced. Maybe it was just a combination of physical needs and—

And what?

He'd never been a player. For some reason, he'd never gone through that rampaging hormonal stage that afflicted almost every adolescent male to a greater or lesser degree. Sex for sex's sake had never interested him. He placed a higher value on male-female interaction than that. His friends had mercilessly kidded him about his values.

Throwing back the sheet that clung to his body, he sat up, moving his shoulders and stretching. Last night had been a workout all its own.

He realized that her scent was still lingering on his skin. He needed coffee and a shower. And something to do.

As if in response, his pager went off. The small blue item vibrated along the nightstand, coming close to the edge. He picked it up before it fell, looking at the numbers that were displayed.

Christian smiled to himself. It looked like Mrs. Scalli was finally ready to have her twins. It couldn't have happened at a more opportune time. Drawing the phone over to him on the bed, he dialed the number on the pager. A minute later, he was assuring a very distraught Mr. Scalli that he was already on his way to the hospital.

The summer she had turned seven, as a special treat her mother had taken her to a local production of *Peter Pan*. It was her first play. She could remember sitting in the audience, completely enthralled as she watched Peter fly around the stage.

But what had really stuck out in her mind over the years was one of the musical numbers: Peter, posturing and singing "I Won't Grow Up." The tune went through her head now as Cate sat in her car, parked across the street from a sprawling, custom-made house. Except that in this case, the words were "I Won't Get Involved." But even as the refrain repeated itself over and over again in her head, Cate knew she was in danger of doing just that. Of getting involved.

Last night she and Christian had had hot, cleansing, teeth-jarring sex. And she wasn't the type to do that casually. Not even with a gorgeous, full-blooded Navajo doctor.

Cate sighed, shaking her head. Ever since she'd found out she wasn't who she thought she was, nothing made sense to her anymore.

She'd left his bed early, wanting to avoid any conversation. Wanting to avoid the disappointment she felt certain to come. So she'd quickly gathered up her things, dressed hurriedly in the bathroom—so hurriedly that she didn't realized she'd left behind her thong underwear until she was halfway home—and left. Rushing toward sanctuary.

Finding none.

Once in her apartment, she'd showered, changed and faced the dawn with a cup of poorly made coffee and so many questions ricocheting inside of her, she didn't know where to start. So she hadn't.

She didn't need this extra complication in her life. So she did what she always did when she didn't want to be alone with her thoughts. She got busy.

A call to the hospital had told her that "Jane" was still unresponsive, still unconscious. She decided to go into the office despite the fact that it was Saturday.

But somewhere between getting into her car and arriving at the Santa Ana building, she'd turned her vehicle to the more exclusive region of Bedford.

Specifically toward the development called Spy Glass Hill. It was an older community, secure in its affluence amid a city known for its rich citizens.

It was where Joan Cunningham lived with her family.

Spy Glass Hill was aptly named since the developer had placed his lots on a hilly region that allowed for a breathtaking view of the surrounding area and the ocean that lay just beyond. It was said that on a clear day, the island of Catalina could be seen sunning itself like a contented, tame whale.

Cate drove up the hills slowly, looking at the signs, searching for where she needed to make turns. She took a wrong street once and had to go down the entire length before she could backtrack. She tried to enjoy the scenery and unique buildings, but in her present frame of mind, it wasn't possible. There was too much going on in her head.

Joan's house was almost at the top of one of the hills. The white-columned residence looked as if the architect had had it lifted straight out of the history books. Or a movie.

She half expected Scarlett O'Hara to come racing out the front door, holding her skirt high and laughing as she flirted her way through innocence.

Cate turned off the ignition and settled back to wait for someone to come out of the house. She needed to catch a glimpse of her mother's family. More than that, she needed something to tie her to an existence other than the one she had.

Chapter 27

The minutes moved slowly, pulled along on a wagon with square wheels. Eventually, an hour passed, drunkenly meandering its way into the second one.

Cate could feel every one of those minutes as they catatonically inched by. She'd lost count of the number of times she'd told herself to start the car again and leave.

Something made her stay.

The morning sun had risen and begun to warm the interior of the car, forcing her to first crack, then roll down the window on her side. Monotony hovered over her like an oppressive cloud. She didn't dare play the radio for fear of calling attention to herself. Like a sneak thief casing his next job, she remained enshrouded in silence.

What was she doing here? Cate demanded of herself impatiently. Had she gone completely off the deep end? She was behaving irrationally. Last night certainly proved that. Making love with a stranger. And all this nonsense about searching for her identity was just that. Nonsense.

Annoyance mounted as she shifted in the car, trying to keep her legs from cramping up. She knew who she was, damn it, and it wasn't some shrinking violet, jumping at her own shadow. She was Big Ted Kowalski's daughter—his daughter of choice, she underscored—and it was about time she started acting like that again.

What would he think if he saw her here, skulking around, waiting to catch a glimpse of a woman who wouldn't give her the time of day? She remembered what disappointment looked like when it spread itself over his broad face. She'd never seen it directed at her, but if he were alive…

She was out of here, Cate decided abruptly.

As she reached to turn the key in the ignition, a movement across the street caught her eye. Her fingers on the key, she looked in the direction of the house.

The front door was opening.

Her hand retreated from the key.

Instead of only one person, as she'd hoped, five emerged from the house. Moving in single file, they regrouped on the front step. She'd already met the older of Joan's two sons and she knew what Ron Cunningham looked like thanks to the records that Jeremy had forwarded to her. She hadn't been very impressed by Cunningham's picture. He'd looked austere. In person, Ronald Cunningham cut a far more dynamic figure. Tall, sturdy-looking, he had a thick head of hair that was just beginning to turn silver from its natural chestnut brown.

The son she hadn't met, William, looked like a younger version of his father. The daughter, Rebecca, was the youngest of the trio. She appeared to be a composite of both her parents, dark-haired like her father, thin like her mother.

She was also the apple of her father's eye.

It was easy to recognize the signs. Ron Cunningham had his arm around his daughter's shoulders and they were talking like friends. It made her miss her father. Joan followed behind the duo, flanked by her sons. Alex walked a little ahead, as if he wanted to get this over with. He seemed impatient.

Like me, Cate thought.

All five were dressed in subdued colors, blacks and navies. Wherever they were going, it was formal.

A funeral? Whose?

Cate made a mental note to try to check the recent obituaries just as she heard Rebecca laugh. Cate's attention was drawn back to the girl and Ron Cunningham. Again nostalgia shimmered through her as she recalled similar moments she had shared with the man she'd thought was her father.

She would have given anything to have that comfortable frame of mind restored, to think of Ted and Julia as her parents and nothing else. But it was too late. She knew better, she thought as she watched the five people get into the silver-gray Mercedes sedan. Joan got in the front beside Ron. Her children sat in the back. Rebecca took the seat directly behind her father. Alex sat behind his mother, with William in the middle.

Odd person out?

That makes two of us, William.

A wistfulness swirled through her as she watched. *That would have been my family. If she'd kept me.*

But even as the thought occurred to her, doubt followed.

Maybe not. Maybe if she'd kept me, she would have never met Ron Cunningham, never married him.

Maybe Joan would have had to take another path as a young single mother. She might have had to drop out of school and go to work to support the two of them. She knew nothing about Joan's parents, but she did know that not everyone was lucky enough to have their families stand behind them. All she had to do was look to her current case to know that.

And if her birth mother had kept her, she would have never known Big Ted and Julia. Never felt the sheer power of their love, never known the pride she'd experienced at being the daughter of a man who was not only well respected, but also well loved in his wide circle of friends.

Shock was responsible for taking her on this odyssey, Cate thought. The shock of losing her mother, of having her world shaken not just by death but by the discovery that what she'd thought was the truth, wasn't. With her very foundations knocked out from beneath her feet, she'd wanted desperately to connect to something, even if only for the sake of connecting.

And maybe she still would, but whether or not she did, that didn't diminish what she'd had up to this point, Cate told herself with newfound conviction. A happy childhood. Because two people had loved her more than anything in this world.

Maybe instead of anger, she owed Joan a vote of thanks. It was something to think about.

Four doors slammed, almost in unison. The Mercedes, still waiting to receive its official license plates, rumbled to life. The next moment, the sleek vehicle was backing down the driveway. Once parallel to the garage, the car took to the street.

She doubted if any of its occupants even noticed her car, or her. Why should they? She wasn't even a speck on their radar. And maybe, her conscience whispered, it should stay that way.

But the stubbornness she now realized she had learned rather than inherited from Big Ted and Julia made her want her due. She wanted to be recognized by Joan. At least privately.

Cate sat in her car for a long moment, thinking, her conviction vacillating. Leaning toward talking to Joan one more time. She supposed there was no question about it, she was stubborn. And added to that, she didn't like the idea of facing life alone.

That was both her strong point and her failing. She needed to be part of something. Independent, she still needed to know there were links she could turn to, links that joined her to something greater than herself. Links to family, to the bureau.

And to Christian?

The second the thought came to her, she pushed it away. Her mouth hardened as she finally turned the key in her ignition.

No, not to Christian. Definitely not to Christian.

That had just been a vulnerable episode, nothing

more. She'd stumbled last night, but she was on her feet again and she was going to remain that way.

She realized that her hands were clutching the steering wheel tightly and she forced herself to loosen her grip.

Okay, so she was human, but that was all last night had been about, Cate reasoned. Being human. She'd enjoyed a healthy physical relationship with Gabe. Since his death, she hadn't been with a man, hadn't even gone out on a date. It was only natural for her body to yearn to experience that same sort of wondrous release she'd enjoyed with Gabe. Especially when confronted with temptation. And Christian Graywolf was nothing if not extremely attractive in every sense of the word. She'd been attracted to him from the first.

There was nothing more to it than that.

Cate sighed, willing the tension to leave her body. It was time she made herself useful. With renewed determination, she guided her vehicle along the winding path down to the outskirts of the development. Once outside, she took the road that would lead her to Santa Ana.

Mrs. Scalli had an amazingly short time of it, especially given that this was her first pregnancy.

Of course, Mrs. Scalli probably didn't think so, Christian mused as he drove his car toward the private landing field of John Wayne Airport.

His ears were still ringing with her screams. For a small woman, Lorraine Scalli had a lusty set of lungs. As did the twin boys she'd given birth to after only three and a half hours of labor.

It seemed to him that everyone on the floor, especially her husband David, was relieved that her labor had only lasted as long as it did. It wasn't uncommon for first timers to take almost a day, if not more.

Christian grinned. Everyone would have been deaf by then.

As soon as she was in the recovery room and he was certain everything was all right, he'd left Mrs. Scalli and her new family in good hands. Namely Simon Neubert's. Over the last two years, he and Simon took turns covering for each other.

When he'd called the obstetrician at his home, Simon had reluctantly agreed to step in. Simon's reluctance no doubt stemmed from the fact that he didn't want to leave the owner of the female voice he'd heard in the background. He could just about make out that the woman was pouting over Simon's pending departure. For as long as he'd known him, Simon had hardly ever been without female companionship. The man had incredible stamina.

Christian figured the man could do with a break.

As could he, he reasoned. At least mentally.

He didn't usually travel to the reservation this late into the weekend. Normally, he took a commuter flight Friday evening so he could spend two full days at the clinic.

But he needed to get away. Needed to touch base with his roots. The need had been building all day and it was now at almost critical mass.

Because she wouldn't get out of his head.

The shower he'd taken this morning hadn't helped. It hadn't eradicated her scent. He swore that it was still there, clinging to his skin if not his clothes. Clinging to his mind. There seemed to be nowhere he could go to escape it.

Or her image, which kept popping up in his head at the most inopportune times.

Christian told himself that it was just because she'd been the first woman he'd slept with since Alma. He wasn't exactly treadworn and experienced in the way so many of the men he knew were. There had only been a couple of girls before he'd dedicated himself completely to Alma. In light of that, it was only natural that making love with Cate would linger like this on his mind. After all, only a few hours had actually passed.

And the woman made love with the vigor of a Viking princess.

They'd both made love with a passion he'd never ascribed to the act before. Alma, because of what she'd endured when she was younger, was reticent when she made love. Holding back, as if she was afraid of someone no matter how gentle he was.

Cate had been fearless.

There had been a frantic element in her lovemaking and it had brought out the same in kind from him. They'd made love as if it was their last chance. As if they were both fleeing from something.

Or was that *to* something?

No, he decided as his plane took off. In his case, he hadn't been searching for anything, except perhaps for respite. A time-out from the demons that haunted him. Oblivion.

He sighed, never comfortable with lies, even his own. There was more to his own reaction than that. He might have gone into the evening looking to be numbed, but making love with Cate had had the opposite effect. Rather than become numbed, he'd caught on fire. And become aware of sensations for the first time in three years.

Become aware, too, that in so doing, in making love with Cate, he'd betrayed the memory of a woman who had regarded him as her one true salvation.

He tried to convince himself the evening had been a mistake. A little detective work on his part had gotten him Cate's address. He'd sent flowers to her apartment to silently convey his thanks and his apology.

And now he was going back to the reservation, to the cemetery, to say he was sorry to Alma. Sorry that he had failed her. Failed her in so many ways.

Chapter 28

"He's here, you know," Henry Spotted Owl said, his voice rumbling from deep within his wide chest.

Juanita looked up from the latest reports she was reading, reports that would hopefully help her to upgrade the school she'd dedicated herself to for the last twenty years in one form or another. All she needed now was to rattle a few cages, raise a little money to help with the funding. That shouldn't be any more difficult that say, turning water into wine.

Sighing, Juanita sat back and rubbed her forehead, willing away yet another headache. Wasn't she supposed to be more carefree in the second half of her life? Not hardly.

"Which 'he' would that be?" she asked.

"Christian."

The short reply, without fanfare, surprised her. As did

the information. Juanita removed her glasses, sliding them up onto her head where they spent most of each day.

"No, he's not." Christian would never be on the reservation without letting her know. He always stopped home first.

Henry sank his still-powerful frame down onto the sofa and reached for the remote control. Pressing the power button, he brought life to the rectangular box that had sat dormant until this moment. "Mary White-feather said she saw him."

Juanita raised her voice to be heard about the commercial that had come on. "When?" Mary Whitefeather was their own personal communication system. If anything was happening on the reservation, Mary was somehow always the first to know.

Henry's eyes were sealed to the screen. The corners of his mouth, already down, drooped a little further in disapproval. He went to the next channel. "A little while ago."

This just wasn't like Christian. Something was wrong. She could feel it. "Was he at the clinic?"

Two more channels came and went before Henry answered. "She said he was walking somewhere. She called out to him, but he didn't hear her."

Mary was getting on in years, although no one was really certain just how old she was. The numbers she gave changed every year. There was no doubt in Juanita's mind that in the not-too-distant future, Mary would be the same age as her own son.

Disturbed, Juanita frowned. "Christian never comes on a Saturday. It's always on a Friday evening." She looked at Henry for confirmation. "He always wants to get in two full days at the clinic."

Henry's wide shoulders moved up and down beneath the colorful green-and-yellow shirt he wore, a gift made for him by the mother of one of the boys he worked with at the gym. He wore it proudly. He went to yet another channel, then paused. A woman was going into labor on one of the medical programs. Birth of any kind had always fascinated him. "Hey, I'm just the messenger."

Juanita realized that she must have sounded as if she was snapping at him. She hadn't meant to. Lately, she hadn't been sleeping that well. Half-formed dreams about Christian that vaporized with first morning light kept plaguing her. Were they warning her about something? "What do you think it means?"

For all of Henry's stories, he was basically a simple man. He slanted a look toward Juanita. "It means that Mary Whitefeather saw him walking. Don't look for omens."

"I wasn't looking for omens, old man." The omens usually came looking for her, Juanita thought.

But they'd had this discussion before and Henry didn't believe in the old ways as she did. She found it amusing that she should be the one to look to the past while he embraced the present. A present that had widows gifting him with shirts and various other tokens of appreciation. "I was just trying to figure out why he would be on the reservation without first stopping here."

Amusement filtered into Henry's leathery features. He paused his channel-surfing to give momentary attention to a program about the Painted Desert. "Maybe he didn't want you asking a lot of questions."

Juanita took exception to his implication. "I leave my sons alone."

"You don't have to ask questions with your mouth, Juanita. You do it with your eyes."

"So I should close them when Lukas and Christian are here?"

Henry inclined his head. A commercial break had come on. He went in search of something interesting to fill in the ninety-second slot. "It's a thought."

Juanita looked at her older brother with no small affection. How would she ever have faced life without him? He'd helped her plug up all the holes these past twenty years, usually without being asked. But if she said as much to him, he'd be on the next train off the reservation. Gratitude embarrassed Henry unless it came from some widow who was eager to show him just how grateful she was.

"Would you like me to tell you what to do with that thought?"

Henry grunted, working his way back to the nature program one channel at a time. It never occurred to him to press in the actual numbers on the remote and speed up the process. "Didn't anyone ever teach you to respect your elders?"

"When I find an elder, I will. You're younger than I am." And there were times when she felt that was actually true. Henry managed to somehow have more energy than she could muster.

"Not tonight. Tony and Jack are giving me a run for my money," he said, mentioning two of the boys who had been with him for a couple of years now. When they'd started, he'd had to tie their trunks around their waists with rope because the trunks were so large. The boys had since grown into them and filled out considerably. So much so that Henry complained he had to chase some of the local girls away. "Those boys can box." Juanita knew this was high praise. Henry never wasted his time with flowery rhetoric. "We might even have an Olympic contender on our hands with one of them." He paused for a moment, then lowered the volume on the set. He looked at his sister. "He's all right. Stop worrying."

As if she could. Juanita shook her head. "They never told me how. That wasn't covered in the Mother's Handbook."

She had a feeling she knew where Christian was. Where he always was when he wasn't at the house or the clinic. With Alma. Or at least her final resting place. The fact that he was probably there bothered her even more than his being on the reservation without communicating with her.

She glanced over to the far corner of the room, where John had sat this entire time, a silent figure more given to observing than speaking. He was a lot like her firstborn, she thought fondly. They could have very easily been actual brothers.

There was a book opened on John's lap and he looked to be reading. Even so, she knew he was taking in every word. He always did.

"John?"

The teenager raised his deep brown eyes from the page and looked in her direction. "Yes, ma'am?"

She'd told him to call her Mother when she'd first taken him in, right after the accident. For all intents and purposes she had taken over the role of mother in his life. But although he loved her as much as any son could love his mother, the word "Mother" just would not come to his lips. Not after he'd lost his. So he called her "ma'am" and she let it go at that.

"Would you please go to the cemetery for me and see if Christian's there?"

John was up in an instant, marking his place before closing his book and neatly putting it in the middle of the coffee table.

"And if he is?" Henry asked as John crossed to her. "What then?"

"Tell him to come home. That he's worrying his mother," Juanita said simply to both her brother and John. "It's cold outside. Take a jacket."

John took his jacket from the coatrack by the front door and slipped it on quickly. "Yes, ma'am."

The door closed. Juanita exhaled a long breath, feeling as if she'd just crossed a tightrope. There was no sense in worrying about Christian, but she couldn't help herself. It was nice to have John to fall back on.

"He's a good boy," she said with pride.

"He's got a girl, you know."

Juanita raised an eyebrow at the information. "You're just a walking news bulletin tonight, aren't you, old man?" Henry made no response. He was busy watching what sounded like a band of coyotes, howling, on the program he'd temporarily allowed to grace the screen. She knew he was waiting for her to ask. "All right, who is she?"

"That part I don't know," he told her honestly. Her dismissive snort had him defending his position. "But I know the signs." He chuckled then. The sound was more like a rusty cackle. He enjoyed being one up on Juanita in this department. Usually his sister was the first to know about something like that. "You're slipping."

"And you're hallucinating." She picked up the report again.

"Have it your way," he said in that infuriating way of his that told her he knew he was right and was allowing her to delude herself.

Juanita made the attempt to go back to reading the report. It was useless. Her mind kept getting stuck on isolated words, refusing to allow her to link them together.

With all her heart, she wished she'd never brought Alma into the house. If she'd insisted that the girl be sent to her great-aunt in Texas when her father had fled the reservation, none of this might have happened. And right now, Christian would still be that happy boy she remembered with longing.

John shoved his hands deep into the pockets of the jacket Juanita have bought for him last winter. He quickened his pace as he entered through the wrought-iron gate that stood at the front of the cemetery. Some of his friends didn't like coming here in the daytime, much less after dark. They claimed that the cemetery was haunted by troubled spirits.

He himself had never subscribed to legends like that. Dead people didn't come back to visit. They moved on. Just like his parents had. He liked thinking that they were both now in a better place than the one they'd known while they were alive. For them, it had taken death to escape the reservation. For him, the path that would get him to some place better would be school. Just like it had been for Lukas and Christian. He admired both his adoptive brothers and wanted desperately to emulate them.

To that end, he studied every free moment he had. Every moment he didn't spend with Lily.

He was crazy about her the way he never had been about any other girl. In a way, though he'd never say anything, that gave him a bond with Christian. He understood what Christian felt, or thought he did. If he lost Lily the way Christian had lost Alma, he'd be here, too, not looking for her spirit, but just trying to connect to her resting place.

Moving amid the tombstones, John made his way over to where they had buried Alma and her daughter. The moon was behind a cloud tonight, but he could just about make out the figure of a man sitting on the ground.

John's mouth curved in a grim smile. Juanita had been right. Christian was here, sitting beside the headstone he had bought.

The night was breezy and the faint murmur of a deep male voice rode on the wind. John couldn't make out the words, but he didn't want to interrupt. It didn't seem right. So he hung back and waited.

The minutes ticked by. Finally, because he knew Juanita would be worried, he cleared his throat. The moment he did, Christian turned in his direction. Silently, he raised an eyebrow as John came forward.

"Your mother sent me," John explained. "She says she's worried and that you should come home."

That was just the problem, Christian thought, gaining his feet and brushing the dirt from his jeans. Since last night, he was no longer a hundred percent sure just where home was.

"How'd she find out I was here?" It wasn't really a question, just idle curiosity as to the source this time. Christian knew that word traveled very fast on the reservation.

"Mary Whitefeather told Uncle Henry she saw you."

Mary Whitefeather. One of their stellar reporters. Christian laughed softly. "We had communication down to a science on the reservation long before the Internet came along." It was time to leave, anyway. The night was growing colder. Forcing a smile to his lips, he looked at John. "So, how's the studying coming along?"

"Glad you're here," John said in earnest. "I need a little help with math."

Christian nodded. "You got it. By the way," he began as he turned toward the gate and led the way out of the cemetery, "how would you like to come to the clinic tomorrow and help me out?"

"Is the fox clever?"

He'd picked that up from Henry, Christian thought. Uncle Henry had a saying for almost everything. "No question about it. All right, be up at six."

John groaned, but his smile never faded.

Chapter 29

"You've got more than math on your mind," Christian commented later on that evening.

After coming home from the cemetery, Christian was relieved that he was not about to be subjected to any lengthy inquiry by his mother as to why he hadn't let her know he was coming. She'd just looked at him with that smile of hers and said "hello." That smile that told him she was glad he was home and that she sensed he needed his space. As far as mothers went, she pretty much set the standard.

A long time ago, he'd discovered that when things seemed to be at their most tangled, he could best work out problems that were plaguing him in his own life if he saw beyond them and tried to help someone else. Tonight, as he'd attempted to sort out the confusion in his head regarding the night he'd spent with Cate, John had come along and fit the bill.

Despite his genuine desire to get ahead, the teenager his mother had taken into her home and heart seemed very distracted as they tackled the problems he'd pointed out in his advanced-algebra text.

So after a while, Christian had suggested a break and they went outside.

They were standing, mostly in silence, on the porch that Lukas, Henry and he had built as a surprise for Juanita when she was away at a school conference. It was one of the few times he could remember ever seeing his mother cry.

In answer to his question, John shrugged and gazed up at the sky.

Christian looked at the teenager's rigid profile. Something was definitely up. He leaned against the railing. "Want to talk about it?" He left the door open without prodding, waiting to see if it would be shut, or if John would step through.

Still not facing him, John took a deep breath. "I've been thinking…I want to get married."

Whatever he was expecting to hear, it definitely wasn't remotely close to this. Christian thought back to himself at that age. At seventeen, his heart had already belonged to Alma, but the rest of him had been torn. On the one hand, he'd wanted to take care of her, on the other, he'd wanted to be free, to experience at least some of what life had to offer.

Looking at John, he could sense that same sort of wavering in the boy. A foot planted in each world, he thought.

"Married, huh?" Christian hid his surprise and concern. "To anyone in particular?"

John closed his eyes and an image came to him that he both resisted and embraced. He'd never felt more confused in his young life. "Yes."

Maybe he was reading things from his own past into John's tone, but he didn't hear the enthusiasm he would have normally associated with the declaration. "You don't sound sure."

"I am," John protested, but because he had never lied to anyone, felt bound to add, "except…"

The word had trailed off into the night. Christian looked at the younger man, waiting. "Except?"

"I want to be free, too." It was almost a protest. A protest against being locked into a box. "I want to find my way off the reservation. Be a doctor like you and Lukas." John rubbed his forehead with the heel of his hand, as if that could somehow make his doubts disappear. His desire to become a doctor was complicated enough with all that was involved. Love just increased complications. "I don't know. This girl, she has me all twisted around."

Christian wasn't about to alienate John by saying he was too young to know love. Some people weren't and John was very intelligent. Love didn't always come when you were in your late twenties, sometimes it came before. But even if John felt the kind of love that was lasting, that didn't mean he had to take all the giant steps that were mapped out for adults who felt the way he did.

Christian chose his words slowly. "Love is a wonderful thing, John. It can make you feel ten feet

tall." He studied his adopted brother's face as he spoke.
"But make sure that you stay true to yourself first."

Right now, everything just felt hopelessly confused.
John could swear that he kept hearing her voice in his
head. Telling him things he didn't want to hear. Making him feel guilty.

And yet he loved her.

Sighing, John shoved his hands deep into his pocket
as he turned to face Christian. "What do you mean?"

Looking into John's eyes, Christian felt as if he was
seeing himself at that age. His past came rushing back
to him. He'd almost made a mess of his life. The only
good thing was that he had hung on to his ambition,
thinking that it would get them both to a better place
in their lives. If Alma had had her way he would have
been working at the reservation's one lone gas station,
pumping gas and running the tiny convenience store.

"Don't be pressured to do something just because
you're afraid of losing that love. At this stage, you
need to grow up a little bit, live on your own. Taste life
a little, before you commit to one woman. If that love
is strong—if it's worthy of you both—it'll still be there
once you finish college."

He didn't often talk about Alma, and never to John,
even though John and Alma had been distant cousins—
or perhaps because of it. But maybe it was necessary.
For the boy's sake.

Christian flashed a self-deprecating smile. "Maybe
if I'd followed my own advice years back, I wouldn't
have felt so responsible for Alma, or been so ill-
equipped to help her. I would have realized that your
cousin had a lot more problems than I was able to help

her with on my own at that age." Christian blew out a breath, staring into the night. And into his own dark soul. A pain existed there that he wasn't sure if he would ever conquer. "And I certainly wouldn't have brought a child into the world to suffer the fate she did."

Rousing himself, Christian looked at the tall young man beside him. Immobile, quiet, John hardly even seemed to be breathing as he listened. "Any of this making any sense to you?"

John nodded grimly. But he knew what Christian was saying was right. He just needed the courage to see it through. And not to melt at the sight of her tears, or give in when she railed.

"Yes," he murmured. "Yes, it is."

"Good." Christian moved away from the railing and John followed suit. Christian put his arm around the boy's slim shoulders. "Now, let's go inside. We've got an early morning ahead of us."

"Still six?" John asked.

Christian grinned, opening the door. "Still six."

This time, John's groan was a little less audible. Christian laughed, giving him a little shove, sending John through the doorway a little faster than the teenager had intended on going.

"She's awake."

Cate had just barely had time to open her cell phone. She certainly hadn't identified herself. Neither had the person on the other end of the phone. Instead, the woman had gone directly to the reason for her call.

Although her head felt as if it was still half-enshrouded in a fog, there was no need for Cate to ask who was calling or who the "she" was. She recognized Lydia's voice. The woman sounded far too excited for there to be any mistake as to whom she was referring.

Jane Doe was conscious.

What a time to have overslept, Cate upbraided herself. Right now, she should be in her car, pulling up into the parking lot behind the federal building, not scrounging around, trying to find a pair of elusive shoes that she knew she had on when she'd walked through the door yesterday.

Or had that been the day before?

Finding a box of long-stemmed roses on her doorstep when she'd come home late Saturday had completely thrown her off. There'd been no card, no indication who they were from, although she'd surmised they came from Christian. What she couldn't figure out was why he'd sent them. To say here's to the beginning of a wonderful friendship? Or thanks for the one-night stand? Or were they some kind of consolation prize?

Nothing made sense to her.

Sunday had seen her serving a self-imposed prison sentence in her apartment, determined to empty out every single box and find a home for its contents. What else did one do when one had insomnia?

"Did you hear what I said, Cate? She's awake," Lydia repeated. "Katya's awake." The last was declared several decibels higher.

Cate found one shoe in the kitchen under the table. Rather than put it on and hobble around, she held it in her free hand as she went in search of its mate.

"Katya?"

"Katya," Lydia echoed. "At least that's the name

the officer on duty said she gave him. He walked in to check on her and she was staring at him with these wide eyes. When he tried to talk to her, she began babbling at him, crying. But he's pretty sure that's the name she said. She pointed to herself when she said it."

Her other shoe was wedged inexplicably under the sofa. After fishing it out, Cate quickly slid on both shoes, never losing the thread of the conversation. She hurried into her jacket, switching the phone from ear to ear as she worked the sleeves. "And he's sure she didn't say anything else?"

"Nothing that he understood," Lydia told her. "I'm on my way down to the hospital. Meet me there."

"See you in a few minutes," Cate responded. Breaking the connection, she slid the cell phone into her pocket. Just before leaving the apartment, she checked the shape of her service revolver, then straightened her jacket.

It was Monday morning and she was late. Something that had happened perhaps a handful of times in her life, and never since she'd joined the bureau. But she'd only drifted off to sleep after four in the morning, still thinking about the roses. Six o'clock came and went, leaving her asleep. So did seven.

At a few minutes after seven, a dream she couldn't remember less than two minutes after she'd opened her eyes had her bolting upright in bed. All she could remember was the sense that she'd been drowning. Drowning in giant rose petals. Red ones.

The numbers on the clock beside her bed had her instantly jumping up a second after they'd registered. She had already dashed into her clothes when Lydia called.

At least her apartment was finally straightened out, she thought as she locked the door behind her. But that wasn't the only thing she'd accomplished last night. After spending most of it unpacking and wrestling with her thoughts, she'd come to two decisions. One, she was going to make one more attempt to get Joan to admit to being her mother, and two, she was going to get a dog for companionship. Both had something to do with the fact that she could recognize her own weaknesses.

The former came from her need to be acknowledged, not just tossed into the garbage like last week's entertainment magazine.

Her decision to buy a dog was a little more complex. It had to do with vulnerability. With her mother gone and the foundations that defined her life eroded, she felt incredibly alone. She'd needed to feel someone's arms around her, to feel that she *wasn't* alone. So when she found herself occupying the same space as Christian, something had just happened. She'd given in to the attraction she'd felt and the need that was eating her up alive.

She was certain that if she hadn't felt this lonely, this vulnerable, she would have never made love with Christian. She would have been able to find the strength to withstand the strong attraction she felt toward him. That was where a dog came in. A pet would fill some of the void she felt.

A German shepherd like the one she'd had as a child, Cate decided.

At least she had a plan, she thought as she took the on-ramp to the freeway.

* * *

"And you still haven't gotten any more out of her?"

Cate heard Lydia's voice before she turned the corner. Her partner and the police officer were standing directly outside the young girl's room.

The police officer who had been guarding the girl shook his head adamantly. His moon face was affable, but not without confusion. Every thought he had registered across it, and right now he seemed perplexed. Cate hoped the man never allowed himself to be talked into playing poker.

"Nothing that I understood," he confessed. "Mostly, she's just crying. When she does say something, it's in some other language." Wide shoulders rose and fell. "Damned if I know what it is."

"Thanks, we'll take it from here." Lydia nodded at Cate. "Morning."

It had taken two cups of coffee, purchased on the fly, to get her eyes to remain open. Cate found herself suppressing a yawn even now. "If you say so."

Despite her excitement at what she hoped was the beginning of a breakthrough, Lydia slanted her partner a look of interest. "Put in a late night?"

"Still unpacking." The weekend felt like one giant blur of boxes, roses and murky dreams. She realized suddenly that she'd been remiss. "I meant to call you and thank you for dinner."

Hand on the doorknob, Lydia paused and waved away the words. "Nothing to thank me for. Lukas told me not to quit my day job. That I'm pretty much a failure when it comes to matchmaking."

Cate shrugged. "We're just not in the market for that."

"We?" A light came into Lydia's eyes as she led the way into the ICU. "Did you and Christian discuss it?"

Only a seriously hearing-impaired person wouldn't have heard the hopeful note in Lydia's voice. And she had perfect hearing. Cate carefully edited her answer before speaking. "Outside your house. When we went to get our cars."

"Oh." Disappointment slid like heavy dew off the word. Feeling sorry for her, Cate almost said something, but stopped herself at the last moment. No sense in having Lydia entertain any false hopes. What had happened Friday night had been a fluke.

Right?

Lydia squared her shoulders as she looked at the young girl in the bed. Their would-be witness was conscious now, watching them with large, frightened brown eyes.

"How are you with languages?" Lydia asked Cate.

"I'm not exactly a linguist." Cate made eye contact with the girl and offered her a smile. "I know Spanish."

"So do I. Just enough to order a limited amount of food," Lydia said. "Somehow, I don't think that's the language the guard heard."

"And Polish," Cate added.

Lydia glanced in Cate's direction. "Now, there's one you don't stumble across every day," she commented. Just then, the girl ventured a few hesitant words. They became more urgent as she finished. Lydia looked at Cate. "Anything?"

"Sounds like it might be Czech, or maybe Ukrainian." At the mention of the second, there was a flicker of recognition in the girl's eyes. "Ukrainian?" Cate repeated. She saw the same reaction. "I think we might have a winner," she told Lydia.

Taking out her cell phone, Lydia flipped it open. "Let's see if the department has anyone available who speaks Ukrainian."

Slavic languages were similar. At times, if a person knew one, they knew another. Her father had been able to make himself understood in half a dozen languages, or so he liked to tell her.

She supposed she had nothing to lose. It was worth a shot, Cate thought.

Coming over to the bed, she took the girl's hand and very slowly, in clear and distinct Polish, told her not to worry. That they were here to help her. She ended by asking if the girl understood.

An eagerness they hadn't seen before highlighted the girl's face. *"Tak."*

Lydia slapped her cell phone closed without completing her call and quickly crossed back to the bed. "What did you just ask her?"

Cate's eyes were on Katya's. She was still holding the girl's hand, trying her best to convey reassurance. "If she understood what I was telling her."

"And that word I just heard her say, that was a yes?" Lydia cried eagerly. Cate nodded. "Oh, Cate, I could kiss you. Ask her how she got there. Ask her—"

But Cate had already begun questioning the girl in a tone that was low and soothing. Despite that, despite her assurances to the girl, tears began to run down Katya's cheeks. Her words were cut short by sobs that all but choked her.

"What are you doing to my patient?"

Cate stiffened. She didn't have to turn around to know that Christian had entered the room. Damn, she'd hoped to have more time to pull herself together before having to face him again. Say like half a decade or so. But she'd never been one to run from anything, even her own confused feelings or the very real possibility of embarrassment. So, after allowing herself one short, bracing breath, she looked over her shoulder at the man she'd made love with on Friday night.

Christian strode into the room, immediately taking charge of his territory. As per his instructions, he'd received a call from the head nurse on duty that the girl had finally regained consciousness. The second he'd heard, he'd driven just inside the speed limit to get here. He'd wanted to examine her before word reached Lydia and her people.

He should have known better.

Cate raised her chin, her eyes defiant. "Comforting her."

Christian frowned. "Funny, she doesn't look very comforted."

She wasn't about to get embroiled in any kind of verbal sparring match, nor was she going to let him pull rank on her. He might be the girl's doctor, but they had a responsibility to bring whoever had done this to her to justice. Not to mention that there undoubtedly were other lives at stake. Maybe many more lives at stake.

"That's because she's remembering what she went through," Cate informed him.

Damn but she looked like a firecracker about to go off. What was it about these bureau women? Even as he wondered, Christian couldn't help thinking that she looked magnificent with her blazing eyes.

"How do you know that?" he challenged. "The nurse said she didn't speak any English."

This was getting too personal and she resisted. She didn't want to get personal with him, not any more than she already had. This was the time for retreating, not advancing.

But she had no choice.

"She seems to be able to speak a little Polish," Cate finally said.

"Christian—" Lydia came to stand between the two "—let Cate talk to her."

Though he loved her, he gave Lydia the same look he'd given Cate. Here, at the hospital, his responsibility to his patients came first, ahead of his loyalty to those he cared about. "I don't want her getting upset, Lydia."

He might have been talking to Lydia, but it was Cate who answered. "My guess is that this girl has been through something a hell of a lot more upsetting than being asked a few questions. Maybe if she feels she can tell someone who understands, she might start healing."

The moment stretched out as he studied Cate. "So now you're a psychiatrist?"

"I'm whatever I need to be in order to close this case and keep girls like Katya from becoming punching bags and worse for the scum of the earth," Cate replied crisply.

"Christian, could I see you for a minute?" Lydia requested. Not waiting for him to answer, she took hold of his arm and draw him over to the side. Away from Cate and the girl in the bed.

For a second, Christian continued looking at his sister-in-law's partner. He hadn't realized, until this very moment, just how unprepared he'd been to see her after the other night. Though he masked it well, running into her like this made him feel as if he'd just received a blow to the solar plexus. It took effort to continue to breathe evenly.

Lydia had his ear as soon as she'd drawn him over to the side. "Is there something going on here I should know about?" She was asking as both an agent of the bureau and as his sister-in-law, although the latter had to take a back seat to the former. Nothing could be allowed to get in the way of this case. Nothing.

He nodded toward the girl in the hospital bed. "She's obviously regained consciousness and—"

"No," she fairly snapped, annoyed. He knew what she was talking about, she thought. Why was he pretending otherwise? "I mean between you and Cate. Did something happen after you left our place Friday?"

Yes, something happened. I think the sky fell in. His face was impassive as he said, "We went out for a drink."

For just a split second, Lydia Wakefield, FBI agent, took second place to Lydia Graywolf, sister-in-law. Her eyes brightened. "Really?"

He was *not* going to go there. "Lydia, I can't have you and your partner badgering my patient."

Her eyes narrowed, pinning him. "Right now, I'm badgering you."

A dark look reminiscent of the one she'd seen only once before, at Alma's funeral, descended over his face. "Don't," he warned.

Lydia raised her hands just enough to indicate surrender. "All right, have it your way. I'll give you space. But not when it comes to her," she added, indicating his patient. "I need to have her questioned. We've already lost too much precious time while she was unconscious. Christian, think," she insisted when she saw that she was losing him. "There could be lives at stake. Lives of girls just like her." She played her trump card. "Do you want me to show you the videotapes? Do you want to see what those girls are made to do?"

"No." The very thought of what could be on those tapes made him physically ill at the same time that anger flared through his veins. He set his jaw. "All right. I'll give you ten minutes." Five was the normal time limit. Five minutes per hour at an ICU bed. "But no more. She needs her rest and I don't want to take a chance on her having a relapse."

But Cate had used her time well while Lydia had hashed things out with Christian. She'd spent it talking to the girl. Communication had been halting. Katya was Ukrainian and there were words she didn't know in Polish. Plus she was growing very tired.

Although she wanted to press on, Cate knew she couldn't. But she did feel she had something for them to go on. Leaving Katya's side, she came up to Lydia and Christian just as he was granting them permission to go ahead.

"No relapse," Cate said. They both looked her way. "Katya's told me enough for now."

Lydia was at her side immediately. "Well?" she demanded eagerly. "Do we have any idea who's behind all this?" She asked the question even though she knew there was little hope of getting a positive answer.

"We might," Cate allowed. Christian shot her a suspicious look, or maybe she was just reading into it. She wasn't trying to be coy, she just wasn't sure of the information the young girl had given her. But there were ways of tracing and verifying it. "I did find out what happened to her. Old story." It was nearly as old as time. Different faces, different methods, same results. Slaves for the highest bidder.

"She and her sister were told that they could have a wonderful life in America if they would just help gather together some of their young friends to go along with them." Her lips twisted in a mirthless smile. "It was a 'package deal' they were offered. There were twenty of them in all, all from her village. The oldest was sixteen." Cate tried not to let her mind paint pictures as she spoke. "They were brought over here in one of those large metal freight boxes."

Christian stared at her. It sounded too horrible. "A box?"

She nodded, pressing her lips together. "The ship transporting them docked in San Diego. They were sick and frightened by the time they got there. No one cared," she said grimly. "They were taken to the first of half a dozen or so locations. The girls were separated, threatened that if they didn't do as they were told, they would be killed and their parents would be horribly tortured before being put to death. Seems the man at the top of the pyramid is powerful with a long reach, or so she overheard one of the guards say." Cate had seen and heard a great many horrible things during her time at the bureau, but this very nearly overwhelmed her. "Katya says she doesn't know where her sister is right now."

Lydia listened quietly, taking in the information. Her time at the bureau had taught her to be wary of Trojan horses. As awful as it seemed, the girl could have been deliberately left behind with misinformation. "Why did they leave her?"

Cate had asked Katya the same thing. And her stomach had twisted when she heard the answer. "Because she refused to appear in one of those videos we found. She was afraid that her parents might somehow get to see it and be ashamed of her. The scum in charge of the filming beat her when she wouldn't do what he told her to."

Cate paused and took a breath, the queasiness in her stomach increasing. She refused to give in to it. "From what she says, she thought that he believed she was dead when he left. She told me she stopped fighting and lay very still, hoping he'd finally leave her alone. He beat her to show the others what happened if one of them disobeyed him." She looked at Lydia, knowing she wasn't supposed to admit this out loud to another agent. Unable to keep her peace. "I'd like to kill him."

"Take a number." And then Lydia forced a grim smile to her lips. "He'll go down," she promised.

Christian looked at his sister-in-law sharply. Just how big a role was she planning to play in this? "Why don't you report this back to your assistant director and have them take it from here? This is obviously international."

Cate looked from Christian to Lydia. Neither one seemed to notice her for a moment.

Again she got the feeling that there was more going on between the two than she understood.

Since Lydia had seemed eager to get her and Christian together the other night, she could only assume that what was between them had to do with family loyalty, not any kind of sexual attraction. Most likely, Christian was feeling protective of Lydia, like a younger brother might toward the sister he cared about.

She liked that about him.

She liked a lot of things about him, a small voice reminded her. Maybe so, Cate silently countered, but she couldn't allow that to cloud her resolve not to get entangled with him.

You slept with the man. I'd say that was getting pretty entangled.

Cate blocked the voice out. She turned toward the girl, who was still watching them with wary eyes. "I'm going to stay with her awhile."

"Don't you think you've questioned her enough?" Christian protested. He took the girl's pulse. It was reedy and irregular. "I told you, she needs her rest."

"No argument," Cate agreed, surprising him. She liked that, too, she thought, catching him off guard. God knew he'd caught her off guard Friday night.

"Then why…?"

"Because I think she'll feel better if there's someone here who understands her. I might not be able to understand everything she says, but I'm willing to bet it's probably better than anyone else on the floor is able to do."

Lydia nodded. "I guess it's lucky for us you're Polish."

Cate felt Christian's eyes on her as she agreed, trying her best to sound offhand about it. "I guess so."

She knew he was thinking about the line she'd said the other day to him, about having to endure Polish jokes for no reason. She supposed, since she'd been raised Polish, that did give her some claim to it, even if she really wasn't.

"Kay-ate."

She looked toward the girl and crossed back to her bed. She asked her if she needed something.

Christian watched as a warm expression came over Cate's face. Saw her squeeze the girl's hand and nod. He couldn't hold back his question. "What?"

"She just asked me to find her sister for her."

There was sympathy in his eyes as he looked at the small girl. He felt the same kind of anger he imagined his sister-in-law was grappling with. People who took advantage of such innocence should be destroyed. Painfully. He supposed that feeling was at odds with the oath he'd taken, but given a chance at the man who had done this, he knew which way he'd lean.

He looked at Cate. "Tall order."

Cate nodded, then amended, "Maybe not so tall."

"How do you mean?" Lydia wanted to know.

"She gave me something to work with just now."

Lydia appeared as if she was ready to jump out of her skin as she literally grabbed Cate's arm and tugged on it. "What? What did she just tell you?"

Her eyes swept over Lydia and Christian. "The name of the man who originally approached her. She just remembered it."

Lydia fisted both hands and jerked them down in a victory sign. "Yes, Virginia," she cried, "there is a Santa Claus."

Chapter 30

Several hours later, when he was finished with his morning patients, Christian went to the intensive care unit to see how Katya was coming along. Easing open the door, he found that Cate was sitting right where he'd left her. Beside the bed and holding the girl's hand.

Somehow, it didn't surprise him to find her there. He was beginning to realize that there were a great many qualities that he and this woman shared. Seeing something through was one of them. Quiet compassion was another.

After crossing to the bed, he picked up the chart that hung at the foot of the bed and flipped it open to the last entry.

"How's she doing?" he asked her mildly.

Cate had seen his reflection in the window as he'd

opened the door. Her pulse had accelerated at the same time. Just like a schoolgirl's, she thought. Where was this going to go? She had no answer.

"Better, I think. She's been sleeping most of the time." Cate rotated her shoulders and realized she'd gotten a little stiff. She needed to find herself a gym around here and start working out again. Her body missed a regular schedule. "Fitfully, but I think that's because she's dreaming." She saw him glance quizzically in her direction. "I can see a lot of eye movement going on beneath her lids," she explained. "She doesn't like what she's dreaming."

Getting up, Cate wrapped her hands around her arms, drawing them in close to her. "I can't even begin to imagine what it had to be like for her." A bittersweet expression played across her face as she leaned over Katya and brushed the hair away from the girl's face. "She should be dreaming about her first kiss, not…"

Cate's voice trailed off, ending in a sigh. She hated the fact that Katya had been robbed of that, robbed of being able to enjoy first love the way only the innocent could.

Christian paused to take Katya's pulse, then glanced at the monitor to make sure everything was recorded properly. "Life isn't always fair." Very gently, he placed the girl's hand back down on the covers again. "At least you found her in time."

"Right, focus on the positive."

She realized there was a touch of bitterness in her voice and she struggled to bank it down. He had a point. If she hadn't found her when she did, Katya would be dead. Besides, wasn't that what she always tried to do? Focus on the positive? Why was she balking because he told her the same thing? And why was everything continuing to scramble inside of her like this whenever she looked at him? If anything, Friday night had been about eliminating needs, not increasing them.

"I guess that's all we can do," she added quietly.

Shoving her hands deep into her pockets, Cate watched him for a long moment as he attended to the girl. Common sense said leave well enough alone, but then, she'd never been a great one for common sense. Deciding she had nothing to lose, and maybe even something to gain, she finally asked, "Were the roses from you?"

Christian looked up from the chart and she couldn't tell if he knew what she was talking about or not. Now he had a poker face, she thought. "I received a dozen long-stemmed roses on Saturday. When I got back from the office, they were on my doorstep. No card, except for the one the florist always includes, telling you how to care for the flowers." A half smile played on her lips. "I suppose I could have the box dusted for fingerprints, but that won't help if they were delivered by messenger."

His eyes met hers. Damn, but she couldn't tell what he was thinking. So much for that bit about eyes being the windows to the soul. Unless his soul had moved.

"They were from me."

"Why?"

He never flinched. "Why not?"

She wasn't about to back away. "Answer my question first."

He gave a half shrug, returning the chart back to the hook at the foot of the bed again. "It seemed like the thing to do."

Maybe to him, but not to her. Not like that. "Without a card? I didn't know if you were saying last night was great, or last night was a mistake, here's a consolation prize. Nice knowing you."

He found that there was something immensely appealing about her when she began to get worked up. "Which did you want it to be?"

She blew out a breath, curbing her exasperation. "God, you should work for the bureau. You bob and weave with the best of them."

He returned the compliment with an easy smile that found its way straight to her gut. She realized that her pulse hadn't leveled off yet. On the contrary, it seemed to be elevating. No two ways about it, the man was bad for her. Bad for her concentration.

"So do you."

Okay, so he was putting her on the spot, asking for her answer. Couldn't say she hadn't asked for this. Cate took a chance. "I guess I would have liked for it to be the former—" And then, afraid he might misunderstand—not completely sure she understood it all herself—she quickly added, "With no strings."

He played the moment out a little longer, just to see her reaction. "And if it's the latter?"

She raised her chin, her eyes narrowing just a touch. "Then I would have expected you to be man enough to tell me face-to-face, not hope I'd put two and two together and somehow get the message."

There was one more option. The one he'd been toying with originally. Because the one worried him and the other, well, he found himself not really wanting the other. "Maybe when I sent them, I wasn't sure which it was."

Past tense. He was using past tense. Did that mean he knew his mind now? Knew how he wanted to proceed? Damn it, why couldn't her pulse stop racing like this? "And now?"

He turned his back to the patient, for now blocking out everything in the room except for the woman he was talking to. The woman he'd made love with. The woman who had stirred things up inside of him to the point that he wasn't sure if he could find his way safely back again.

Or even wanted to.

"And now we take it one step at a time." He watched her face as he told her, "I do know I want to see you again. Whether that's wise—"

"Why does it have to be wise?" Cate countered. She was not only asking him, but herself as well. She was playing devil's advocate out loud. "Why can't it just be?" The more she spoke, the more she knew that this was what she believed, what she wanted. "One step at a time, one moment at a time. If there's anything I've learned in these past few years, it's that the moment is all we have. Because the next moment could bring huge changes you wouldn't believe."

He thought of Alma. How one moment he was a married man with a baby, the next, he was a widower grieving over the deaths of his wife and daughter.

"I'd believe," he said softly.

She could tell he had a story. A story he wasn't ready

to tell. Lydia had merely hinted at it, saying that her brother-in-law was a widower. She supposed she could try getting more information out of Lydia, but it wouldn't really count unless it came from him. Because if he confided in her, they would be establishing a basis of trust. A beachhead from which to build. He had to trust her enough to share his pain with her. And he didn't yet.

She thrived on challenge. "Someday you're going to have to tell me about that." And then she realized how that might have sounded. "Assuming there is a someday."

"Someday," Christian repeated, for the moment leaving it at that.

Lydia looked around at the people sitting at the table. Except for her mother, everyone she considered part of her family was here. And she had something to tell them.

It burned on her tongue all through dinner. With every second that went by, she was having a harder and harder time containing her excitement. She always felt this way when things were finally taking on a positive shape.

And things were very positive right now.

The name Katya had said she'd overheard one of the other men use turned out to belong to someone presently working at the American embassy in the Ukraine. The hunt to bring down what amounted to a white-slavery prostitution ring had taken on international proportions that extended far up the food chain. It had taken some doing on her part, but after much haggling and opposition, A.D. Sullivan had finally agreed to send her to the Ukraine. Once there, she was going to bring back Brad Baker, a twenty-six-year veteran of the diplomatic corps with a spotless record and a nondescript life.

"I guess he got tired of just being the reliable man in the shadows. Greed got the better of him," Lydia said to the others, still refraining from saying that she was going after him.

"The man should be boiled in oil," Juanita commented in disgust as she leaned back in her chair. She sat at the head of the table, surrounded by Lukas, Lydia and John on one side and Henry, Christian and Cate on the other.

It took effort on her part not to stare at the new face at her table. When she'd extended the thinly veiled mandate for her sons to come for dinner the following evening, declaring that it had been a while since they had both graced her table at the same time, she of course had meant that Lydia was to come, too. It hadn't crossed her mind that Christian would bring anyone with him. He never did.

So when he walked through the door with the young blonde behind him, she'd thought at first that it was Lydia. She had to admit that her daughter-in-law's people did all look alike to her. But she quickly realized that this wasn't her daughter-in-law, but someone new.

Someone who had come with Christian.

Lydia made the introductions, saying the woman, Cate Kowalski, was her partner, and for a moment, Juanita thought she'd made a mistake and a wave of disappointment had followed. Ever since Alma's suicide, she'd been waiting for Christian to come around.

But the moment she saw the way her younger son looked at the newcomer when he thought no one else saw, she knew she hadn't made a mistake after all. It seemed that perhaps he was finally on his way. Her sharp eyes saw that there was more going on here than anyone wanted to say. Perhaps even more than either one of them was aware of.

During the course of the dinner, she set about probing the situation with her subtle questions. Somewhere before the meal was over, she decided that she liked this young woman. The more she thought about it, the more certain she was that Cate was the girl she'd dreamed about. The blond woman who would come to change her son's life. The dreams she remembered were rarely wrong.

Lukas knew how much this case meant to his wife. He nodded as she paused in her narrative. "Looks like it might finally be coming to a conclusion."

Lydia took a breath, her eyes on Lukas's face. This was what she'd been leading up to. "It definitely will be on that track as soon as I bring the bastard back in chains."

Lukas put down the glass he was raising to his lips. "You?" He frowned at the thought of her having to fly overseas. "Can't they send anyone else?"

"I don't want them to send anyone else," Lydia protested a little too heatedly. "This is my case, this is what I've been working toward." She glanced toward her mother-in-law, confident that Juanita would understand. The strong-willed woman thought in terms of right and wrong, not male and female. Besides, the Navajo were a matriarchal society, which made Juanita an ally. "After all the time and legwork I've put into the case, I need this sense of closure. I need to bring down whoever's responsible. I have to be the one who goes."

"No, you don't," Christian said firmly. "You know you can't go."

All eyes at the table looked toward him.

Henry shifted in his armchair. "Don't you think you're a little out of line, Chris?" he asked mildly. "If Luke isn't against Lydia flying over there…"

Christian saw the warning look that came into Lydia's eyes. She was silently pleading with him. And he was torn. Torn between his oath as a doctor and his loyalty to his brother. Not to mention what he felt as a member of the family. To let her go, to have her risk not just her life but the life of the child she was carrying, he didn't know if he could live with himself if anything happened to either one of them because of his silence.

There was a time when rules had to be bent and consciences followed, even if that was not the most popular way to go. He looked at his brother first before turning toward his uncle. He did his best to shut out Lydia, knowing that to look at her would only cause him to falter.

And he had to say this.

"That's because Lukas doesn't know."

Chapter 31

"Know what?" Lukas demanded, looking from his brother to his wife. He had absolutely no idea what to think, what could possibly be going on between his brother and Lydia, or what they had been keeping from him.

The others were silent, waiting.

Christian still wanted to leave the telling up to Lydia. News like this should come from a man's wife, not his brother. He hated the position he was in. "Don't you think it's about time you told him?"

"Told me what?" Lukas demanded again. He was on his feet now, his attention focused on his brother. "What the hell is going on here, Christian?"

Christian rose to his feet as well, not wanting to be at a disadvantage. It wasn't all that many years ago that they'd faced each other over raised fists in the boxing ring that Henry oversaw. Then it had been a healthy way to get rid of aggression. If this came to blows now, the results might not be so healthy.

She'd never wanted it to come to this. And she'd never dreamed that she'd get Christian in trouble. Lydia got in between the two men. Facing her husband, she cried, "That I'm pregnant."

The news, something that ordinarily he would have greeted with bottomless joy, stunned him now. Lukas stared at her. "How long have you known?"

"Not long." Her voice was a great deal quieter than it had been a moment ago. "A month maybe."

"And you?" Lukas turned to his brother, no less amazed. "You knew, too?"

He knew that tone, Christian thought. It was the calm before the storm. "Yes."

An angry cloud descended over Lukas's features. "And you didn't tell me?"

Juanita stood, afraid of where this could lead. Afraid of words that wouldn't be able to be taken back.

"Calm down," she ordered both her sons. "I won't have shouting in my home."

"Too late," Henry commented more to himself than to her. Juanita shot him a dark look before turning back to Lukas and Christian.

"This can be worked out," she began. Lukas was slow to anger these days, but when he got mad, it was a fierce sight to see. And the path back was not always an easy one. "We're family."

Lukas snorted at the words. "Well, maybe someone should have told *him* that." He jerked a thumb at his brother.

Because he could easily place himself in Lukas's shoes, Christian kept his own temper and tried to explain what had happened. "Lydia came to me as a patient, Lukas. She asked me not to tell you. You know I can't violate a trust."

Lukas clenched his hands at his sides to keep from striking out. He didn't know who he was angrier at, his brother or his wife.

"What about the trust between us?" he asked his brother. Thoroughly disgusted, he threw down his napkin and strode toward the door.

Anxiety telegraphed through Lydia as she saw him opening the door. Walking out on her. "Where are you going?"

"Back to where things make sense to me." He grabbed his jacket off the coatrack and didn't bother to put it on. "Bedford."

The slamming door punctuated his statement.

Lydia raced after him, knowing they couldn't just leave it this way. They had never, ever had an argument, much less one of this proportion. She knew she couldn't just wait for him to cool off. She had to make him understand why she did what she did, and why she'd made Christian promise not to tell him first.

"I'll make him see it wasn't your fault," she promised Christian, then looked at Juanita just before she left. "I'm sorry. I'll make it up to you."

"Don't worry about me, worry about Lukas," Juanita advised.

Without another word, Lydia hurried after her husband, the door closing behind her. The next moment, they heard the sound of a car starting up.

Well, that had gone less than well, Christian thought in disgust. He glanced toward Cate. "That was our ride."

His mother gave him one of her looks, the kind that seemed to penetrate clear down to the bone. He congratulated himself for not flinching. "What's the matter with you? You know better than to come between a man and his wife," his mother said.

He made no excuses, sticking only to the facts. "I urged her to tell him, but my hands were tied."

Juanita shook her head. There was a place for professional ethics, but this was about family and family always came first, no matter what. "There's always wiggle room."

It was an argument not to be won, especially since his heart wasn't entirely in it. So rather than try to back up his position, Christian merely nodded and then looked at Cate. "I'd better get you back."

She knew he thought she felt uncomfortable, but in an odd way, she wasn't. She was witnessing the natural fallout between family members who cared about one another. It made her feel extremely nostalgic and wistful, but not uncomfortable.

"How?" she asked. "The car just left."

"I can take you," Henry volunteered. He was already moving his chair back. The legs scraped against the wooden floor. "Truck's not much to look at," he admitted, referring to his '89 pickup, "but it can get you from here to there."

"That's all we need, Uncle Henry," Christian told him. After walking over to the coatrack, he got Cate's coat off the peg, then took his jacket. He slipped it on quickly and held out Cate's for her.

She slid it on, very aware of his hands as they guided the jacket onto her shoulders.

"Go after your brother," Juanita urged him. "Make peace." The expression in her eyes was somber. "You owe me that."

And he'd have no peace of his own until he achieved a truce, Christian thought. His mother would see to it. Like the dutiful son he was, he nodded and then kissed her cheek.

Cate queued up to take her turn. "It was a very nice dinner." About to shake the woman's hand, she was surprised and pleased when Juanita embraced her instead.

"Up to the entertainment portion of the evening," John quipped, standing behind his adoptive mother.

Juanita gave him the same kind of warning glance she'd given Christian. It was obvious to Cate that the woman made no differentiation between the sons who were part of her flesh and the one she'd chosen to take to her heart.

"It'll be better next time," Juanita told her at the door just before closing it.

The woman's words replayed themselves in Cate's head as they followed Henry to the truck. She eyed at Christian. "Did I just get invited back?"

Before Christian could reply, Henry looked at her over his shoulder. His many wrinkles melded into one another, arranging themselves around the smile that formed on his lips. "Sure sounded like that to me."

All in all, Cate thought, it had been one strange day. When she'd gotten up this morning, she never thought she'd be invited to meet Christian's mother. Despite their last conversation in the hospital, she hadn't even been sure that she would ever see Christian outside the hospital again.

Even when he'd said that the invitation came at Lydia's suggestion, it hadn't diminished the magnitude of the gesture. Christian didn't strike her as a man who did anything he didn't want to.

She watched him now as they drove away from John Wayne Airport, where they'd landed not half an hour ago. "So that was what was going on between you and Lydia."

At a light, Christian glanced in Cate's direction. It was the first thing she'd actually said to him since they'd left his mother's house. Henry had brought them to the small airstrip where he and Cate, Lydia and Lukas all boarded the same commuter plane back to Southern California. The silence before the engines started up had almost been deafening. But Christian had known better than to talk. Lukas had looked far too angry to approach, so they had all kept their distance as well as their peace.

The rattle of the plane was the only sound that was heard the entire return flight.

Cate didn't envy Lydia right now. Lukas had every right to be angry. This was his baby as well as hers. A pregnancy wasn't the kind of thing you kept from the man you loved, no matter what the job called for.

"What do you mean?" Christian asked, a wary edge to his voice.

"She'd told you about the pregnancy and didn't want you saying anything to Lukas."

"Yes, why?" The wary tone remained.

She shrugged. "There were times when the two of you would exchange looks and I thought that maybe…"

"That maybe what?" He spared her one glance before turning back to the road. She could see that he didn't care for what she'd left unspoken. That made two of them. Which was why she realized she was so relieved to find out that this was about keeping a pregnancy secret rather than an affair.

"That I was bedding my brother's wife?" Even saying it left a bad taste in his mouth. "Is that what you think of me?"

"I wasn't sure what to think," she told him honestly. After all, she hadn't known him all that long. And yet there was a part of her that felt she had known him a long time. There were things about him that just jibed with her soul. Timeless. "But that was a pretty tough situation she put you in."

"She had her reasons."

And her reasons had put him in hot water with his brother. A smile curved her mouth as she regarded him. "You're pretty loyal, aren't you?"

He slowed down at the next light. It had turned yellow, then quickly went to red. He stopped just in time. "Family is all there is."

"When you have one."

"You had one, Cate," he reminded her, stepping on the accelerator again. "Seems to me they loved you a great deal." Her father had gone to great lengths to keep her from finding out that she was adopted because he hadn't wanted to risk losing her. That spelled love in his book. "Sometimes love makes you do stupid things because you're afraid of losing that love."

There was something in his voice that caught her attention. "You speak from experience?"

"Maybe." But it wasn't something he was about to go into with her. Not yet, perhaps not ever. There had to be more between them before then. He slanted a look toward her. "Would you like to come over?"

She knew what he was asking. Knew all along, no matter how she tried to tell herself otherwise, what her answer would be.

Because she'd been hoping for this from the moment he'd asked her to fly to the reservation with him.

"Yes."

The house was too quiet.

The silence was driving Lydia crazy. Lukas hadn't said a single word to her since they'd left his mother's house, no matter how hard she'd tried to get him to talk.

As he turned toward the staircase, she all but threw herself in front of him, blocking his path. When Lukas began to turn away, she grabbed his wrist and forced him to face her.

"Talk to me, Luke," she half pleaded, half demanded. "I can't take this silent treatment much longer."

That was when he finally looked at her. She'd never seen his eyes look like thunder before. "Talk to you? Why should I talk to you? You wouldn't talk to me."

"What are you talking about? I always talk to you—"

"Not about the baby," he shot back.

She blew out a shaky breath. "Please understand. I just needed a little more time."

It didn't make sense to him. "Why, Lyd? Why did you need more time? And how could you keep this from me? I'm your husband. It's my baby, too. I had a right to know, a right to enjoy it from the very first minute you were sure."

She closed her eyes, trying to hold back tears that were suddenly pressing so hard against her lids. It was a sign of weakness. She didn't want to cry.

She did her best to make him understand. "Because if I told you, you'd have the same objections that Christian had tonight. You wouldn't want me to go to the Ukraine. You wouldn't want me to follow this case through."

He set his jaw hard, staring at her as if he'd never seen her before. And maybe, in a way, he hadn't, he thought sadly. Maybe he'd been blind before. He never put her second. But she had done that to him. "And is the case more important than us?"

"No, but—" Lydia sighed, then tried another approach. "I need to tell you about Susan and then maybe you'll understand why I did what I did."

He was angry and he wanted to remain angry. But he loved her, really loved her, and if there was something she could say to subdue the anger, the pure hurt he now felt inside, he was willing to hear her out.

"All right," he said, sitting down on the bottom step, "tell me about Susan."

She sat down beside him and told him about her cousin. Told him about the promise she'd made to herself when this case began to evolve the way it did. She left out nothing.

"I can't help it, this case means a great deal to me. And these girls are so young, Lukas. You should see

Katya—" Tears rose in her eyes again. "They need someone to fight for them. They have no one."

"No, not no one," he told her quietly. With his thumb, he brushed away the tears that had leaked down her cheeks. "They have you."

She swallowed, afraid that she'd somehow misunderstood. "Then it's all right with you?"

"No," he told her honestly, "it's not all right with me." If he had his way, he'd keep her beside him, under lock and key. But then she wouldn't be the woman he'd fallen in love with. She wouldn't be Lydia. "But you need to do what you need to do." He framed her face in his hands, worried already. "Just promise me, you won't take any undue risks."

She raised her hand. "I promise. Only 'due ones.'" God, but she loved this man. "I'll only be gone a few days. Just long enough to bring Baker in. Sullivan's already working on getting the State Department to fire Baker if this checks out." And then her smile softened. "You're wonderful, Lukas."

"Yeah, yeah." The import of the earlier discovery was just now sinking in. Extreme pleasure washed over him. He could hardly believe it. "So, pregnant, huh?"

She grinned. "Yup."

He rose to his feet, taking her hand in his. "Would you like to celebrate?"

"With all my heart." She threaded her arms around his neck as he lifted her up into his arms. "I like it a lot better when we agree." She buried her face in his neck.

He kissed her hair softly, then began to go up the stairs. "Yeah, me, too."

Chapter 32

This time, there was no pretense, no need to make excuses to Christian or to herself as to why she was in his apartment or what the rest of the evening would hold. She felt as if it had been building up to this from the moment he'd come to pick her up for the unexpected trip to meet his family.

"Why did you bring me there?" As he shut the door behind her, she asked him the question that had been hovering in her mind ever since he'd called earlier to see if she was interested in going. She hadn't wanted to ask him before for fear that the invitation would be withdrawn. "To your mother's house," she added when he made no response.

"It's mine, too," he told her quietly. He felt as if his gut was tightening into a knot, just looking at her. There was no point in pretending. He wanted her. More now than the first time. Because then there'd been curiosity involved. Now there was only knowledge. And desire. "Mine and Lukas's, or so Mom says. Just because we've moved here doesn't mean that's still not home."

Why did he refrain from telling her things? Was he afraid they'd become too close if he did? She pushed, but only a little, leaving him space. "That still doesn't answer the question."

"No," he agreed. He adjusted the lights, turning them lower. "It doesn't." Christian turned to face her, his eyes drawing her in. "Does every question have to have an answer?"

A stubborn glint came into her eyes at the same time her mouth curved. He could feel her smile moving him. "I'd like it to. Unless the conversation's about Einstein's theory of relativity," she said flippantly, "in which case—"

"In which case," Christian pronounced, slipping her coat off her shoulders and down her arms as he pressed a soft, fleeting kiss to the side of her neck, "you talk too much."

"It only seems that way because you're so quiet." Freed of her coat, she turned around to face him. Her limbs already felt heavy, as if she were drugged while, in contrast, her pulse raced wildly. Anticipating. Her eyes searched his face, looking for a clue, for a sign. "What are you thinking about?"

Only a hint of humor entered his eyes. "That you talk too much."

"What else?" she prodded, her breath whispering along his face.

He could feel his body warming. Yearning. "That I want to make love with you. That I've wanted to all evening." His breathing grew shorter as his desire lengthened. "That I'm sinking into quicksand when I promised myself never to do it again."

Cate was positive her heart had just leaped up into her throat. But if that was true, how could she still speak?

"It's not quicksand," she told him. Her eyes held his for a long moment, even as she felt his hands beginning to roam over her, probing, touching, causing her pulse to feel as if it was in danger of breaking the sound barrier. "I won't let you go under."

The promise almost made him smile. "It could already be too late."

Even as he said it, he thought that it was. Because there were things happening inside of him, feelings being stirred, feelings that had very little to do with sex and everything to do with the coming together and sealing of two souls.

Cate leaned into him. "Pessimist," she teased, her lips grazing his just lightly enough to arouse him. She could feel his need pressing against her. Felt her own mounting even before her skirt and blouse had left her body and found the floor.

Her heart hammered against his fingertips as he removed her bra. He filed his hands with her breasts, sealed his mouth to hers. Their breaths and desires mingled, merged.

Feeling shaky, needing to anchor herself to something before she found herself sinking to the floor, she wrapped her fingertips around his biceps. They felt like rocks. She held on to them as best she could while she pressed her mouth against his for all she was worth. Drinking in the life-sustaining passion she found there.

Her head spun. Her fingers tightened on his arms. A fire broke loose in her belly, feeding the craving that was taking hold of her.

She found herself being moved back. Step by step. Christian kept moving forward, his mouth assaulting hers, his hands traveling up and down her body, reducing everything he touched to a consistency of warm Jell-O until he had her back flat against the wall with no room for escape.

As if she wanted it.

The wall felt cool against her naked back. His body felt hot against the rest of her.

And all the while, she was aware of an eagerness inside of her, an eagerness that only kept building, doubling, until she felt it would burst out of her pores.

Her head spinning almost dangerously now, Cate worked his clothing loose, taking buttons out of their holes, tugging at zippers and buckles, until she had finally gotten rid of the barriers of material that kept him from her.

She ran her hands over him as if she'd never touched a man before, never felt that wild surge through her veins that only intimacy brought.

His skin was hot as it moved against hers and she felt her own flesh sizzle. She could swear that it felt even hotter on the inside than it did to the touch. Anticipation was responsible for that. Anticipation at what was to come.

At least, she thought she anticipated it. And yet,

when it began, she found that she was unprepared for the onslaught that followed. Unprepared for the siege that he lay to her body.

Christian pushed her against his sofa, easing her fall with his arm tucked under her.

His mouth roamed over her face, her neck, her breasts, claiming each place he passed, making it his own. Making her his own.

She twisted and turned against him, eager to have him anoint her everywhere. Eager to have the flames grow even higher as his lips and tongue teased, suckled, moistening that which was already moist.

And then, somewhere amid the haze that had claimed her brain, she realized that she was being only the recipient, not the instigator. It went against everything she had ever believed herself to be. Summoning energy from some far-off recessed place, she pulled herself together, determined to return the favor. Or the exquisite torture.

He was unprepared for it.

She could tell the moment she began. The look in his eyes gave him away. Seeing it gave her a sense of power as well as delight. Fortified, she forged a trail along his torso with her hands, with her mouth, and delighted in the response she felt. When he moaned, she thought she was going to explode.

Unable to hold back any further, she splayed her body over his, positioning herself so that his entry would be almost effortless.

Damn but she was more than a handful, he thought. More than he had bargained for. The thought sent rays of sunshine through him, giving light to the dark.

His eyes on hers, filled with desire and wonder, Christian thrust himself into her.

The climax that came, seizing them both in its grip, was more intense than anything they'd experienced with each other so far. It absorbed more of them than it had before. And brought with it a sense of overwhelming awe.

He could feel her heart slamming against his as she spiraled up with him, reaching.

Reaching.

And then they were floating down again. And paradise was a memory.

His arms closed more tightly around her during the descent than the ascent. Because before it had been due to passion, but now it was because of the tenderness that was washing over him. He realized that he liked holding her like this, liked feeling their hearts linked.

The strings he claimed were not there, the strings he wanted to resist more than anything in this world, tightened around him.

He didn't care.

Maybe later he would, when energy returned. bringing with it baggage filled with remorse and other useless emotions. But not yet. Not yet.

Cate raised her head, a slightly dazed, bemused expression on her face. She rested her head on the hand she had pressed against his chest. Her eyes were on his.

"So, you think the Angels have a chance at the pennant next season?"

He didn't know about the Angels, but he was beginning to wonder if he did. With a laugh, he cupped the back of her head with his hand and caught her mouth with his own. Her lips still tasted sweet, even blurred with the imprint of his.

He grinned at her when it was over. "I don't really follow baseball."

"Too bad." Did she seem as breathless as she felt? To her ear, she sounded like an unseasoned runner who had just attempted a five-mile run. "Everyone should have a sport to call their own."

One side of his mouth rose in a half smile. "This yours?"

He saw her eyes darken. Had he insulted her? He hadn't meant it that way.

"I told you," she said, "I don't do this kind of thing on a regular basis."

"I didn't mean to insinuate that." And then he paused before asking, "Why me?"

For a moment, she only looked at him. And then a smile came to her lips. He thought it was like the sun coming out from behind a cloud. "Now who's asking questions?"

"Why me?" he repeated, needing to know.

Chemistry, attraction, they were all good words, but that's all they were. Words. And there was something more at play here.

"I don't know," she told him honestly. "Maybe because something in your soul talked to mine."

She'd said the wrong thing. Or maybe the right thing, she amended, because the look in his eyes changed instantly. He released her and fell back against the sofa. She didn't know whether to curl up beside him, or get up and get dressed.

The question answered itself as she felt his arm

close around her. Drawing her to him, to his warmth. "I was married once."

"I know." Her words were slow, measured, as if she was feeling her way around. "Lydia told me."

He tucked his other hand under his head, looking at the ceiling. Looking at the past. "What else did Lydia tell you?"

"Nothing. She said it was your story to tell."

"No," he answered quietly. "It was Alma's."

She waited a beat before asking. "Was that your wife's name?"

"Yes." He glanced at her beside him. "It means soul."

She nodded, an almost shy smile gracing her lips. "I know. I took Spanish in high school."

He looked back up toward the ceiling again, not seeing it.

"I thought she took mine when she died." And then, abruptly, he rose up on his elbow and looked down at Cate. He felt as if he was standing on the very edge of a precipice, staring into the abyss. Wondering if he was going to fall. "Alma killed herself. And she killed our daughter."

Shock waves resonated through her. For a second, Cate forgot to breathe.

Chapter 33

The horror of what he must have had to endure slammed into her with the force of a Mack truck. Cate sat up and stared at him in disbelief.

"Oh, God, Christian, I am so sorry. What happened?" The question rose to her lips before she could stop it. She had no right to pry into his pain, even if she hoped to ease it. She was quick to try to erase her words. "No, wait. You don't have to tell me if you don't want to."

He realized that he wanted to tell her, to let her into the dark part of his life that he normally didn't share. He didn't explore why. Alma's death wasn't something that he talked about. Not with someone outside his own family. He doubted if any of the people he worked with at Blair Memorial knew very much about his past, other than his record as a physician. Certainly not this.

He took a deep breath and released it.

"I'd known Alma all of my life. She was beautiful, bright, but she had these demons. ..." His voice trailed off for a moment and Cate thought he'd decided against saying anything further. But then he continued. "Demons she couldn't conquer and I couldn't help her with."

Christian turned his face toward her, drawing her closer. "Alma's father abused her for years, starting when she was a child. In every way possible." He saw horror wash over Cate's face and knew she understood. "She didn't tell anyone until we were teenagers. When I found out, I told her father I'd kill him if he ever touched her again, but I think it was Uncle Henry who was the reason why he disappeared." A slight smile curved his mouth. "Uncle Henry had 'a few words' with Alma's father." That was the way the old man had put it, but Christian was certain that fists had been involved. "Henry was a lot more formidable than I was back then.

"After that, my mother took Alma in, tried to make things right for her. But Alma was like a sparrow with a broken wing that could never heal." The years came rushing back to him. It was hard trying not to react. They'd left their mark on him. "She was afraid her father would come back, afraid to be left alone. She begged me to take her with me when I went away to medical school." He could still hear her voice, pleading with him. "And I loved her, so I took her with me."

He took another breath, then blew it out, as if fortifying himself against the rest. "We got married before I graduated. Had Dana almost immediately." His voice softened when he mentioned his daughter. Sometimes, saying her name was almost too hard for him to bear. Her little life had been snuffed out almost before it had begun.

"I honestly thought that would do it for Alma, that it would make her put her past behind her. For a while, it did. She stopped drinking, tried to be a good mother to our daughter." He'd been so hopeful back then. Hopeful and happy, convinced everything would turn out well. "And then she started slipping back." He set his mouth grimly, putting the blame where he felt it belonged. On his shoulders. "I was too busy to see it, but things just kept getting darker and darker for her.

"There wasn't any one thing I could even look back on and point to that sent her over the edge. Maybe it was everything. But I thought things were good. I'd just been accepted by Blair Memorial, we were making plans…" He paused, trying to pull himself together. Trying not to let the past take him apart.

"That last weekend, I went back to the reservation to help out at the clinic. She insisted that she and Dana come with me because she didn't want to stay behind in our house." A bittersweet smile played on his lips as he thought of the place he had long since sold. "I bought her that house to make her happy. Her first real house."

But it hadn't made Alma happy. And he would never know what would have. Pain began to crowd his chest, chasing away the air as he went on. But he refused to stop until all the words were out.

"I went to the clinic, figured I'd be there most of the day. After a while, Alma waited until everyone was gone, then she left with the baby. When she didn't come back, no one thought anything of it at first. Everyone just assumed Alma was visiting someone on the reservation, showing off the baby."

His throat tightened, making it hard to talk. He pressed on, his whispered words hollow. "And then some of my mother's neighbors came. They said that Alma had walked out onto the tracks just as the train was coming. She had Dana in her arms. The engineer saw them, but there was no way he could stop in time. He almost derailed the train trying."

Christian had to pause to work his way past the years that had gathered in his throat, all but cutting off his air supply.

Beside him, Cate lay perfectly still, listening. Horrified.

"I kept thinking that if only I had seen it coming, if I hadn't been so wrapped up in my own world, in becoming a doctor…"

Cate thought her heart was going to break. Reaching out, she brushed away the single tear that had managed to break free and had slid down along the side of his face. She felt as if she was looking into the mirror of her own pain when she had lost Gabe.

"It's not your fault." She said it so fiercely, he looked at her. "Just like Gabe getting killed in the second tower wasn't mine." She said the question that came into his eyes. "I was supposed to take some time off and go with him when he was sent to New York for that meeting. We both worked for the bureau together," she explained. "Gabe wanted to make a holiday of it, but at the last minute, I changed my mind and decided to finish up some work. I told him we could go to a bed-and-breakfast inn the following weekend instead."

She moved her shoulders in a vague shrug. "The following weekend never came." Her eyes met his. "For the next full year, I just wanted to die. Couldn't understand why I was still alive and he wasn't." The question had haunted her, waking and sleeping, for all that time. "I wouldn't let anyone comfort me, but eventually I realized that some things just happen and there's nothing we can do about them."

Without a word, Christian turned his body toward hers and drew her into his arms. Still silent, he sought the comfort he saw in her eyes. Sought to give her comfort for the pain she'd felt as well.

This time, the lovemaking was more tender, less frantic though no less intense in its effect. And somewhere in the night, two broken souls came together to form one new whole one.

"You're not going?"

Cate stared at Lydia incredulously the following Monday morning. It was the first day back into her own world. The weekend had been spent with Christian in his. More specifically, in his apartment, where she wore his shirts when she bothered to wear anything at all, cooked for him and tried to pretend that the outside world, both past and present, didn't exist. That there was nothing beyond the moment. And him.

But Monday came, as it was wont to do, with Monday's responsibilities, dragging the world in its wake like some giant, off-kilter pull toy. She'd gone to her apartment in the wee hours of the morning for a change of clothes and a shift of attitude. She'd succeeded in one out of two.

Being with Christian like that, making love when the spirit moved them, enjoying just sharing the same space, the same air, had made her fiercely yearn for life again the way it could have been. The way she'd once planned for it to be.

It was hard now to pretend that there were no strings and that she was happy about that. Because she desperately wanted those strings.

But nothing could be resolved now and so she placed her desires on hold as she walked into the room she shared with the others on the task force.

The first words out of Cate's mouth had knocked her for a loop, given Friday's scene in Juanita's house— not to mention what she knew to be Lydia's frame of mind.

Maybe she'd heard wrong.

But Lydia looked completely serious when she delivered her news. Cate realized she didn't look upset.

"I decided that for once everyone else was right," Lydia told her. "I was allowing this case to consume me. To turn me into an obsessed person. And this case shouldn't be about obsession." She moved her shoulders beneath her fawn-colored jacket in a vague gesture of surrender. "Whether I bring the case to a close or you do doesn't matter. What matters is that it *is* brought to a close." A very maternal smile found its way to her lips as Lydia splayed her hand over her still very flat belly and the baby she knew was there. "I owe something to the life I'm carrying, too." She dropped her hand to her side with a resigned sigh. "Susan would understand."

But Cate had her hand up like a police officer halting the flow of oncoming traffic. "Back up." She stared at Lydia, sure she wasn't hearing correctly. "Me?"

Lydia nodded. "I talked it over with Sullivan. He was reluctant at first, but I got him to agree to it. He's very impressed with you." If he was, Cate thought, it was all Lydia's doing. "Besides, you know Slavic languages."

"I know Polish," Cate was quick to correct. "That hardly qualifies me to travel through the Ukraine."

Lydia's eyebrows drew together in a puzzled expression. "Then you'd rather pass?"

"Hell, no." If Lydia wasn't going, then she wanted to. Desperately. This was true hands-on field work in its purest sense. She would actually see the results of what they were doing here, behind the scenes. "I just want you to know my limitations. Of course I won't pass."

There was nothing else she would have wanted more than to bring one of the key men in this filthy enterprise down and to justice. She didn't fool herself into thinking that arresting Baker would be the end of it, but it might be the beginning of the end for this particular monster.

"The hard part," she confided to Lydia, "will be to keep Baker unbruised during the trip home." She realized that she might be jumping to conclusions. "I take it that your investigation didn't clear Baker."

Again Lydia shook her head. "It nailed him. Made him the right man in the right place." She told her about the final nail in the coffin. "I showed an array of photographs to Katya yesterday. She picked him out of the crowd without any hesitation. He's our man, all right."

"Now we just have to get him stuffed and mounted." Since there was this kind of evidence against Baker, she knew the State Department would be quick to distance itself from the man. So his butt belonged to the bureau. "When do I leave?"

Now that it had been finally put in motion, the ball was rolling fast. "As soon as you can get your passport updated and throw some clothes into a suitcase."

"I'm already gone." She was halfway toward the door before she paused to look over her shoulder at Lydia. "Does Lukas know you're passing on this?"

"Yes." This had been decided between them first, after a very long, satisfying night. She'd decided that maybe she'd allowed her work to take precedence over what really mattered in her life. Sullivan hadn't been pleased at first at the change in plans, but he had accepted her reasons once he knew them. And now she was faced with a desk job for the next eight months. But she had survived worse. And the grin on her husband's face had made it all worth it. "And he's very relieved."

"I just bet he is."

Cate lost no time in getting home.

On her way back to the office, Cate decided that no one's nose would be out of joint if she took a small detour and stopped by the hospital first.

Her intention was to check on Katya, who was being released soon.

And to see Christian.

She looked for Christian first. After a couple of inquiries, she tracked him down to his office, where he was still seeing patients.

The nurse at the reception desk was not the same woman she'd met previously. This one appeared to be efficiency personified and was not about to interrupt "the doctor" while he was in with a patient unless she was about to go into labor and give birth to triplets right in the waiting room in the next five minutes.

There was a hint of a British accent as the nurse told her, "If you just leave your card, I'll be sure the doctor gets it."

"No, I—"

And then Cate abruptly stopped. Maybe it was better this way, she thought. The weekend had been wonderful, but it was just two days out of a lifetime. Maybe she was making more out of the situation than it warranted. Than Christian would have wanted her to.

She needed to put things in perspective.

The problem was, things were moving so fast, it was hard to see everything in its proper light.

"All right." Cate took one of her cards out of her pocket and wrote down, "See you when I get back," across the back of it. With a faint smile, she handed the card to the nurse and left the office.

Cate squared her shoulders as she hurried off. *Okay, now focus on what you're supposed to do. Bring back the bad guy.*

She was halfway down the corridor, on her way to the exit, when Christian finally caught up to her. Grabbing her arm, he turned her around to face him.

"What's this?" he wanted to know, holding up the card. "I walked out with my patient and Joyce handed this to me." He looked down at it. "'See you when I get back," he read. "What's that supposed to mean?"

"I wanted to tell you in person, but your nurse is very protective of you. She didn't want to interrupt you and I couldn't wait around. I'm in a hurry."

A flash of impatience flirted across his face before he blocked it. Christian drew her over to the side, out of the path of foot traffic.

"In a hurry to go where?" he asked.

"Lydia changed her mind about going to the Ukraine. I'm taking her place."

All sorts of concerns and thoughts began to pop up throughout his head, crowding his mind. "Just like that?"

She nodded. "That's how it happens sometimes. Long spates of nothing, followed by frantic moments. We have to move fast, before this guy gets word that something's wrong and maybe starts destroying evidence."

He didn't want her leaving, didn't want her going to a foreign country where she would be even more exposed to danger than she already was. But he had no right to tell her not to go. No right at all.

"How long will you be?"

She pressed her lips together and shook her head. "Not sure." Not long, she hoped.

Words rose in his throat. Words of caution. Crazy words, asking her to stay. He struggled to hold them in check, but he could feel himself losing the battle.

Christian frowned. "I know I don't have a right to say anything."

She didn't want him to tell her not to go…and yet…

"I think my letting you know kind of gives you the right."

He said the only thing he knew he could, fairly. "I don't like you going."

"I know." She could feel her heart lighting up. He cared. At least a little. "I won't say it's as safe as crossing the street, but it is necessary and I'll be careful."

His frown deepened. "It's not always a matter of being careful." He didn't know if he liked what was happening. Control over his life was slipping from his fingers again. But he couldn't make himself back away. At least, not yet. "You know, I think that for the first time, I realize what Lukas has to go through with Lydia." He took her hands in both of his. And didn't want to let them go. "Call me when you get there."

"It might be the middle of the night before I get the chance," she warned.

He laughed shortly. "I'm not exactly a stranger to middle-of-the-night calls." He grew serious again. "And even if I were—call."

"Okay. I'll see you." She began to walk away, but then he caught her by the wrist, turning her around again. Her eyes searched his face. "Something else?"

"Yes. Something else."

And before she could ask what, Christian swept her into his arms. Kissing her long and hard.

Chapter 34

Her knees were the first to abandon her.

Forgetting for a moment that they were standing in the middle of a busy hospital hallway, Cate threw her arms around his neck.

She sank deeper into the kiss, wild sensations scrambling her pulse and turning everything upside down. Alarms went off in her head. If she didn't get him to stop kissing her right now, she knew she wasn't going to be responsible for what came next. Exercising supreme control, she ended the kiss.

It took more than a few erratic beats of her heart for her bearings to return. Cate drew in a breath and released it again before she trusted herself to speak coherently and above a squeak. She wished she was home, in bed.

With him.

She did her best to reunite herself with a smattering of composure. "Wow. Will that be waiting for me when I get back?"

He thought about being cagey, about holding back. About his own survival, all of which dictated a flippant retort. But this was about absolute moments. And the thought that she might not return completely decimated all the safeguards he told himself he should be reconstructing. Instead, he smiled warmly at her, remembering their weekend and wanting to feel that there would be others to savor with her. "Count on it."

Cate pressed her lips together, still tasting him. Why wasn't there more time? "Then I'll be sure to come back."

Abruptly turning on her heel, she hurried off to see Katya before she said anything more stupid than that. Or dragged Christian off to a supply closet to jump his very provocative bones.

"What will become of me?" Katya asked the question haltingly, mixing what she knew of Polish together with the brand-new English she had been picking up.

The girl was like a sponge, Cate thought. Despite what had happened to her, she was eager to learn, eager to have a life.

Pressed for time, Cate still answered her, both in Polish and then in English, hoping that somewhere between the two languages, the girl would understand and continue to find hope. With hope anything was possible. Cate knew that firsthand, because somewhere in the barren garden of her own soul, hope had begun to sprout again.

"You'll be taken into the child services system."

The words meant nothing to Katya and Cate didn't know the term for it in Polish.

Katya read into her friend's tone and drew her own conclusions. "Is orphanage?"

Cate heard fear surrounding every syllable. "No, it's much better," she said quickly. Because the situation demanded it, she cut to the wished-for happy ending. "And then, after a while, maybe a nice couple will adopt you."

Katya's brown eyes widened and there was a spark of hope in them. "You? You adopt?"

Cate's heart felt heavy. The word no came automatically to her lips, but she suppressed it. There was no way she could stand being the one to squelch Katya's hopes. So she began to turn the question, the idea, around in her head. She certainly hadn't been thinking, even remotely, of adopting or even of having a child of her own at this point in her life. But Katya needed someone.

And *she* needed someone.

Maybe one need could cancel out the other one and they could both be the better for it. It was worth thinking about. "I'll look into it."

Katya cocked her head, her long brown hair spilling over one shoulder. "Is yes?"

"We're a long way off from yes," Cate cautioned, then explained. "It isn't up to me." She saw that she was losing Katya in both languages. So she smiled, nodded and, fondly imitating Katya's accent, said, "Is 'maybe.'"

Katya understood the word *maybe* and how far it

was from *yes*. But she smiled because it was also far from *no*.

"*Maybe* is good," Katya concluded.

She'd spent more time than she'd meant to. In both places. Which meant that she was late.

Jumping into her car, Cate peeled out of the parking lot. She took to the road, making sure she was doubly vigilant at all times. One eye on the lookout for the flow of traffic in front of her and one eye watching for the sight of any approaching police vehicle behind her.

She got back to the field office in what she felt could very well have been record time.

The minute she walked into the task force room, she saw Lydia coming toward her like a shot. Something was up. She didn't need a news bulletin to tell her that.

"Did you listen to the news?" Lydia asked her when she was still halfway across the floor.

Cate shook her head. "I was trying to enjoy this CD I bought a week ago. Didn't know when I would get a chance to listen to it again." She knew now that she should have switched on the all news station instead. Lydia had never looked so grim. "Why?"

The news was as grim as Lydia's expression. "There's been a bombing at the American embassy in the Ukraine. Sullivan says they're checking to see if some terrorist organization is claiming responsibility."

"Damn," Cate muttered, then looked at Lydia as several of the others gathered around them to listen and share. "What else could it be?" Questions began occurring to her. Questions that had to be answered. Questions she was almost afraid to ask. "How many casualties?"

The reports were still coming in and conflicted with one another. Lydia was rooting for the lower numbers, but even one was one too many. "Enough."

"Baker one of them?"

Lydia shook her head, feeling helpless. "We don't know." Sullivan had placed several calls to the ambassador, who had been touring a museum at the time the bomb had gone off. So far, the ambassador hadn't called back. "He hasn't been accounted for yet."

Cate did a worse-case scenario. "Which means Baker might have used this as a cover-up to cut his ties and escape."

"He'd only do that if there's a leak in the bureau and he found out we were after him." There had already been one security overhaul eighteen months ago. Right now, things were as airtight as they could get. She didn't want to entertain the thought of another leak.

There was another explanation. "Or the people he's dealing with made things too hot for him," Cate pointed out. "Anyone involved in what amounts to the kidnapping and selling of children doesn't exactly have the moral makeup of a Boy Scout." Thoughts raced through her head as she weighed options as well as their accompanying repercussions. "In any event, I don't see how it changes anything for me. He's either out there to be found or dead, in which case I need to bring the body back."

Not to mention questioning everyone who'd ever had anything to do with the man since he'd gone over there, she added silently. As another thought occurred to her, she looked at Lydia.

"I'm going to need to take someone with me." She was thinking out loud and saw that Lydia wasn't following her. "If Baker is dead, I want someone from the M.E.'s office with me to make sure the body belongs to Baker and not some poor schmuck he decided to use as a body double." More than likely, if the bombing was started as a cover-up, Baker's body would be burned to the point that recognition would be difficult if not impossible without an expert.

Despite the gravity of the situation, Lydia couldn't repress the bemused smile that came to her lips. "'Schmuck?'"

Cate raised and lowered her shoulder in a dismissive gesture. "You pick up things on the job."

Lydia grew serious again. What Cate said made sense. The more she worked with her, the more respect she had for the way the younger woman's mind operated. "I'll go talk to Sullivan, tell him what you need."

Glancing down on her desk, Cate saw that a boarding pass had already been dropped off for her. "It's going to have to be quick, Lydia. Unless someone's willing to give me one hell of a crash course in forensics."

"On my way," Lydia declared, already rushing toward the door. To her surprise, Cate fell into place beside her. "I'll walk with you."

"Why?" Lydia shifted slightly to one side, making room for her partner. "Don't you don't trust me to find my way down the hall?"

"It's not that." Cate searched for the right words. "I wanted to ask you something." She sidestepped several agents coming from the opposite direction. None of their faces registered. "Off the record."

Lydia wondered if this had anything to do with Christian. Cate hadn't said a word about what had happened after they got off the plane on Friday. Had the two of them gotten together? "Shoot."

Cate talked fast, wanting to get it all out before being interrupted. "Katya's due to be released from the hospital soon. She'll go into the system after that. We all know how that can be." She pushed on before Lydia could say anything one way or another. "What do you think of my adopting Katya?"

Lydia stopped walking and looked at her. Her puzzled expression gave way to one of compassion. "I think it's an impulsive idea."

Because she liked Lydia, she took no offense. Instead, she pushed forward with her thoughts on the subject. "She doesn't have anybody, Lydia. I've looked into her family and no one there knows what happened to her parents. Dead most likely. That means she's alone. Alone, scared and she has a language problem."

"Timmons, the newbie we've got guarding her," Lydia added in case Cate didn't know to whom she was referring, "says he's been trying to teach her some basic stuff. The girl's a fast study."

Cate nodded. It wasn't anything that she hadn't already discovered for herself. "Yes, I know. Still doesn't change the fact that she is alone. Who's going to want to adopt a fourteen-year-old girl who's been traumatized the way Katya has and has a language barrier to boot?"

Lydia resumed walking down the hall to Sullivan's office. "You never know, we might find a Ukrainian couple. After all, Katya's not the only one who's ever come from that country. Look, one problem at a time, okay?" she said, tabling the discussion. "We'll tackle the question of what to do with Katya once you get back."

"Count on it."

Her words echoed back to her. Cate realized she'd used the exact terminology that Christian had earlier. No matter what else was going on, she just couldn't get him off her mind for more than a few minutes.

She wondered what he would think of this idea of hers and if it would affect their situation. Or even if they had a situation, she amended. She was well aware that emotions always spiked when an element of danger was involved, and they both knew she was facing it, big time.

Maybe once she was back, the excitement, the thrill would be gone. And he would back away from any implied commitment.

They'd reached Sullivan's office.

"Want me to come in?" she asked just as Lydia knocked on the door.

Lydia grasped the doorknob, turning it. She gestured for Cate to go first as she opened the door. "It's your idea."

Five hours later, Cate was on an international flight bound for Kiev, the capital of the Ukraine, and sitting next to Dr. Walter Phelps, a mid-level member of the medical examiner's office. Sullivan had pulled strings that allowed them to circumvent the long, tedious security-check process at the airport. They were allowed to board the plane the moment they arrived at the terminal.

Nonetheless, anyone could see that the man sitting next to her was far from a happy camper. He hadn't said much, but had been fidgeting the entire time he'd occupied his seat.

"I'm missing my daughter's basketball game."

The half-whining declaration came out of the blue. Cate looked at him and realized that he was holding tightly onto his seat rests. His knuckles were so white, they looked as if they were about to break through his skin at any moment. Takeoff had been almost an hour ago. From the looks of it, Walter hadn't loosened his grip in all that time.

"First international flight?" she guessed.

"First any-kind-of-flight," he confirmed. "I don't get out much," he added defensively.

She smiled at him, trying to bring him around and hoping to allay his fears. "Except to basketball games."

If he sighed any harder, he would have been classified a type-two hurricane. "Not this time."

Maybe a compliment might help him bear up to this. And calm down a little, she hoped. "I wouldn't have asked for anyone if I didn't need them, and they wouldn't have given me you if you weren't good at what you do."

"That'll teach me," Walter mumbled through clenched teeth.

Cate took off the kid gloves and gave it one more shot. "You know, it's the pilot who flies that plane. Pulling off the armrests really doesn't affect the flight one way or another."

Walter scowled at her and went on clutching the armrests.

Giving up, Cate began planning her next move once they were on the ground again.

Chapter 35

Unlike some people she knew, Cate never liked throwing her weight around, never enjoyed being pushy. She only became that way when all else failed.

All else had failed now.

The people she found herself dealing with from the moment she deplaned, both the Americans in charge at the embassy and the Ukrainian agents who had been sent over from Interpol, expected a woman to defer to their authority. She gave the people from the embassy a little slack because of what they had undergone in the past twenty-four hours. As far as she was concerned, the Interpol agents were deserving of no such consideration.

It was as if officials from both groups were determined to keep her on the outside. She was just as determined not to stay there.

Her patience quickly grew short as she tried to gather information as to the events preceding the explosion. In their meandering, conflicting responses, both groups directed their words to the medical examiner she had brought with her.

Until Cate, exasperated, utterly out of patience and afraid that she had already run out of time, assumed the commando persona she'd seen work so well for her father. She became hard as nails.

They had gathered in the section of the embassy that had miraculously escaped any damage. Specifically, in the shaken vice ambassador's quarters. When she once again requested to see Baker's body, the vice ambassador looked at Walter and in a distant voice said, "Perhaps tomorrow we can honor your request if that's all right with you."

Walter in turn looked at her with miserable watery eyes. He'd already shared his allergy history with her. She had no doubt that the awful smell of smoke, which persisted in hanging in the air, had caused it to kick into high gear.

She didn't have time to offer him her sympathies. Sitting on the edge of her seat, curbing an almost insurmountable desire to tell the four other men in the room just what she thought of their slightly older than eighteenth-century views, Cate took over. "Gentlemen, I would appreciate it if you addressed your answers to my questions to me, not Dr. Phelps. And no, it's not all right if we see the body tomorrow. If you really have found Mr. Baker's body, we need to see it immediately. As in *now*," she emphasized.

The Interpol agent with breath like rotting garlic

smirked at her. When he spoke, his English was as flawless as his thinking was flawed. "You seem to be very eager to view a dead body, Ms. Kowalski. This passion you have, one could almost interpret it to be a touch of necrophilia."

If he meant to fluster her, he was going to have to do a lot better than that, she thought. Her eye contact never wavered. "Necrophilia means that I have an erotic attraction to dead bodies. I assure you that all I want to do is make sure that Mr. Baker is really dead."

The vice ambassador inclined his head, confused. His hand shook as he brought the end of the cigarette he was holding to his lips and dragged in the nicotine. "Why all this interest in one undersecretary? There were a great many more important people hurt in this bombing—" His voice broke. When he looked at her, it was with the eyes of a man who had stared into hell and seen his reflection there. "Why aren't you investigating what happened?"

"There are people on their way to do just that," she assured him. "But that's not my assignment. My only job is to find Baker, verify his identity and bring him back home."

The vice ambassador exchanged looks with the rather thin man at his side. She'd been told Lewis Seager ran the embassy. Had he also run something else? she couldn't help wondering.

"Just Baker?" Seager asked.

"Just Baker," she repeated.

The other Interpol agent hadn't spoken yet. She wasn't even sure if he understood English. Dressed in a suit that should have been on a man one size smaller, he leaned forward and fixed her with a look. "Why?"

Her smile was perfect. And impersonal. "I'm not at liberty to say."

His partner snickered. "You Americans are tight-lipped."

"Yes," Cate agreed. "We are." Rising to her feet, she looked directly at the vice ambassador. She was aware that Walter got up behind her, ready to move the moment she did. She got the feeling that he would be as relieved to leave this room as she would. "Now, if we may see the body…?"

The vice-ambassador continued sitting in his chair, as if his legs no longer supported him. The cigarette he kept drawing to his lips was almost an ember by this time. He glanced at Seager.

Seager took his cue, stood up and turned on his heel as if he'd been practicing marching all day.

"This way."

Cate was relieved that the two Interpol agents had elected to remain behind.

Cate struggled not to gag. The smell of death was everywhere within the room. Walter, she noted, had no such problem. This was his element. Thank God it wasn't hers. The thought of becoming so anesthetized to the dead appalled her.

There were twelve bodies in the makeshift morgue that had been hastily put together in the basement of the embassy building. Miraculously, it had escaped damage. Seven of the bodies were Americans, the rest were locals working at the embassy.

She was told by Sally Reynolds, the weeping woman who had taken over for Seager, that the locals were all hoping to someday make the trip across the ocean and see the country for themselves.

"And now they never will," Sally sobbed, lifting up her rimless glasses and wiping her eyes with a worn, graying handkerchief. "This is Mr. Baker."

Cate looked at the body. His face was so badly burned, it hardly bore resemblance to a human being. "How do you know?"

Sally's hazel eyes clouded over again. "The ring." She indicated his left hand. Except for parts of his face, the rest of him had not been burned. Cate leaned closer and saw that the ring in question was a college graduation ring. From Princeton. What a horrible waste of a once-promising life, she thought.

"He was very proud of that ring," Sally told her.

She left a few minutes after that and Walter got down to work.

Cate's stomach revisited her throat almost immediately. "God, this is a grim business," she muttered.

Walter looked as if he would start humming at any moment. For the first time since she'd met him, he looked content. Wearing a leather smock over his clothes, his sleeves rolled up, it was obvious that he enjoyed his work.

"Gotta have the stomach for it," he told her cheerfully.

Cate was already edging her way to the door. There was just too much death in this room to suit her. It was the kind of place that gave her nightmares.

"Well, you obviously do." Her hand was already on the doorknob. "I'm going to see what I can find out."

Walter raised his eyes from the corpse on the cafeteria table that had been brought down for them. "You're leaving?"

She didn't want him panicking. "Just going exploring," she assured him. "I won't be gone long."

She was almost out the door when Walter's mild voice called her back. "You might want to know that he didn't die in the explosion."

Everything inside of her went on alert. Care crossed back to the table in long strides. "Talk to me," she ordered.

"Baker was already dead. Strangled. Obviously no one's going to strangle him after he was burned." He pointed a gloved finger to the man's neck. "Those are ligature marks."

Bingo. "Walter, when we get back to the States, dinner's on me," she declared happily. "Anything you want. Sky's the limit."

"Can I bring my wife?"

"You can bring your daughter's basketball team if you want to."

He regarded her for a second, then shook his head and got back to work. "Never saw anybody so happy about someone being strangled before."

"Because it just proves to me that we're on the right trail."

And it also suggested, she added silently as she left the room, that the embassy bombing might *not* have been the act of terrorists, especially since no group had come forward claiming responsibility. She had a very strong feeling that the bombing had been the work of someone trying to cover up Baker's death. And cover up the trail to the white-slavery ring.

Now all they needed to find out was who had killed Baker.

Cate packed as much work into the next few hours as she could. Their return flight was already booked and her time was limited. She talked to everyone from the embassy she could find. The impression she came away with was that no one really paid much attention to Baker. He'd been described as "a little odd" by several of the people who worked directly with him. Even Sally Reynolds agreed with that assessment, albeit reluctantly because the man was dead.

It was Sally who gave her the address to Baker's one-room apartment, located less than a mile from the embassy.

Wanting to avoid unnecessary contact with strangers and the questions of a possibly nosy landlord, Cate used her own "keys" to get into the apartment and pick the lock. When she walked in and closed the door behind her, she wasn't surprised to discover that the small place looked as if it had suffered the ravages of a tornado.

Everything within the apartment had been taken apart and shattered. If there was anything to be found here, it was long gone.

Still, her training required her to search for herself rather than assume the worst. She sifted through everything, looking inside slashed pillows, broken lamps, paging through books whose spines had been broken and that now littered the floor like so many tiny sagging pyramids, their pages mashed against the floor-boards.

It took her almost two hours to reach the conclusion she'd come to upon entry. There was nothing in the apartment to remotely suggest that the late Brad Baker had ever been involved in a white-slavery ring.

Her cell phone rang, making her jump.

"Where are you?"

The sniff at the end of the question gave the man's identity away. Walter's allergy was going strong.

"On my way back," she answered. She knew better than to give her location away. Any form of electronic communication could become a party line without notice.

Flipping her cell closed, she turned to walk to the door. Her heel caught on a piece of the comforter that had been dissected. Trying to regain her balance, she dropped her phone. It hit the bare floor beside the bed with a thud.

The sound registered, nudging at a memory, as she picked the phone up.

Why did that sound so familiar?

And then she remembered. When she was a child, she'd had a secret hiding place beneath one of the floorboards under her bed. She kept her diary there, as well as a few assorted "treasures." The board made the same kind of sound when she knocked on it, which was how she'd been able to locate it in the first place.

Cate's heart was racing.

On her hands and knees, she began to knock on first one length of board, then another, following each well under the bed as she tried to duplicate the sound she'd heard.

Locating it took time and she kept glancing toward the door, afraid that the landlord might come in for some reason.

And then she heard it, that funny little hollow noise. Cate stopped breathing as she tried to pry the board loose with a butter knife she found on the floor. It came up easily.

"And we have a winner," she murmured to herself, hardly believing what she was seeing. Beneath the board was a small, narrow hollow space, no more than five inches wide and eight inches long.

Big enough for a small metal box.

She pulled on her last pair of rubber gloves. Her hands shook slightly as she withdrew the box and placed it on the floor beside the opening. There was no lock, as if Baker was arrogant in his belief that no one would find it. And if she hadn't been a little girl with secrets once, no one might have.

She held her breath as she lifted the lid. Inside the box was a small rectangular object that could have passed for a key chain. The inscription 256 MB was faintly scratched across the back. She knew a wealth of data could be stored inside. There were also several photographs and what looked like an address book. Flipping through it, she saw names, dates, amounts, followed by a combination of three different letters on three quarters of the pages. The desire to run back to her hotel room nearly overwhelmed her.

But training won out, forcing her to take out the device she liked to refer to as her spy camera. As quickly as she could, she photographed the contents of each page. Just in case.

Finished, she deposited what she'd found into her purse. And then she got the hell out of there.

The first full breath Cate drew was when her plane touched down at LAX. The entire return flight, she half expected to be hauled back to Kiev by either Ukrainian security or the two men she'd met from the Ukrainian Interpol. While Baker's body was in the cargo area of the plane, the papers he'd undoubtedly believed were his insurance policy were safely with her. She hadn't even mentioned finding them to Walter and no word was sent back to the field office, beyond a confirmation that they were taking the flight back. And that she had news.

Lydia and Sullivan met the plane. One look at Lydia's face as she and Sullivan approached told Cate that the woman somehow sensed that the mission had been a success. As always Sullivan had a poker face.

Lydia looked at her, a hopeful note in her voice as she asked, "We got 'em?"

"We got 'em," Cate declared. Taking out the sealed envelope that contained everything from her purse, she addressed Sullivan. "This is everything we were look-ing for. Names, dates, everything," she repeated. Then almost gleefully added. "Let the dismantling begin."

Hooking her arm through Cate's, Lydia gave her a quick, warm squeeze. Lukas was right. It didn't mat-ter who did the job, as long as it got done. "I knew you could do it. Just the same, I've been holding my breath the entire time, waiting for something to go wrong."

"Sometimes things actually do go right," Cate said.

She grinned at Sullivan. "You just have to have a little faith."

Sullivan gingerly separated the two sides of the manila envelope, then withdrew the book. He looked at a few pages, then returned the book to the envelope again. He raised his eyes to look at Cate. "Did you read the entries?"

Maybe she was getting paranoid, but Cate thought she heard something in Sullivan's voice. Something not quite right. "No," she finally answered.

There was enough hesitation in her voice to trigger a reaction.

Disbelief filtered through her as she saw the glint of steel. A second later, she realized that she was looking down at a weapon in Sullivan's hands. His coat was draped over it to hide his gun from public view, but it was definitely there.

The expression on the man's face never changed. "I think you have, Special Agent Kowalski. Which means that the four of us are all going to have to go for a little drive."

Chapter 36

Parking at LAX was hell. Despite all the expansion the airport had undergone in the past few decades, that was more or less a given.

But there was nothing out of the ordinary about that. Anticipation of cruising up and down the rows, searching for a spot hadn't been the reason for the turmoil Christian had endured for the last forty-five miles. Anticipation of another sort was the cause of his unrest.

Christian had tried to talk himself out of what he was doing even before he'd gotten into his car at Blair Memorial. He'd tried over and over to tell himself that it was too soon, that he was being rash and that, damn it all to hell, he didn't *want* to be involved with anyone. He'd made himself that promise, sworn it over and over again over the course of the past three years.

So what was he doing here, parking his vehicle in what amounted to the north forty?

The electronic doors leading into the terminal opened as he approached them. He walked through, a man who very well might be on his way to his own funeral.

What else could it be but a funeral? There was too much going against his getting involved with anyone, not the least of which was that he didn't want to leave himself exposed to the possibility of feeling like one of the walking dead again. It had taken him too long to get back to functioning properly.

And then there was the guilt to grapple with. Guilt that he could have feelings for someone else when he'd been so firmly convinced that his heart and soul would always belong to Alma.

Funny, her face wasn't as vivid as it used to be when it materialized in his mind. There was guilt about that, too. Guilt that his thoughts kept drifting over to Cate. Guilt that the lovemaking they'd enjoyed had made him feel so alive, so vital.

He wanted to be with her again.

And set himself up for a fall, an annoying voice whispered in his head. The annoying voice was right. There were a hundred arguments against coming here to meet Cate's plane. A hundred arguments, large and small. But in the final analysis, they all seemed to bounce off him like hail falling on concrete. He hadn't even been able to mount enough of an argument to keep himself from starting up his car and taking the 405 on-ramp that would eventually lead him to the airport.

And for once, traffic seemed to be light. It was as if someone was paving the way for him.

Or was he reading too much into this?

Leave, damn it. Save yourself now before it's too late.

It was already too late, he thought. Too late because he *did* have feelings for Cate. If he didn't, what was he doing here?

The answer was simple, he thought cynically. Driving himself crazy.

Striding up to the arrival-departure board, he looked up and scanned the flight numbers. He didn't have to refer to the piece of paper in his pocket, the one containing the information Lydia had given him. The flight number was embossed in his brain.

That had been his final hurdle. Asking Lydia. He'd almost balked, then forced himself at the last minute to talk to her. To her credit, his sister-in-law had made no comment when he asked when Cate's flight was arriving. Which made the largest comment of all. That she'd expected this.

Well, Lydia might have expected this, but he sure as hell hadn't.

Cate wasn't even his type.

Cate was nothing like Alma. Oh, granted, there was this small part of her that might have been thought as needy because she wanted to connect to her birth mother, but he had a feeling that wasn't the way she was normally. Cate could just take life's pitches all in stride. He'd seen enough of the independent, take-charge woman she was to know that she was not a clinging vine who only fixated on the wrong that had been done her rather than the opportunities coming her way.

That had been Alma's problem, he thought. Alma just couldn't seem to pull herself up, no matter how hard everyone tried to help her. No matter how much he loved her. The only thing she had succeeded in doing, especially in death, was to pull him down.

Until Cate had happened in his life.

After scanning the board, he finally found the right flight. Cate's plane had arrived early. It had already landed a full fifteen minutes ahead of schedule.

Cate could be anywhere in the terminal by now.

Christian muttered a curse under his breath as he hurried to the gate where she was to have deplaned. It was a long shot and in all likelihood, she might have already hooked up with Lydia and left. Lydia was very efficient that way. No, wait, Lydia had mentioned a body that was being transported from the embassy. That meant that she and Cate had to wait for the cargo to be taken off the plane.

He breathed a sigh of relief. With any luck, that gave him some time to find her.

He thought of calling her cell, but given the din in the terminal, he doubted if she could hear it unless she was listening for it. Or it was set to vibrate. He supposed it was worth a try. Taking out his cell phone, he began to dial her number.

And then he saw her. All the way across the terminal. Astonished, he flipped his phone closed and returned it to his pocket. In the middle of a crowded terminal, he could pick her out as if there was something inside of him that was tuned in only to her.

Weaving his way through the crowd, he began to move in her direction.

She wasn't by herself. She wasn't even with just Lydia. There was a man of about thirty-five, forty, with hunched shoulders standing beside her. Both he and Cate were looking at another man who was apparently with Lydia.

He'd been so intent on coming here, on seeing her, that he hadn't thought she'd be traveling with anyone. He didn't like audiences. For a second, he wavered, toying with the idea of retreat after all. It wasn't as if this was the last time he'd ever see her.

It might be, given half a chance. Once you begin retreating...

Damn it, he hadn't come all this way on the 405 freeway just to go back with his tail between his legs. He remembered life before Alma's suicide had ripped him apart. A life he'd just begun to glimpse again.

Because of Cate.

Christian made up his mind and pushed forward again. Striding across the crowded floor, working his way around and through groups of people, he never took his eyes away from the prize.

Look at me, Cate. Look at me.

As he cut the distance between them, Christian became aware that there was a very strange expression on Cate's face, one he'd never seen before.

She looked wary as she regarded the man in front of her.

He'd seen that same look on a child, regarding a needle, anticipating the pain that was to come. Trying to brazen it out.

Something was wrong.

Christian lengthened his stride, a gut feeling urging him on.

"Cate," he called out. She gave no indication that she'd heard him and he tried again, raising his voice this time. "Cate!"

He saw her head jerk up as she searched the area for him. Saw, too, that the man she'd been regarding so oddly half turned, startled, before he swung back around toward her again.

This was it, Cate thought. Now or never. She knew that if she didn't make use of this opportunity, there wouldn't be another one. Having been in the dark only a few minutes ago, she now knew too much. They all did. And Sullivan would have them eliminated.

She thought of Lydia and the baby she was carrying. Of Walter and the basketball game he'd lamented missing. She thought of Christian. Everything raced through her brain in less than an instant.

As did the desire to live.

There wasn't time to draw her weapon. She lunged at Sullivan, grabbing the hand with the gun in it. Sullivan's coat fell, exposing the gun.

Christian's heart rose in his throat. The man was going to kill Cate.

"Get out of the way!" he shouted, sprinting across the last little bit of distance.

The warning was intended for both Cate and Lydia, as well as for anyone else who might be in the line of fire. The words were hardly out of his mouth as Christian made a flying tackle, bringing down the man with the gun. The latter was a good six inches taller than he was, but the element of surprise was definitely on his side.

The gun, no longer raised overhead, went off just as

a gaggle of LAX security personnel converged around them out of nowhere, all running to the center of the disturbance. Screams came from the crowd and panic descended over the area.

And nowhere was its effect felt more than in Cate's chest. Christian had come flying out of nowhere a second before the gun had gone off.

Where had the bullet gone? The question throbbed in her head.

Oh please, don't let it have hit Christian, she prayed.

All Christian knew was that he had to disarm the other man. He made a grab for Sullivan's elbow, then his wrist, determined to get the gun away from him.

In an instant, both Cate and Lydia had drawn their weapons, even as guns were bring drawn on them.

Cate never took her eyes off the two men on the ground. It took everything she had not to give in to the urge to shoot Sullivan. It wasn't so much an act of self-control as it was fear that she might hit Christian instead.

"It's over," Cate cried, loathing clawing at her throat. "You're surrounded, Sullivan. Give up now and they might take that into consideration." Although, given the nature of his offenses, she sincerely doubted it. Too bad that having someone drawn and quartered was against the law, she thought, because if anyone ever deserved to be, it was Sullivan. He'd used his position not only to line his pockets, but to betray them at every turn.

"Hey, you, drop your weapons," the man who was very clearly the head of airport security ordered. He worked his way to the center of his people, both hands on his service revolver.

"FBI," Lydia countered, holding up her badge. She looked around for the man who had initially cleared both her and Sullivan for entry when they'd arrived at the terminal less than ten minutes ago. "Sergeant Bigelow here?"

When the man stepped forward the next moment, he stared at the scene, especially at Sullivan. "I thought you were all on the same side."

Lydia shook her head, still unable to fully process what had just gone down. She'd worked beside Sullivan for more than two years. Trusted him. What the hell had happened? "I thought so, too," she said quietly.

Getting to his feet, Christian jerked Sullivan to his, as well. The very action cost him. He could feel pain searing across his rib cage as if someone was dragging the sharp end of a spear against his skin.

Relieved that he was all right, Cate threw her arms around Christian's waist. She caught her breath when he winced. Stepping back, she looked at him quizzically. The next moment, fear replaced joy. From beneath the opening of his jacket, she could see that blood had begun to discolor Christian's shirt.

The bullet *hadn't* missed him, after all. "Oh, God, you're hit."

Dazed, confused, Christian looked down and saw the growing splotch of dark red that was spreading out on the left side of his shirt.

That would definitely explain the light-headed feeling that was swirling around him, he thought. "I guess I am."

Chapter 37

Afraid that he might pass out on her, Cate wanted to prop him up. But she was afraid of touching Christian. Of making the pain worse for him. He wasn't even supposed to be here.

She could only stare at him, at the wound, in accelerating disbelief as she fought back tears. "What are you doing here?"

"Bleeding," Christian replied succinctly. He'd never seen his own blood before and he stared down at the stain in complete, almost detached fascination. It seemed to border on the surreal.

His head kept whimsically winking in and out.

Coming to life, Walter elbowed Cate aside and quickly tore open Christian's shirt.

"Looks like the bullet went clean through," he announced as if he was still talking into the tape recorder he always employed during the autopsies he conducted. He looked first at the man who had come to their rescue, then at Cate. "But this needs to be cleansed and bandaged immediately." He saw the incredulous look on Cate's face. "What? I didn't always just cut up corpses. I had to go through medical school first, just like every other doctor." He looked back at the ring of security people. "You got anything like a first aid kit available?"

"Sawyer, go get the doctor a first-aid kit," Bennett, the head of security, ordered. He had the voice of a retired cop and the bearing of a tired bloodhound.

Moving to the center, Bennett kept his service revolver trained on Sullivan. Sawyer returned with the kit almost immediately and handed it off to Walter, who quickly got started.

As the crowd of rubberneckers around them grew, Lydia took the opportunity to place a call to the regional office to report this latest strange twist of events. She still kept out her own gun, ready to use in case things turned ugly again.

She nodded at Cate, then held out the cell phone to her as the phone on the other end rang. "You want to do the honors?"

Cate barely glanced toward her partner. Her eyes were fixed on Walter's hands as the M.E. swiftly cleaned up Christian's wound.

"Not interested in honors," she told Lydia. The next moment, Lydia was on the line with the regional director. Cate tuned her out. "You sure you know what you're doing?" she asked Walter. After all, if he made a mistake in his regular line of work, it didn't really matter. The subject was already dead.

It mattered a lot here.

Walter raised his eyes from his work long enough to give her an offended look. "This isn't exactly a triple bypass I'm performing. I'm just cleaning up his wound." He snorted dismissively as he applied a liberal dose of peroxide to the wound in Christian's side. "Even you could do this."

Cate drew in her breath as she watched Christian's skin momentarily pucker in response to the pain. "Because you're helping him, I'll let that go."

In her mind's eye, the scenario replayed itself. It could have gone at least a dozen different ways. And she could envision Christian getting killed almost each and every time.

Fear and horror pushed words out of her mouth. "What the hell were you thinking?" she demanded heatedly. "Don't you know better than to aim yourself like a baseball at a man with a gun?"

"Okay, break it up, nothing to see here," the security personnel were saying to the crowd, dispersing them.

Cate was vaguely aware of flashes going off. Had the media been called in? She didn't know. She didn't care. She just wanted Christian to be all right.

"Usually, yes," Christian replied. He measured out each word carefully as he bit back the desire to groan.

The hole left by the bullet hurt like a son of a gun, he thought. He'd never had so much as a hangnail before and heretofore had been unacquainted with physical pain beyond having the wind knocked out of him on several occasions when he boxed in Uncle Henry's gym. He didn't much like it.

"But the gun was aimed at you," he pointed out. Christian left it at that, feeling he had no further need to explain.

He thought wrong.

"Having Sullivan shoot you wouldn't have helped me any," she cried. She threw her hands up, knowing she was just going to have to find a way to cope with this and block out the thought that he could have been killed. "Oh, damn it all, you're the heroic type on top of everything else."

"Wait until Lukas hears," Lydia said to him fondly, covering the cell microphone opening with her hand. "He'll really skin you."

"He'll have to catch me first." The joke fell a little flat as another shaft of pain skewered its way through him. "He was never very fast on his feet." He looked at Cate and told her, "As a boy, I used to beat him every time."

"And I should be beating you." Cate doubled her fists at her sides, struggling with the urge to swing at him at least once and drain the stress from her. *He could have been killed, and it would have been your fault.* "Never, ever do that again."

She was serious, he thought. As if he'd had any other choice once he realized that she and Lydia were in danger. But he humored her. "I promise the next time I see someone hiding a gun under their coat and aiming it at you in the airport terminal, I won't tackle him."

Cate shook her head. Tears had come out of nowhere, stinging her eyes. She blinked several times to keep them from falling. Success was only minimal. She used the back of her hand to get the rest. "Your mother's right. You should have been a lawyer."

"That's not what she said," he reminded her. He'd pointed that out the last time.

"I'm done here," Walter announced, lumbering back up to his feet. He left the first aid kit open on the bench, confident Security would see to it.

"Thanks," Christian muttered, rebuttoning his shirt.

Walter looked at his only living patient in the past five years with not a little pride. To his surprise he realized that he missed the satisfaction this part of the job provided. Dead people never said thank you.

"But you need to go to a hospital to have that x-rayed—" Walter indicated his handiwork "—to make sure there's no internal damage. I'd make that my next stop if I were you."

"There's no internal damage," Christian told him evenly.

Cate laughed shortly. "So now he has X-ray vision, as well." Her mind working rapidly, she turned to her partner. The latter slipped her cell phone back in her pocket after she concluded her conversation with the regional head of the bureau. "Lydia, if I give you Dr. Doolittle here, can you take Sullivan to the field office?"

The smile on her lips said that nothing would give her greater pleasure. "Even without Dr. Doolittle."

Walter's chest rose indignantly. "Who are you calling Dr. Doolittle?"

Cate flashed a wide grin at him. "It's a term of affection, Walter. An endearment. Thanks for bandaging up the hero." She nodded at Christian.

"You're welcome," Walter mumbled.

"You need anything from us?" Bennett asked once Lydia had her weapon trained again on the handcuffed Sullivan.

How the mighty have fallen, Lydia thought. And it didn't have to be. Sullivan had been a good man once, or so she'd heard. Thirty years with the bureau. All of it down the drain now. And for what? Money? Vicarious excitement? Or was there something even more base at the bottom of all this?

She wasn't sure if she even wanted to know.

Lydia smiled at Bennett. "An escort to my car wouldn't be out of order."

Walter moved over beside her as Bennett pointed to three of his people, selecting them to do the honors.

"See you at the field office later," Lydia said to Cate before leaving. "Much later," she underscored in a lower voice that just carried between the two of them.

"What about you?" Bennett asked Cate once the others had gone. "You need anything?"

She looked at Christian. His complexion was paler than she'd ever seen it. "Where's your car?" It took him a moment to remember the lot number.

Cate looked at Bennett for clarification. "All the way in the back," he told her.

In that case, it was much too far for Christian to walk in his present condition. But there was no way he'd consent to being taken to the hospital by ambulance. Besides, she knew he would undoubtedly prefer going somewhere he was familiar with. Which meant Blair, and that was more than forty-five miles from here. No ambulance would go that distance. They reported to the hospital closest to the point of pickup.

She thought of a solution. "One of those cute little transport cars to drive us over to his vehicle."

Christian bristled. "I can walk," he protested. He rose from the chair, gaining his legs unsteadily.

If someone blew on him, he'd fall over, she thought. Cate quickly positioned herself beside him and slung his arm over her shoulder for leverage. She wrapped her free arm around his waist. "Of course you can."

Christian did his best to glare at her. "You're humoring me."

She turned up her face to his and pasted a wide smile on her lips. "Yes, I am."

He would have pulled away from her. If he could. "I don't like being humored."

Cate turned as the cart came into view. "I'll keep that in mind."

"It's true what they say," Cate decided after having been a silent witness for the past two hours. "Doctors do make the worst patients."

With no small sense of relief, Christian pulled the zipper up on his pants. It was nice to have them back on again after having endured being wrapped up in a smock for the past couple of hours. Stiffly, he reached for his bloodied shirt. Cate beat him to it and held it out to him.

He moved very carefully as he gingerly slipped first one arm and then the other into the sleeves. Taking possession of his shirt, he slowly began buttoning it. Over his protest, they'd given him something for the pain and he now felt as if he was moving in slow motion.

"You try sitting around in that abbreviated tablecloth and see how you like it." He balled it up and tossed it into a container for dirty linens. "Don't see why I couldn't keep my clothes on."

He knew the rules as well as anyone, had stood on the other side of them every time but now. She knew he was just blowing off steam. Maybe discovering his mortality had made him angry.

"Maybe because all the nurses wanted a thrill," she cracked. He gave her a dark look. "Well, that bullet might have missed all your vital organs, but it certainly made a direct hit on your sense of humor." She picked up his jacket for him and slung her purse strap over her shoulder. She gamely took hold of his arm. "C'mon, hero, I'll take you home."

They made their way out through the back entrance to the E.R. More than a few people called out to him as they went.

He acknowledged each one with a nod, then looked at Cate. He wasn't sure if he was up to her continued ministering. It conflicted with his invulnerable self-image. "Don't you have to go to work and make a report or something?"

"It'll keep." There was no hurry now. Especially since she'd heard from Lydia that she and the team had found the other girls and they were being taken care of. She kept her arm tucked through his until they reached his car. Cate made a point of opening up the passenger side, then waiting until he got in. "In light of the fact that we now have at least one of the key behind-the-scenes people, I think the powers that be can wait a little while for me to make my report."

He fumbled with his seat belt, unaccustomed to having it at his right. "So, it was Sullivan all along?"

"Looks that way." Cate started up his car and it purred to life. "That would explain how they were almost always one jump ahead of us. He was warning them." She backed up slowly, knowing he was scrutinizing how she was handling his baby. "The funny thing was, he did some jumping of his own because he leaped to the conclusion that I'd discovered he was in on it. The truth was, I never had a chance to take a look at that disk. I was in too much of a hurry to get it out of the country. Since he was the one I was turning it over to, he could have just waited it out and dubbed a copy, leaving himself out of it."

Everyone was fallible, he thought. It was all just a matter of time. "I guess when it's your neck on the line, you don't always stay clearheaded."

She eased the car onto the main thoroughfare. "Speaking of clearheaded—" she spared him a look "—you never answered my question."

He pointed to the road. Dutifully she looked back at it. "Which one? You've been firing questions all afternoon."

"The original one. What were you doing at the airport?"

Cate flew through a light that was on its way to red. He wouldn't have done that, he thought. That was the difference between them. He was more cautious than she was. Maybe that was one of the elements that made her so appealing. "I distinctly remember answering you. I said 'bleeding.'"

She frowned. He was stalling again. Was that a good sign? "What were you doing there before then?"

"Saving your life," he said simply.

Yeah, she thought. *He had been. And maybe in more ways than one.*

Chapter 38

"You don't have anything in your refrigerator."

Cate pushed the handle, letting the door close on its own. The inside of his refrigerator had been the picture of barrenness. There weren't even any old, soggy take-out containers drooping sleepily in the recesses of the shelves. It was as if he'd just bought the appliance and plugged it in that afternoon.

She'd headed for the kitchen after settling him in the living room, determined to feed his body as well as his spirit. She'd struck out on the first count.

"Food is the last thing on my mind."

Cate frowned. She'd left him in the living room, but he was standing behind her in the doorway. The man just didn't know when to stay put.

She turned and faced him. "But you need to keep up your strength."

Christian laughed, shaking his head. "Wow, that must be some kind of record. You just went from sounding like a crack FBI agent to my mother in less than two and a half seconds."

"Special agent," she corrected. Gently, she herded him back to the living room, where she discovered that she could lead an injured man to a sofa, but she couldn't make him sit. "The term is special agent."

The smile on his face was just the slightest bit lopsided and did not belong to a man who was in the kind of pain she knew he had to be in. She'd once caught a slug dead center in her bulletproof vest and it had hurt like hell. The impact had momentarily knocked her not only off her feet, but out cold.

And then she remembered, they'd given Christian something at the hospital for the pain.

Was that what that funny little smile on his lips was about? The one that was burrowing itself right into the pit of her stomach, upheaving absolutely everything in its path? It was obviously responsible for his lack of common sense, because every injured person knew one had to lie down after the ordeal he'd just gone through.

When she thought about the fact that the bullet could have hit something vital... She pushed the thought away as fast, as hard as she could. She couldn't do the same with the man. Christian had somehow managed to eat up all the space, all the air between them, and suddenly she was the one on life support, not him.

"Special agent," he repeated. His eyes were teasing her even as they seemed to touch her. "Tell me what's so special about you."

She lifted her chin, putting on one hell of a nonchalant performance. "I can press close to my own body weight and I can toss a man into bed."

The lopsided smile spread—both across his lips and to her insides. "Sounds promising."

She rolled her eyes and tried to keep from laughing. "What did they give you?"

He lightly feathered his fingertips along her cheek. Causing tidal waves of emotions to form. "Something to clear my head."

Cate held her ground as best she could. "And suck out all the brain cells, obviously."

From where he was not so steadily standing, it seemed to Christian that the painkiller had killed more than just the physical pain he'd been experiencing. It killed the other as well. The emotional pain he'd been dealing with all this time. Killed it so that he could allow himself to silently ask what he was running from in such a hurry.

Maybe just about the best thing that has happened to you in a long, long while.

He blinked and realized that Cate had left his side as he'd been examining this new revelation. She was all the way across the room, on her way to the rear of the apartment. "Where are you going?"

She paused to answer. His head was spinning a little, but he caught up to her in less than a beat. Because he swayed slightly, Cate took hold of his arm. He saw a shade of alarm mixed with disapproval in her eyes.

Or was that desire?

Mirroring his own.

"To the bedroom," she told him, "to turn down your

bed." If worse came to worse, Cate decided, she could push him down onto the bed. She doubted he'd offer much resistance in his present state. He'd probably be out within moments. Or, at least she hoped so.

She also wished he'd stop looking at her like that. He was making her forget all her good intentions. Instead, her thoughts kept reverting to something that had nothing to do with common sense and everything to do with fulfillment.

"Why?" he asked, his breath tantalizing her as he leaned in. "Did I proposition you?"

She wasn't sure if he meant the question seriously. "No," she laughed, moving the comforter back off the bed. One good flip, she thought, that was all it would take. Gently so as not to hurt him.

"Okay." He took a deep breath, squaring his shoulders. "Then I will."

Turning, she was about to put her plan into action when he surprised her by pulling her to the side. In less than a very hard heartbeat, she found herself against the wall with a muscular arm on each side of her, barring any chance for a quick getaway.

He looked at her for a long moment. So long that Cate felt that she was in imminent danger of completely losing herself. The last trace of laughter faded as a deep-seated longing came to claim every part of her.

It seemed to get worse, not better each time. Because each time built on the last, growing higher, stronger. Making her feel as if she were capable of touching the very sky. Damn, what had she allowed herself to get into? She was a virtual prisoner, held captive not just by his body, but by his eyes.

"Marry me."

She saw his lips moving, thought she heard the words, except that she knew she couldn't have. Was that just her inner thoughts projecting themselves? And even so, she couldn't be thinking that. Not after what she'd been through. Her life wasn't about strong, lasting intimate bonds any longer.

It wasn't? an inner voice mocked.

She cleared her throat and tried to look like the same woman she no longer was. "What?"

"Marry me," he repeated, saying the words so softly she could feel them moving along her skin as well as hear them.

Rather than push him away and chance having him fall over, she suddenly ducked down, escaping beneath the barrier of his arm.

"You're delirious." Cate pulled out her cell phone. "I'm calling your brother."

Very deliberately, Christian took the phone out of her hand. "Lukas is already married. I don't want to marry him."

He was holding the phone above his head, making it impossible for her to reach. She tried once, but unless she wanted to kick him in the shin, the phone was going to remain out of her reach.

"And you don't want to marry me," Cate insisted.

"Sure I do." He tossed her cell phone onto the nightstand on the other side of the bed, then blocked her access to it. "And before you start talking about the painkiller they gave me, all that did was kill my inhibitions." He framed her face with his hands. "And strip away the cobwebs."

God, but he could make her want him faster than morning coffee was brewed. She had to keep reminding herself that he was hurt and that one more tumble in bed wouldn't lead anywhere. Except to an ecstasy that she found addictive.

"Tell you what," she said gamely, trying to step away from him and toward the doorway. "You sleep on it and we'll talk about it in the morning."

For a man who'd been shot, he was awfully agile, she thought in frustration as he blocked her escape one more time. Filling her path with him and her own desire. "How about I sleep with you and we'll talk about it now?" he proposed seductively.

Compared to her insides right now, jelly was firm. Still, she mustered all the outward resolve she could and pointed to the mattress.

"Christian, bed," she ordered in the sternest voice she could.

"Yes, ma'am."

Just when she thought he was actually going to obey, Christian hooked his arm around her waist and pulled her down to the bed with him, his lips on hers.

But the kiss that threatened to incinerate her abruptly halted as he stifled a curse. When she'd fallen with him, her elbow had accidentally come in contact with his wound.

Cate quickly scrambled away from him, kneeling on the bed as she stared at him. What was wrong with her? She was the adult here right now, because the painkiller had obviously reduced him to the behavioral level of an adolescent who'd had a double barrel of hormones shot through him.

Remorse and guilt formed the two ends of the rope that tied her up into a knot. "Oh, God, Christian, I'm sorry. Look, I told you—"

He caught her hand before she could get off the bed. "I'll live," he told her firmly, then his voice softened again. As did the look in his eyes. "Make love with me, Cate."

He was out of his mind—and he was driving her out of hers. She didn't know how much longer she could hold out. An entire host of emotions had been put into play this afternoon, not the least of which was the fear that she could have lost him. Permanently.

"Christian," she protested, "you've been shot."

His grin was nothing short of absolutely wicked. "Not there."

With a laugh that was only half surrender, Cate sank down beside him, shaking her head. "No one told me you were insane."

He grazed his fingers along her throat, tilting her head up toward him just a fraction. "It's a well-kept secret."

"Must be," she breathed.

The sensations she'd been trying to keep in check suddenly dashed out like riders in a nineteenth-century land rush, bent on claiming a section of territory to call their own. It was hopeless and she knew it. She wanted him just as much as he seemed to want her. Probably more. And that ache in her chest, the one that had bloomed full grown when Christian had asked her to marry him, she recognized it for what it was.

Silently, she damned it even as its tapering fingers dug into her soul, holding her prisoner.

"I'll be gentle," she promised, surrendering to the

inevitable. The next moment, he was kissing her. Or she him. Order didn't matter.

She could feel his mouth curving against hers even as the kiss deepened. The proposal he'd uttered was forgotten.

At least, she thought, by him.

Her hand was shaking as she finally inserted her key into the lock of her door. Cate stifled an impatient curse. It had taken her three tries to get it into the hole. She'd dropped the key twice.

God, what had he done to her?

Made wild, passionate love to her body and completely blown away her mind, that's what he'd done. You'd think a man who'd just been shot and then pumped full of medicine would have the decency to pass out once she'd gotten him home, not perform like some robust lover who'd been deprived of any sort of female companionship for the past three years.

Just thinking about him made her body hum.

Walking in, Cate flipped the lock closed behind her. And still felt vulnerable, still felt exposed. She leaned against the door for a moment, not bothering to turn on the lights.

He'd proposed to her.

Okay, the painkiller had proposed to her, but the words had come out of his mouth, using his voice. And for one wild, insane moment, she'd wanted to shout yes. To lean over as far as she could on her colorfully painted carousel horse and grab the brass ring.

To hold it to her chest with both hands and pretend everything would be wonderful.

With a sigh, she stepped out of her shoes and crossed the floor. Wishing with all her heart that she didn't know as much as she knew about life. She knew what happened when you began to believe in happily ever afters. Reality came to hit you across the face with a five-day-old fish, bruising you even as it polluted the air.

She'd made her escape the moment Christian had fallen asleep. Escaping from him, from his apartment and from the terrible things she knew were lying in wait for her the moment she became stupid enough to believe everything could work out.

She looked around her apartment, wanting to hide. Wanting to flee. Too bad she'd finally unpacked everything. It would be a lot easier if everything was still in boxes, ready to go.

Like she was.

Working her lower lip, Cate could feel her mind chasing around, desperately searching for something to focus on. Something to get her through this rocky patch until she could deal with it better. Until she could get back to her old self again. Strong and cynical and devoid of hope.

Her thoughts turned to the one thing that she could always rely on to pull her out of an emotional tailspin.

Work.

Squaring her shoulders, she crossed back to the front door and slipped on her shoes again.

Chapter 39

Lost in thought, Lydia looked up from the computer screen. Surprise immediately filtered over her features. She glanced at her watch. It was almost six. Time for their shift to leave, not show up. "I didn't think you were coming in."

Cate shrugged out of her coat and draped it over the back of her chair. "It took longer at the hospital than I thought."

Lydia nodded, taking in the explanation as far as it went. She really hadn't been thinking about hospital downtime when she'd asked.

"I guess even doctors have to wait." She'd already called the hospital herself to find out, but she wanted to give her partner leeway to talk. She sensed Cate needed to. "So how is he?"

Magnificent. Cate banked down the single-word

reply. It didn't do him justice, anyway, and it would just give Lydia an opportunity to pump her.

"The doctor said there were no internal injuries. Christian should be good as new in a few weeks." *Actually, he's that way now.* Cate struggled to keep a smile from spreading on her face.

"Good to hear. The whole department's buzzing with the news about Sullivan." Unable to hold back any longer, Lydia rose from her chair, rounded their desks and hugged her. "You did good." Somewhere in the middle of the hug, a stiffness registered. Lydia released her and took a step back. "Something wrong?"

If she even said a single word on the subject, if she so much as mentioned that Christian had proposed, she knew the dam would break and everything would come rushing out. And Lydia wouldn't understand. Wouldn't understand why she was so afraid. Aside from an argument or two, Lydia and Lukas were happy. As far as she knew, Lydia had *always* been happy.

So she took the easy way out, otherwise known as the coward's way out, and shook her head. "Just a little stressed, that's all. That and jet lag," she added for good measure.

If the answer left Lydia suspicious, she gave no indication.

"Then maybe you'd better return these some other time." Before Cate could ask her what "these" referred to, Lydia reached into her pocket and produced several pink telephone message slips, which she deposited on the desk. "According to Hawkins who took the calls, this woman's been calling all afternoon." Lydia regarded the small pink pile with professional curiosity. "An informant?"

Picking up the message slips, Cate quickly went through them. The same name was on each and every one. Joan Cunningham.

It didn't make any sense. Joan didn't want to have anything to do with her, she'd made that abundantly clear. So why was she suddenly calling her?

Cate folded the slips and put them into the middle drawer of her desk. "No, just someone I met."

Lydia made no effort to question the statement. "Maybe she saw you on the news."

It felt like her brain was the inside of a blender that had gone amok. She looked at Lydia, confused. "On the news?"

She nodded. "It seems like we all made the evening news. The little media vultures must have been hiding in the airport woodwork. They commemorated that little action sequence that took place between Sullivan, Christian and you. And me," she added as an afterthought. By the time she'd gotten back to the office, the others on the task force were more than happy to tell her all about it. The story was replayed within the half hour. She'd seen it on three different channels so far.

Cate groaned in response.

"Maybe you'll get your own groupies," Lydia laughed.

Cate slid down further in her chair, not happy about the turn of events. "I sure as hell won't be able to go undercover anytime soon."

Lydia was puzzled. There were special agents who

went undercover, but that wasn't anything her detail did. "Undercover? What brought that on?"

Cate shrugged, looking around her desk. Now that she was here, she didn't know what to do with herself. She couldn't seem to focus any better here than she could at home.

Why the hell did he have to propose, even if he was half out of his head?

"I was just thinking about a change, that's all."

Something *was* wrong. "You're just settling in here," Lydia protested.

"It was just a passing thought." Opening the drawer, she took out the messages again. The only way to find out what was going on was to call. "I'd better return her call before she calls again."

Sensing she needed privacy, Lydia rose from her desk. "I'm going to get some coffee—tea," she corrected herself, then realized that wasn't enough. "Herbal tea. Hell, I hate herbal tea." She sighed, shaking her head. "This is going to be a very long pregnancy," she murmured as she walked away.

Bracing herself, Cate pressed the numbers that would connect her to the initial reason for her transfer. God but that felt as if it had been a million years ago. As she made the call, she realized that that, too, had somehow gotten pushed into the background. Especially after she'd seen the way Christian's mother had interacted with John. Juanita treated the teen no differently than she did either one of her sons.

Watching the woman had made her think of Julia and Big Ted. Of all the times they'd shared together. Not just the vacations, but the small moments as well.

Ted and Julia were her parents in every way that counted. They might not have donated any of their genes, but they'd given her their time, their love. And growing up, she had embraced their heritage. They had been her foundation, her roots, not whoever her birth parents were. She knew that now.

Looking back, she could only shake her head. She hadn't been herself for a while. The shock of learning she was adopted had done that to her. But she was better now. And proud to be who and what she was. Big Ted and Julia Kowalski's daughter. No amount of DNA could change that.

The phone on the other end barely rang once. And then she heard an uncertain voice saying, "Hello?"

"Joan?"

"Cate." She said her name breathlessly and with something that almost sounded like relief. "I know you must be wondering why I've been calling you."

Cate looked at the messages. Five in all. "I can take an educated guess." Joan had probably seen her that day she was parked across the street from their house. "You called to make sure that I won't suddenly pop up and embarrass you in front of your family." Odd how important this had been to her just a short while ago. And now it didn't matter. She didn't need that acceptance anymore. Because she'd accepted herself. "You don't have to worry, I won't."

"You won't?" Joan sounded surprised and almost bewildered.

Leaning back in her chair, Cate smiled to herself. She looked at the empty space on the side of her desk. That would be a good place to put that photograph of her parents she'd yet to unpack. "No, I've decided that you don't owe me anything. You already gave me more than you'll ever know."

"I don't follow."

"By giving me up to the Kowalskis, you gave me the opportunity to have a wonderful childhood. They were really very good people."

"I'm so glad." Cate thought that the woman honestly meant that. But then Joan went on to say, "But that's not the reason I called. I saw you on the news earlier."

"Yes?"

She heard Joan take a deep breath before saying, "I realized that you could have been killed and then I would never have the opportunity to get to know you."

That didn't make any sense. "I thought that you just wanted me to leave you alone."

"No, what I wanted was to have my life go on the way it had been. But things don't always work out that way. People get sick, they die…" She began to speak more rapidly with each word. It was as if she felt if she didn't say this quickly, her courage would falter and she wouldn't say it at all. "Cate, there hasn't been a day that's gone by in the past twenty-seven years that you haven't been on my mind. That I haven't wondered where you were, if you were happy. What you looked like. But that day you came into my hospital room, I just wasn't prepared. My world was already shaky. I thought I was going to die. I was scared and I needed support. I was afraid that if anyone found out that I'd had a baby and given her up for adoption, my whole world would just fall apart."

She knew that the operation had been a success and

Joan's cancer successfully removed. But nothing else had changed. Her husband and children were still the same. Her circumstances were still the same. "And now?"

"And now I've decided to stop being such a coward. I've already told my husband and he was upset that I hadn't told him before, but he didn't condemn me the way I thought he would. My mother-in-law and her blue blood is going to be knocked for a loop, but that can't be helped, and frankly, I'm tired of living my life walking on eggshells. If it's not too late, I would really, really like the chance to get to know you."

"It's not too late." She was surprised that she felt a tightness in her throat after telling herself that this didn't matter. "I think that something can be arranged." She made a date to meet Joan for lunch at a popular restaurant the following Monday.

And just like that, she thought, she had a mother. Another mother, she amended, because Julia would always have first claim to that title.

Cate was just about to hang up when she heard Joan's voice in the receiver. "And Cate—"

Cate brought the receiver back to her ear. "Yes?"

"Thank you for not hating me."

Hate had never entered into it, even at the height of the rejection. "The Kowalskis raised me well."

"Yes, it seems that they did."

Hanging up, Cate regarded the telephone in silence for a moment, thinking how strange life was. When she'd pushed for this, she'd met with nothing but rejection. Now that she'd made her peace and backed off, Joan had come to her, bearing an olive branch.

She had exactly sixty seconds to savor her new-found peace before Lydia came back to her desk. "Cate, the regional director wants to see you ASAP."

Turning away from her desk to face Lydia, Cate groaned. This was the height of so-called rush hour. "I'm not sure I can endure L.A. traffic right now."

Lydia grinned. "Then you're in luck." Cate looked at her quizzically. "Because he's upstairs."

Her day was catching up to her. Suddenly weary, she rose to her feet. "We'll see how lucky I am after we talk," she said, leaving the room.

There were commendations in her file.

Commendations in her file and a newly found mother who wanted to establish ties after all. Not bad for a day's work, Cate thought as she drove home an hour later.

She deliberately didn't allow her thoughts to go any further, to encompass the real center of her day. She wasn't about to even toy with the idea that the proposal might have had a ring of truth to it.

More than likely, when Christian woke up and found her gone, he would be either relieved to be alone, or would have no memory of the proposal he'd uttered in the heat of his delirium.

Exhausted, all she wanted was to take a hot shower and drop into a warm bed. Hopefully in that order.

She pulled into her parking space slightly askew. She was going to regret this tomorrow when she had to pull out again. But right now, she wasn't up to straightening out the vehicle. After locking the doors, she made her way to her apartment, already visualizing the water coming out of the showerhead.

"I was beginning to think that you were never going to come home again."

Instantly awake, Cate swung around, one hand on the hilt of her service revolver, ready to pull it out and fire.

Christian stepped out of the shadows. She removed her hand from her gun, but the tension that had seized her refused to leave. She waited a beat for her heart to shimmy down out of her throat and let her speak.

"I had a lot to do," she said slowly. "Why aren't you in bed?"

"It's empty."

"Of course it's empty," she snapped. She just wasn't up to this. Her nerves suddenly felt brittle enough to snap like the two ends of a dried-out wishbone. "You're not in it."

"No," he corrected. "What makes it empty is that you're not in it."

Oh, please, please, go away. Don't do this to me. Don't make me bleed all over again.

Christian nodded toward the door. "Are you going to open it and invite me in, or do you want Mrs. Noble to watch us?"

She had no idea who he was talking about. "Mrs. Noble?"

"The woman in the apartment across the way." He indicated the neighbor's window. "I've been out here so long, she came out to ask me if there as anything she could do." A smile curved his mouth. And her insides. "I've got a feeling that she likes to keep up on things. So if I kiss you out here…"

"C'mon." Against her better judgment, Cate unlocked the door and allowed him to follow her in as a little voice taunted, You'll be sorry.

Chapter 40

"My mother called me," he told her as Cate shut the door behind them and flipped on the light.

The call had woken him up. For the first few seconds, he'd had trouble concentrating on what his mother was saying. All he was aware of was that Cate had left his bed again. He'd thought they were beyond that.

Apparently not.

He followed her into the living room. "Seems we made the five o'clock news in Arizona."

Cate felt as if she was suddenly all thumbs inside. She was no longer tired, just edgy. And confused. "Here, too."

He watched her as she moved around the room, a bird with nowhere to land. "She wants to know if you're all right."

That was a matter of opinion, Cate thought while forcing a smile to her lips. Forcing herself to sound nonchalant. *You proposed to me. Do you even remember that?* She didn't know if she wanted him to or not.

"Tell her I'm fine." When in doubt, turn the tables, Big Ted had taught her. "How does she feel about having raised a hero?"

"She told me I did the right thing." He was waiting for her to sit down before he did the same. So far, it was like waiting for Godot. "She also told me that John almost ran off with Lily."

Cate stopped moving around and looked at him. This was a new name. "Lily?"

"A girl on the reservation. More like a woman-child." Thinking back, he realized that John had wanted to talk about Lily that night at the cemetery but had stopped himself at the last minute. He should have pushed instead of thinking the boy would tell him in his own good time, Christian thought. Sometimes people needed to be pushed. "He was trying to protect her."

"From?"

"Herself, mostly." It was amazing how alike Lily and Alma were. Except that for Lily, there was still hope. "I talked to him, told him not to think he can fix everything, that he can be there for her when she needs him, but he has to make sure that he's strong enough himself first. That takes growing."

Something he had learned the hard way, Christian thought. But at least he'd finally learned it.

Cate nodded. "Good advice."

His eyes held hers. "Yeah, I should have followed it myself when I was his age."

She knew him well enough to know that this was a huge admission on his part. Her expression softened. "Think he will?"

"We learn by our mistakes and by example. Barring that, Uncle Henry will sit on him if necessary until John makes the right decision. Mom's doing what she can for Lily. I think it'll be all right." In fact, he was willing to bet on it. With those two in one's corner, very little could really go wrong.

She felt as if they were waltzing around the subject. And it wasn't that she didn't like waltzing, but there was a different melody playing.

"Did you come here to give me a news bulletin?" When he said nothing, she felt she had her answer and filled in the blanks. "Look, if it's about what you said to me earlier, I know it was the painkiller doing the talking, so you don't have to worry—"

He cut her off before she could get carried away. Or say something he didn't want to hear. "I will if you turn me down."

He didn't get it, did he? He'd gotten swept up in the heat of the moment, nothing more. "Christian, we were in one hell of a situation before. That tends to pump up the adrenaline, make you think you feel things you don't." Because she wasn't getting through to him, she tried something he was more familiar with. "It's like with your patients, the ones who fall in love with you. They're not really in love with you, right?"

The look on his face was pure innocence. "They're not? Well, there goes my ego."

She laughed, some of the tension draining from her. And then she sobered as she looked at him more closely. "You're different. Why?"

She was the reason he was different. Cate, and the fact that he had finally given himself permission to forgive himself.

He draped his arm over her. "Different how?"

"Freer. Less solemn—no, not solemn, that's it. You're not solemn." The shadow of pain had left his eyes, she realized. "Maybe you should consider getting a refill for that painkiller."

His mouth curved as he looked at her. She knew it wasn't the painkiller, he thought. It was just an excuse she was using because she afraid to face the truth. He could relate to that.

"It's already out of my system." When she opened her mouth to say something, he placed his finger to her lips, silencing the protest. "Trust me, I know about these things."

Her shoulders moved beneath his hands in a half shrug. "Then I don't understand."

His eyes pinned her. They both knew she was lying. "What's not to understand? I love you—did I forget to mention that?"

She felt like a bowling pin that had just been mowed down. Her throat tightened so much, she could barely squeeze out the single word. "Yes."

He didn't have practice at this sort of thing. But he'd learn, he promised himself. He'd learn. "Okay, consider it mentioned. We'll get back to that part." He took her hands in his, as much to make contact as to keep her from fleeing. She had a strange look in her eyes. "I want you to marry me. I want me to marry you. Nothing very complicated about that—unless you don't feel about me the way I think you do."

Her stomach and brain had just simultaneously launched into the spin cycle. "I don't know what I feel—"

"Scared?" he supplied.

She took a breath and then nodded. "Yes."

"Confused?" he guessed.

"Yes." Never so confused in her whole life, she added silently.

"Like you want to run away?"

She wanted to say no, but this wasn't a time for lies. "Yes."

He grinned broadly and she caught herself thinking that he looked almost boyish. No, not boyish. More like a teeth-jarringly sexy hunk who reduced her knees to the consistency of water.

"Congratulations," he said, "you're in love, adult-style. Either that, or you think someone's out to get you, in which case, you're still right. Because I am. But only in the nicest possible way."

As much as she wanted this, she could feel disappointment looming on the sidelines, ready to swallow her up again. Panic had her pulling away from him. "Don't you get it? This isn't a joke and I don't want to be in love."

His grin faded a little around the edges as he grew serious. "Not really a matter of choice. You either are, or you aren't."

"If I'm in love—" She looked up toward the ceiling, trying to collect herself. Trying not to cry. "Don't you see? Loving someone leaves you open to all sorts of awful things."

She was focusing on the down side. That wasn't like her. "Only if they betray you or they die. I'm not about to do the first. As for the second..." His voice trailed off as he shrugged. "I can only promise you the same thing you can promise me. Today. Right now." And then the smile returned as he nodded heavenward. "I'm working on a deal regarding immortality, but it still has a few wrinkles to iron out."

She wanted to laugh. She wanted to cry. Most of all, she wanted him. But she was so afraid of taking that final step. Of admitting what she was feeling out loud. "This isn't a joke."

"No, it's not," he agreed. "It's very serious. *I'm* very serious. Those days you were in the Ukraine, doing your special-agent thing, I tried to get back to normal. Back to life without you." The effort had been doomed from the start. "I didn't like it. Life didn't feel right. *That's* what I was doing at the airport. To see for myself just how I felt the first second I laid eyes on you.

"When I did, my pulse leaped. And I liked it. When I saw you start to grapple with Sullivan for the gun, I got that same awful feeling I had when I heard that Alma was killed. Except this time I was there, witnessing it. And I wasn't about to let anything happen to you." He spoke earnestly, firmly. All he knew was that he had to make her understand. "Alma wasn't my fault, I know that now. But if I let you slip through my fingers, that *will* be my fault. Nothing comes with absolute guarantees in life, but I can absolutely guarantee that I will love you for the rest of your life or mine. Whichever comes last."

He took her hands in his again. "Love me, Cate. Love me just a little. I'll make up the difference."

"I'm scared, Christian."

"Me, too." He drew her into his arms, holding her against his chest. Stroking her hair and thinking how he never thought he would ever feel this way again. Ever. It was enough to make a man humble. "But if we're scared together, there'll be someone to talk to in the middle of the night."

He felt her words against his chest as she spoke, creating circles of warmth. "You make it hard to say no."

"Then don't say no." He drew her back so that he could look at her face. So that he could silently plead. "Say yes."

Every single bone in her body was saying yes. She was surprised he couldn't hear. "If I say yes, will you go home and go to bed?"

"No," he said honestly, "but if you say yes, I'll go to your bed."

She grinned, threading her arms around his neck. "I guess that's a start."

He moved to kiss her, then pulled back. "Just so we're on the same page—is that yes you love me or yes you'll marry me?"

Mischief entered her eyes. "You'll have to torture me to find out. And I warn you, I've been trained to resist by the very best."

"We'll see." He took her into his arms and kissed her. Kissed her so deeply that she felt as if her very core was in meltdown.

"Yes," Cate breathed, finally, finally letting herself go. She felt as if she had wings and could touch the sky. "Oh, yes."

"We already know that part," he murmured against her mouth just before he deepened the kiss again. "But don't stop saying it. I like the sound of it."

Everything you love about romance...
and more!

Please turn the page for Signature Select™
Bonus Features.

Bonus Features:

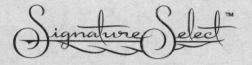

BONUS FEATURES

Searching for Cate

A day in the life...
of Marie Ferrarella

Ever wonder how authors spend their days? Here's your chance to peek inside the life of author Marie Ferrarella, who shared her description of a day in her life.

My days can only be described as typical, if *typical* means to encompass the word *insanity*. For most people, dragging a comatose body up at four in the morning five days a week comes under the heading of torture, not typical. However, that's when I get up. No, I don't live on a farm, I live with a man who somewhere in his family tree absorbed a rooster. He has always gotten up before God invented dawn— usually to exercise before he goes to work.

My daughter, unfortunately, takes after him. She works seventy miles from the house so, traffic being what it is, she needs to leave by 6:30. Jess has never been as fast as I have, so she gives herself a lot of time. I get up to make breakfast for both of them, to pack a lunch for my husband, Charlie, and then, after he leaves at six, I walk the dog. I'm back by 6:30 to say goodbye to Jess.

Between 6:30 and 7:00 I like to get in a little exercise if possible, and eat breakfast. I write a rough draft of my chapter between 7:00 and 8:30. Also in that timeframe, I usually get my son, Nik, up for school and clean up after everyone (it's like living with three versions of the Tasmanian devil).

Depending on the weather, I usually spend between fifteen to thirty minutes taking Charlie's cacti and succulents out of the garage, into the sun (his hobby, my work; my autobiography will be entitled *Taking the Cacti for a Walk*). Contrary to popular belief, a great many succulents and cacti are delicate so if it's too sunny they have to be brought in again relatively quickly.

I spend the next two hours doing whatever errands need to be done: grocery shopping, going to the drugstore, taking my mother-in-law to various doctors (she has a number of ailments and is confined to a wheelchair), taking the cars (we have four) to the mechanic, my dog in to make the vet richer, etc. (And you thought my life wasn't glamorous.) If I'm not taking my mother-in-law to the doctor, I go over to see her daily to get her mail, take out her garbage and do whatever chores she needs done. I'm home by 11:30, have my lunch, return any phone calls on my machine, check my e-mail and am back at the computer "making magic" by 12:30.

I write until 3:00. Then I bring in the plants and start dinner. My husband's usually home by 4:30. We eat, I do dishes, clean up and go back to writing until the chapter "feels right." I watch TV and usually fall asleep during the last fifteen minutes of *Law & Order*—I've never seen a first-run ending yet (thank God for videotapes). That's around eleven.

The next morning, it starts all over again.

Native American Legends
of the Navajo

Navajo legends have been around for as long as the people themselves. No one knows just when the first legend came about, but they are part of the proud people's heritage. Stories handed down from their grandparents are what link the Navajo to their ancestors and what connects them to the generations they know are to come. They represent tradition, roots, pride, all told in the simple story form that appeals to the child in all of us.—MF

Spider Rock

Before the counting of the days, in a place that was home to the Dine, known to the White Eyes as "The Navajo," Spider Rock was formed. Some say it stands 800 feet, some say more. It touches the sky and is the home of Spider Woman, the goddess who to this day watches over the Dine. It was she who sent Monster-Slayer and Child-Born of Water to seek out their father, Sun-God, so that he could show them how to slay the monsters who roamed the earth, and were a threat to the Dine. The Dine were very grateful and called Spider Woman their goddess before all others, as it should be.

Pleased by their worship, Spider Woman asked her husband, Spider Man, to construct a loom so that the Dine women could weave cloth and clothe themselves and their children. This was done and it was good. Throughout the generations, the Dine women work their looms, remembering the goodness of Spider Woman.

Spider Woman was a stern goddess. The Dine elders warned their children that if they did not behave, Spider Woman would cast down her web ladder, ensnare the bad children in it and carry them up to the top of Spider Rock, where she would eat them. Legend had it that the top of Spider Rock was white with the sun-bleached bones of children who had misbehaved. So great was their fear of being carried off that the Dine children always behaved and listened to their elders.

One day, a Dine boy strayed from his home within the cliffs, where the flood waters and his enemies could not reach him. Instead, he walked the land and came across an enemy who wished to do him harm. The enemy chased him right to the base of Spider Rock. The boy had nowhere to run and he thought he would surely die. Suddenly, a silken cord came from the very top of Spider Rock. Having no choice, the boy grabbed the cord and found himself magically pulled up to the very top of the Rock, leaving his enemy far below. When he reached the top, the boy found no bleached bones, no one waiting to eat him. Instead, there was food and drink waiting for him.

When he had eaten his fill, he rested. Upon waking, he discovered that his mysterious benefactor was none other than Spider Woman. She had seen his dilemma and fashioned the magic cord to rescue him. He was very, very grateful for her kindness and remained with her until the danger at the base of the rock was no more. Once his enemy was gone, he used the magic cord to lower himself to the ground again, then raced back to his people in the cliffs. He told all who would listen that Spider Woman had saved his life and praised her to the end of his days.

The Journey to Rainbow's End

A long, long time ago, so long that no one remembers just when, First Woman the Goddess was created—she was fully grown in four days. She was so beautiful that all the Dine (Navajo) braves were in love with her. But she did not love any of them, only the handsomest of them all, Sun-God. However, she did not think that he even noticed her.

But he did. One day, when she was alone, he came up behind her and tickled her neck with a large, feathery plume. Immediately, she felt as if she was surrounded with warm sunshine. In this magical way, she became Sun-God's wife. He was the father of her first child, a son.

Soon afterward, First Woman was sleeping beneath an overhanging cliff, and a few droplets of water fell on her. They were from Water-God. This was the way he fathered her second child, also a son. Because the boys were born so close together, everyone called them the Twins of the Goddess. All three lived in a beautiful canyon together.

It was a time when giants roamed the earth and one such giant was Great Giant, who was very evil. He ate every human who came across his path. When he saw First Woman, his heart was so taken with her that he did not eat her, but loved her. But she would have nothing to do with him.

Great Giant was very jealous of her. She knew he would eat the Twins if he saw them, so one day, when he was coming, she quickly dug a hole in the middle of her hogan and hid her sons. She covered the opening by putting a flat sandstone rock on it, then spread dirt over it. That day, the Great Giant did not find her children.

Another day, Great Giant came and saw small footprints around the hogan. He demanded to know where the children who made them were and if they were hers.

Brave First Woman told him she had no children. When he wanted to know who had made the prints, she said she had. She told him that she was lonely for children, so she made the prints herself with the heels of her hand and the tips of her fingers and pretended they belonged to her children. Great Giant believed her and went away.

As the Twins grew bigger, First Woman knew she could not hide them much longer. She prayed for help, and the Spirit who had made First Woman appeared with a bow made of cedar wood for Sun-God's child. She told her son that it was time for him to learn how to hunt.

First Woman told Sun-Child that he had to make another bow and arrows for his brother. Sun-Child said this was good and that he and his brother wanted to hunt for his father. He asked First Woman who his father was because all this time, he did not know. It was time for him to know and she told him that his father was Sun-God and that he lived far away in the East.

A bow and many arrows were made for Water-Child, as First Woman had asked. The Twins began their long journey to find Sun-God, but they could not find him and returned to their mother.

"If he is not in the East, he must be in the South," she told her sons, and they went on another long journey to find him. But again, they did not find him and had to come home. First Woman told her sons to look to the West and if Sun-God was not there, then they must try to find him in the North. She did this to keep them safe because if they were on their journey, Great Giant would not find them here with her.

But finally, the Twins returned very unhappy because they could not find Sun-God in any of the places that First Woman had sent them. They thought their mother was lying to them. When she saw how upset they were, she told them the truth. She said that their fathers, Sun-God and Water-God, live far away in the middle of the great Western Water. The journey there was dangerous. The trail went through great canyons where the walls of the cliffs clapped together and could crush them as they passed.

And even if they made it through the great canyons, they would not be able to cross the Grand Canyon and certainly never be able to cross the water to reach their father's house in the middle of the Western Ocean.

But the Twins insisted, so she taught them a song of protection. The words of the song were "We are traveling in an Invisible Way to seek our fathers, the Sun-God and the Water-God." This she told them to sing four times, because four was the magic number.

The Twins sang the song each day as they traveled. One day, as they were walking, they saw a small hole in the ground and heard someone say "Ssh!" four times. When they looked into the hole, they saw that Spider Woman was there, beneath the earth. She told the Twins not to be afraid of her. She was their grandmother and welcomed them into her home, but the hole was very small and the Twins said they could not fit through it. Spider Woman told them to blow once toward the East, once toward the West, once toward the South and then once toward the North. They did as she told them and the hole became just big enough to let them pass into her home.

Inside Spider Woman's home they saw bones bundled up on the walls just the way spiders wrap flies in their webs. Spider Woman told them not to be afraid. The bones belonged to evil men that she had killed.

They sat and talked for a long time. Spider Woman told the Twins of the dangers they would encounter on their journey and taught them songs for their protection. She also gave each twin a magic Feather-Plume. She told them to hold it before them as they walked. They must hold it straight up or sideways and it would allow them to walk forward in safety.

Before she walked them from her lodge, she told them to be on the lookout for a little man with a red head and a striped back. He would look like a sand scorpion, only bigger. He would help them on their journey.

They walked again and after many days, the Twins heard a voice coming from the ground. It was the little man Spider Woman warned them about.

He said that he could help them, and said the Twins should put their hands down on the ground and spit into them four times. Then they must close their fists to save the spit until they came to the Great Water, where they had to wash off the spit.

The Twins spit into their hands as the little man told them. They closed their hands, then said goodbye. Soon, they came to the canyon walls that smashed themselves together. They repeated the prayers that Spider Woman had taught them, holding the Feather-Plumes sideways. The clapping walls stopped just long enough for the Twins to walk through.

They walked many days, then came upon a jungle of sharp reeds. The reeds were so thick, they could not pass through. The Twins sang the song Spider Woman taught them, touching the very tips of the reeds with their magical Feather-Plumes. The reeds turned into cattails and were so happy to be cattails that they parted and made a path for the Twins to walk.

The most curious part of their journey was when they came to the giant cliff. They walked around its rim, only to come back to where they had started. They could not go forward. So again they sang the songs their mother and their grandmother had taught them. They closed their eyes and prayed. When they opened them again, a magnificent rainbow had appeared. They walked across the rainbow, which brought them to the other side of the Grand Canyon.

The Twins continued walking West for a long time. Finally, they came to the Great Water. It was so big, they thought they would never reach Sun-God's Turquoise House in the middle of the Great Water.

They walked down to the beach to the edge of the water and did as the little man with the red head had told them—they washed the spit off their hands, singing and praying as they did so. The rainbow appeared again. A great big Rainbow Bridge stretched before them from the beach to the Turquoise House.

The twins raced onto the Rainbow Bridge. Their fathers, Sun-God and Water-God, were waiting for them. Together they all went into the Turquoise House, which was at the end of the Rainbow Bridge.

How The Wood Tick Became Flat

Many moons ago, before your great-grandmother's great-grandmother was ever born, giants roamed the earth and animals spoke to the Dine, known to the white man as the Navajo.

On one such day, Coyote was out for a walk when he met Old Woman. She asked where he was going and he told her nowhere in particular, he was just roaming around. She warned him that there was a giant in the area. A very big, mean giant who was closer than he thought. Coyote wasn't afraid because he had killed many giants and said he would kill this one, too.

He thanked Old Woman for the warning and went on his way. A little while later, he found a broken branch that looked like a club. He picked it up, in case he met the giant and needed a weapon. Feeling very happy, he whistled as he walked. Soon he came to a cave and decided to explore it, so he walked in.

A few feet into the cave, he found a woman crawling around on the ground. When he asked her what was wrong, she told him that she was starving and could no longer walk. Seeing his stick, she asked him what it was for. "To kill the giant," he told her. Even though she was very weak, she began to laugh. "Silly Coyote, you are already in the giant's belly."

"No, I am in a cave and so are you," Coyote protested.

"No," the woman said, "I am in the giant's belly and so are you. That was no cave you walked into. That was his mouth. Do not feel bad, many have walked in. But no one has ever walked out. He is very, very big."

Upset, Coyote threw his stick down, left the woman and continued walking. Soon he came upon more people, lying near death on the ground. "Help us," they cried when they saw him. "We are starving to death."

The Coyote looked around and then he laughed. "Silly people, if we are all in the giant's stomach, then these walls are made of meat and fat. We can cut pieces from the walls and eat them."

The people were surprised at the solution. They had never thought of that. Coyote laughed and said that men were not as smart as animals, and he was the smartest animal of them all.

He took out his hunting knife and began to cut chunks of meat and fat from the walls. He fed the starving people, then went back to the first woman he had met to feed her. Soon the people felt much stronger. But they were still sad because they were trapped.

"Do not worry," Coyote told them. "I will kill the giant. I will stab him in the heart and then we will all be free."

He looked for the heart and came upon what looked like a volcano, all puffy and beating hard. Certain he had found the heart, Coyote began to stab and cut at the volcano.

"Coyote, please do not stab my heart," the giant cried. "If you stop, I will open my mouth and you can go free." But the Coyote would not leave his new friends and continued to stab and cut until he had made a deep hole in the giant's heart. Lava began to flow from the hole. The ground beneath the people's feet began to move. It felt like an earthquake.

"Run!" Coyote cried when the giant opened his mouth. They all ran to the opening before it closed again forever. The last to run was the wood tick. The giant's teeth began to close again, almost on top of the wood tick. Coyote reached in just in time and pulled the wood tick through the tiny space at the very last second.

"Look!" the wood tick cried in distress. "I am all flat!"

"Yes, you are," Coyote agreed. "And you will be flat from now on. But you are also alive. Be happy about that."

And the wood tick remained flat and happy from that day on.

Here's a sneak peek...

The Measure of a Man
by
Marie Ferrarella

*Coming in September 2005 from Silhouette
Special Edition*

CHAPTER 1

Smith Parker frowned deeply. Not at the woman in front of him, but at the situation. This was not where he expected to be at this point in his life.

At twenty-nine, Smith had expected to be doing something important. At the very least, something more significant than changing lightbulbs in the hallway of one of the older buildings at the very same university he'd once attended, nurturing such wonderful dreams of his future.

A future that definitely did *not* include a maintenance uniform. But this was the same university that had abruptly turned his life upside down, stripped him of his scholarship, money awarded through a work-study program and thus his ability to pay for the education that would have seen him rise above a life involving only menial jobs.

An education that would have allowed him to become something more than he was now destined to be.

In a way, Smith supposed that he should be grateful he was working, grateful that he was anywhere at all. There had been a stretch of time, right after he'd spiraled down emotionally and sleepwalked through his exams, causing his grades to drop and him to leave the university, that he had seriously considered giving up everything and meeting oblivion.

Ultimately it was his love for his parents, who had loved him and stood by him with unwavering faith throughout it all, that had kept him from doing anything drastic. Anything permanent. He knew that ending his own life would in effect end theirs.

So he had pulled back from the very brink of self-destruction, reassessed his situation and tried to figure out what he could do with himself.

20 The answer was just to pass from one day to the next, drifting without a plan, he who had once entertained so many ideas.

To support himself and not wind up as a blot on society's conscience, he'd taken on a variety of dead-end, lackluster jobs, doing his best but leaving his heart out of it. Some of the others he worked with felt that a job well done was its own reward, but he didn't. He did them well because that was what he was getting paid for, nothing else. He did them well because that was his nature, but one position was pretty much like another. When his father's health had begun to fail, any tiny speck of hope he'd still entertained about eventually returning to college died. He'd needed to help out financially.

When this unsolicited offer had arrived out of the

blue, asking him to come down to the university to apply for the position that began at something higher than minimum wage, he'd taken it only because of the money. There had been no joy in it, no secret setting down of goals for himself to achieve anything beyond what he was offered.

He was seriously convinced that, for him, there was no joy left in anything. Being accused of something he had not done and verbally convicted without being allowed to defend himself had killed his spirit.

So he did his work, making sure that he was never remiss, never in a position to be found lacking by anyone ever again.

But today, his mind had wandered. Just before beginning his round of small, tedious chores, he'd seen a landscaping truck go by. The truck's logo proclaimed it to belong to a local family company that had been in business for the past fifteen years. Seeing it had momentarily catapulted him into the past.

That had been his goal once. To have a business of his own. Something where he was his own master, making his own hours, responsible for his own success. Evaluated and held to high standards by his own measure, not whimsically made to live up to someone else's, someone who might, for whatever reason, find him lacking through no fault of his own but because of something they themselves were dealing with.

The truck had driven around the corner and disappeared. Just as his dreams had.

He'd returned to his chores in a dark frame of mind. Even so, he went through the paces, giving a hundred percent, no more, no less.

He'd spent most of the morning dealing with a clogged drain incapacitating the university's indoor pool. The smell of stagnant water was still in his head if not physically with him and admittedly he wasn't exactly in the best frame of mind, even though he was tackling a far lesser problem.

So he hadn't been paying attention when he set up the ladder and worked the defunct bulb out of the socket in the ceiling. He'd only used the ladder instead of the extension pole he normally employed because someone had apparently made off with the pole.

Even the hallowed halls of Saunders saw theft, he'd thought.

It seemed ironic, given that was the offense he'd been accused of all those many years ago. Theft. When he discovered that the pole, an inexpensive thirty-dollar item, was missing, he couldn't help wondering if this would somehow come back to haunt him. Would the head of the maintenance department think he'd taken it for some obscure reason?

Once a thief…

Except that he hadn't been. Not even that one time he'd been accused by that pompous, self-centered jerk, Jacob Weber.

Smith looked down now at Jane Jackson's face, biting back a stinging retort that was born of defensiveness and the less-than-stellar mood he was in. She was right, he'd been careless, which made his mood even darker.

Still, he couldn't just bite her head off, not if she didn't deserve it. That wouldn't be right and he'd made a point of always abiding by what was right, by walking the straight and narrow path even when others veered away from it.

He always had.

Which made that accusation that had ruined his life that much more bitterly ironic.

So he blew out a breath, and with it the words that had sprung to his tongue, if not his lips. Instead, after a beat, Smith grudgingly nodded his head. "You're right. My fault."

Since he'd just admitted it was his mistake and not hers, the anger Jane had felt heat up so quickly within her died back. Leaving her feeling awkward.

She looked up at Smith—he had to be almost a foot taller than she was—a little ruefully, the way she did each time their paths crossed. She remembered him. With his dirty-blond hair, magnetic brown eyes and chiseled good looks, he would have been a hard man to forget.

Smith Parker had been in one of her English classes when she'd attended the university. The one taught by Professor Harrison. Back then, she'd had a bit of a crush on Smith. Maybe more than just a bit.

She'd been trying to work up the courage to say something to him, when suddenly, just like that, he was gone.

The rumor was he'd been caught stealing things from one of the girls' dorms, forcing the university to take away his scholarship. She'd heard that his grades dropped right after that. And then he was gone.

Shortly thereafter, she went on to meet and then to marry Drew.

She hadn't thought about Smith in years until one day, not that long ago, she'd seen him hunkered down against a wall in one of the classrooms, working on what appeared to be a faulty outlet.

Standing there that day, looking at him, she couldn't help wondering if he remembered her. But the brown eyes she recalled as being so vivid had appeared almost dead as they'd turned to look at her. Like two blinds pulled down, barring access to a view she'd once believed was there. There was no recognition to be found when he looked at her.

Or through her, which was how it had felt.

Still, because of the incident in his past, because of the shame that was attached to it, she was never comfortable around Smith. Because she knew about it, it was as if she'd been privy to some dirty little, dark secret of his. She found pretending not to know him the easier way to go.

She cleared her throat as he stood beside the ladder, looking at her. "Are you all right?"

He half shrugged at the question. "Yeah, thanks to your quick hands."

Something shivered through her as he said that, although she had no idea why. A smattering of those old feelings she'd once secretly harbored about him struggled to the surface.

Jane pushed them back. She wasn't that girl anymore. Wasn't a girl at all, really. A great deal of time had gone by since then and she'd discovered that the world was really a hard, cold, disagreeable place. If it wasn't, then people like the professor could go on about their chosen professions, professions they loved, until they ceased to draw breath.

And if the world wasn't such a disagreeable place, she wouldn't have made such an awful mistake, wouldn't have allowed herself to fall so hard for a student two years ahead of her. Wouldn't have impulsively married him instead of thinking things through.

She shrugged, that same awkward feeling she always felt around Smith returning to claim her. "I've got a five-year-old."

Smith looked at her blankly as he moved the ladder a good foot away from the path of the door. He hadn't really been around any kids since he'd been one himself. The explanation she'd given him created no impression in its wake.

"I don't follow."

She smiled. No, she didn't suppose he did. She'd nosed around a little and discovered that Smith was very much alone these days. No children, no wife, no attachments whatsoever. The world she lived in, even without the constant demand of bills that needed paying, was probably foreign to him.

"Danny is a little hyper." She considered her words, then amended them. "Actually, he's a lot hyper."

Smith moved his head from side to side slowly. "I still don't—"

He *really* didn't know anything about kids, did he? "Okay, let me put it to you this way. Danny never really took his first step. He took his first leap—off a coffee table."

She remembered how her heart had stopped in the middle of her throat. One minute her son had been crawling on the floor beside the table and she'd looked away for a split second. The very next minute he'd clambered up not only to his feet but to the top of the coffee table where he proceeded to take a fearless half-gainer on wobbly, chubby legs while gleefully laughing.

"I was just lucky enough to be there to catch him." She'd all but sprained her ankle getting there in time to keep him from making ignoble contact with the floor. A smile curved her lips as she remembered another incident. All incidents involving Danny fared far better when they were relived than during the original go-round.

"And last year, during the holiday season, I was walking through a department store with Danny, holding his hand. Which left his other hand free to grab the branch of one of the trees they had just finished putting up. He got hold of a string of lights and if my mother's radar hadn't kicked in, the tree would have gone over, flattening another customer." She'd swung around just in time to right the tree. The shoe department manager, whose area it had been, hadn't looked very happy about the matter, despite the smile pasted on his lips.

Smith tried not to notice the way her smile seemed to light up her face. And curl into his system. "Sounds like you have your hands full."

And her life, she thought. "Keeps me on my toes, that's for sure."

He knew she worked full-time. Did five-year-olds attend school? He'd never had a reason to know before. He hadn't one now, he reminded himself. This was just conversation and now that he thought of it, he was having it more or less against his will.

Still, he heard himself asking, "Who watches Danny when you're here?"

Kindergarten would be starting for Danny soon. Another hurdle and rite of passage all rolled into one to go through, she mused. But for now, he was still her little boy and she was hanging on to that for as long as possible.

"Some very exhausted day-care center people." The cost of which, she added silently, ate huge chunks out of her weekly paycheck. But it was a good day-care center and Danny seemed to be thriving in the environment, which was all that mattered. She couldn't ask for anything better than that.

Except, maybe, a father for the boy. But that wasn't ever going to happen. For Danny to get a father, she would have to start dating again. Have to put herself out there emotionally again. After the mega-disaster that was her marriage, she had come to the conclusion that she and love had nothing in common.

Unless, of course, she was thinking of love for her son. Or the professor.

Smith caught himself studying Jane. Minding his own business to a fault, he knew very little about the lives of the people around him. He'd never pictured Jane with a son. Hadn't really thought of her as married, either. But that was because she still used the same last name she'd had when they were students in English class together. He'd been aware of her from the first day of class. The cute little redhead with the pale green eyes, soft voice and perfect shape. He'd even come close to asking her out. Back then, he'd thought anything was possible.

But that was before he learned that it wasn't. Not for him.

Smith glanced down at her hand and didn't see a wedding ring. Was she one of those independent women who didn't care for outward signs of commitment? Or hadn't acquiring a husband along with a son been part of her plan?

"Don't you miss him?" he asked.

She wondered if Smith had always been this abrupt or if getting caught and then having to leave the university had done this to him. What was he doing here, anyway? If something that traumatic had happened to her, she certainly wouldn't have come back, asking for a job. She would have starved first.

Maybe that was what he was faced with, she suddenly thought. Compassion flooded through her. "Miss him?" She didn't quite understand what he was driving at. "I see Danny every morning and evening."

Smith shook his head. His own mother had stayed home to raise him, returning to the work force only after he entered middle school. "No, I meant, wouldn't you rather stay home and take care of him?"

A soft smile flirted with the corners of her mouth. "In a perfect world, yes." And then she laughed shortly. The world was so far from perfect, it was staggering. "But if I stayed home, the cupboard would get bare incredibly fast."

"Your husband doesn't work?"

Smith had no idea where that question even came from. For that matter, he didn't even know why he was talking to her. Ordinarily he didn't exchange more than a barely audible grunt with people he passed in the hall. Especially the ones he recognized from his initial years as a student. Those he avoided whenever possible.

Only Professor Harrison was the exception. But that was because the man seemed to insist on taking an interest in him. Long ago, he'd decided that the professor, like his parents, was one of the few good people that were scattered sparingly through the earth.

He noticed that Jane stiffened when he mentioned the word "husband." Obviously he must have hit a nerve.

"I have no idea what my husband does. And he's my ex, actually."

The very thought of Drew brought with it a wealth of silent recriminations. Looking back now, she had no idea why she had been so stupid, not just to put up with his infidelities, which he'd never really made much of an effort to hide, but with his abuse, as well. A self-respecting woman would have never stood for any of that, especially the latter.

Smith saw her jaw harden. Time to back away. He hadn't meant to get into any kind of verbal exchange with Jane, much less wander into personal terrain. In general he'd found that the less he interacted with people, the better he liked it.

He imagined from her tone that she felt the same way, at least in this case. It probably embarrassed her, sharing something so personal with a maintenance man. He doubted very much if she even remembered him. Or would remember him ten minutes from now.

After all, in his present capacity, he was one of the invisible ones. One of the people that others looked right past, or through, without having their presence actually register on any kind of conscious level. People, like bus drivers, waitresses, hotel workers and gardeners, who were there to serve and make life a little easier for the people who felt themselves above them.

Hell, he'd been guilty of that himself once. Filled with high-powered dreams and drive, he'd seen only his own goals, not the people who toiled around him. Working just the way he did now.

"Sorry," he apologized, his voice monotone. "Didn't mean to sound like I was prying. None of my business, really."

Because of all the baggage her marriage had created, not the least of which was Drew's vanishing act and with it, her alimony and child support payments, Smith had hit a very raw spot. She hated being reminded that she had been such a fool. And that because of her poor choice, Danny wouldn't be able to have the things that his friends did. Right now, he didn't notice, but soon, he would. And that was all her fault.

"No," she snapped, "it's not."

Embarrassed, afraid that he might say something else, Jane abruptly turned on her heel and hurried down the still-darkened hallway. The sound of her three-inch heels clicked against the vinyl until they finally faded out of earshot.

For a second Smith thought of following her and repeating his apology, but then he shrugged to himself. If he did that, he'd risk getting involved, however peripherally. It was the last thing he wanted or needed. Right now, it was hard enough just getting through the day.

Whistling under his breath, he got back up the ladder and finally attended to the bulb that he had originally set out to change.

As Smith began to climb back down, he saw Professor Harrison opening his door very slowly and peering out. Unlike the first time, the door completely cleared the space without coming in contact with the ladder. If Jane hadn't come out like gangbusters, Smith thought, she wouldn't have rocked his ladder and there would have been no need for any kind of verbal exchange to have taken place.

And he wouldn't have noticed how pale and beautiful her eyes still were.

32

The professor looked up at him, as if startled to see him there. He shifted the files he was carrying to his other side. "Oh, Smith, I almost didn't see you."

"A lot of that happening lately," Smith murmured nearly under his breath.

Gilbert looked up toward the ceiling and saw the new bulb. He shaded his eyes and smiled broadly. "Ah, illumination again. I knew I could count on you, Smith."

The professor made it sound as if he'd just slain a dragon for him, or, at the very least, solved some kind of complicated mathematical equation that had eluded completion up until now.

Smith frowned. "It's just a bulb, Professor. No big deal."

The expression on the professor's face said he knew better. The old man was getting eccentric, Smith thought. The next words out of the man's mouth seemed to underscore his feelings.

"Better to light one candle, Smith, than to curse the dark."

That was probably a quote from somewhere, Smith thought. What it had to do with the situation was beyond him, but he didn't have the time or the inclination to discuss it. He'd had enough conversation for one day. For a week, really.

"Yeah, well, I've got to be going…" Taking the two sides of the ladder, he pulled them together, then tilted it until it was all the way over to the side. It was easier to carry that way, although by no means easy. He silently cursed whoever had taken the extension pole. "I've got another 'candle to light' over on the third floor in the science building."

About to leave, he felt the professor's hand on his arm.

"Something else I can do for you, Professor?"

Gilbert looked at the young man for a long moment. There was a time when Smith Parker had been one of his more promising students. He'd been like some bright, burning light, capable of so much. And then, just like that, the light had been extinguished. His pride wounded, Smith had dropped out of Saunders after those charges had been leveled against him, charges he could never get himself to believe were true. But Smith had left before he'd had the chance to try to talk to him, to see about making things right again.

"Smith, have you given any thought to your future?"

It wasn't what he'd expected the professor to say. And it certainly wasn't anything that he wanted to get into a discussion about. "Yeah, I have. Right after I replace the other bulb, I'm having lunch," Smith replied crisply. "Now, if you'll excuse me."

The professor dropped his hand from Smith's arm.

Before there could be any further conversation, Smith hefted the ladder beneath his arm and made his way down the hall.

...NOT THE END...

34

Look for the continuation of this story in The Measure of a Man *by Marie Ferrarella, available in September 2005 from Silhouette Special Edition.*

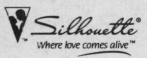

SAGA

USA TODAY bestselling author

Dixie Browning

A brand-new story in
The Lawless Heirs miniseries...

FIRST TIME HOME

Reeling from the scandalous ruin of her
career and love life, Laurel Ann Lawless
escapes to North Carolina and turns to
relatives she's never met. She soon feels
a strong sense of belonging—with her
newfound family and her handsome
new landlord, Cody Morningstar.

*Available
in September.*

Bonus Features:

**Author Interview,
Recipes
and
Lawless Family History**

Where love comes alive™

If you enjoyed what you just read,
then we've got an offer you can't resist!

Take 2 bestselling
love stories FREE!

Plus get a FREE surprise gift!

Clip this page and mail it to Silhouette Reader Service™

IN U.S.A.
3010 Walden Ave.
P.O. Box 1867
Buffalo, N.Y. 14240-1867

IN CANADA
P.O. Box 609
Fort Erie, Ontario
L2A 5X3

YES! Please send me 2 free Silhouette Special Edition® novels and my free surprise gift. After receiving them, if I don't wish to receive anymore, I can return the shipping statement marked cancel. If I don't cancel, I will receive 6 brand-new novels every month, before they're available in stores! In the U.S.A. bill me at the bargain price of $4.24 plus 25¢ shipping and handling per book and applicable sales tax, if any*. In Canada, bill me at the bargain price of $4.99 plus 25¢ shipping and handling per book and applicable taxes**. That's the complete price and a savings of at least 10% off the cover prices—what a great deal! I understand that accepting the 2 free books and gift places me under no obligation ever to buy any books. I can always return a shipment and cancel at any time. Even if I never buy another book from Silhouette, the 2 free books and gift are mine to keep forever.

235 SDN DZ9D
335 SDN DZ9E

Name	(PLEASE PRINT)	
Address	Apt.#	
City	State/Prov.	Zip/Postal Code

Not valid to current Silhouette Special Edition® subscribers.

Want to try two free books from another series?
Call 1-800-873-8635 or visit www.morefreebooks.com.

* Terms and prices subject to change without notice. Sales tax applicable in N.Y.
** Canadian residents will be charged applicable provincial taxes and GST.
All orders subject to approval. Offer limited to one per household.
® are registered trademarks owned and used by the trademark owner and or its licensee.

SPED04R   ©2004 Harlequin Enterprises Limited

COMING NEXT MONTH

Signature Select Collection
LOVE SO TENDER by Stephanie Bond, Jo Leigh and Joanne Rock
Why settle for Prince Charming when you can have The King?
It's now or never—Gracie Sergeant, Alyssa Reynolds and Ellie
Evans can't help falling in love...Vegas style! Three romantic
novellas that could only happen in Vegas.

Signature Select Saga
SEARCHING FOR CATE by Marie Ferrarella
A widower for three years, Dr. Christian Graywolf's life is his
work. But when he meets FBI special agent Kate Kowalski—a
woman searching for her birth mother—the attraction is
intense, immediate and the truth is something neither Christian
nor Cate expects. That all his life Christian has been searching
for Cate.

Signature Select Miniseries
LAWLESS LOVERS by Dixie Browning
Two complete novels from THE LAWLESS HEIRS SAGA.
Daniel Lyon Lawless and Harrison Lawless are two successful,
sexy and very sought-after bachelors. But their worlds are about
to be rocked by the love of two headstrong, beautiful women!

Signature Select Spotlight
HAPPILY NEVER AFTER by Kathleen O'Brien
Ten years after the society wedding that wasn't, members of
the wedding party are starting to die. At the scene of every
"accident," a piece of a wedding dress is found. It's not long
before Kelly Ralston realizes that she's the sole remaining
bridesmaid left...and the next target!

Signature Showcase
FANTASY by Lori Foster
Brandi Sommers doesn't know quite what to do about her
sister's outrageous birthday gift of a dream vacation to a
lover's retreat—with sexy security consultant Sebastian Sinclair
included as the lover! But she soon discovers that she can do
whatever she wants....